PIECES
OF
ME

Also by Kate McLaughlin

What Unbreakable Looks Like
Daughter

PIECES OF ME

A NOVEL

Kate McLaughlin

WEDNESDAY BOOKS
NEW YORK

This book is for everyone out there with dissociative identity disorder, including a long-ago friend whose struggle I didn't see.

It's also for Steve, because of all he does so I can live my dream. Love you.

Published in the United States by Wednesday Books, an imprint of St. Martin's Publishing Group

PIECES OF ME. Copyright © 2023 by Kate McLaughlin. All rights reserved. Printed in the United States of America. For information, address St. Martin's Publishing Group, 120 Broadway, New York, NY 10271.

Book design by Michelle McMillian

www.wednesdaybooks.com

The Library of Congress Cataloging-in-Publication Data is available upon request.

ISBN 978-1-250-26434-3 (hardcover)
ISBN 978-1-250-26435-0 (ebook)

Our books may be purchased in bulk for promotional, educational, or business use. Please contact your local bookseller or the Macmillan Corporate and Premium Sales Department at 1-800-221-7945, extension 5442, or by email at MacmillanSpecialMarkets@macmillan.com.

First Edition: 2023

10 9 8 7 6 5 4 3 2 1

Some of the thematic material within contains discussions of suicide, child abuse/sexual assault, and alcohol abuse, as well as mentions of vaping, smoking, and sex.

ME

*It is the power
of the mind
to be
unconquerable.*

—SENECA

ONE

*W*ake up.

I snuggle deeper into the blankets, trying to push away the voice in my head. Everything feels light and muffled, the edges of my brain lined with cotton balls. I cling to the last vestiges of a dream, holding on even though I can't quite remember what it was or why it was so good.

You need to wake up.

With a sigh, I open my eyes.

The world takes its time coming into focus. First, I hear the traffic outside, slightly muted. Daylight flickers through the fluttering of my eyelashes. Too bright. A slight ache presses against the inside of my brain. I snuggle deeper into the pillow to ease it, squishing my eyes shut, but it doesn't matter. I'm awake.

My mouth tastes like old sour wine and my throat is scratchy in a familiar way. I don't remember drinking or vaping last night, but I must have been. The two usually go together for me. Normally I stay away from vaping or smoking, but there's something about when I'm feeling loose and free that makes me want them. Did I go out last night? The last thing I remember is going to class yesterday. It must have been one hell of a party.

I thought I'd conquered drinking. I've avoided situations with alcohol for this very reason—blackouts aren't a good sign, and I've had them, like, a lot.

The pillow beneath my head is soft and smells slightly spicy—like gingerbread. There's a sweetness to it, vanilla and sunshine on clean skin. I could smell it all day. Taking a deep breath, I bury my face deeper in the soft flannel.

Wait. I don't have flannel sheets on my bed.

Where am I?

I open my eyes wide. I'm at the edge of the bed, staring at a rug. A couple more inches and I'd be on the floor. I raise my head. The bookcase against the wall is filled with books that aren't mine. An unfamiliar phone on the bedside table says it's ten o'clock. As I roll onto my back, I realize I don't recognize the room, or the boxers and T-shirt I'm wearing.

Or the guy asleep beside me.

Shit.

I sit up. He doesn't stir. Confusion keeps me there, staring. I'm not afraid as I look at him. He's actually kind of cute—if you like long, skinny guys with riotous curls and angular faces. I could cut myself on that jaw, or at least sharpen a pencil. He's got an amazing profile.

I should be panicking, wondering where my clothes are.

Planning my escape. Instead, I sit here, on this comfortable but messy bed, and watch a stranger sleep. I mean, I don't know if I'm here by choice or if he brought me here while I was drunk. Did we have sex?

I'd like to believe I would remember *that,* but as I scour the recesses of my brain, I can't. I have fuzzy memories of his smile, his laugh. But no bad feelings. That gingerbread smell is all him, I think. But I don't freak out. *Not again,* I say in my head before giving it a rueful shake.

There's a knock on the door. I turn my head as it opens. There's a girl at the threshold. She's tall and willowy—like a model—with long dark hair and wide blue eyes. She looks like she should be in a tampon commercial. Or toothpaste. Something where she has to flick her hair and smile a lot. She's not wearing any makeup and her skin is perfect. I want to hate her, but when our gazes meet, I smile.

"Hey, girlie," she says. "I thought you might be up." She hands me a cup of coffee.

"Just," I say. "Thanks." I know her, but I don't—like I met her in a dream or saw her on TV. I must have been way wasted last night. I take a sip. It's good.

She smiles at the guy sprawled beside me. "Did he snore?"

Cradling the mug in my hands, I shake my head. "Nope. I think he talked, though." Did he?

"It was nice of you to let him crash with you. He really would have slept on the floor."

So, no sex, then. Probably? "That would have been ridiculous. This bed is huge."

She nods, eyeing me strangely as I take a drink. "You okay?"

I nod. "Mm-hmm. Just a little groggy, y'know?"

"Yeah, sure." She doesn't look convinced. "Okay, I'll be in the kitchen if you want to join me for a vape."

The last thing I want is to suck on a vape pod, but I don't tell her that. She leaves the room, closing the door behind her. The second the latch clicks I'm off the bed and at the desk, pawing through the papers and notebooks to see if there's anything that can help me figure out where I am.

This isn't the first time something like this has happened to me, but it's the first time I've come to in a place completely unfamiliar. Usually I'm at home or with Izzy. Safe, but confused and foggy. I stopped going to parties because of stuff like this. Obviously, I forgot that last night.

There's an envelope addressed to Connor James on the desk. I assume that's my bedmate. If that's true, and the rest of the information is correct, then I'm on West 152nd Street in New York. At least I'm still in the city.

The room spins a little around me. There's a noise in my head kind of like the crackle of static—the hum of a radio station turned down so low I can't make out the words. I still don't know how I got here. None of this is familiar. And yet . . . it's not exactly completely strange? These people seem to know me. They haven't chopped me into pieces or used my skin to make furniture. Not yet, anyway. More importantly, I feel comfortable with them. I still haven't jumped into full-on panic mode. I feel safe, which is saying something, because a lot of times I don't even feel safe at home.

Oh, shit. Mom. She'll be worried if I didn't call her last night. I always try to let her know if I'm going to stay out.

I glance around and spot my backpack on the floor. I squat down and grab my phone out of the front pocket.

"Fuck." It's dead. How can that be? It was fully charged yesterday after class. Unless I recorded the entire weekend on video, it should still have *some* juice. Then again, if I did record stuff, that will help me remember.

"You okay?" asks a gravelly voice.

I look up. He's awake, sitting in the middle of the bed with his arms slung around his knees. He's got a wicked case of bed-head and his eyelids are heavy, dragged down by the length and thickness of his eyelashes. My fingers twitch—I want to draw him. If ever there was a face that should be put to canvas, it's his. He's really, *really* beautiful.

"My phone's dead," I say stupidly.

He lifts his chin in the direction of the desk. "There's a charger in the top drawer. You can use mine if you need to make a call."

"Thanks." I stand as he gets off the bed. He moves like liquid—a combination of long-limbed grace and confidence. He's lanky in his black T-shirt and sweatpants—all shoulders and legs.

An image of us dancing drifts across my mind, hazy and slightly out of focus. He made me laugh, I think. Or maybe I made him laugh. I don't remember. I like him, though. I know that. He's self-deprecating and sweet.

I knew you'd like him, whispers a familiar voice. I blink. My "internal voices" have always been pretty vocal, but this one is particularly clear.

"Are you sure you're okay?" he asks. "You seem kinda . . . out of it."

"Wow," I hedge. "That's a great thing to say to the girl who let you share the bed instead of sleeping on the floor."

His cheeks flush slightly as he averts his eyes. "I didn't mean it as an insult." His gaze meets mine once more. "You just seem . . . confused."

It's obvious he's a really nice guy and I don't want him to decide he made a mistake letting me into his house. "I think I had too much to drink last night."

He's still for a moment. "Did you." It's not really a question, so I don't answer it. "Yeah, maybe you did."

Oh, shit. But it's kind of good as well. At least it explains things. "Yeah. I'm sorry if I did anything stupid. I didn't, did I?"

"No," he says softly. "Nothing at all. And you don't need to worry—you left me with my virtue intact."

What? Oh, he's joking. Right. I try to hide my sigh of relief, because I don't want him to be offended. I mean, if I slept with a guy who looks like him, I'd want to remember it. "Good," I say. "Because I'd hate for Mr. Darcy to think you're of loose character."

He grins at that. "*Pride and Prejudice.* I like it."

I glance at my phone. Still dead. At this rate I'll be here making an idiot of myself all day. I'm wearing his underwear, for God's sake. I mean, it doesn't get much more intimate than that, does it? And I'm wearing his *Cyanide & Happiness* T-shirt. I mean, I assume it's his. It's kind of snug, so it's not made for someone with boobs.

I'm not wearing a bra. Where the hell are my clothes?

Connor grabs a phone off the desk, unlocks it, and hands it to me. Next, he opens a drawer and pulls out a charging cord. He gives me that as well. "I'm going to get a coffee. You want anything?"

I shake my head.

"I'll get your clothes out of the dryer, too," he says, as if he can read my mind.

"Thanks." I force a smile. My face feels tight, my eyes, wild.

He smiles slightly and leaves the room. Alone, I can finally breathe normally. First, I plug in the charger and my phone. That little charging symbol eases my anxiety so much it's almost laughable. Then, using his phone, I dial my mother's number, gnawing on my thumb as it tries to connect. It rings three times.

"Hello?"

I can't begin to describe how it feels to hear her voice. It's so freaking good I want to cry. "Hey, Mom."

Silence, then a small sound, like a hiccup. "Dylan?"

"Yeah." I run my hand through my hair—it's sticking out around my head like tangled cotton candy. Way too much product in it. "I'm sorry I didn't call last night."

"Last night? Oh my God." I can hear her breath shake as it rushes out. "Where are you?"

I frown. She sounds really freaked out. Like, *really* freaked. "The city. I'm sorry if you tried to call, my phone was dead."

"Your *phone* . . ." She has that "no excuse" voice of hers on. Come on, I'm not a baby anymore. She doesn't even blink if Mark stays out all night. Yeah, I still live at home to save money, but I'm almost nineteen.

"It must have died last night. Anyway, I'm with friends and I'm okay. I'm going to head home soon. I have that project due Monday that I need to work on."

"Dylan . . . What day do you think it is?"

"Saturday," I reply, resisting the urge to add a joking "duh."

She makes that noise again. "It's not Saturday, sweetie."

I frown. "Yes, it is."

"It's Monday."

"What?" No. "That's impossible." The world tilts around me, and I grab the desk chair to keep from falling.

"Honey," she says, her voice raw with concern and irritation, "you've been missing for three days."

TWO

There's something seriously wrong with me.

I think.

Whatever it is, the doctors can't quite figure it out. At fourteen, I was diagnosed with depression. When I was sixteen, another therapist thought I had severe anxiety disorder and probably ADHD. My brother thinks I'm a drunk, and my mother thinks I'm bipolar. My last shrink diagnosed me with borderline personality disorder shortly after my eighteenth birthday, even though I don't really think my moods are that extreme.

What do I think? No one's bothered to ask. Mostly I think I'm crazy. I know it's not the politically correct thing to say, but it's how it feels. Like there's a connection in my brain that doesn't work the way it's supposed to. It just shorts out. Either that, or I'm dying.

I definitely feel crazy after I hang up with my mother. I sit on the floor of this strange but not strange room and stare at the phone in my hand. "Three days," I whisper. How could I have blacked out for three fucking days?

I like to drink. I spent an awful lot of the last couple of years absolutely wasted, but I stopped doing that almost six months ago. I'd had too many blackouts, and I couldn't stand it anymore. I've lost almost twenty pounds—weight I'd gained from drinking and prescription drugs. Physically, I feel good. Why would I go back to that?

"You okay?" Connor asks again. I look up. He stands over me with a cup of coffee in his hand and a worried expression on his face. He sets a small pile of clothes on the bed, including a bra. He washed my bra. I should be mortified, but it's the least of my concerns.

"Have I been here three days?" I ask, not caring how it sounds.

He blinks those impossibly thick eyelashes. He probably thinks I'm out of it, not knowing the answer myself. "Yeah."

"How?"

He sits down on the edge of the bed, elbows on his knees, mug in his hands. "What do you mean?"

I turn toward him and reach for my own coffee. Maybe it will sharpen my brain, get rid of these cotton balls. "How did I get here?"

"You really don't remember?"

I shake my head even as images start to flood my brain. It's like someone's setting photographs on a table for me to look at, or a movie montage. "A coffee shop?"

He smiles, some of the concern fading from his gaze. "Yeah.

I told you I liked your drawings, and we started talking comic books. Jess invited you back here. We hung out and then you left, but you came back saying you'd been locked out and asked if it'd be cool if you stayed a bit."

I can see it in my head, flickering behind my eyes. "And you believed that I'd been locked out?"

He laughs. "Well, yeah. Why else would you say it?"

"If a guy did that to me, I'd assume he was looking to hook up."

"Oh, shit, no." The laugh turns nervous. "I didn't think you were looking for that."

Surprise floods me. He's serious. "But I slept in your bed. I invited you to sleep there with me."

Pink floods his cheeks. "A friend of Jess's crashed here last night. I was going to sleep on the floor. You said we might as well share the bed—there was nothing . . . sexy about it. We talked for a bit and then fell asleep."

That plays with what the girl—Jess—told me. "A girl invites you to sleep with her and you don't hope you're going to get some?"

"I'm not an asshole." He stares at me, a little indignant, but mostly bewildered. "You really don't remember, do you?"

I shrink in on myself, suddenly ashamed. Tears fill my eyes, hot and ugly. I blink them away. "I don't really remember anything. It's like a dream." I look at him again. "How drunk was I?"

"You weren't," he says with a shrug. "You had a couple glasses of wine, that's it."

That wasn't possible. "Was I stoned?"

His face hardens. "Did I roofie you, you mean?"

"No." I need to explain. "I'm just trying to find a reason why the last three days are nothing but a fog in my head."

We sit in silence for a moment, and I let out a shaky breath.

"You're really upset," he says.

No shit. "Wouldn't you be?"

"Are you on meds?" he asks. Guess he figures he doesn't need to answer my question.

I don't want to be honest, but I can't help it. What difference does it make at this point? If I say no, he's probably going to tell me I should be. "Yeah."

"Do you have them with you?"

I check my bag. I usually have a day's dose with me in case, but the pill container is empty. "No."

"Maybe that's it. Going off your meds messed with your head."

"But it's only been a couple of days without them." I tilt my head. "No, I've messed up with them before and they've never caused something like this." But when these blackouts happen it's not uncommon for me to have forgotten to take my pills.

Shit. I really thought my memory loss was because of booze. Honestly? I'd *hoped* it'd been because of booze.

He shrugs. "Hey, I'm only trying to help. I'm not a doctor."

I shouldn't believe him. He could have drugged me, but that feels wrong. Looking at him, I feel like I trust him even though I don't know anything about him. *I'm* the problem here, not him.

"I need to get home," I say. I can't believe it's Monday. "I was supposed to turn in a project today." I'm going to be lucky if my instructor gives me even half credit for it. Fuck. Why is life so hard for me? Other people juggle way more than I have on my plate and pull it off. Why do I always feel like I'm being left behind, running to catch up all the time? High school was never this hard and I hated it. Art school should be easy for me. Art is the one thing I'm good at.

"Where do you live?" he asks. "I'll drive you."

I don't want to tell him. That's the unwritten rule, right? Never tell a hookup where you live. "You don't have to do that."

"Yeah," he says, rolling his shoulder back. I hear a pop. "Kind of feel like I do."

I'm too mopey to fight. Too tired and confused. And honestly, I think he just wants to get rid of me. Can't say I blame him. I nod. "Okay. Thanks. I live in New Rochelle."

"I'll let you get dressed. Then we'll go. You can charge your phone in the car." He leaves the room and I quickly change out of his clothes into mine. They kind of smell like him now. I can't believe he did my laundry. Are these people for real? Because it's not lost on me how incredibly lucky I am that they seem to be nice. Good. I know how much badness there is in the world—what girl doesn't? We're told about it and all the things we're supposed to do to avoid it from before puberty.

If I'd been raped while out of it, they'd say I deserved it for going off with strangers. It would be my fault for wearing black underwear, or red lipstick.

Your fault for just being a girl. I push that voice aside. I try not to wonder if he's posted photos of me online, or if I'm the star in his private porno.

Dressed, I grab a brush off the dresser and yank it through the tangles in my hair until my shoulder-length, choppy, pink-streaked hair looks close to how it usually does. I feel better in my own clothes—striped jeans and a black sweater. Part of me wants to keep freaking out, but I can't seem to do it. Not fully. Another voice in my head is soothing me, saying it's going to be okay. It's only a glitch. I'm safe, I'm okay. *Nothing bad has happened and nothing bad is going to happen.* The rest is just icing.

I listen to that voice. It's right, after all. Okay, so I had some weird glitch. A combination of wine and being off my meds. The memories will come back to me and I'll laugh about this later.

I leave the bedroom, my practically dead phone in hand. Connor and Jess are in the kitchen, talking quietly at the table. They stop when I walk in, and look up in unison.

"Bet I can guess what you're talking about," I joke.

Jess looks away, but Connor doesn't. He just smiles. "You ready to go?"

"You really don't have to drive me. I have a train pass."

"We've been through this already." He stands up. He's almost a full head taller than me. He offers me a to-go cup. "I made you a new coffee. You didn't drink the other one."

"Thanks." I take a sip—it's exactly the way I like it. I guess this isn't the first time he's fixed a cup for me either. "Listen, I want to thank you both for being so nice to me. I know I seem crazy right now—"

"Don't worry about it," Jess cuts me off, with a tight smile. "Is Lannie even your real name?"

Lannie? I haven't heard that in a long time. "Dylan," I reply. "Lannie is what my dad used to call me."

Her smile relaxes a little. "Okay. Well, nice meeting you, *Dylan.*" She gets up and leaves the room, coffee and vape in hand.

"She's mad," I say, when it's just me and Connor. One more thing for me to feel bad about.

"She's confused, not mad," he counters, then jangles his keys. "Let's get you home."

It's a nice, but old, apartment they live in. They've got it decorated in a fairly boho kind of way. A lot of color and fabrics and mismatched prints. It's the second floor of a walk-up in a fairly decent neighborhood. "Who lives on the bottom?" I ask as we descend the stairs.

"My cousin," he replies. "My grandfather owns the building."

My eyebrows rise. "Convenient."

"I'm not complaining." He presses the key fob to unlock a black Jeep Renegade. I have a flash of having been in it before, only in the back seat. Connor and Jess are up front and there's someone else in the back with me. We're all singing along with the song playing.

My head swims—like I've gotten up too fast. I give it a little shake to clear it before opening the passenger door and stepping in.

"Oh, also, no smoking in the car."

"I don't usually smoke," I tell him. "Or vape, or anything else."

"Except when you drink," he comments.

I buckle my seat belt. "Yeah, well, I thought I'd given that up too, but I guess not."

"I'm pretty sure you've been mostly sober this weekend."

Really? "I'm not making this up."

Our gazes lock. "I'm not saying you are," he says, voice soft. "Look, it's pretty obvious you didn't do any of this on purpose. No one can fake how pale you were after you talked to your mom."

"Wouldn't you be freaked out if you lost three days?"

"Yeah." He puts the Jeep in reverse, turning to look out the rear window. "Especially three days as awesome as the last three were."

My stomach clenches at the tightness in his voice. I'm not the only one struggling to understand this. "And you swear we didn't have sex?"

He presses the brake hard enough to give us both a little jerk. "You really find that hard to believe, don't you? That I was able to control myself, despite your overwhelming allure?" It's not mean, the way he asks, but there's definite sarcasm.

Heat fills my face. "It makes me sound like a total narcissist, doesn't it?"

"A little." With a grin, he backs the car out onto the street.

"You really think these last three days were awesome?" I feel stupid even asking.

"Yeah, I do. I'm sorry you missed them."

"Me too." I am. I really am.

"Well," he begins, his attention focused on the road. "Maybe we can try again sometime."

I smile as I glance out the passenger window. "Maybe."

And that voice in my head whispers, *Definitely.*

—

Where I live in New Rochelle is only about fifteen miles from Connor's apartment, but it takes almost forty minutes to get there in New York traffic. That's the price you pay for being relatively close to Manhattan, and my mother was determined to live as close as she could and still give her kids a house and a yard. Every once in a while, she'd get offered an acting job on—or off—Broadway, or a photo shoot, something to make her feel relevant just when she was beginning to think people had forgotten about her.

My parents divorced when I was eight. That's when we moved to New Rochelle and my dad left for LA. The house my mother bought had belonged to some investment banker who skipped the country. The bank foreclosed and Mom managed to buy the house, which was on the water and even had a pool, for a relative steal. The house is huge, but there's also the whole "keeping up appearances" thing to consider. My twin brother and I each have our own en suite bathroom, and we have two guest rooms in addition to the room Mom took as her office.

"There's something I should tell you about my mother," I tell Connor when we're almost there. He's not going to escape meeting her and I don't want it to be any weirder than it has to.

"Is she going to have the cops waiting for me, or something?" he asks with a nervous smile.

"No. Well, probably not." I check the charge on my phone and try to ignore how many missed calls I have. Guilt makes me look anyway. Most of them are from Mom, the rest are Izzy and a few from Mark. "My mom is kind of famous."

"Kind of?"

I sigh and turn the screen off. "You remember that show from the eighties, *Addison Grant*?"

"I've seen reruns, yeah."

"My mom was Addison."

He laughs. "Get the fuck out. Your mother is Jennifer Tate? Seriously? I saw her in *Spring Break Slaughter*. It's a classic."

I nod. "Yep." We still live off the money from those awful movies, and the show. Especially the show. Thank God for syndication and nostalgia channels, because Mom hasn't had a lot of screen time since. Not because of crap like the *Spring Break Slaughter* franchise, but because she took most of my life off to be with me and my brother, particularly after the divorce. My parents separated as nicely as they could given Dad's affair. He didn't press for custody—just really generous visitation. And Mom didn't push for support for herself, only us. She got to keep what was hers and he kept what was his.

But lately Mom has started looking for parts again. God, I hope my superb fuckery didn't make her miss out on an audition. She's already missed out on too many opportunities because of me and my broken brain. I can't handle any more guilt. I feel like I'm ready to explode and I already take meds for this shit.

"That's cool," Connor allows. "Random, but cool. Do you act, too?"

I close my eyes. Was that a not-so-subtle dig? Like, maybe

I was acting this morning, or this entire weekend? "No. My brother does." Mark is in his first year at Juilliard. He had *Addison* to thank for the tuition. Mom is good with money.

"What do you do?" he asks.

"I'm in art school." And making a mess of it. College is more stressful than I thought it would be. It made the holes in my head . . . deeper. The city is loud and busy, and no one ever really stands out. At my high school I was one of the kids at the top of my class, but now . . . there are easily a dozen people as good as me, and at least half a dozen that are much better. I don't need to be the best, but I want to make something of myself that's outside of my mother's shadow. I don't want people to think that I've been given stuff because I'm her kid.

I want to be *good* at something.

"I'm not surprised. You're really talented."

"I am?"

"Yeah." My surprise must be all over my face, because he adds, "I saw your sketchbook."

"Thanks." I don't usually show that to just anyone. I wish I could remember the time I spent with him if it was enough to make me show him my art. My private art. "What about you?"

He glances at me in surprise that turns to disappointment. "Right—you don't remember. I want to be a writer."

I frown as a foggy image oozes through my memory, as if someone turned on a TV in the back of my brain. "You're writing a book, right?"

"Yeah." He looks so happy that I remember. I'm such a shit. How can I remember that and not anything else? And why does it feel more like something I watched happen than something I experienced?

"Take the next left," I say as we approach an intersection.

Connor takes the turn and raises his eyebrows as we continue down the street. "Wow. Nice neighborhood."

I shrug. "Yeah. If you like country clubs, I guess."

"Never been to one."

"Me either, but there's one not far from here. The beach is nice in the summer, though." We drive a little farther and I point. "This one."

He doesn't say anything as we pull into the drive, and I'm glad. Our house is great—Spanish style, cream stucco—but it can come across as pretentious, especially after I name-drop my mother. I only told him because I've had too many friends meet her and freak out because they didn't know. And then things get weird. They'd act differently around her and then my "issues" would inevitably drive them away. Until Izzy.

Connor turns off the engine.

"What are you doing?" I ask, suddenly panicked as he unbuckles his seat belt.

He looks like it should be obvious. "Walking you to the door."

"No, you're not."

"I'm not just dropping you off and driving away." His expression is incredulous as he gestures with his hand. "I don't even really know if this is your house."

I wince. "I deserve that."

"I didn't mean . . ." He sighs. "I feel partly responsible for whatever this is. Just let me do this, okay?"

Let him, one of my voices whispers.

I shrug. "Okay."

He follows me as I get out of the Jeep. Before I make it to the front door, it flies open and my mother rushes out. It's October and she's in a T-shirt and jeans with her hair in a ponytail. She looks closer to thirty than fifty, all tanned and toned. I have her pale blond hair, but that's about it. The rest of me looks like my dad's side of the family. Mark takes after Mom, which is why he's looking to be a movie star and I'm . . . not.

She grabs me in a hug so hard it hurts. "I am so glad you're okay," she whispers.

"I'm sorry," I mumble. It sounds stupid, but I don't know what else I can say.

I feel the moment she looks at Connor. She goes stiff and releases me. Her "public" face slips into place. I dread seeing it. It's her "I don't trust you" face—the one she wears with reporters. "Who's your friend?"

Mom can look intimidating when she wants to, and she obviously wants to, but Connor smiles and offers her his hand. "Connor James, Ms. Tate. Dylan stayed with my cousin Jessica this weekend. I offered to drive her home."

Nice of him not to say I was at his house. Not that Mom would be all that upset. By the time she'd turned nineteen, she'd already been a part of two different Hollywood "it couples," and I'm pretty sure she had sex with both of those guys, though I've never asked.

Mom accepts his hand. Her expression softens a bit. "Thank you, Connor." And because she's not rude: "Would you like to come in?"

"No. Thank you, though. I've got to get back." He turns to me. "Maybe I'll see you around?"

He can't *actually* want to see me after this. No, that's wishful thinking on my part. If he wanted to stay in touch he would have asked for my number.

"Yeah," I say. "Maybe. Thanks for the ride."

He smiles again and walks back to the Jeep. Mom steers me toward the front door, but I stop to look back as Connor drives away.

Mom closes the door behind us after we enter the house. My brother, Mark, sits on the stairs in jeans and a sweater. He looks like he stepped out of a fashion magazine, all chiseled jaw and perfect hair.

"Have a good weekend?" he asks. His jaw is tight and his eyes glitter with anger.

I set my backpack on the floor. Suddenly, I'm exhausted, and I still have to get that assignment done tonight and hope Professor Eckford doesn't give me a big fat zero on it. "What do you want me to say, Mark? I didn't disappear on purpose."

"No," he says, standing. "You never do anything on purpose. You just keep fucking up by accident and expect the rest of us to deal with it. Were you drunk?"

"Mark." Mom's tone has an edge of warning.

"Whatever," he says in disgust. "You're almost as bad, because you let her get away with it. Dylan, Mom's been worried sick about you. For *days*. There's even an Amber Alert out for you. Guess you can explain to the cops how you didn't disappear on purpose. Oh, and you'd better call Dad. He was going to fly out early to look for you." He turns and stomps up the stairs. A few seconds later, the door to his room slams.

I'd almost forgotten Dad was coming to visit for our birthday. Mark and I are turning nineteen on Halloween; just a few more weeks.

I glance at my mother. She looks as tired as I feel. "Did you really call the police?"

She nods. "I'll have to let them know you're home safe." A soft sigh escapes her lips. "Connor seems nice."

"I wasn't drunk." All I have is Connor's word and how I feel, but I *know* it's true. "I swear."

"I believe you."

At her simple declaration, tears burst from my eyes and stream down my face. I throw myself into her arms, sobbing like a stupid kid. "Mom," I croak through the tears. "What's wrong with me?"

"I don't know, sweetheart," she tells me, rubbing my back. She sounds tired. So tired. "But I promise we'll find out."

THREE

On the train the next morning, I stare at my reflection in the rain-splattered window. I have this weird disconnect from my face—like the features are familiar but not mine. This must be one of those moments that I've read about or seen in movies. When the main character has done something that makes it so they no longer recognize themselves, like an epiphany. Only, I don't have any life-changing realization as I stare into my eyes and wonder what's going on behind them, so I pull out my phone and text Izzy instead.

Me: I'm sorry. Can we talk later?

I stare at the screen, focusing on the words and not the reflection of my strange face. Staring at himself is what got Narcissus in trouble.

A bubble pops up on the screen.

Izzy: Okay.

It's all I need to ease the knot of tension coiled between my lungs. I lean my head back against the seat and close my eyes.

She's going to tell you she doesn't want to be your friend anymore, whispers an internal voice. It fills my mind despite the music flowing from my earbuds.

Shut up, I think, but I'm already paranoid that it's right. Izzy's finally going to be done with me.

It's going to be okay, another voice insists. That's the one I'm going to listen to, because I have to. If I listen to the other one, I'll fall apart.

I get off the train at Grand Central and switch to the subway. As usual, the station is filled with bodies. There are the regulars, moving fast, focused on where they're going, and there are the tourists, who stop in the middle of the thoroughfare. Avoiding them is almost impossible. Look, I get it: There's a lot to see in New York. But get the hell out of everyone's way while you gawk at it.

The subway platform's no better. One minute for the next train. We pile into the cars, pressed together like tapioca pearls in bubble tea. I hold on to the bar as the train speeds through the dark tunnel. When I emerge aboveground again, I'm only a couple of blocks from school and the rain has stopped.

Professor Eckford, one of my favorite instructors at school, looks up when I knock on his office door. He's in his forties and has something of a scruffy Justin Timberlake vibe. Izzy thinks he's hot, but I just think he knows his shit. Besides, I'm pretty sure he has a boyfriend.

"Dylan," he says with a slight smile. "The prodigal has returned, huh?"

"Yeah," I reply. "Sure." I have no idea what he's talking about. "Can I come in?"

He gestures to the row of chairs directly in front of his desk. "Please. I'm assuming you're here to discuss the assignment that was due yesterday?"

I set it on his desk. It's not my best work, but it's done. "I understand you'll probably take points off for it being late. I'm sorry. It wasn't . . . intentional."

He looks at me—really looks. "What's going on with you, Dylan?" He folds his hands on top of my work. "Really. What's up?"

I shake my head. There's this throbbing on the right side of my skull and all this noise inside, like somewhere there's a TV with the volume up and no one will turn it down, but it's in a foreign language so I don't even understand the show.

They won't shut up. I really wish they'd be quiet. Is it normal to feel like the inside of your head is a New York City apartment building?

"I don't know what's going on, Mr. E," I reply honestly, blinking away the fog that's trying to cover my mind. "I've got a doctor's appointment this afternoon to hopefully figure it out."

"I spoke to your mother. She tells me you've been blacking out."

I draw back. Why the hell would Mom tell him anything?

"I'm not a drunk." Not anymore, and even when I was, it wasn't like this. What happened with Connor wasn't the same. Wasn't like any blackout I'd experienced before.

His expression doesn't change. "I didn't say that you were. Blackouts happen for other reasons."

"Like tumors," I supply. I'm terrified it's cancer. I haven't said that to anyone. But yeah, what else could it be? An aneurysm? A clot? A brain-eating amoeba?

"Let's not go there," he suggests with a gentle smile. "I'm glad you're going to the doctor. Your grades have slipped a bit since the first of the semester. Maybe this will help you get back on track."

"I hope so. I don't want to mess this up." It's only my first year. I can't fail this soon. Art is the only thing I truly love to do, and I need to have it in my life. Without it, there's no point in anything else.

God, you're so dramatic. Take a pill or something. I blink. The voice broke through the noise in my brain and now there's . . . silence. Like a circle of people is gathered around me waiting to see what I'm going to say or do next. I almost prefer the noise.

Professor Eckford is still watching me, oblivious. "You're a talented artist, Dylan. Nothing can take that from you."

A stroke could—like a stroke caused by brain cancer. I take a deep breath, because I haven't gotten to the point where I can dry-swallow my antianxiety pills. "Are you going to fail me on the assignment?"

"No. Health issues are valid excuses for late work." His eyes narrow a little bit. "You look tired. Maybe you shouldn't have come to class today."

"I'm okay." I'm not, though. Being here makes me nervous. Anxious—like I have ants bustling beneath my skin.

He nods. "All right. Is there anything else you'd like to discuss?"

"Do you . . ." I hesitate. "Do you ever feel like you don't know yourself?"

"Excuse me?"

"Do you ever look in the mirror and not recognize your face?"

"Maybe? I think the image we have of ourselves is different from what we actually project." His expression has changed. He's concerned now. "Do you not recognize yourself?"

I shouldn't have said anything. I gather up my books. "I'd better go. Thanks for being so understanding."

"No worries. And, Dylan, I hope you know I'm always here if you want to talk."

I nod, rising to my feet, backpack clutched to my stomach. "Thanks." I leave the office and start down the corridor toward my first class. Around me, other students move with and against the flow of traffic, their voices competing to be heard. The noise drowns out the sound of my thoughts, but it makes my head hurt more.

"Dylan."

I turn. Coming toward me is my best—my *only*—friend, Izzy. She's got her dark hair in two braids and is wearing combat boots with tights and a short kilt. When I asked if she wanted to meet later, I meant later today, not within the hour. From the set of her jaw, she's more than annoyed, and I have no idea how to apologize for bailing on her.

"Iz," I begin, "I'm so sorry . . ."

She holds up a hand. "Yeah, I know."

I wince, even though I deserve it. This isn't the first time I've had to apologize for letting her down. I hate it, but it probably won't be the last, either.

"Where were you?" she demands as we fall into step together. "Mark said you shacked up with some guy for the weekend?"

Wait a second. "You talked to Mark?"

"Who do you think called to let me know you weren't dead in a ditch, that you'd just fucked off?"

"I didn't 'fuck off' on purpose," I counter, defensive.

That's it, stand up for yourself.

"Then, what, it was an accident? 'Cause that's some pretty passive selfishness going on."

"Yeah." That sounded lame, even to me. "Izzy, I have next to no memory of anything that happened from Friday night to Monday morning."

She hesitates, but her dark eyes narrow. "Are you drinking again?"

I know why people keep asking me this, but I'm a little tired of it. "No. I don't know what happened. It's all foggy. Honestly, I didn't ditch you on purpose. I promise."

Izzy softens. She's known me for a long time, and we've been through a lot together. "What's going on with you, D?"

Tears burn the back of my eyes. I try to blink them away before they can ruin my makeup. "I don't know. I wish to God I did. Mom's taking me to the doctor after class."

"Another one?" Her tone is doubtful. There have been a few, and nothing has changed.

"She's going to ask them to do a scan of my brain."

"Shit."

"Yeah."

"You want me to come with you?" she asks.

I nod, suddenly unable to stop the tears from coming. Izzy steers me into the bathroom and into a stall. She rips a wad of toilet paper off the roll and hands it to me. "Here." She knows better than to hug me—I'm not big on being touched, and her sudden compassion is already more than I want.

"Thanks." I dab at my eyes and blow my nose. I'm so tired. And the noise in my head won't stop.

"So, was he cute?"

I throw the tissue in the toilet and dig out my mirror to check my mascara. "Who?"

"The guy you didn't ditch me for." She smiles, letting me know we're okay.

I chuckle. "He was, but I doubt I'll see him again."

"Why not?"

"Would you want to date a crazy girl who wakes up in your bed one morning and has no memory of the time you spent together?"

"You were in his bed?"

Right. Mark didn't know that part. "That's where I woke up. He says nothing happened."

Her mouth twists in the way it always does when she thinks something's bullshit. "And you believe him?"

"I do. He didn't give off the creepy vibe."

I expect her to say something about all guys being creepy, but she doesn't.

"What's his name?"

"Connor," I reply. "Connor James."

She takes her phone and starts typing. She shows me the screen. "That him?"

"Yeah." It's a picture of him in sunglasses, laughing at something. It's not the kind of thing you post if you're trying to look cool, which makes me like it even more. "That's Connor. He lives in the city."

"He's cute. For a white boy."

I laugh. When we were fifteen, Izzy went through a phase where she only wanted to relate to her African American side and every boy who wasn't black was "cute for a ___." I haven't heard her say it in a long time.

"Doesn't say he's in a relationship."

I roll my eyes. "Don't."

"You should friend him."

"No. What I should do is get to class." Sighing, I lean back against the cool wall. "He smelled good, though." Most of the boys at school smell like paint or photo chemicals.

Says the girl hiding in a toilet stall.

"The ones to avoid always do," she says wistfully.

"Oh? Is there someone delicious I should know about?"

She looks away, but not before I see the guilt on her face.

"Oh, shit." I give my head a little knock against the wall. I *knew* this was going to happen. As soon as she told me she'd spoken to him I should have pounced. "You've got a thing for my brother."

Her cheeks turn pink. "It's just a crush. It'll go away."

I sigh. I'm not one of those people who freak out when friends crush on Mark. I guess he's a good-looking guy. And he's a great brother—when he's not being an ass. Izzy's been around for years; she's seen my twin at his worst, so it's not like she doesn't know what she's getting into.

"Does he like you?" I ask.

Izzy shrugs. "I haven't asked. And you're not going to either, got it?"

I nod and check my watch. "We're going to be late."

She opens the stall door. I walk out first. A couple of girls by the sink give us odd looks, but we just share a grin as we exit the bathroom.

We walk to class together. I'm glad we go to the same college. Sometimes I think she's the glue that helps me keep myself together—mostly.

"Meet you after class?" she asks when we stop at the door to her History of Photography class. I agree and manage to sneak into the room two doors down—Intro to Pop Surrealism—before Ms. Kennedy closes the door. She smiles at me as I brush past her. This is one of my favorite classes. I definitely have an appreciation for pop and lowbrow art. Lori Earley and Caia Koopman are two of my favorite contemporary artists.

I check my phone before putting it on silent mode for class. Suddenly my cheeks hurt from smiling.

I have a friend request from Connor James.

—

The doctor Mom made an appointment with is Maria Bugotti, a neurologist who had a cancellation spot open up on her schedule, otherwise I would have had to wait a few weeks to get in to see her as a new patient. It helped that Mom had been referred by a mutual friend.

The doctor's office is in a clinic not far from Montefiore New Rochelle Hospital. When we first arrive, Mom and Izzy and I sit in the waiting area, where I fill out paperwork before being taken into Dr. Bugotti's consultation room. I sit in front of the desk and gnaw on the side of my thumb, tearing at a bit of cuticle with my teeth.

We only have to wait a few minutes. As soon as Dr. Bugotti walks in, she shakes Mom's hand and introduces herself.

Mom smiles. "Thank you for seeing us, Doctor. This is my daughter, Dylan, and her friend Izzy."

The doctor turns to me. She's got to be over six feet tall and her eyebrows are perfect. Like, completely symmetrical and full—not a stray hair in sight.

She offers me her hand and I take it. "Hello, Dylan. Nice to meet you. Please, sit." As she lowers into her chair, she slips on a pair of reading glasses and opens the file on top of her desk. "So, Dylan, you've been having trouble with memory loss?"

I nod. "Yeah. I've lost hours before, but this is the first time I've lost days."

Her expression remains the same. My shoulders relax a little. If she's not freaking out, I won't freak out. "Can you tell me what happened? Start with what you do remember."

I tell her about going to the coffee shop, then waking up at Connor's.

"Was it a total amnesic episode, or do you have some idea of what's transgressed?"

"Both? I have some foggy images in my head of things that happened, but it feels like they happened to someone else."

The doctor nods, making notes on the pad in front of her. "Are you on any medications?"

My mother gives her the list of what I'm currently taking and what I've taken in the past. Dr. Bugotti frowns. "That's quite a lot. You've been treated for anxiety, depression, bulimia . . . You were tested for schizophrenia?"

"Yes," Mom says before I can. "But she doesn't have it."

The doctor looks between the two of us. "So, you've been having issues for several years now."

"Yes," I say quietly.

"She's always had an active fantasy life," Mom reveals, obviously nervous, maybe a little defensive. "We thought she was just an imaginative child, you know? I mean, it runs in the family. It was the anxiety and depression that hit us."

"Why didn't you take Dylan to a neurologist before this?" There's no accusation in Dr. Bugotti's tone, just polite interest.

Mom flushes all the same. "We were going to, but that's when she was diagnosed with social anxiety and depression. The medication seemed to help."

Your mother doesn't need to talk for you.

The voice makes me sit up straight. "For a while," I add. "Look, Doctor . . . I have memory issues and sometimes the world seems like it's out of focus, or off balance. If I'm crazy, then I'm crazy, but there's something wrong with me and it's affecting my life and my family." I glance at Izzy. "My friends."

"I hate that word," Mom whispers. She gets upset when I call myself crazy.

"And you just want to know what it is," Dr. Bugotti supplies, sparing a small smile for my mother, before focusing on me again. I like that she's looking to me for answers.

"Yes. I used to drink—a lot. I guess that's self-medicating, right? Well, that helped for a bit, too. Or at least made me too numb to care. And I was able to blame the blackouts on that, but I don't drink anymore, and I don't take drugs that haven't been prescribed to me. Shouldn't the pills make me better?"

"In the case of mental health conditions, sometimes it's a matter of finding the right medication."

I gesture to the piece of paper on her desk. "Haven't I tried most of them?"

She smiles slightly at that. "A good representation, at least."

"Dr. Bugotti," Mom begins, leaning forward, "we've seen therapists, psychiatrists, specialists, holistic practitioners . . . No one has been able to give us the answers that work. I just want someone to figure out why my little girl is having such a hard time."

Izzy reaches over and takes my hand. She squeezes my fingers. I squeeze back.

"Of course you do, Ms. Tate. Dylan's well-being is my priority as well. We can begin with an MRI of Dylan's brain so we can eliminate any physical causes of the blackouts and take it from there. Meanwhile, Dylan, are you under any increased stress lately?"

They always ask me about stress. "I've been struggling a little in school. I'm trying to catch up."

She smiles. "I remember that feeling. Try to take some time for yourself to relax, all right? And make sure you're getting enough rest."

They always tell me that, too. The only difference with Dr. Bugotti is that she hasn't taken my blood pressure or weighed me.

"Are you currently seeing a therapist?"

"Dr. Raymond Jones," Mom tells her before I can.

"Do you like him?" Dr. Bugotti asks me.

I glance at Mom before shaking my head. Dr. Jones keeps wanting to talk about my parents' divorce and my relationship with my father. He's always talking about my "repressed anger" and "feelings of abandonment."

"He . . . doesn't listen to what I say. He tells me what I'm feeling, as if he knows my mind better than I do." I hadn't realized until now how much that annoys me.

"Well, then let's get you a referral for someone new."

She makes a note and continues asking me questions. I try to answer as honestly as I can.

"Is there any reason for these blackouts that you can think of?" Dr. Bugotti pauses with her pen over the paper. "Any injury or trauma past or present?"

"Injury." "Trauma." The words flood my head with images. I have to be careful not to squeeze Izzy's hand too hard.

Tell her no, says a voice, loud and clear in my head. *Tell her no, NOW.*

"No," I reply, voice strained. I clear my throat. "None that I can think of."

None that I can remember.

We sit there a few minutes more and—finally—it's over. She didn't ask me about self-harm or if I have suicidal thoughts. It's a relief. But I never realized before how I really, really want this to be something I'm making up, or something mental. If it's a tumor or something . . .

I'm not ready to die.

"I'll make an appointment for a scan and we can go from there once we have the results," she tells us. "And I'll have my assistant call with the referral for a new therapist. I also want to rule out that these episodes aren't side effects of medication."

I hadn't even thought of that. I mean, I've heard of meds making people feel crazier than they already are. Could it be something that simple? Maybe I should stop taking my meds.

When the appointment is over, Mom and I thank Dr. Bugotti and leave the office. Izzy falls into step beside me.

"You do *not* stop taking your pills," Mom tells me on the way to the car. It's like she can read my mind sometimes. "She said it might be the cause, and until we know otherwise, you're not adding going cold turkey on top of it."

"She thinks I'm crazy," I blurt, then frown. Why had I said that?

Mom looks at me like she can't believe I went there. "No, she doesn't."

"She does." I open the passenger door. "You heard her. This is all to rule out physical causes. That means she doesn't think there are any physical reasons for me to be like this."

"She's a doctor, D. They have to be vague." Izzy shakes her head. "You think she's going to say, 'Right, let's see if it's cancer'? She doesn't want to freak you out."

"You're not crazy and it's not cancer," Mom insists.

I glance at Izzy in the back seat and back to my mother. "It's something," I remind her.

"It's a chemical imbalance." She starts the car. "Something they can treat with the right meds or a procedure."

She's terrified—I can see it. I can almost smell it, it's so overwhelming.

How much is she paying for Dr. Bugotti and these tests? How much has she already paid? How much of her life has she missed out on, or dates has she had to break because of me?

She'd be better off if you were dead.

I frown. WTF? Where had that come from? "Maybe it is my meds," I suppose out loud. "I *am* glad she's going to refer me to a new therapist."

Mom nods. "I wish you'd told me you didn't like Dr. Ray." I wait for her to ask if I'm having "dark" thoughts, but she doesn't. She's still too hung up, too afraid that it's something she can't fight.

"I didn't want to complain," I tell her. I didn't want to be a burden. Didn't want to be difficult.

When we arrive back at the house, I step out into the windy day. Beyond our large backyard, the tide pounds relentlessly against the beach. I imagine myself as the water, powerful and relentless. In truth, I feel like the beach. I'm tired of being continuously hit by life's crap. It's not even like I have a bad life. My brain's just fucked up.

"You look like you could use a nap," Izzy says as we walk inside.

I look at her—she's a little out of focus. I blink, but it doesn't help. "I . . . Yeah." Maybe I am tired. I feel a little loopy as I kick off my shoes. "Will you think I'm horrible if I lie down?"

"Nah. Your mom asked me to stay for dinner, so maybe I'll hang out with Mark for a bit." She takes my coat and hangs it in the closet with hers.

I smile. "You do that." If my twin breaks her heart I'll fucking kill him.

She hugs me. Hard. "It's going to be okay," she whispers.

Hugging her back, I have to blink back tears. "I hope so," I reply, voice hoarse and low.

Izzy pulls back, hands on my shoulders. She gives me a determined smile. "I *know* so. Whatever happens, you're going to be great. And I'm going to be there with you."

Words desert me. If I open my mouth I'll start crying, so I only nod and hug her again.

"I'll wake you up in an hour or so," she promises as she leaves me to join my brother.

I rub my forehead, making my way up the stairs to my bedroom. As soon as I've closed the door, I climb onto my bed and close my eyes. The noise in my head rises and blurs and . . . disappears.

A chilled breeze lifts my hair off my shoulders. I wake up freezing.

I'm on the beach, knee-deep in the tide and wading deeper. My socks are soaked, and my jeans and shirt are damp. Salt spray hits my face, cold and sharp.

What the hell?

My hands are cold and stiff—I can't feel my nose. I stumble back on numb feet, and turn and run from the water, to dry sand. How did I get here? Why am I here? I'm alone—no Izzy or Mark. No coat or shoes on the sand either. I look up—the curtains in my room are open, but there's no one there. What am I expecting? To see myself staring down at me?

I hug myself for warmth as I jog back to the house. I slip through the patio doors and strip off my socks before hurrying upstairs. My teeth chatter, I'm so cold. The last thing I remember is lying down. I glance at my phone on the bedside table—it's only been an hour.

An hour. I'm not even safe in my own freaking house for an hour.

In my bathroom, I turn on the taps in the shower and strip off my clothes. The hot water feels good and I stand under the spray for a long time. When I'm done and dressed again, there's a knock at my door. Izzy sticks her head in.

"I heard the shower and figured you were up," she says. "Wanna watch a movie or something before dinner?"

"Sure," I say. Anything to distract me. I don't tell her about my little adventure. I don't plan on telling anyone. Maybe I was only sleepwalking. People do that. I used to do it as a kid, didn't I? I think so. Yeah. Mark and I both did it. Sometimes Mom would find us playing or roaming around together, fast asleep. Obviously, the stress and anxiety of what I've been going through lately has me falling back on old habits.

Yeah, sleepwalking. That's all it was. Harmless sleepwalking, and not an attempt to walk out into the ocean and drown myself.

You weren't sleepwalking, whispers that familiar voice. I shiver. What if it's not a tumor, and it's not my meds? What if it's something else? What if I can't be fixed?

FOUR

So, what's wrong with you?" my brother asks after we drop Izzy off at her house later that night. It's late and dark and the only light inside the car comes from the dash. It's nice because I don't really have to see his expression, which I'm pretty sure is wary at best.

"Not sure yet." I fiddle with the radio. "They're supposed to do a scan."

"They didn't offer up any ideas? I mean, it was a freaking brain doctor."

I keep looking for a station. The noise of scanning reminds me of the inside of my head. I like it. "She said it could be my meds."

"That would be weird, though, right? You've been on those for a while."

I shrug. "Maybe I've been on them too long. Who knows? I just want them to figure it out."

"You seriously blacked out for three days?" I can feel the weight of his attention in his glance.

"Yep." The radio blips past a commercial for a local pizza place. "I've gotten a few moments of the weekend back, but it's like it happened to someone else."

"I still think that asshole drugged you."

"Connor's not an asshole." Is there no good music on? It's all been talk, country, or religion so far.

"Yeah, okay." Mark's not convinced, and that's okay because I am. "What do you think, then?"

Maybe it's stupid, but that he asks makes my eyes tingle. I am not going to start bawling. He'll get upset if I start crying. He always does.

"I guess maybe I could have messed up my brain with all the drinking."

"Like how people who've done too many drugs can spontaneously hallucinate?"

I glance at him. "Known many drug addicts, have you?"

"I saw something about it on a documentary. But you didn't drink enough to cause lasting damage. Did you?"

"Maybe. I dunno. I think Mom's afraid it's cancer."

"That would suck."

"Sure would." I finally find a station I like and sit back in my seat. "But then I'd be dead, and you guys wouldn't have to worry about me anymore."

He takes his eyes off the road long enough to shoot me a scowl. "What kind of fuckery is that?"

I shrug. It was a stupid thing to say. "It's true, though. If I wasn't around, Mom wouldn't have the hassle of worrying about it anymore. And you wouldn't be mad at me all the time."

"I—I'm not mad at you. Not all the time. God, you're such a drama queen. I bet you've even fantasized about your funeral. You've probably imagined me throwing myself on your casket."

"Of course you'd make *my* fantasy all about *you*."

"So, you have thought about it." He makes a scoffing noise. "I knew it."

"And you haven't?" I challenge.

Mark swears. "Most people don't sit around obsessing over the tragedy of their own demise."

"So, you have thought about it," I parrot mockingly. I can't help but chuckle at the expression on his face.

"I'm more normal than you are, freak," he says. He's only teasing, though.

"Be glad freakishness isn't genetic." I sigh. I'm tired of talking about it. "So, what's going on with you and Izzy?"

"What do you mean?"

"You're never going to get an acting gig if that's the best you've got." I look out the window at the passing night. I love nighttime. Ever since I was little I've loved seeing lights in the darkness. I guess it reminds me of Christmas. There's something so pretty about twinkling lights—even traffic.

He ignores my dig. "Has she . . . said anything about me?"

I could torture him, tell him no, but why should the two people I care for most be lonely and messed up just because I am?

I really *am* a drama queen. But I'm not a jerk.

"She likes you, too," I reveal with a laugh. "And I'm okay with it, if that was your next question."

"It wasn't."

I smile. It was, and it's nice. Mark can be an ass sometimes, and I know he thinks I can be a pain, but neither of us wants a world without the other in it. I'd do anything for him, and he'd do anything for me. If I told him to stay away from Izzy, he would. But I don't have the right to ask that of either of them.

My phone dings. I pull it out of my pocket and check the screen.

Unknown: Feeling better today?

I don't recognize the number.

Me: Who is this?

Unknown: Connor. Sorry.

Connor. My stomach flutters. How did he get my number? I must have given it to him, but of course I don't remember.

Me: Yeah. Thx.

Connor: Can I call you?

Me: Out. Call you in 10?

Connor: Sure.

"Who's that?" Mark asks.

I put my phone away. "No one you know."

"The asshole?"

I roll my eyes. "Again, he's not an asshole. An asshole wouldn't have driven me home." An asshole wouldn't have done my laundry.

My brother snorts. I'm beginning to think he has a sinus infection with all the noise he's been making. "He would if he wanted to know where you and your famous mother live."

"He didn't even know about her before we got home. And besides, Mom's not famous. Not anymore."

"She's famous enough," he insists.

"What does that even mean?"

"You shouldn't trust this guy."

"Not with my life, no. But I trust him as much as I trust any guy I've just met." Okay, maybe I trust Connor a bit more than that.

"I don't know how you've avoided a serial killer before this." Could he be more condescending?

"Because they all found out you're my brother and decided I've suffered enough."

"You're crazy."

"I thought we covered that already."

"I didn't mean—"

I hold up a hand. "I know what you meant. Relax. And leave Connor alone, okay? He's a nice guy, and when he realizes what a mess I am, he won't want anything to do with me anyway, so you don't have to worry."

A long silence passes.

"Hey," he says softly. "I'm sorry. If you like this guy, cool. I'm just . . . I'm worried about you, D."

Tears prickle the back of my eyes, hot and sharp. I blink

them away. "Me too," I confess. "I want to figure it out so I can deal. Not knowing's the worst."

"You're going to be okay."

I'm not sure if he's trying to convince me or himself, so I don't say anything. The rest of the drive—what little there is left—passes with only the radio as a soundtrack. I'm relieved when we pull into the driveway.

"So, you're really okay with me and Izzy?" he asks as he switches off the engine.

"Knock yourself out." I stifle a laugh at the stupid smile on his face as I get out of the car. I try not to run into the house, and inside I toe off my shoes—which don't want to come off. I rush upstairs, but then force myself to wait until I've caught my breath to make the call.

Connor answers on the second ring. "Hey."

"Hey." I sound like a parrot.

"It's only been nine minutes and seventeen seconds."

I grin as I sit down at my desk. "Want to hang up and I'll call you back?"

"Nah, it's okay."

I lean my elbows on the scarred, wooden surface. "How did you get my number?"

"You gave it to me. Is that not okay?"

I like the way he talks, his choice of words and how easily they seem to fall off his tongue. "No, no. It's fine. It's good, really. I just . . ."

"Don't remember."

I close my eyes. *Idiot.* "Um . . . yeah."

"I didn't mean to embarrass you." His voice is low, gravelly. I like it.

"You didn't. I do it to myself."

"Did you go to the doctor?"

"Yeah." I open my sketchbook. "They want to run tests."

"That's what they do. How else are they going to pay for all that malpractice insurance?"

He's weird. I like that, too. "I just want to know what's wrong with me."

Maybe then you'd stop fucking talking about it all the time.

Mentally, I give the voice in my head the finger.

"It would be great if it was that easy, right? Like, someone just comes up to you and hands you a letter. 'Here's what's wrong with you.' Think of all the time you'd save in therapy. You could get right to it."

I smile. "I'd be scared it wouldn't only be one thing. They'd probably give me a list."

He chuckles. "I don't think so."

Selecting a pencil from my pink skull pencil holder, I start sketching. I don't want to talk about my brain anymore, but it's nice to talk to someone who doesn't seem to think it's that big a deal.

"Do you ever sleepwalk?"

"Sleepwalk? Nah. I talk, apparently."

I remember saying something similar to Jess but don't actually remember him doing it.

"I think I sleepwalked today. I remember lying down on my bed and the next thing I knew I was on the beach." I shiver at the memory.

"I guess you could have woken up in worse places."

"I was standing in the surf in my socks." I'm not going to tell him that I think I might have planned to walk out farther.

"Shit. How cold was that?"

"Very." I'm drawing him from memory and the jaw doesn't feel right. I erase and retry. "Thanks again for bringing me home yesterday."

"I wasn't about to let you take the train given how freaked out you were."

"Still, I appreciate it."

"You're welcome." A heartbeat later, "So, can I see you?"

I drop my pencil. "What?"

"You heard me."

"Yeah. Okay." If I'm not dying, that is. If they don't lock me up.

"Maybe this weekend? We can do something closer to you if you want."

He wants to hang out. Only the two of us? "Like what?"

"I dunno. Like a movie, or something? Get some food. Just hang out. Maybe this time it'll be worth remembering."

Is it weird how much I appreciate him making a joke of the whole thing? "I'm pretty sure it was worth remembering last time, my brain just didn't get the text."

"So, Saturday? I can call you Friday to make plans."

"Sure." And, before I lose my nerve, "You can call before that, if you want. I mean, it *is* only Tuesday." Look at me, flirting.

Connor chuckles softly. "Maybe tomorrow? Same time?"

"Sure. If you want."

"I'll talk to you then. Good night."

"Night." I end the call and set my phone on the desk before picking it up again. I go to Connor's page and bring up

his photo album. I scroll until I find one of him—with Jess—
that I really like and use it as a reference as I draw. A couple
of hours later, my hand starts to cramp, and I realize how
late it is. I need to go to bed, but I'm really happy with how
the portrait looks so far. Getting a good likeness of someone
is only half getting the features and dimensions right. The rest
is all about the shading and values—you have to re-create the
planes and hollows of the face with nothing more than pencil
lead and the illusion of light and shadow.

Leaning back in my chair, I yawn. I'm exhausted and I
have class tomorrow. I start to flip my sketchbook closed, but a
passing page catches my eye. It's a character I've been drawing
recently, even though she's been in my head for as long as I
can remember. With long blue hair, sultry eyes, and a curvy
body, she's pretty much the antithesis of me. I don't remember
drawing this. It must have happened over the last few days,
because I have work from last week just before it. One more
thing lost to the void, I guess.

I've written something on the page, and as I read it, my
heart skips a beat. Somewhere along the line I'd given her a
name.

Lannie.

—

My MRI is scheduled for Monday afternoon, and tomorrow—
Friday, is my first appointment with my new therapist, Dr.
Christine Zhao. She emailed Mom a questionnaire for me to
fill out, so I do that on the train on my way home from class
instead of texting Connor like I want to. He called me last

night and we talked for at least an hour about our favorite books and movies. Nothing about my head or how messed up it is.

I've got a crush brewing. It's probably not going to end well—my love life has been pretty disappointing thus far—but I'm not so jaded that I'm not going to try. Besides, I like Connor. Like, actually *like* him as a person.

I stare at the questionnaire and try to focus on the words printed across the paper. The first page is personal information. Then I see this:

Symptoms (check those that apply):

• Difficulty falling asleep • Difficulty getting out of bed	• Difficulty staying asleep • Persistent tiredness
Average hours of sleep per night _____ • Lost interest • Irritability • Panic attacks • Anxiety • Avoiding friends • Avoiding places • Outbursts of anger • Excessive worry	• Feeling numb • Isolation • Rapid shifts in mood • Trouble leaving home • Feelings of guilt • Feelings of fear • Feeling worthless • Sadness
• Feeling helpless • Not feeling like self • Difficulty concentrating • Increased energy • Dizziness	• Feeling hopeless • Acting unlike self • Confusion • Decreased energy • Racing thoughts

• Large gaps in memory • Thoughts of self-harm • Intrusive thoughts	• Nightmares • Thoughts of harming others • Flashbacks

• Feeling lack of control   • Hearing voices when no one else is present   • Confusion as to what is real   • Persistent intrusive thoughts, impulses and images   • Feelings that your body is being controlled by another   • Difficulty meeting the expectations of others

Fuck me.

There's not an "all of the above" option, which, honestly, would really help. Not only would it be efficient, but it would make me feel less messed up for wishing there was one.

But who doesn't feel hopeless sometimes? Who doesn't have anxiety or trouble sleeping in our current social and political climate? What young person doesn't feel like their body is being controlled by other forces at times?

Okay, maybe not that one. My pen hovers. I don't want to check it. I've checked almost every fucking selection on the page. But they can't fix me if I'm not honest. I have to be honest.

You don't have *to be honest.*

I ignore the voice and answer the questions the best I can. I don't know what it all means, but that's for the doctor to figure out, right? I mean, she'll talk to me before drawing any conclusions or attempting a diagnosis. They always do. I just hope this time it's the right one. I'm tired of getting my hopes up, doing the work, and then still being fucked up.

"Kaz?"

A voice makes me look up. The person has stopped right beside me. It's a girl in her early to mid-twenties. Huge blue eyes rimmed with black. Dark skin, arched black eyebrows. Nose pierced. Pretty in a punky way—like an Indian Tank Girl. My heart gives a hard thump against my ribs. I don't know her, but she looks like she knows me.

"Sorry?" I say, blinking.

She sits down beside me. She smells like leather and amber. Something about it tickles the back of my brain. That scent. Warm skin. Soft lips . . .

I blink again. The world goes out of focus, like my head is wrapped in wool, and snaps back in—sharp and clear. She smiles at me and I feel my lips curve in response. It's weird because it's me but not. It's like . . . like I'm a puppet in my own skin. Like some part of my brain knows what to do even if I don't.

"I know it's you." Her breath smells like mint. "I'd know you anywhere."

I don't remember her name, but it's obvious she knows me. "Oh?" My voice sounds rough yet coy.

"Well, yeah. You're pretty memorable."

She's turned toward me, blocking me in, making the world small and all about her. It's a very intimate gesture. A flush creeps up my neck. Nerve endings tingle.

"Nisha," I echo aloud the word whispered in my head.

Her smile grows. Her teeth are perfect. "You do remember."

No, not really, but I *feel* something. Something strong and wonderful and . . . sexual.

WTF?

I'm straight. I've always been straight. I've never wanted to be with a girl, but at this moment, I want the one sitting next to me, and it's because I've been with her before. The phantom feel of her fingers lingers on my skin.

How could I have totally flipped my sexuality and not remember it? Is this schizophrenia? I don't know enough about it to even guess. Could we have hooked up when I was drinking?

That she's a girl doesn't freak me out. Well, it does a little, only because it's not something I really ever thought about. What freaks me out is the same old issue—that I don't remember. And what little I do recall feels like something that I watched, not something I experienced.

If I was religious, I'd wonder if maybe I was possessed.

"Give me your phone," Nisha commands.

I hesitate, but my body doesn't, handing over my phone as if this were completely natural. She smiles, and her thumbs tap against the screen. "I'm adding myself to your contacts. Now you have no excuse not to call."

"Text yourself so you have my number." Why does my voice sound like that? In my head it's even scratchier.

Her glossy dark gaze meets mine. "You sure? I'll definitely use it."

My lips lift at one corner. "I hope so." I watch her type.

Our fingers brush when she hands the phone back to me. A jolt of electricity hits me straight in the chest. Some of the glint leaves her eyes, deepens into something else.

"My stop is next," she says. "Want to come home with me?"

I do. I really, *really* do. I have to fight the part of me that wants to go. The world slips out of focus once more. I blink as my head starts to swim. I don't know what this is, but if I let it take me, I will be gone and I don't know for how long. I promised Izzy we'd hang out tonight. "I can't," I manage to get out. I grip the edge of the seat to keep myself from getting up.

Bitch. That raspy voice rings in my head like a car crash. Anger swirls through my brain—not of me but *at* me. My right temple throbs with the beginning of a headache. My vision blurs as a shadow sweeps through me like a cloud passing in front of the sun.

The train slows.

"Another time," Nisha says, not bothering to hide her disappointment. She smiles, though, when she leans over and kisses me on the mouth. I don't even have time to respond before she stands and steps into the aisle. "Call me. Maybe I'll still be available." She winks and walks toward the nearest exit as the train comes to a halt. She doesn't look at me as the doors open and she steps out.

I look out the window as disappointment and resentment settle in my stomach. My hand lifts—palm pressed to glass as the train begins to move. Nisha turns her head and our gazes lock. A little smile tilts her full lips as she waves. My heart warms as I feel my mouth smile back. I watch her for as long as I can, but she's gone when the track takes a turn.

We've got her number, I think, like I'm trying to placate myself. *We'll call her.*

The noise in my head subsides. The headache is still there, but not so bad. I close my eyes and lean my head back against the seat. Two stops later and I'm off the train, standing on the platform in the crisp afternoon, blinking against the sun.

Mom's waiting for me in the parking lot. She looks relieved to see me. Did she sit here waiting for me that Friday I disappeared with Connor? No. This picking-me-up thing is new. Normally I take an Uber from the station, or if it's nice I walk.

"Hey," she says when I climb into the passenger seat.

"Hey." I put my bag on the floor.

"How was your day. Anything happen?"

I hesitate. She sounds so hopeful. "No," I lie. "Nothing." I tell myself not to feel guilty. Mom doesn't need to know I ran into a girl I don't remember having sex with.

And what does it say about me that I'm more freaked out about not remembering having sex with her than I am about my surprise bisexuality? I don't care who people love as long as it's consensual. But . . . I think something like that ought to be memorable.

There's nothing forgettable about Nisha. So why don't I remember? Feels disrespectful of me not to know what happened.

"Oh, good." Mom's relief is palpable.

"Yeah. It was a good day." I force a smile as I buckle up.

She takes my hand in hers. "You're going to have a lot more of those real soon. I know it."

My mom is beautiful. It's what got her on TV and gets her stared at when we go out. But lately, the fine lines around her eyes have gotten deeper. She looks exhausted and it's all because of me.

I'm not going to cry. I swallow the tears instead. "I hope so."

She lets go of me to concentrate on driving. "We should celebrate that it was a good day. How about pizza?"

"Sure." Let's celebrate that I'm a lying shit.

"Did Izzy have class today?"

"She was done earlier than me."

"She's supposed to come over tonight, right? Why don't you call her and see if she wants to join for dinner? We'll pick her up."

Izzy's the only person I can talk to about this, so I don't need any more incentive to text. She responds within a few seconds.

"She's down," I say. "Says to give her five minutes."

"It'll take that long to get to her. You want to order the 'za? We'll pick it up on the way home. Oh—text your brother and see what he wants."

I roll my eyes. "He'll want what he always wants—meat, meat, and more meat, with extra cheese. Then he'll complain about having to work out to make up for it."

She laughs. "You're right. Go ahead and order it. I trust you. You've got my card number, yeah?" Mom made sure a long time ago that both Mark and I had credit cards linked to her account. We're allowed to use them for food and school stuff without question. Any bigger purchases have to be cleared first.

Yeah, we're lucky. Really lucky. I know that. And I know if the tabloids found out about my "episodes" I'd be just another train-wreck offspring of a former teen star.

"Mark got a callback for that commercial," Mom tells me as I place the order on the restaurant's app.

I glance at her. "That's more cause for celebration than me, don't you think?"

She smiles as she watches the road. "He didn't want me to say anything. He thinks it will jinx it."

I shake my head. "Right, because the world works like that."

"Don't let on I told you."

"I won't." I submit our order and then check my messages. There's one from Connor.

Connor: Call you later? Think about what you want to do tomorrow.

I smile. I've texted with him enough to realize he never uses abbreviations or slang or shorthand. He went off on a rant the other night about how illiterate our generation is. It was cute.

Me: Sounds good.

"Is that Connor?" Mom asks.

"Yeah. How did you know?"

"Your smile."

Ugh. "I'll have to work on that."

"I think it's nice. Are you still going out Saturday night?"

"Yeah."

Her humor fades. "We need to put one of those apps on your phone so I can find it if anything happens."

"Connor's not going to abduct me, Mom. I'll give you his number if you want."

"I don't mean Connor. I mean . . . in general."

It feels intrusive, but I get it. In fact, I'm relieved she suggested it. It would be different if I knew what I was doing, but . . . I don't.

"I'll do it now," I tell her.

Her shoulders visibly drop. "Thank you."

"I don't mean to make you worry, Mom."

"I know that, sweetie. And I know I can't lock you in your room until we find out what's going on. We just have to figure this out as we go. I promise I won't spy on you."

I think about the things I've forgotten. What else have I lost? Is there someone else I've had sex with? Should I get tested for STIs? What have I done? *Fuck.*

"Maybe you should," I suggest. "Maybe I should get one of those chips they put in dogs."

"Oh, honey," she says with a laugh—like I've made a joke.

I'm not joking.

FIVE

That must have been so freaky," Izzy says later that night as we lie on my bed. "Are you sure you had sex with her?"

I nod, propped up on my elbow on my pillow. "I remembered flashes of it—like I was watching a movie."

Her eyes sparkle as she looks at me. "What was it like?"

Heat fills my face. "I'm not sure." I'm not going to tell her I think I liked it. That part of me wants to do it again. I'm not going to tell her because I don't know how to make her understand when I don't even understand myself.

"You're bi." She slumps back against the pillows she has piled against the footboard. "God, this makes you so much more worldly than me. I'm jelly."

I arch a brow. "Yeah, because that makes so much sense."

Izzy grabs her phone off the comforter and starts typing.

"Okay, this forgetting shit is getting old, right? Let's see what it could be."

"You really don't want to do that," I warn her. Like I haven't already looked.

She ignores me. "Here we go—confusion and memory loss. Possible causes are: drugs, head injuries, infections, hypothyroidism, diabetes, mental illness, liver failure, stroke, brain tumors, syphilis, HIV . . ." She looks up at me, eyes wide.

I smirk. "Told you."

"Balls, D. That's some serious shit." She sets the phone facedown on the bed. "You don't have any of that crap. It's nothing they can't fix."

She says it as if nature wouldn't dare defy her. I envy that confidence. Mom has a friend who had a stroke in her twenties that messed her up hard. She's in her forties now and still has problems from it. "It might be, Iz. I'll burn that bridge when I get to it. Right now, I just want to find out what it is." I always used to roll my eyes when people said not knowing was the hardest part, but it's true. Or, at least it's true until you know, then knowing's the hardest part.

"How long after the MRI will you have to wait?"

"I don't know. Probably a week? Maybe less if they're not that busy, I guess." I shrug. We look at each other, silent. She's worried about me. So am I.

There's a knock at my door.

"Yeah," I call.

The door opens to reveal Mark. He's wearing jeans and a T-shirt, but he looks like he's about to get headshots done. Like, he's carefully disheveled with just enough scruff to look older than he is. He leans against the doorframe and crosses his arms, showing off his muscles.

"You guys wanna watch a movie or something?"

I turn to my friend. Does she know this display is all for her benefit? Her cheeks are flushed as she checks her phone. "Actually, I'd better take off. I have early class in the morning."

My brother straightens. "Want a drive?"

"Yeah, she does," I tell him, drawing startled glances from them both. Oh, please. Even if I didn't know they were into each other, I'd know now. Neither are great at subtlety.

Izzy smiles. "That would be great, thanks."

He turns his attention to me. "You coming?"

I smile. "Nope." I'm not the least bit offended by how happy he looks to hear it. I say goodbye to Izzy and close my door when she's gone.

Alone, I sit down on the bed and lean back against the headboard. I pick up my phone and go into my contacts and find Nisha's name. I delete her information. I don't know what's wrong with me, but I'm pretty sure she doesn't deserve to be involved in it. Plus, I'm still freaked out by the whole thing and my mixed emotions around it.

Why did she call me Kaz? That's one of the details I didn't share with Izzy. I haven't heard that name in forever. Kaz was the name of one of my imaginary friends when I was a kid. I had a few of them. Kaz was always the one I blamed when I got into trouble. No matter what it was, I always told my parents that Kaz made me do it.

Kaz was fun and daring and not afraid of anything. I wanted

to be more like her, but that was years ago. Did I use that name so I could pretend to be braver than I am? Pretend to be something I'm not? I've never considered myself duplicitous, but . . .

It's not the first time I've lied about my name. I did it to Connor and Jess too, and I've done it to other guys in the past. Guys I met at parties and didn't want hassle from, or guys I knew I wouldn't want to see again. But it seems weird that I would pull Kaz out of a hat after all this time, though I guess I thought it would be easy to remember?

And the way I reacted to Nisha. There was something inside me that was happy to see her. I obviously didn't give her a fake name hoping we'd never see each other again.

I'm about to search "symptoms of a stroke" when my phone buzzes with a message from my father.

Dad: Hey, kiddo. How's it going?

Me: Pretty good. Haven't woken up in any strange places. You?

Dad: I haven't woken up in any strange places either.

Me: Bet Angie appreciates that.

Dad: Smart-ass.

Angie is his wife. I refuse to call her my stepmother because it's not like I've spent any real time with her, or like she's been a mother to me. She's only ten years older than I am, so . . . yeah. Anyway, it's no secret he was sleeping with her while married to my mother, so if we can't joke about it, it's going to stay a point of betrayal. I could do that, but what's the point? Mark and I agree our parents are happier apart and we're happier with them apart, so being bitter seems pretty useless.

Me: Can't wait to see you.

Dad: Me too. Bella's first trip to New York. You'll have to spend a day with us—or more.

Bella is my stepsister. She's five and such a force of nature. I've spent time with her before, but mostly we interact when I video-chat with Dad. She's finally old enough to remember stuff we've done or talked about, and she gets excited about talking to me and Mark. She's like chaos in a cute package.

Me: Done. We'll take her trick-or-treating.

Dad: Awesome. Guess what? Travis is going to meet us for a few days.

That's a surprise. Travis is my uncle—Dad's brother. I haven't seen him in years. Haven't thought about him in forever. Once our parents divorced, Uncle Travis slowly dropped out of our lives. I always liked him. He spent a lot of time with us when Mark and I were little. He used to buy me a lot of presents.

Me: It'll be great to see him again. Where are you staying?

Dad: We found a great Airbnb in the Village. There's an extra room if you want to stay over. I want to have time with both you and your brother—together and one-on-one. I want to hear about everything going on with you.

He wants to know about my "episodes." I'm getting tired of talking about it, but I guess he deserves to hear it from me.

Dad and I text a little while longer. He tells me about the show he's working on, part of the reason he's going to be in New York for a couple of months. They're filming in several different locations in the city.

Dad: Gotta run. Dinner's ready. Take care of yourself, kiddo. I'll check with you in a few days. Love you.

Me: Love you too.

After, I plug my phone into the charger. I pack up the textbooks and sketchbooks I need for tomorrow, along with my pencils and other supplies. Then I grab some clothes out of my closet. There's a long black sweater with the tag still on it that I don't remember buying. It's cool, though. Mom must have bought it for me. I pair it with some leggings and boots—toss the tag in the trash.

I contemplate texting Connor, but I have work left to do for class tomorrow. I send him a funny GIF instead, put my phone on silent, and sit down to work.

By eleven thirty I'm ready for bed. I'm frigging exhausted.

I barely have the energy to wash my face and brush my teeth. By the time my head touches my pillow, it's already spinning toward sleep.

I dream.

I walk down a long gravel driveway, canopied by tall maple trees, their leaves brilliant shades of red, peach, and gold. At the end is a large Victorian house—rose stone with black trim. Overblown garden plots are everywhere, sprouting flowers of impossible colors and size. I stop to admire giant teal lilies spotted with orange and pink. A fuzzy black bee with oil-slick eyes glances at me before flying away.

There's a flutter of movement in the corner of my eye, and I turn toward the building to see someone duck behind the curtains in a second-floor window. There's a black feathery wreath on the front door above a knocker shaped like a crow skull. I move toward the veranda and climb the steps.

There's a woman curled up on a covered swing, reading a book. She has a granny-square afghan over her legs, and her dark red hair is piled up on top of her head in a way that looks like it might fall at any second. She looks up as I approach, her gold eyes widening in surprise. She sets her book aside.

"Hi," she says. "What are you doing here?" Her voice is rich and clear and familiar to me in a way that makes me smile.

"Just visiting," I reply. "Can I go inside?"

"It's your house. Knock yourself out."

I turn to the door—it's open. I walk inside. The interior of the house is as eclectic and awesome as the outside. The furniture is Victorian, but bright—very pop-goth. The walls are covered in art of various styles and eras. I look at it all in awe as the frames build toward the high ceiling.

"Hullo."

Standing on the bottom stair of the wide, winding stair-case on the left side of the room is a little girl. Her braids and the way she's dressed remind me of the Wednesday Addams costume I loved as a kid. Her eyes are huge—almost too big for her face—and her mouth is a perfect little cupid's bow. Her skin is flawless porcelain, with shades of blue and rose just below the surface.

"Hi," I say. "What's your name?"

"Guess," she challenges with an impish smile. "I bet you can't." Her cuteness is only accentuated by her English accent.

I smile. I know the answer. "Alyss. Your name's Alyss."

Her eyes lose some of their sparkle. She's not pleased I guessed so easily. "We're all mad here," she says.

I take a step toward her. "Like in Wonderland."

"Maybe."

My gaze travels up the stairs. At the top, someone jumps back from the railing before I can see them clearly.

"What's upstairs?" I ask.

"Nothing."

"I want to look." I move closer.

Alyss steps in front of me, blocking my progress. She only comes up to my chest. "You're not allowed up there," she tells me.

I smile at her. "But it's my house. I want to see them."

Her eyes narrow. "You don't want to fuck with me, Dylan."

"What are you going to do?" I challenge. "Bite me?" She's only a kid.

Suddenly, she smiles. Only, it's more like a baring of teeth. Her mouth and teeth start to grow and keep growing, stretching her face to impossible proportions. Her teeth morph from perfect and square to sharp and jagged, glistening under the chandelier. Her jaw opens, unhinging as her mouth keeps growing, until there's barely anything left of her except this gigantic, gaping maw of wet, threatening mouth.

I can't move. "What the hell?"

Alyss lunges, teeth snapping.

I wake up with a cry. I sit up in my bed, gasping for breath in the dark. Seconds pass; then there's a soft knock at my door. It's Mom.

"You okay, honey?" she asks.

I nod, my heart still pounding in my throat. "I'm okay. Bad dream."

She yawns. "Want to talk about it?"

"No, thanks though. Go back to bed."

"You sure?"

Another nod.

"Okay. There's plenty of room in my bed if you need it." She smiles and blows me a kiss before closing the door.

As I lie back down, I consider her offer. I'm tempted to take her up on it as I pull the blankets up around my chin.

Alyss's delighted giggle rings deep inside my head.

—

Dr. Zhao's office isn't far from the train station. There's been a lot of renovation going on in New Rochelle lately, and she's located in one of the older buildings close to the hospital that have been modernized and fixed up. There are other doctors there too—the whole thing is like a mental health center.

A directory inside the door tells Mom, Izzy, and me where

to go. When we get to the office on the second floor, the waiting area is small but comfortable. There's tea and coffee and a large selection of reading material. The three people staring at their phones barely glance up when we come in.

"You guys don't have to wait with me," I tell them.

They both give me "that" look. I sigh as they sit down, and walk over to the reception window. The guy behind the glass doesn't look much older than me. He smiles before opening the partition. I tell him my name and give him my insurance card. Of course, he has papers for me to fill out. He gives me a clipboard and tells me to attach the questionnaire I've already answered.

"Do you need help with that?" Mom asks when I sit down next to her.

"It's pretty straightforward," I reply. Besides, I'm almost nineteen, not nine. It's just my medical history, medications, etc. I fill out the forms as fast as I can and hand them back to the guy at the window along with my credit card for the copay.

My appointment is scheduled for four o'clock, and it is one minute past when a tall woman with shoulder-length black hair and brown eyes opens the door to the main office.

"Dylan?" she asks with a kind smile.

I stand up.

"I'll be right here if you need me," Mom says.

Inside, I cringe at her utter momness, but after all the crap I've put her through I owe her more respect than that. I give her a slight smile before walking away. She looks worried. And hopeful. So does Izzy. I feel slightly sick seeing their expressions. They're both afraid for me.

Dr. Zhao holds the door for me and follows behind once I've crossed the threshold. I begin walking down a brightly lit corridor.

"Take a left," she instructs, and I do as she tells me. "Straight ahead."

Her office is large, with a wall of windows that let in the October sunshine and give her a view of the street below. There's a solid wood desk facing the windows and a seating area diagonally across. My choices are one of two large armchairs or a love seat. I take one of the chairs.

Dr. Zhao closes the door. "Welcome," she says.

"Thanks." I curl my hands into loose fists on my thighs. I don't know what else to do with them.

"Do you mind if I record our session? It allows me to go back and make sure I didn't miss anything during the original conversation."

I glance at the camera in the corner of the room. "Will anyone else see it?"

She shakes her head. "Only me."

I shrug. "Sure."

"Wonderful." She switches the camera on and sits down across from me.

"Dr. Bugotti sent me your medical records and will be sending me a copy of the MRI results, but I'd like to hear from you the symptoms you've been experiencing."

"I filled out the questionnaire."

"Thank you, and I'll take a look at that after, but right now I'd like to just talk some, if that's okay."

I nod. "Sure."

"How long has it been since you've had a therapist?"

"Not long. I had one, but Mom and I agreed that he wasn't doing much for me."

"How so?"

"I don't feel like he really listened to me. I had this voice in my head telling me he didn't understand."

She looks at me a second, pen poised over her notebook. "Sounds like you made the right choice for you, then. What happened that prompted you to seek therapy again?"

I take a sip from the water bottle I brought with me. Where to start? "I woke up in a strange place and have no real memory of the three days before that."

Her expression doesn't change, so I can't tell what she thinks. "Was that the first time anything like that had ever happened?"

"For that long, yeah."

"But it's happened before to a lesser extent?"

I nod. "Everyone has those autopilot moments, but I can have hours that are just gone—or are foggy."

"When was the last time you remember it happening?"

"The other day I woke up on the beach, standing in the ocean."

"Woke up? Did it feel like you were sleepwalking?"

"It felt . . . it felt like I'd been walking around without knowing."

She writes something on the pad. "When you have these memory losses, how do you cope?"

"What do you mean?"

"Do you get upset? Try to make yourself remember?"

"I guess I get a little upset, yeah. Sometimes I can remember bits of what happened. Mostly I get mad because I've missed out."

She smiles. "That would be frustrating, I imagine."

"It can be." I scoot forward on my chair. "I'm scared I've had a stroke. Mom's friend had one when she was young."

"Have you had any of the physical symptoms of a stroke?"

"I don't think so."

"Well, Dr. Bugotti will determine if that's a legitimate concern. Has anything bad ever happened during one of these episodes?"

"Not that I know of." I frown. "I met up with a girl who I think I might have . . . had sex with."

Again, no reaction beyond looking at me with that direct focus. "You don't remember the encounter?"

"No, but it was obvious she knew me."

Dr. Zhao sets down her pen. "Dylan, do you have any problems with substance abuse? Drugs? Alcohol?"

"I used to drink a lot in high school, but I don't do that much anymore."

"What happened that made you adjust that behavior?"

I look away. "I blacked out at a party and came to having sex with a guy." Does she think I'm a slut? I'm starting to feel like one. I shouldn't shame myself, I know this.

"A boy from your school?"

I swallow. "Yeah. The captain of the football team. Not my type at all."

That gets a reaction. Only a pause, but it's something. She tilts her head. "How old were you at the time?"

"Eighteen."

She nods. "What happened?"

"Um, he finished, and I took off. I haven't gotten drunk since." My hands shake slightly. I haven't had any hangovers, so it must be true. "It's pretty embarrassing."

"I understand. Was that your first sexual experience?"

"No."

DO NOT TELL HER THE TRUTH.

I rub my forehead as a headache begins to build. "I don't really want to talk about that."

"Okay. We don't need to talk about anything you don't want to discuss. Let's change the subject: What was it like for you growing up?"

"What do you mean?"

"What was your childhood like? Was it happy?"

"Mostly. My parents divorced when I was young, but that's a good thing. Though, it does suck not getting to see my dad much."

"You and he have a good relationship?"

"We do."

But you wouldn't if he knew the truth, whispers a voice in my head.

She's going to ask, warns another.

I blink. I'm suddenly off-kilter—like I stood up too fast.

"What about your mother?"

"She's great."

She asks me something else and I respond, but I don't know what either of us said. I don't like this. I feel like I'm being pulled out of my own body.

"Have you ever thought about harming yourself?" Dr. Zhao asks.

I try to focus on her. I have to blink a couple of times and really concentrate. The throbbing in my head worsens. Fuck, it hurts. I dig my fingernails into my palms, focusing on the pain.

"Dylan?"

"Yes," I say, leaning back as the world comes into focus again. "I used to pull my hair out." Mom bought me a bunch of awesome wigs. I still have them.

"Trichotillomania," she calls it with a nod of her head. "It's common among teenage girls. Do you still have the compulsion?"

"No."

"Good." She taps her pen against the pad. "Do you have a large social circle? A lot of friends at college?"

"Not really. I like to think I'm friendly, but I don't make friends easily. My friend Izzy is the only one I spend a lot of time with. Oh, and I've started talking to Connor some."

"Connor?"

"The guy whose house I spent the three lost days at. I thought he'd figure I was crazy and run screaming, but we're going out tomorrow night."

"Well, that's nice. Are you nervous?"

"A little, yeah. I feel weird not remembering spending the weekend with him." I cross my legs. "He probably could have taken advantage of me, but he didn't. Most guys would have."

Dr. Zhao gives me a little smile. "Do you think so?"

I laugh. "Yeah. Most guys I've known only care about getting their dicks wet." I blink. That was crass. Honest, though.

"You don't have a very positive opinion of men."

"I guess not." Before she can ask why, I say, "I haven't been sleeping that great lately."

She hesitates, but only for a split second. "Tell me about that."

"I go to bed at a decent time, but I still wake up tired. I feel like I dream a lot—and I'm aware of it."

"Lucid dreaming? You're aware that you are in a dream and can often alter the events or surroundings you're in?"

"Yeah. And sometimes it's like I'm watching a movie play out on a screen inside my head, but other times I'm in the movie. It's weird. Last night I had the freakiest dream about this amazing house and a creepy little girl." I tell her about Alyss.

Dr. Zhao arches a brow. "That sounds like something out of a horror movie. I know you're an artist. Are you a fan of surrealism?"

I nod. "Mostly pop surrealism."

"Perhaps that carried over into your dream." I have no idea what to say, so I say nothing. "What do you think was upstairs that Alyss didn't want you to see?"

"Other people," I reply, confidently. "But I don't know if she was protecting them from me, or me from them."

"You described the house as if you liked it. Did you feel safe and welcome there?"

"Yeah. I felt like it was mine. My grandmother used to say that if you dreamed about a house it was likely a representation of your own psyche."

She smiles. "That's one thought, yes. I lean toward the interpretation of dreams being subjective upon the dreamer, and it does sound as though this house was a reflection of your personal tastes, as was Alyss."

"So, who are the people hiding in my attic?" I ask with a grin.

"Perhaps if you have the dream again you might give the little girl something to nibble on other than you."

"I don't think she wanted to hurt me. She wanted to take me inside her—you know, like when cartoon characters end up inside a whale? They're just whole and fine inside the belly of the thing? That's what she wanted to do to me."

The older woman tilts her head. "Any idea why?"

I shrug, but somehow, I know the answer. "To keep the others safe from me. Or me safe from them." As if on cue, I hear a tiny echo of Alyss's laughter in my head.

"Do you ever have the sensation of dreaming while you're awake?"

My eyes widen as I meet her gaze. "Yeah. Sometimes."

"What does that feel like?"

"Like someone else has control of me and all I can do is watch."

"How long does it last?"

I shrug. "It depends. A few minutes, maybe? Sometimes longer." That feeling of dizziness returns and I try to blink it away. The room drifts out of focus and I feel myself receding, drawing back into a warm, dark place inside. I can't stay here. I have to go back, but I'm so freaking tired. I don't want to be out. I want to stay in here where it's safe.

"Dylan?"

I blink. Dr. Zhao smiles at me like nothing's happened, like I didn't zone out on her. "Sorry?"

"I said our time is over for today. I'd like to see you again next week if that's possible."

I glance at the clock. That was fast. It didn't feel like an hour. "Yeah, okay."

She tells me to make an appointment at the desk out front and stands up. I follow her to the door, smile, and thank her for seeing me, even though I know she's getting paid a crap ton of money for it.

As I walk down the hall toward the door to the waiting area, my phone buzzes in my pocket. I pull it out and see a text from a number I don't recognize. I open it and stop dead in my tracks. It's from Nisha.

I can't wait to see you.

That's not what has my heart pounding, though. It's not the first message from her. There's a whole text exchange between us—or at least I assume it was us, because I sent her a selfie *while fucking lying in my bed last night.* My stomach drops as I read the things we said to each other. Flirty things. Sexual things.

I want to turn around and run back to Dr. Zhao. I want to show her the texts and tell her I don't remember sending them. I want to make her tell me why I can't remember.

But I don't. Not because I'm afraid, or ashamed, but because there's a part of me that doesn't want to know.

SIX

W e're double-dating tonight."

I turn away from the bathroom mirror to look at my brother, who stands in the middle of my room. My eyeliner is only half done. "Excuse me?"

"Iz and I are going out with you and this Connor guy."

"No, you're not."

He folds his arms across his chest. "Yeah. We are."

I turn my attention back to the mirror to finish my eyeliner. "Izzy won't go for it."

"It was her idea."

"Bullshit."

"It's true." This comes from Izzy as she steps into my bedroom.

I stare at her in the mirror. "What the fuck, Iz?"

She shrugs. "I want to meet this guy. Make sure he's as great as you think. You'd do the same."

"I'd ask first. You two just decided to crash my date without asking? Like I'm twelve?" I can't believe this. I really can't.

Izzy at least looks a little bit ashamed, but not Mark. "That's right," he says. "Your judgment can't always be trusted, D, and you know it. This way Mom doesn't have to worry about you."

I draw back. "That's a low fucking blow."

"But true," he argues. I don't respond because he's right. "Look, please just accept it and finish getting ready. I'll tell him when he gets here."

"No, you won't."

Mark sighs. "You don't have a choice. Either you go with us or I tell him you're not going at all."

I want to punch him in his smug face. "You wouldn't be so mean. And it's not like you can really stop me."

"Mean has nothing to do with it. I'm not spending another three days with Mom freaking out like that. *I'm* not spending another three days freaking out like that." His voice cracks.

Since I can't guarantee everything will be okay—that I will be okay—I really can't argue with that. I want to scream and throw things, but that will only make me look crazy. I know, because it's happened before. Rage bubbles inside me, compounded by the BPD. It makes all my emotions that much *more*. Plus, I feel like shit for making him and Mom worry.

My brother's not done. "Have you even considered that maybe this Connor guy is hoping you'll black out again? He could do anything to you. For all we know, he already did and is selling copies of the video online."

"He's not."

"You don't know that. You don't know anything about

this guy. I don't care what you feel where's he's concerned. I'm asking you to fucking *think* for once."

"Get out," I say, teeth clenched.

Mark sighs. "D, I'm not trying to be an asshole—"

"That's too bad. Imagine what you could achieve if you really applied yourself."

He and I stare at one another. If he thinks I'm going to break first, he doesn't know me at all. He doesn't look angry, though. He looks . . . tired and worried.

He turns away. Mumbles something to Izzy, who is watching me like she's trying to telepathically make me understand where they're coming from. I walk away, seething inside. I know where they're coming from. They love me. They're worried about me.

They don't trust me. Let's be honest, I can't trust me either. I'm mad at myself as much as them, but I can lash out at them.

Does my brother think I like putting the people I care about through this shit? Does he think it's fun wondering what the hell is wrong with me? That it's a laugh waking up in strange places, wondering what I've done? Maybe he just wants to keep that from happening. Maybe he wants to protect me, but by taking away my choice he's just making it worse.

We could always sneak out.

Yeah, I could. But then what? Mark counters by calling the cops? Even if he didn't, Mom would be upset. That seals the deal.

This is so humiliating.

Makeup done, I sit down on my bed and call Connor. He's probably already on his way.

He picks up on the second ring. I can tell he's driving. "What's up?"

"I'm giving you a chance to back out," I tell him.

"Why would I do that?" He sounds genuinely confused.

"Because my brother and his sort-of girlfriend have invited themselves along tonight." I can't call Izzy my best friend right now. I just can't.

He doesn't even hesitate. "They want to check me out, huh? I guess I can understand that."

"You can?"

"Yeah." And then, "Wait. Were you hoping I'd bail?"

"No." All the fight leaves me, and I slump against the pillows. "I'm just mad they invited themselves without asking."

"Don't worry about it. I'll be there in . . . eleven minutes, according to the app. Tell your brother to make himself pretty for me."

I'm still laughing when we hang up. If I wasn't so angry still, I would go and tell Mark just that. Instead, I fuss around with my hair. I freshened up the pink dye yesterday and it looks good with my brown eyes. I put a little curl product in—just enough for some beachy waves.

I'm downstairs looking for a jacket when Connor arrives. He actually comes to the door. Mom arches a brow when he rings the bell. "Someone raised him right."

When I open the door, Connor's on the steps in jeans, a sweater, and a wool coat. His hair tumbles over his forehead. He smiles and my stomach flutters a little. He looks at me like we're in this together. I appreciate that.

"Hi," I say. "Come on in."

He says hello to Mom and makes conversation. When Mark

and Izzy appear, he offers Mark his hand. My brother accepts the handshake—thank God. If Mark is rude to him even for one second, I'm going to lose my damn mind.

He shakes Izzy's hand next and introduces himself before I can. She's polite too—more than Mark. At least she looks uncomfortable with the whole situation.

"How 'bout I drive?" Mark suggests. More like "How 'bout I take control of the entire night?"

Connor shrugs. "Sure." He glances at me with a smile. "By the way, your hair is awesome."

"Oh," says Mom. "I hadn't even noticed you dyed it again. It does look good, Dede."

None of them had noticed—not even Izzy. That Connor did makes me like him even more. "Thanks," I say.

Mark and Izzy get their coats and we head out. Mom stops me as the others step outside.

"I know you're mad at your brother," she says, "and I don't blame you, but he only wants to keep you safe. Try to have fun, okay?"

I nod. "I will." I'll have fun if it fucking kills me.

Outside, it's chilly, but clear. I huddle in my thick faux-fur coat as I hurry toward Mark's car. Connor opens the door for me. "I'm still trying to impress Mr. Darcy," he jokes.

I grin. "It's working." I climb into the back seat and he closes the door, coming around to the other side to get in. Mark didn't open the door for Izzy, I notice. I wonder if that bugs her. Probably not.

If Connor's uncomfortable, he doesn't show it. He fastens his seat belt as Mark starts the engine, and immediately turns to me. "Have you been to the lowbrow exhibit at MoMA yet?"

"No. I want to, though."

"I'm going next week, if you want to come with."

I see Izzy's head turn slightly as she eavesdrops. The exhibit was one we'd talked about going to, but she wasn't that excited about it. Photography's more her thing. "That's so your jam, D," she says.

"That would be fab," I tell Connor. "I'm out early on Thursday."

"Awesome. We can meet there and grab some food after if you want."

I look at him. It's dark in the car except for the dashboard lights and the streetlights outside. I can't see his face that well, but he seems to be genuinely interested in hanging out with me. I like that.

"I didn't think you were into art."

"I'm working on an idea for a graphic novel set in a surrealistic world. I thought the exhibit would give me some inspiration."

"Graphic novel, huh?" Mark glances in the rearview mirror. "Sounds like something you'd be into, D."

I roll my eyes. He's trying too hard, and I'm not going to forgive him that easily. "Do you have an artist?" I ask Connor.

"No. Know of anyone?" I catch a glimpse of his smile. I've started a few graphic novels of my own, but I've never gotten very far because I'm not that great with words. Having someone to collaborate with would be amazing.

"Maybe," I reply, trying not to sound too flirty. "I'll have my agent call yours."

Connor laughs.

We go for dinner first. At least Mark asked where everyone wanted to go. We end up at a Vietnamese place not far from the movie theater. It's not fancy, but the food is delicious.

"So, Connor," Mark begins, dipping a spring roll into sauce. "What do your parents do?"

I put down my chopsticks. "Seriously?" I ask.

Connor just smiles that little smile of his. Does anything ever annoy him? "Mom's a doctor and Dad's a structural engineer."

"They must do pretty well for you to go to college to study writing."

I glare at Mark. What a douchebag thing to say. "What?" my brother asks, a stupid look on his face. Really?

Connor mixes some hoisin and sriracha together in a little bowl. "About the same as if I'd chosen to study acting."

I almost choke on my bubble tea. Even Izzy can't help but laugh. Mark flushes. "And burn," he says, but at least he's not being a jerk about it.

After that, things are a little more comfortable. We talk about movies we like as we slurp down bowls of pho and discuss reviews of the one we're going to see. It's a Marvel movie, so it's not like it's art-house fare. We're all excited about the cast and characters and are already predisposed to liking it.

After dinner we walk the short distance to the theater. We make it right as the trailers start.

"This is my favorite part," Connor tells me, leaning close as we sit down. "Lame, huh?"

I shake my head. "I like them too." I offer him some of my candy.

The trailers are good and the movie's pretty fun. The best

part? Mark keeps his mouth shut through the entire thing. Or at least he does to me. I hear him whispering to Izzy a few times, and her laughing in response. They like each other so much and it makes it hard to stay mad at them, because I know one of the things they have in common is that they both care about me.

It's about ten thirty when we arrive back at the house.

"You want to come in?" Mark asks Connor, like he's giving permission or something.

Connor shakes his head. The bottom of my stomach drops. "I think I'd better head. Thanks, though." He looks at me. "I'll text you about MoMA?"

"Sounds good," I say.

Nodding a little awkwardly, he begins to back toward his car. My brother's not even going to leave us alone long enough for me to say good night. *Asshole.*

That's the moment when I'm confident I won't hear from Connor again. Bad enough that I'm the chick with the faulty memory, but now that he's met my overprotective brother . . . God, he probably thinks we're all *Flowers in the Attic* or something.

"He seems all right," Mark allows when Connor's taillights disappear down the drive.

"Yeah," Izzy agrees. "He's nice."

My lip curls as I look at them. "Fuck you both."

They stare at me. Mark's mouth opens, but I stop him before he can speak. "You humiliated me tonight," I tell them. "I don't care what your intention was, the result's the same, and I kind of hate you right now. Both of you."

Izzy looks like I've punched her, and I don't care. I turn

on my heel and stomp into the house. Mom comes out of the living room.

"Did you have a good time?" she asks.

"No," I tell her. "I didn't." As I stomp upstairs, I hear Izzy and Mark come in. Mom says something to them and Mark answers, but I don't bother trying to listen. I go to my room and close the door. Maybe I'll just go to bed. Hopefully I'll wake up somewhere else and this night will join the list of others I've forgotten.

My phone dings. I dig it out and look at the screen.

Connor: Meet me on the beach behind your house.

I can't freaking believe it.

Me: Now?

I count the seconds until he answers.

Connor: Ten minutes.

I smile, the anger draining out of me. He could want to meet to tell me he never wants to see me again, but I don't think so. Most people wouldn't bother with that kind of courtesy. I hear Mark and Izzy go to Mark's room and close the door. From their hushed voices I know they're talking about me. Whatever. I wait a couple of seconds before slowly—and quietly—opening my door. I tiptoe downstairs. Mom's nowhere to be seen—probably back in the living room. I almost creep out without talking to her, but I can't do it. I find her sitting on the couch watching a movie. She looks happy to see me.

"I'm fine," I tell her and give her a kiss on the cheek. "I'm going for a walk on the beach. I have my phone, so you can track me if you want."

Mom smiles. "Just give me his phone number, sweetie."

I don't know how she knows. I just accept that she does and do what she asks. I put Connor's number in her phone.

"I won't tell your brother," she adds as I get up to leave. "But let me know if you're going to be late." After all I've put her through, she still trusts me. I swallow thickly.

"I love you, Mom."

"Oh, sweetie." She gives me a hopeful smile. "I love you too."

—

I find Connor sitting on the log we use when we have bonfires on the beach. The wind blows his hair around his face. He's wrapped in a thick fleece blanket.

"Cold?" I ask.

He shakes his head, squinting up at me with a smile. "Nope." He opens the blanket. "I'll share."

I hesitate, but then it's almost like someone shoves me from the inside. I stumble in the sand, lurching toward him like a scared zombie. If he notices, he doesn't let on. He just waits for me to sit beside him.

He drapes the fleece over my shoulders, and I pull it snug around me. It also pulls me snug against him. We're pressed together from shoulder to foot. He's warm and smells good.

Normally, I'd start to feel nervous, even anxious, being so close, but this is nice.

"I'm sorry about tonight," I say.

I feel his shrug. "It's not that big a deal. I get why they're overprotective. If Jess was going out with some guy she'd spent three days with that she couldn't remember, I'd tag along too." And then, "They were pretty nice, though."

"They said the same thing about you."

"So, there. No harm no foul." He nudges me. "This is better, though."

"Even though it's cold?" I ask with a laugh.

He turns to face me. "I'm not cold. Are you cold?"

At that second? Looking into his glittering eyes? Hell, no. I am definitely not cold. "No," I murmur.

He leans in like he's going to kiss me but stops. "Just for the record, you're going to remember this, right?"

I could be offended, but I'm not. I smile. "You better make it unforgettable then."

Connor laughs. I see his teeth flash in the moonlight. And then his mouth is on mine and my smile melts away. His lips are cool, his breath warm. His nose is cold.

"I've wanted to do that since you answered the door," he confesses when we come up for air. Our faces aren't even an inch apart.

"I'm glad you finally did." I touch my forehead to his.

He nudges my nose with his, tilting my head up so he can kiss me again. This time he pulls a hand free of the blanket to cup the back of my head. I shiver, sliding my own hand inside his coat to rest against his chest. He's warm and firm beneath my palm—his leanness is deceptive. I feel strong muscle under his clothes.

He makes a noise in the back of his throat that makes me shiver. He pulls me closer. Our legs entwine, bodies shift until we face each other, my legs draped over his, torsos pressed together. There's a very strong part of me that wants to take him to the sand and rip off all his clothes. There's another part, nervous and afraid of the way I feel right now.

Just relax, my head whispers. *You're safe.* He's *safe.*

I can tell Connor's enjoying himself as much as I am. I mean, it gets to a point where it's pretty obvious with a guy. He doesn't push it, though. I guess he's decided just to enjoy it too. After all, this is technically our first date.

What if I wake up tomorrow and don't remember this? I know we joked about it, but . . .

I'm not going to think about it.

I break the kiss and bury my face in his neck, breathing in his smell. It's one of the strongest senses that humans have. If nothing else, I'll remember this.

Connor hugs me, presses his cheek to mine. We sit like this for what feels like forever, holding each other. We don't talk. I don't even really think. I just enjoy. There's only the crashing of the surf and the cold salt air and us, safe and warm inside this cocoon he made.

Finally, he lifts his head. "I have to get going," he says. "My parents are taking me out for breakfast in the morning."

I don't want to leave the warm hollow between his jaw and shoulder, but I make myself. "Do you still want to go to MoMA this week?"

"Yeah." He brushes my hair back from my face with a smile. "Can I call you tomorrow?"

I nod. "Thank you."

"For what?"

"For this. For treating me like I'm normal. I was pretty mad at Mark earlier. I still am, but this . . . getting to hang out with you, was really great."

He takes my face in his hands and kisses me again. My heart throws itself against my ribs as though it's the first time our lips have touched. I'd be embarrassed if I didn't like the feeling.

"Can you find your way back?" I ask when we finally break apart and stand up from the log. One of my legs is asleep and my butt hurts and I don't care. I'd Frankenstein-walk for a month if it meant I could kiss Connor whenever, and as much as, I wanted.

"I'm good." He steps away.

"Your blanket," I say. He's left me draped in it.

"I'll get it from you later," he says. "My way of making sure you have to see me again."

I stand there, grinning like an idiot, wrapped up in fleece that smells like him. "Text me when you get home."

He tells me he will and kisses me once more before walking away. I watch until the darkness swallows him. Then, wrapped in my cozy blanket, I jog back to the house, slipping in through the sliding back door.

Mom's not in the living room anymore, so I head straight for the stairs to go up to my room. I freeze when I hear Mark's voice.

"She didn't answer?" he asks, softly.

"No," Izzy replies. There's sadness in her voice. "I guess she's asleep."

"Or hates us," my brother offers.

"You don't have to sound so fucking pleased about it," she shoots back. I smile as I hide in the shadows. Izzy might be crushing on my brother, but she's still my friend.

Mark sighs. "I'm not happy—trust me. Dylan's my twin, remember? For the first few years of her life I was her best friend and she was mine. You think I like treating her like I don't trust her? Because I really don't, Iz. I fucking *hate* it. I hate not being able to make everything right for her. I hate that she has all these problems that I can't fix. And I really hate—" He takes a breath and has to lower his voice. "I hate when my worry for her turns into resentment."

It's hard to breathe, listening to him.

"We can't control her. We shouldn't even try." Izzy comes further down the stairs and I tuck myself as deep into my little dark corner as I can.

"And what? Let her go out and get hurt?"

"I know, I know, but if you keep trying to boss her around, she's going to resent you too."

I can't see him from where I'm hiding, but I don't need to. I can imagine him running a hand over his face like he does when he's tired and stressed out. "I don't know what to do."

"Talk to her. That's what I'm going to do. Hopefully she'll listen."

I will. She knows I will.

"Yeah. Come on, I'd better take you home."

I wait until they've left before I leave my hiding spot. I

shouldn't have listened in. I'm lucky I didn't hear them talking shit about me instead of saying how bad they feel.

Mom's light is on when I go upstairs, shining through the crack under her door. I knock and stick my head in.

"I'm going to bed," I tell her.

She's under the covers already, her blond hair in a loose topknot. She's wearing an old pair of pajamas she's worn ever since Dad moved out, and is reading a novel, her glasses perched on her nose. She smiles at me. "Okay. Did you have a nice walk on the beach?"

I grin. "I did. Good night, Mom."

"Good night, sweet girl."

In my room I get ready for bed—put on pajamas and brush my teeth and all that. I climb into bed with Connor's blanket, pulling it up around my chin so I can inhale his scent.

I'm shopping on my phone for art supplies when Connor texts me that he's home. Feeling sure of myself, I snap a selfie with the blanket and send it to him. I'm starting to second-guess myself when he sends me a photo of himself in bed, his eyes heavy and his hair a tousled mess.

Connor: I'VE NEVER BEEN SO FUCKING JEALOUS OF A PIECE OF FABRIC.

Me: Lol. I've named him Mr. Darcy.

Connor: THE BASTARD

I grin and pull the blanket tighter.

Connor: Good night, D.

Me: Good night, C.

I put my phone on silent and turn off the screen before turning off the lamp on my bedside table. Then, with Mr. Darcy pulled up to my nose, I roll onto my side, tuck up my knees, and close my eyes. In my head, I play kissing Connor on the beach over and over, reliving every moment until my entire body hums with tension.

I can't remember the last time I touched myself. Can't remember the last time I wanted to, but something inside me sighs when my fingers slide between my thighs. I can smell Connor on the blanket, and as I move my fingers, I pretend they're his. It's almost embarrassing how little time passes before I shudder and moan into my pillow.

Wow.

I'm not overly sexual. I'm not a virgin—not at all—but most of my sexual experimenting has been done inside the confines of relationships, or at least hookups with people I knew—blackouts not included. Still, I haven't often enjoyed the whole process. Sometimes I did, but more often than not I was kind of "meh" about the whole thing. I guess that's why my reaction to Nisha caught me off guard. But my reaction to Connor?

If the last two minutes were any indication, I am *not* meh about Connor. Maybe that's sad, that I'm almost nineteen and I'm only now getting excited about sex. Regardless, out of the entire fuck-show that has been my life lately, it's something to be happy about, so I'll take it.

It doesn't take me long to fall asleep after that. My body is like warm rubber, loose and relaxed. I feel myself drifting on a warm breeze, not thinking about anything in particular, not worrying. I'm just me, and I'm completely okay with it. I can't remember the last time I felt this way.

I knew you'd like him, whispers a familiar voice. I hear the smile in her words.

I do, I silently reply. *I really do.*

She wraps her arms around me in a warm, comforting hug. Love and acceptance radiate out of her. I can't quite see her face, but I catch a glimpse of her blue hair. I snuggle into her embrace and deeper into the Connor-scented folds of Mr. Darcy with a contented sigh.

I want you to always feel like this, she whispers. *I love you, Dede.*

I smile. I'm not sure who she is, but I love her too.

SEVEN

I have no expectations of my MRI on Monday. It's not like they can give me any answers right away. I have to wait until Dr. Bugotti and I guess some other people look at it. That's going to take at least a week.

I really hope I get some answers then. But for now, I wait, and get the test done. I have to leave class early that afternoon to get there, and I'm surprised to find Izzy waiting outside for me.

"Hi," she says when she sees me, looking me directly in the eyes.

"Hi," I respond. I'm not sure how this is going to go. As far as I know we haven't spoken since Saturday. I don't think I've had any blackouts since then, but it's not like I'd know.

"So, I know you're like, mad at me, but I know your MRI is today and your mom already said I could come along."

I shrug. "Okay. And yeah, I was. You and Mark ganged up on me."

"He didn't handle it right. He should have talked to you instead of forcing you into it." She sighs. "He's just worried about you, D. We both are."

"Yeah." I glance away, blinking back the burning in my eyes. "But your worry feels a lot like distrust. I'm sorry you're worried, but that doesn't give either of you the right to treat me like some stupid kid. I feel shitty enough without that."

"I'm sorry." She moves to stand in front of me, so I'm forced to look her in the eyes again. "Really. The last thing I want is to hurt you. You're my best friend. I just want you to be okay. For what it's worth, you were right about Connor. He's really great."

"Yeah. He is." I'm not so upset anymore. I sniff. "I need you—of all people—to be on my side, Iz. Even if that means sometimes Mark doesn't like it."

She smiles. "I'm always on your side, idiot. Even when *you* don't like it."

I choke on a laugh. "Yeah, sure."

"So, we're good?"

Nodding, I fight tears again. "We're good."

We take the train to meet Mom, who then drives us to the hospital. The wait is longer than the actual procedure. Nothing exciting about it—I wait, then I'm put into a tube and wait a little longer, before they bring me out and I get dressed and go home. All very anticlimactic given how much I've stressed about the whole freaking procedure.

Izzy comes back to the house with us. Mark's car is in the driveway when we pull in.

"You can hang out with Mark while I work on my painting," I tell Izzy when we get to my room. "I don't mind."

She flops onto her stomach on my bed. "That's okay. I'll stay with you."

I look up from adjusting my easel. "Did you two have a fight?"

"No. I just want to hang out with you. Girl time."

"Iz, you don't have to choose between us." Mark and I still haven't spoken about the night of our "double date" and I don't know if we ever will. He's moved on to pretending it never happened and I've decided to wait until the right moment to remind him that it did. Regardless, he's my brother and I love him, even if he's an asshole. There's no need for Izzy to be in the middle of that.

"I know. Hey, this sketch of Connor is freaking amazing."

I preen under her praise. "Thanks. I spent a long time on that."

"Has he seen it?"

"So he can think I'm a crazy stalker? Uh, no."

She laughs. "There's a lot of great stuff in here. How do you manage to switch styles like that?"

"Like what?"

She gets off the bed and brings the sketchbook over to where I stand in front of my easel. She shows me the sketch of Connor and another of a girl with a grunge-goth kind of look. Besides one having been done in graphite and the other in colored pencils, they look like they were drawn by two different people. Connor's sketch is lifelike, but the other has a more comic-book feel.

"Maybe someone else drew in my book," I say. I don't remember drawing the girl.

"Did someone else draw this one?" she asks, skipping ahead

a few pages to a stylized portrait of another girl done in what looks to be alcohol markers. Again, it's different from the other two, and not the sort of different that comes just from switching mediums.

"I guess I've been experimenting with other styles," I say, and go back to adding masking fluid to areas of my watercolor canvas.

Izzy closes the book. "D, I've been doing some research."

Oh, shit. "On my symptoms?"

She nods. "These sketches kind of support it."

"Okay, what is it?"

She holds the sketchbook to her chest like a shield. "Have you ever heard of dissociative identity disorder?"

"Like in *Split*?" Great movie. I love James McAvoy.

"According to what I've learned that's not exactly a great example, but yeah."

I arch a brow at her. "You think I have other people living inside me?" I don't mean to sound so mocking, but I can't take it back.

"Sketches that look like they've been drawn by different people, losing time, headaches, confusion, memory loss, feeling disconnected . . . they're all symptoms."

"You've been watching too much YouTube."

Izzy grabs my arm as I turn away. "Dylan, I'm serious."

Our gazes lock. "Iz, that's crazy. I'd know if I was more than one person."

"Not necessarily."

I look into her eyes—really look. Shit, she *is* serious. WTF? That kind of thing only happens in the movies. No one really splits into different personalities. Do they?

"No," I say.

"Would you just listen to some of the symptoms?" She pulls out her phone, swipes the screen, and begins to read: "Memory loss, 'coming to' in strange places, feelings of detachment from emotions or surroundings, the feeling that people and surroundings are distorted and unreal, confusion, depression or suicidal thoughts, the feeling that sometimes your body is not your own, headaches, substance abuse." She looks up at me.

My mouth opens, but nothing comes out. I can't make a sound. In my head I'm shouting, because oh my God, so many of those are familiar, but there's a part of me that won't let me say it.

A part of me. And then there's the voices I hear in my head. Voices that aren't mine.

My knees buckle, and I have to grab my easel to keep from falling. "*Fuck,*" I whisper.

"I'm not saying this is what you have, but it's worth looking into, right? I mean, it's better than a brain tumor."

"Is it?" I ask. It's pretty serious shit.

The silence in my head is frightening. It's never quiet in my mind and now there's nothing—like my brain's holding its breath.

"Well, *yeah,*" Izzy says, completely oblivious to the emptiness of my mind. "Lots of people have DID and manage to lead pretty normal lives."

"What causes it?"

Her gaze drops, and I know it's not good.

"It's usually caused by childhood trauma—before the age of seven or so."

I laugh, or at least I make a laugh-like noise. "I didn't have any childhood trauma."

Izzy meets my gaze, and says softly, "That you remember."

"I'd remember that."

"Not if your mind decided you shouldn't."

This is getting ridiculous. "Drop it, Iz."

"Tell me about the trip you guys took to Disney when you were seven."

"What?" That was straight out of left field. "Why?"

"Mark mentioned it the other night. He said it was fun."

"It was."

"He said you got sick on the teacup ride after eating too much ice cream."

Did I? If Mark said it, I must have. "Yeah. Yeah, I did."

She sits down on the edge of my bed. "Dylan, it was Mark who got sick."

"Then why did you say I did?"

"To see if you remembered it."

"Just because I don't remember whether or not I barfed on a ride doesn't mean I have split personalities."

"Tell me anything you remember from your childhood."

A flash fills my head, sharp and quick. A large shadow looming over me. He says something, but I can't make it out. It hurts. It hurts.

StopitstopitstopitstopitstopitstopitstopitstopiTstopITstoPITSTOP-ITSTOPIT!

"Stop it. This is stupid." I shake my head to clear it. "You've known me since we were kids. Wouldn't you have noticed if I was other people?"

"Alters are really good at pretending to be the host."

I don't know what to say. She's going to argue if I protest, and this whole discussion has me off-kilter. There's something I want to tell her, but I can't quite get the words out of my mouth. I can't hold on to them long enough to form them into speech. I feel like if I take a step to the right, I'll step right out of myself.

"I'll talk to Dr. Zhao about it when I see her this week," I blurt. Is it a promise I'll keep? Probably not.

Izzy looks so relieved that I feel instantly guilty. "Good."

"But if she says she doesn't think that's what's going on with me, this conversation is done, okay?"

She nods.

Nice save, whispers a voice. A feeling of relief washes over me from all sides of my brain.

"I really have to work on this sketch," I say. "You can hang out if you want, but I really don't mind if you want to see Mark."

Izzy smiles. "You want me to leave you alone so you can work."

"Yes." I grin. "Please."

"All right. I'll see if he wants to drive me home. I'll meet you tomorrow for lunch?"

"Twelve thirty in the caf."

"Awesome." She gives me a hug, then gathers up her stuff and heads toward the door. She pauses at the threshold. "Love you, bitch."

"Love you too, whore." I don't know when we started saying this to each other, but it's been a thing for years. We haven't done it in a while, and the familiar foolishness centers me.

When she's gone, I sit down at my desk and open my laptop. I go to YouTube and type "dissociative identity disorder" in the search bar. A lot of videos come up. I click the first one that catches my eye—a British girl with brightly colored hair. The description says something about a "switch" on camera.

I watch as she talks about having DID and wanting to get rid of the stigma surrounding it. I like the sound of her voice, and she seems really knowledgeable. Still, it's hard for me to wrap my head around the whole thing.

She begins to explain what it's like to lose time and how she's "woken up" in strange places or situations, not quite sure how she got there. She talks about strangers acting like they know her.

My heart starts to beat a little faster.

When she switches, I realize what the term means. She begins blinking and staring off, and then it's like she spaces out completely, before becoming someone else. It's like someone reached inside her and pulled "her" out of the body and replaced her with someone else. She still looks the same, but her voice and mannerisms are completely different.

This can't be real. It has to be an act. Made up.

But I don't think it's an act. I'm actually watching another person wake up in this girl's body and it scares the shit out of me.

I exit the video without finishing and go back to my easel. I have to get this done for class. I concentrate on creating the right shapes and values on the paper. It's supposed to be a character study. I already knew it was going to be the bluehaired girl I often draw. She's who I'd like to create a graphic novel around. Maybe Connor would help me with that.

I finish the sketch about an hour or so later. My hand's a

little crampy, but nothing that I can't massage away. I step back to get a better view of the overall piece.

When had I decided to make her cry? That hadn't been part of the original plan, but there she is in all her graphite glory, a tear trickling down her cheek, eyes bright and brimming. Her sorrow tightens my throat and chest—not only because she's so sad, but because I know the reason for her tears.

Me.

——

One of the scariest things ever is googling something you *don't* want to have and seeing all the evidence that you *do* have it.

I do this way too much. In the last two months I've diagnosed myself with at least six different diseases, disorders, or life-threatening conditions. Now I can add DID to the list of possibilities. I guess it might be better than a brain tumor in the nonlethal department, but it's still as scary. And just try doing a web search on "DID cure."

There isn't one.

I mention this to Dr. Zhao when I see her for our appointment on Wednesday.

She leans forward in her seat on the couch. "There's no cure for BPD either, but you live your life with that."

"I don't want to have to *live* with things," I shoot back, hotly. "I want to be fucking normal."

"Normalcy is a sociological construct. It is relative to the individual and has no real grounding in reality." She smiles slightly as she says it. "That's what my mother told me when I tried to explain to her how I just wanted to be a 'normal' kid."

"What was wrong with you?"

"Absolutely nothing. I was just very different from my classmates."

"No offense, but there's a big difference between feeling different and *being* different."

Another smile. "I don't give out personal information usually, but I feel like this is important, so I'm going to share it with you. I wasn't born Christine. I was born Christopher." She lets that sink in as I stare at her and feel like a shit.

"And I bet you freaked out when you realized who you really were." Lame, but it comes out anyway.

"I was. But I realized I would never be happy until I dealt with it. There's no cure for many things, Dylan. I didn't need a cure. I needed to accept. I needed to find a way to be happy in my own skin, and I did. Was it easy? No. Was it worth it? Yes."

"Did it feel worth it at the time?" I ask. I've watched videos on YouTube of trans people in various stages of transitioning, and they have to deal with a lot of shit.

"Sometimes, yes. Now, why don't we back up a bit? Why does your friend suspect you might have dissociative identity disorder?"

I list off what I can remember Izzy saying the other night.

Dr. Zhao tilts her head thoughtfully. "How did it make you feel when she told you all of that?"

"Scared. Angry."

"Why angry?"

I have to think about it. "I'm not sure. Probably because I don't want it to be true."

"Is there any reason other than what you've already expressed?"

"Because it means she thinks something horrible happened to me as a kid."

"Did something horrible happen?"

A huge fist pounds against a door in the back of my mind. A door that has so much furniture piled in front of it I can barely see the hinges as they bulge and bow under the force of the blows. Something behind it wants out.

"No," I say sharply—defensive. And then, "Like what?"

She gives a small shrug. "Usually it's some sort of trauma, like abuse or wartime violence."

I laugh. "My life's been pretty cushy, thanks."

Her eyes are dark lasers boring into mine. "What about abuse?"

"My parents never laid a hand on me."

"What about someone who wasn't your parent?"

An image pops into my head—like it's being played on a movie screen—of Mark standing over me, a fierce frown on his face. "Why are you crying?" he demands. "God, you're such a baby. Come on, I'll take you home." I don't know where we are, but we're probably about six. All I know is that the little girl on the screen is hurt. She wants to be safe.

I shake my head as my heart begins to pound. "No."

Dr. Zhao's expression is gentle, kind even. Patient. "Okay. Well, that makes DID an unlikely diagnosis."

I don't think she believes me. I can't stop thinking about Mark's face in the memory. It was a memory, wasn't it? He seems so angry with me. But he's always angry at me, isn't he? Always trying to make me do what he thinks is best. Even though he pisses me off and I scare him, we still love each other. Mark would never hurt me.

"I'd know if I was abused, wouldn't I?" I ask. "I mean, I'd remember something like that."

"Maybe. Our minds can be very protective and sometimes hide things that are difficult for us to deal with."

"Have you ever treated anyone with DID?"

She nods. "I have."

"Do you think I have it?"

"That's not the kind of decision I can make after only two sessions."

I want to get up and leave. I want to change the topic. I want a fucking drink, or a pill—anything to numb myself. Instead, I scoot to the edge of my seat and lean toward her, as if I don't want anyone else to hear, even though it's only the two of us and her camera in the room.

"Recently two people have called me by the wrong name."

I see a flicker of something in her gaze. "What do you mean?"

"Connor, this guy I'm sort of seeing? He said I told him my name was Lannie. No one but my dad calls me Lannie. And this girl on the train called me Kaz, the name of one of my imaginary friends from when I was little."

"Tell me about Kaz. Are they male or female?"

"A girl. She's kind of tough, you know? In my head she was always kind of punky—the kind of person no one messed with." I smile. "She got me into a lot of trouble when I was little."

Dr. Zhao smiles with me. "Why do you suppose you told this girl that was your name?"

I shrug. "She had the same kind of vibe to her, I guess. She acted like she knew me." My face warms when I think of *how* she knew me.

"But you had no memory of meeting her?"

"Not really. But when she talked to me, I got flashes. Like something on a screen or in a book. Like I watched it happen to someone else."

"Does this sort of recall normally happen when you've experienced a loss of time or had a blackout?"

"Sometimes? It's happened when I've been around the people I was with at the time."

She reaches over to her desk and opens the middle drawer. From there she withdraws a folder. "You filled out that questionnaire before our first meeting, and I want to discuss it, but do you mind if I ask you a few more questions first?"

"Knock yourself out."

She hands me a typed sheet of paper on a clipboard and a pen. "Just mark the circles with how often you believe these happen, with 'never' being zero percent of the time and 'always' being one hundred percent of the time. Each circle represents an increase of ten percent."

I look at the paper. One of the remarks is "some people often discover writings, drawings, or notes among their belongings that they do not remember making." *Uh, yeah.*

I fill the form out pretty quickly—it's not something I really have to think about. Dr. Zhao glances over it when I hand it back. I watch her face for some clue as to what she's thinking, but nothing changes.

"You think that most people have voices in their head telling them what to do and commenting on their actions. How do you mean?"

"You know, like parts of your brain arguing over what to do when you can't decide or giving you a hard time if you make a mistake—just the ways we talk to ourselves."

"Do you talk to yourself a lot?"

I laugh. "All the time. Mom used to say I would never be lonely as long as I could talk to myself."

Dr. Zhao smiles. "That must be nice."

"Sometimes," I reply with a shrug. "Like, when I'm looking for something. Not so great when I'm angry with myself, though."

"No? Why is that?"

"I can be pretty hard on myself. Call myself names, that sort of thing." I roll my eyes. "And sometimes they won't shut up."

"They?"

I nod. "Oh, yeah. I have more than one."

"Do they sound like your voice or do they each have their own?"

I realize where she's going with this. Voices are another symptom of dissociative identity disorder. If I tell her they're different she's going to think I have it, but I can't lie to her. She can't help me if I lie.

You can't fucking tell her. She'll find out our secret.

You can't ever tell. You know what will happen if you tell.

"Dylan?" Dr. Zhao's expression turns to concern. "Are you all right?"

"I have to go." Suddenly, I'm on my feet, grabbing my backpack. "I'll see you next week." But I'm not coming back next week. I'll tell Mom it's not going to work out. I'll think of something.

"Dylan—"

I open the door and bolt into the corridor. I practically sprint to the door of the reception area, and I only walk through there because I don't want attention. Once I'm outside the office, I run to the stairwell and out into the parking garage where Mom is parked.

"How did it go?" she asks when I get into the car.

"Good."

"Why are you out of breath?"

"I ran down the stairs. Can we go home? I have a headache."

She frowns as she starts the engine. "You've been getting those a lot lately. We should get your eyes checked. When we get home, maybe you should run yourself a nice relaxing bath. That will help."

It does sound good.

"So, what did you and Dr. Zhao talk about?"

"More of the same. I'm just going to close my eyes, okay? Wake me when we get home." That effectively puts an end to questions.

My head spins as I lean it back against the seat and close my eyes. I want to think about the questions the doctor asked me and what it all means. I want to really focus on things and try to remember, but it's like trying to slice fog.

Hands. Hands on me. Touching me where I don't want them. Oh, God. I can feel them . . . *inside* me. I can feel the roughness, the pain. Smell his breath . . .

"We're home, babe."

My eyes fly open as I suck air through my nose. Home.

I'm home. I'm dressed. No one is violating me. No one smells like mint and something else I can't define. Pepper, maybe?

Mom doesn't even seem to notice that I'm freaking out. It was so real. I could feel it all. When I opened my eyes and he wasn't there I was so relieved and confused.

I know his touch and his smell, but I didn't see his face.

My stomach rolls, a wave of nausea breaking over me. I was abused by a man whose face I can't remember.

It's your imagination. You want so badly to figure out what's wrong with you that you're letting people put ideas in your head. You're pathetic.

Maybe. Or maybe I'm finally figuring things out.

Inside the house I go up to my room. My head really is aching now, so I run a bath like Mom suggested. I drop in a bath bomb that makes my entire bathroom smell like lavender and chamomile and get undressed. Warm water welcomes me, easing the tension in my muscles. I blink, my eyelids growing heavy as the scented water laps around my shoulders.

It will all be over soon.

My phone rings. I open my eyes, confused. I'm still in the tub, but the water is getting cool. Did I leave the tap on? I can hear it dripping . . . *pat* . . . *pat* . . . *pat*.

My head is foggy and still aches as I turn it toward the ledge where I left my phone. I grab for it, my hand wet and clumsy as I swipe the screen. Then I see the source of the dripping sound. Dripping on the phone screen, on the tub, on the floor. My wrists are cut and turning the water crimson.

I scream.

THEM

*I was made up of
a multitude of selves,
of fragments.*

—ANAÏS NIN

EIGHT

Mom hears my scream and comes running. The door to the bathroom opens with a crash only muffled by my wails.

I'm bleeding. I cut myself. How could I not know? I didn't even feel it.

"Mom!" I cry out. "Mom, help me!" I sound like I'm yelling from deep inside a long tunnel, my voice hollow in my ears.

"It's okay, sweetie," she hushes. "You're going to be okay. Mark!"

My head spins, filling with fog. I think she wraps towels around my arms. She talks to me, but I don't understand what she says.

You ruined it, a voice whispers. It's in my head, in that dark tunnel with me. Its breath is on the back of my neck.

I can't focus. Can't concentrate. I'm pulled down into a world of darkness and quiet. . . .

The tunnel snatches at me, tugs at my clothes and hair, tries to keep me, but something stronger has hold of me and yanks me free. I blink as my vision returns.

I'm at the old house in my dreams. I don't know how I got here, but I have a person on either side helping me up the steps. One is Lannie and the other is . . . Kaz. She's changed since I was a kid, but I know it's her.

The woman with the piled-up hair is on the porch, only this time she stands and comes toward me. She looks concerned. Worried. Her expression reminds me of Mom, even though she looks nothing like her. Taking my face in her hands, she gives me a gentle smile and a kiss on the forehead.

"It's okay, baby girl. We've got you. Go ahead and rest."

"I'm scared," I confide. "I hurt myself. I think I'm dying."

Her expression hardens. "You didn't do anything. Someone else acted without my permission, and don't you worry about it. All you have to do is let us take care of you."

Relief washes over me.

"I've got the front," the woman tells the girls holding me. "Take her upstairs. She has a room."

My own room. Nice. I could use some sleep. I'm so tired I can barely hold my head up and my legs feel like they're weighted down with cinder blocks. Every step is a struggle. As if sensing the difficulty I'm having, my rescuers wrap their arms a little tighter around me.

Lannie and Kaz carry me into the house and up the stairs as if I weigh nothing. My legs are so happy to be free of my weight. At the top, Alyss steps aside to let us pass. She doesn't look nearly as creepy as she did the last time I saw her. In fact, she looks almost sad.

"You okay, Dylan?" she asks.

"She will be," Kaz answers in a sharp tone. "No thanks to you. Where the fuck were you, Alyss? You're supposed to protect her."

The little goth girl doesn't back down. "I was with Hannah. She was upset. Now I see why." She meets my gaze. "Been having a bit of a rough day, haven't you, pet?"

I nod. "My arms hurt."

"I'm so sorry," she says. "I ought to have been more diligent. I should have known that if Hannah was upset—"

"She doesn't know who Hannah is," Kaz snaps. "She doesn't fucking know who any of us are."

"Kaz," I whisper, leaning into her. She smells like the cinnamon rolls my grandmother used to make.

She looks at me, surprised.

"Be nice." My eyes threaten to roll back into my head, but I force them to focus on her. "Please."

"Looks like she knows more than you think," Lannie says a bit smugly, as if she's proud of me. "Come on, she's tired."

The two of them take me to a room decorated in shades of wine and cream. There's Modern Gothic–style furniture with that grungy-pop vibe that the rest of the house has, but with a more subdued palette. The bed is massive, with a ton of pillows for me to sink into.

Lannie covers me with a soft, plush blanket. "You can stay here as long as you need," she says.

"I can't," I say. "My mom will be worried. I need to let her know I'm okay."

Kaz puts her hand on my arm. She has pretty tattoos of

spiders, bees, and butterflies on her hands. "Someone else will take care of it, don't worry. It's going to be okay."

She and Lannie exchange a glance that makes me wonder if they're telling me the truth, but I really am *so* tired. Somewhere nearby—almost like a projection on the wall—I see what's going on outside of my mind and body. My mother as the EMTs load me onto the stretcher. Her clinging to my brother, who can't decide if he's angry or scared. He's pale. Mom has blood on her sweater. I hope it washes out. It's one of her favorites.

I hear her tell them she's going in the ambulance with me. It's like listening to a TV in another room. She tells Mark to call Dad.

"*Mark,*" she says when he doesn't move. "Call your father and tell him what's happened. Tell him I'll call him from the hospital."

My brother nods, finally taking his gaze off me. Does he hate me? He swipes the back of his hand across his eyes before tapping his thumbs across the screen of his phone. He's crying. I haven't seen Mark cry since we were kids. I don't hear what he says to Dad, though, because I'm moving. It's almost like floating.

My wrists hurt and I can't lift my arms. I can't move at all.

"Connor," I whisper.

Mom leans down as she hurries along beside me. "What's that, sweetie?"

"Connor. He called. Tell him I'm . . . sorry." Who the hell is this talking out of my mouth? It's not me, but it sounds like me.

"Okay," Mom agrees. "I'll call him. You just rest."

The me on the gurney closes her eyes. I'm passing out from blood loss, I suppose. My head is light and fuzzy.

"Told you," Kaz says from beside me. "You don't need to worry about being in control. Someone else is in the driver's seat. All you have to do is survive the ride."

"Jesus, Kaz," Lannie chastises. They both look pale and tired. That's when I realize something.

Their arms are cut open, the same as mine. They're bleeding. So is Alyss, who stands just inside the door. Behind her are several other bleeding girls. All of us with identical wounds.

We're all one, I realize. These girls are me—pieces of me—and I'm them. They live in this place. In me. It's their voices I hear talking to me. Their experiences I can't remember.

I'm more than one person. If I die, so do they.

My head spins. My eyes roll back into the darkness that swallows me whole.

"She's gonna pop," Kaz says, mimicking Joe Pantoliano in *The Matrix*.

Her hand is still on my arm, her blood mixing with mine. *Fuckfuckfuckfuck* . . .

Lannie's face appears before mine. She smiles and I instantly feel better.

"You're okay," she says. "And if you're okay, we're all okay. Got it?"

I nod. "Got it."

"Good." She pats my shoulder. I glance down at her hand—her arms aren't wounded anymore. There's not a mark on her. Not on Kaz or any of the others either. My arms are the only ones cut, and they don't even look that bad anymore. The blood has slowed.

"She always listens to you more than she listens to me," Kaz remarks.

"That's because she knows I've got her back," Lannie replies without looking at her. Her words calm me. "We're all here for you, Dylan."

"I'm not," comes a voice from the door. It's so loud and mean and sudden I jump.

"Get out of here, Scratch," Lannie commands, her face darkening.

Standing there, just inside my room, is a woman who looks exactly like my mother did when she was younger, except she has buttons for eyes, like the Other Mother in *Coraline*. Big, black buttons that shine with hatred as they glare at me.

"She's put us all in danger," Scratch remarks.

Lannie puts herself between me and this parody of Mom. "*You* put us all in danger. You tried to kill us."

This is the one who made me cut myself. If I were outside of myself, I'd find this whole thing ridiculous. I'd deny it and try to explain it away, but since I'm inside my mind, I watch with a new understanding.

"I don't want you here," I say, finally finding my voice.

They all look at me, each uniquely different face wearing the exact same expression of surprise.

"I have as much right to be here as you do," Scratch challenges me.

"No," I say. "You don't. This is *my* room. I want you gone, now get *the fuck out*."

I can tell she wants to fight me, but it's as though I can push her from the room just by thinking about it, force her out of my space. She drifts back into the hall, and as the small crowd parts, she keeps moving, slipping away into the shadows deep inside the house.

"I didn't see that coming," Kaz remarks, turning toward me with a lopsided grin. "Nice job, D."

Lannie smiles too. All I did was kick an asshole out of my room. Not like I defeated a dragon or anything.

"Is it true?" I ask Lannie. "Did something happen to me when I was a kid?"

She draws back. "I don't know what you're talking about."

"Lannie . . ." Kaz warns.

She holds up a hand. "We're not talking about this. Not now." Then, in a rough whisper, "Not in front of the kids."

There they are—three of them ranging from probably five to nine, peeking at me from behind Alyss. She puts her hand on the head of one of them—a little towheaded blonde who looks to be the youngest, and eerily familiar. I give her a hesitant smile and she immediately buries her face in Alyss's side.

"They're a wee bit shy," Alyss assures me. "But they'll come around, don't worry."

I nod and turn my focus to Kaz and Lannie instead. "I'm tired."

"Yeah, we should let you rest," Kaz says. "That was the whole point of bringing you here. You know, we never meant for you to meet everyone this way."

"How did you mean for it to happen?" I ask.

She shrugs. "We've been trying to get your attention for a long time. You weren't ready yet."

"I'm still not ready," I confess.

Her expression saddens. "No, you're not. But you've got no choice now, chicklet. None of us do."

—

DALI

This wasn't supposed to happen. Not like this. It's my job to take care of Dylan and the others and I almost failed. If Dylan hadn't taken control back when she did, we'd be dead.

Someone had to take control when Lannie and Kaz brought Dylan into the house. Normally one of them takes over when it's needed. I only do it in an emergency, which, I guess if there ever was one, this is it.

What was Scratch thinking? She probably thought she was protecting us by trying to silence Dylan forever, the lunatic. Her methods are extreme, but her heart is in the right place.

Taking control of the body never feels right to me. I don't like to be up front. I like to shepherd over everyone behind the scenes. When Dylan's mother—poor Jennifer—asks questions or speaks to us, I answer as much like Dylan as I possibly can. I'm not as good at pretending as Kaz and Lannie. Fortunately, the woman's too scared to notice the difference. I want to reach out and help her, but it's taking all my strength to keep the body awake. Pretty soon blood loss and sedatives will render us unconscious, and maybe that's for the best. I really don't care for this pain or distress.

This episode is going to change everything for us. For the last thirteen or so years we've been able to keep to the shadows, if that's a suitable description. Kaz and Alyss were already here when I arrived, and Lannie came not long after. I'm not sure when Scratch showed up. Maybe she's always been here, lurking. She might be older than any of us.

It's not easy being a thirty-something in an eighteen-year-old body. Ever since puberty, trying to keep us all united and quiet has been a struggle.

No need to be quiet anymore, I suppose. Dylan knows about us. Over the years I've managed to keep unpleasant memories to a minimum, but even I can't control flashbacks. She's going to start realizing things. She's going to remember situations we've tried very hard to protect her from.

It's going to hurt her. It's going to hurt all of us.

God, I could just *kill* Scratch.

The kids are scared we're going to die. Of course they're scared, they were bleeding like the rest of us. None of us want to die. Well, maybe one or two of us. But even Scratch doesn't want to die. She just wants to make sure no one finds out our secret. Well, too late.

Dylan can't keep on the way she has been, and we can't let her continue in ignorance. She's ready to face her past. She's ready for us, and we need her. The more she accepts us, the easier life will be for all of us.

As the body slowly begins to drift into sleep, I feel the pull of the inner world tugging at me. I need to stay up front a little while longer so I can make sure everything's going to be okay. If I go back now we'll just all be huddled around, anxious to find out if we're going to live or die.

In the distance I hear Kaz and Lannie talking. It's like I'm the driver and they're in the back seat.

"So, we just wait?" Kaz asks. "I fucking hate waiting." I hear the click and hiss of her lighter as she lights a cigarette.

"We stay awake," Lannie replies. "We stay alert. We keep the body going. Dali's still up front."

I want to tell her not for much longer, but I don't have the strength to stay awake and talk at the same time.

"This wouldn't have happened if Izzy hadn't played amateur therapist," Kaz seethed.

Lannie makes a tsking sound. "You know that's not what caused it."

"The therapist then." Kaz sucks aggressively on her cigarette. "It sure as hell wasn't me."

I sigh. She does this a lot—tries to pass the blame. It doesn't seem to matter that she "hooked up" with a girl she met on the train. Somehow, she'll find a way to blame Lannie, or Alyss, or me. She might be right this time, though. Lannie took the body on a three-day vacation and started this fiasco.

But we all knew this day would come, right? Not like we could keep Dylan in the dark forever. It was easier when she had a smaller world, when she wasn't under so much stress. We've all had to adjust.

Scratch doesn't like change. New situations are always perceived as a threat.

"Dylan deserved to have fun," Lannie argues. "That's why I took over. She likes Connor. *You* like Connor."

"Dylan didn't experience *any* of that fun, dumbass. It was all you. And don't presume to know what I like. You have no fucking idea what I like, otherwise you would have let me front."

"She's aware of us," I manage to whisper, silencing both of them. The body's hold on consciousness is almost completely severed. We're at the hospital. We're going to be okay.

"Nothing's going to be the same now," Kaz remarks, her tone ominous. "Everything's going to change."

I shiver as the outer world goes dark. It's like a door being closed in my face. One moment I can see the hospital, smell the hospital—bright lights, medicine, and sick—and the next, it's nothing. I have no idea what's happening.

I glance down at my arms. The blood is completely gone. That's something to be thankful for, I suppose.

Now all we can do is wait and hope that the girl responsible for our lives doesn't die.

NINE

When I open my eyes, I'm in the hospital. I know it's real because my wrists throb with every pulse, and the IV tube brushes against my arm as it feeds blood back into my body. The air around me smells like blood. Like death.

I wish I was still at that strange house. I felt safe there. Accepted. Here, I have to face what I've done—because no one's going to believe Scratch did this and not me.

In my head I see those glossy button eyes glaring at me. That . . . that *thing* lives inside of me and hates me. How can a part of me want me dead?

And how could it almost make that want a reality without my knowledge? Without my consent? That can't be right.

I could call myself crazy, say it's all made up. I could write it off as a dream, but I can feel them inside me. I can feel Lannie and Kaz so close, hovering. Watching over me.

They can't be real. They just *can't.*

We can, Lannie whispers sorrowfully. *We are.*

"Go away," I whisper. "You're making my head muddy."

"Sweetie?" It's Mom, sitting in a chair next to my bed. She must have dozed off. "Did you say something?"

Hot tears spill over my eyelashes. "I'm sorry."

She stands up and smooths my hair off my forehead. "What happened, Dylan?"

"I'm not sure," I reply honestly, sniffling. "Mom, I need to talk to Dr. Zhao."

"She's coming by in the morning. Do you think you can talk to me?"

I gaze up into her eyes and I know she loves me—no matter what. I just put her through hell and she's so glad I'm okay that she can't be mad at me. Do I deserve this kind of love? Maybe not, but she deserves a lot more respect than what I give her for offering it to me.

"I . . ." I swallow. My throat is so dry, my tongue feels like a piece of carpet. "Can I have some water?"

There's a plastic cup on the bedside table. Mom picks it up and holds it for me, guiding the paper straw to my mouth. It's room temp and tastes like chemicals, but it's wet so it's perfect.

"Thanks," I say when I've had enough. I lean back against the pillow. "Mom, I think I have people living in my head."

Her brows knit together. "Like voices?"

"No. Like, people."

Her expression changes, opening her features in face-wide realization. "Multiple personalities?"

"You're fucking kidding me," comes my brother's voice from behind her.

I glance around Mom and see Mark and Izzy standing at the doorway. Izzy looks sad, but Mark . . . he's so angry he's shaking.

"Keep your voice down," Mom chastises him. "People are trying to sleep."

"You don't really believe this shit, do you?" he asks in a lower tone as he walks farther into the room. "Jesus, Mom."

"She has a lot of the symptoms," Izzy tells him. "I've been reading about it."

He turns on her. "Did you tell Dylan about your reading?" She nods and he laughs, a harsh sound. "Great. Now she has something new to run with and get everyone all freaked out over."

I frown at him. "I'm not doing this on purpose—"

"Bullshit!" He's right beside my bed, jabbing his finger in my face. His expression is a mask of ugliness—so much anger and pain. "You've always been like this. You've always had to be the center of attention with your drama and 'poor me' crap. Life can't be about anyone but you. I lost that commercial yesterday, Dylan, and I couldn't tell anyone because all eyes were on you."

"Oh, honey." Mom puts her hand on his arm. "I'm sorry."

Mark doesn't even look at her. "Every day I have to deal with how worried Mom and Izzy are about you. How worried I am about you. Every day we wonder if you're okay, or if something happened and you're in a ditch. You don't think of anyone but yourself and I am so fucking tired of being part of your circus." He shakes his head. "On purpose. Not on purpose. Slut, not a slut. Either way you're fucked up."

The sound of Mom's palm connecting with Mark's cheek echoes through the room like a gunshot. I jump. Izzy jumps. Silence falls, heavy and horrible after that loud crack. Mark and Mom stare at each other—one defiant, one horrified. The redness that blooms on my brother's cheek reminds me of how watercolor blossoms on wet paper.

Mom has never hit either one of us—ever.

"Don't you disrespect your sister like that," Mom whispers. "Don't you talk about women like that. I don't care how angry you are, you do *not* shame."

Mark swallows. "Doesn't make it any less true," he says. "And it doesn't change the fact that you always put her first." He pivots on his heel and leaves the room, fists clenched at his sides, back rigid.

Izzy doesn't seem to know what to do.

"You can go after him," I tell her. "It's okay."

Mom turns to look at her and I can't see the expression on her face, but I can see Izzy's.

"No," my friend says, moving forward to stand beside Mom by my bed. "He needs some time to think. Alone."

I'm pretty sure it's terrible of me to feel as happy as I do that she picked me over Mark. I'm also pretty sure that I don't care. My brother's angry and I get it. I'd be mad at him too, but Izzy's my only friend and I need her right now. I need her more than he does. Maybe it's selfish, but I'm okay with it.

"Connor called," Mom tells me, before clearing her throat. "He wants to visit. I told him tomorrow would be better. Is that all right?"

I nod. I'm not sure what I'm going to say to him. *Sorry for screaming in your ear, but I hadn't realized I'd tried to fillet myself?*

Mom strokes my hair. There's no anger in her face. I almost wish there was. Her love is sometimes hard to live with.

"Do you really think you have other people inside you?" she asks.

Do I? If I say it out loud to her, there's no taking it back because I'm scared. If I say it in front of her and Izzy, then it's real, and I have to deal with it.

I nod. "I've met them. I know how that sounds, but they were so real."

"We'll talk to Dr. Zhao about it tomorrow. She'll know how to proceed."

Tears slip from my eyes. I'm so tired and sore and . . . done. It's like I feel everything and nothing at the same time. "I really am sorry."

"I know you are, sweetheart. I know." She wipes the wet away from my face with her thumb. "Your brother knows it, too. Unfortunately, he lashes out when he's scared. He's like your father that way."

Oh, God. My father. "Does Dad know?" My voice breaks.

She nods, and this time wipes my face with a tissue. "I called him once . . ." She swallows ". . . once we knew you were going to be okay."

Once she knew I was going to live, she means. I guess she would have called him if I died, too.

"Is he mad?" I ask. It's very important to me—or someone inside me—that I know the answer.

"Of course not," she says. "He's worried, like I am, but your father and I love you, Dylan. We just want you to be okay.

And if you do have these . . . other personalities then at least we'll know what we're dealing with."

I can tell Izzy wants to correct her terminology, but she doesn't. "I've been doing some research," she says instead. "I can send you links if you want."

Mom puts her arm around Izzy's shoulder and gives her a squeeze. "Thank you, doll."

A nurse comes in to check on me. She tells us that visiting hours are over, but that Mom and Izzy can stay a little while longer if they like. Apparently, she's going to give me something to help me sleep. That's code, I think, for giving me something that will render me incapable of hurting myself again.

"Can I have my phone?" I ask.

The nurse shakes her head. "Sorry, dear. They're not allowed."

Right, I'm in the psych ward. If only they knew they don't have to worry about me calling dangerous people because they're already in my head.

"Has anyone been in to talk to you?" she asks.

I have no idea.

"There was a doctor who saw her when we first arrived," Mom answers for me.

"Good." The nurse gives me a gentle smile. "You'll have a visit from one of our social workers probably as well. And one of our psychiatrists."

"Dr. Christine Zhao is coming tomorrow," Mom offers.

"Oh, she's in excellent hands then." Another smile at me. I like her. There's no judgment, only kindness. I think the others like her too, because the chaos in my head has calmed. "Do you need anything, love?"

My stomach growls as if on cue. I haven't eaten since lunch. At least, I don't think I have.

We all laugh a little, as if this situation is completely normal.

"I'll see what I can find for you to nibble on."

And then she's gone.

"We're lucky that Dr. Zhao is affiliated with this hospital," Mom remarks.

"How long do I have to stay here?" I ask.

"Until Dr. Zhao decides you can go home, I suppose," she replies. "Hopefully that won't be too long."

I'm going to miss class. I'm going to miss so much.

"Oh, *shit*." I close my eyes. "Connor and I were supposed to go to MoMA tomorrow."

"The museum will be there when you get out," Mom says. Izzy gives me a hopeful smile. I know she's wondering the same thing I am. Will Connor still be around? For that matter, will I?

When all this is done, will I still be me, or will I become one of the strangers in my head? What if one of them takes over? What if I get trapped in that house forever, watching my life go by while someone else lives it?

If it wasn't for the sedatives I'd panic, but all I can do is lie here while the thought goes through my head. I'm powerless.

And someone made me this way.

—

Mom comes back the next morning. She brings me a chai latte that I drink as we take a walk around the ward. Dr. Zhao is coming by later to meet with me and the doctors here. Hopefully I'll know this afternoon when I can go home.

If I can go home. They may decide to keep me here, with the other people who are a danger to themselves and others.

I feel okay—well, I feel stupid and embarrassed and not really secure in my body—but other than that, I'm all right. The voices in my head are quiet. Maybe they're as freaked out as I am.

"Your brother sends his love," Mom says as we pause by a window to enjoy the fall sunshine.

I laugh. "No, he doesn't. But thanks for lying."

She looks contrite—and a little frustrated. "He doesn't understand."

"I know he doesn't. He never has, and I've never really understood him. We don't have to. It's okay, Mom." My brother and I have never fought for too long, and no matter what happens, when it comes down to it, we support each other. He might be angry with me, but he'd come if I called.

"Hopefully they'll let you out today or tomorrow." She touches my arm. "I've been thinking. Maybe you should withdraw from college until we know what's going on and figure out a treatment plan."

"Maybe. Would you get some of the tuition back?" When she nods, I have to admit defeat. "That's probably a good idea." I love art. I love my school, but it hasn't been impressed with me so far. I'd like to be at the top of my game, rather than the bottom.

Mom gives me a quick hug before we walk back to my room. I climb into bed with my new art supplies. I'm not allowed to have pencils, or pens, but they let me have paper and crayons to draw with. The task of drawing anything decently with a freaking crayon has become a challenge I cannot refuse. So far, I'm losing. I draw a quick "portrait" of her in yellow, blue, and peach tones. It's very abstract and . . . waxy.

"I love it," Mom declares.

"Put it on the fridge when you get home," I joke. That's where she used to hang my childhood art.

"I might even frame it," she adds.

"We'll call it 'She Didn't Die.'" It's meant to be a joke, but as soon as I say the words, I wish I could take them back. Mom and I look at each other.

She starts to cry first, then me.

By the time Dr. Zhao arrives we've gone through a mountain of tissues and our eyes are swollen and red.

Dr. Zhao looks cautiously from me to Mom. "Is this a bad time?" she asks.

"No," Mom tells her with a tired smile. "We just finished a perfectly cleansing sob."

The psychiatrist's expression turns less guarded. "Cleansing can also be exhausting. I can come back later if you want."

"No," I say, before Mom can take her up on the offer. "I'd like to talk to you about what happened."

"Do you want me to leave?" Mom asks.

I shake my head. "I need you to fill in the blanks."

Mom looks to Dr. Zhao, who nods. "I have no problem with you being here, Ms. Tate." She takes a seat in the chair closest to the window and crosses her legs. I like the way light reflects off the glossy sheen of her heels.

"I think I have dissociative identity disorder," I tell her.

No change in her expression. I might as well have declared that I love soup. "Why?"

I tell her about Izzy's research. About the dream-house and the people in it. About Nisha, even though my mother's right there. I feel guilty for not telling her about it when I found out.

"I didn't do this," I say, lifting my bandaged arms. "One of the people inside me did. How can someone who is supposed to be part of me try to hurt me like this?"

"They're called persecutors and they can sometimes go to extremes to protect the system to which they belong, but we're getting ahead of ourselves. First, I want to do a couple of diagnostic tests and consult with a colleague who's an expert in dissociative disorders."

"But . . ." I stare at her. "Isn't it kind of obvious? I mean, I've got a house full of people in my head."

Finally, a crack in her armor. She chuckles. "I admit it is a convincing argument, but I wouldn't take your appendix out just because you told me it ruptured. I would do my due diligence all the same."

I suppose. "Does that mean I have to stay here for a while?"

Dr. Zhao nods. "Not long, I hope. It's standard to keep you for a few days after a suicide attempt to make sure you're stable. And if this was the work of a persecutor, I'm concerned they might act out again to protect the others."

"Protect them from what?" Mom asks with a puzzled frown. "From Dylan?"

"Maybe, but usually their goal is to conceal the trauma that caused the dissociation in the first place."

I watch color leach from my mother's face. "What sort of trauma?"

My heart clenches.

"That's what we need to find out," Dr. Zhao replies easily. "But first, let's do the tests." She stands up. "I have them on my cloud. I'm going to pop up to my office here and print them. I'll also call Dr. Mueller and schedule a consult. I'll be back in a little bit."

As soon as she's gone, silence falls over the room. I know what Mom wants to ask.

"I don't remember it, whatever it was," I tell her. "And it wasn't your fault."

She wipes at the corner of her eye with her fingers. How can she possibly have any tears left?

"I keep thinking that I'm responsible for this," she whispers. "That whatever happened to you is because of me."

"Well, that's narcissistic," I reply, lightly enough to make her laugh.

"It is, isn't it?"

"First, we find out what this is, then we deal with why," I decide. "After, we figure out how to fix it." If it can be fixed. What if I can't be fixed?

"If you're going to be here for a few days I'm going to talk to them about phone calls and what you're allowed to have. Will you be okay?"

I nod, but I have no way of knowing, do I?

I scribble on a piece of paper with a red crayon as she leaves the room. It's beige, I notice. How have I not noticed how beige everything is before this? The lack of color is . . . unsettling.

—

Is there anything better in this world than the combination of peanut butter and chocolate? This is the question I contemplate as Izzy and I sit in my bed in the hospital, eating peanut butter cups and reading a Fables graphic novel.

"I love you so much right now," I tell her, licking chocolate from my thumb.

"Love you more." She smiles and offers me another package of delicious candy. How much did she bring with her? "Is it wrong that I have a crush on Bigby?" she asks.

Bigby, aka the Big Bad Wolf, is a character in the Fables universe. "If loving him is wrong, I don't wanna be right," I reply, misquoting an old song by a singer whose name I've never known. I catch Mom singing it sometimes. I think it was on the soundtrack for a movie she was in. She probably died a cheesy but violent and bloody death in it. Hopefully with all of her clothes on.

"I almost forgot. I have something for you."

I sigh, peanut butter melting on my tongue. "Dude, seriously, the chocolate was enough."

She wipes her fingers with a tissue before reaching into her bag. She pulls out a hardcover notebook. It's black with hot pink skulls on it. "For you," she says, handing it to me.

"Cool, thanks," I say. The pages are lined in black, with little pink skulls at the top of each. "I like it." There's a felt-tipped pen with it. I'm allowed to have those because there's not much chance of me using them to hurt myself. It'll be easier to draw with it rather than a crayon.

"In all the research I've done, they talk about the importance of people with DID keeping a system journal."

"Iz . . ." I sigh. I know she means well. "I haven't been diagnosed yet."

She looks at me as though that's a technicality. "Well, if you don't have it, then you have a nice journal. If you do have it, you and the people inside you have a place to express yourselves. Mark picked it out."

I can't quite make myself put it down. "He did?"

"Yeah." She gives me a meaningful look. "You know why he was such an ass, right?"

I nod. I've had a lot of time to think about it. "Because if something happened to me when we were kids, he was there. He was there and I never told him."

"He never saw it." She leans forward. "And that would mean he's let you down."

I clear my throat. "Did he actually say any of this, or are you just trying to make him a good guy and not a douche?"

She grins at me. "Both?" We laugh. "He wouldn't like knowing I'm telling you this, so let's say he's not a douche and leave it at that?"

I don't know why my brother has such a hard time telling me these things himself. I'd have no trouble telling him exactly how I feel if the situation was reversed. And while I appreciate that he feels like he "ought to have known," it's not about him. Something happened to me, and I was so good at covering it up, even I don't remember.

"Have you slept with him yet?" I ask. What the hell?

Izzy's expression mirrors what I feel inside. "Um, no. Though, that's gonna be awkward, don't you think?"

I smile. "Sorry. It's not my business. I don't really want to know."

"Maybe it wasn't you who asked."

"You really want me to have strangers in my head, don't you? Out of all the possible outcomes, that's the one you're hoping for."

"I don't want you to have anything, but it's the least likely to kill you out of the ones you've mentioned."

I hold up my wrists. "Wanna rethink that?"

Izzy takes my hands in hers, turning them palms up. She stares at the bandages on my arms—the right one is slightly smudged with blood—before raising her gaze to mine.

"Whichever one of you did this to my friend, please don't do it again."

I arch a brow. "I don't think they can hear you."

"The ones paying attention hear what you hear."

Jesus, she's really been researching this shit. I should be touched, but I'm more annoyed. She means well, but it feels like one more person trying to "fix" me. I'd like to do that myself.

"Can we talk about something else?" I ask. "Something other than me?"

Izzy doesn't look offended. She leans back against the pillow and shoves more chocolate in her mouth. "Miranda Grayson got arrested."

My jaw drops. "What?"

Miranda Grayson went to our high school. She was one of *those* girls—the stereotypical popular, pretty, snotty girl. Her parents were accountants for billionaires or something.

"What did she do?" I ask.

Grinning, Izzy licks chocolate off her lips. "She got caught shoplifting at Saks."

"Wow." I'm genuinely shocked. "I did not see that coming."

"Kinda sad, right?"

I shrug. "You mean because she could obviously afford to shop there?"

"Yeah. Oh, I heard she also bit one of the cops who arrested her. Right on the face."

I laugh. I can't help it. "Was she high?"

"I don't think so. Just mad that he was arresting her."

I shake my head. "Not so sad anymore. Wow. Miranda got arrested for shoplifting. That's the craziest thing I've heard today."

"Good, because there's something I have to tell you."

I look at the sheepish smile on her face and my heart hesitates before beating again. "No."

The grin grows. "I did sleep with Mark."

TEN

After Izzy leaves, I lose time. There's no other way to describe it. One minute I'm in the bathroom washing my hands and the next, I'm in the common area, wearing different clothes, drinking juice and staring out the window with the journal Izzy gave me in my lap. Someone wrote in it. And it wasn't me.

Is this a joke? I look around for Izzy, or maybe Mark, but nothing. The pages were empty when I flipped through the journal earlier, and I have the pen she gave me in my hand. As soon as I read the first line, I know who the author is.

I DON'T KNOW WHY EVERYONE'S SO PISSED AT ME. IF WE'D DONE WHAT I WANTED, NO ONE WOULD KNOW OUR SECRET AND WE'D BE SAFE RIGHT NOW.

She calls that safe?

SURE, WE'D BE DEAD, BUT WE'D STILL BE SAFE.

I HAVE NO PROBLEM WITH DEAD. DEAD MEANS MY JOB'S DONE. DEAD MEANS I DON'T HAVE TO PRO-TECT A SECRET THAT ISN'T MINE, AND I DON'T HAVE TO WALK AROUND WEARING THE FACE OF A WOMAN I HATE FOR NOT PROTECTING HER KID THE WAY SHE SHOULD HAVE.

Whoa. Wait. Scratch blames my mother for what happened to me? Does that mean some part of me blames Mom for not looking after me? How could she have known? I don't even remember what happened. Not really. I mean, there have been flashes—enough that I have a good idea. Like, what tends to happen to vulnerable little girls when predatory older men are around?

MOST PEOPLE COME INTO THE WORLD AS BABIES, BUT NOT ME. NOT US. THERE'S NOT ONE OF US IN THAT FUCKING HOUSE WHO HAS HAD ANY KIND OF NORMAL, DECENT LIFE, AND IT WAS ALL SO DYLAN COULD HAVE AT LEAST A SLIGHT CHANCE AT ONE. LOOK HOW MUCH GOOD THAT DID. SHE'S A FUCK-ING WRECK, EVEN WITH OUR HELP. AND NOW SHE'S IN DANGER OF REMEMBERING WHY WE'RE WITH HER IN THE FIRST PLACE—THE SECRET I WAS BORN TO PROTECT.

THERE ARE KIDS IN THAT HOUSE. KIDS WHO HAVE ALREADY SUFFERED MORE THAN ANY KID SHOULD. IT'S THEM I WANT TO KEEP SAFE. THEY DON'T NEED TO RELIVE THAT SHIT.

Scratch is why I don't remember? Okay, if I believe in Scratch, I have to believe I have DID. *Really, truly believe.*

Which means my brain created Scratch to protect little me from the secret my abuser forced me to keep.

It's no wonder she hates me. No wonder she seems to hate everybody.

NOW, I'M LOCKED IN MY ROOM AS PUNISHMENT FOR DOING MY JOB.

IT DIDN'T MATTER HOW MANY TIMES I SLAMMED MY PALMS AGAINST THE DOOR. HOW MANY TIMES I SCREAMED, "LET ME OUT, YOU FUCKING BITCHES!" NO ONE CAME.

I REFUSED TO BEG. I HATE BEING LOCKED UP, AND THEY ALL KNOW IT. THEY KNOW I HATE SMALL SPACES. I'M JUST AS ENTITLED TO MY FREEDOM AS THEY ARE. SO, YEAH, I DIDN'T BEG, BUT THE NEXT TIME I SCREAMED "LET ME THE FUCK OUT!" I POUNDED THE DOOR WITH MY FISTS. THEN I STARTED KICKING IT. I KICKED IT SO HARD I THOUGHT I BROKE MY FUCKING TOE.

I WAS ABOUT TO START KICKING AGAIN WHEN I HEARD THE LOCK CLICK, AND IT WAS ABOUT DAMN TIME. STANDING IN THE DOORWAY WAS LANNIE. SHE STOOD THERE GLARING AT ME. AMATEUR. I COULD INTIMIDATE THE SHIT OUT OF HER IF I WANTED. SHE'S NOT THAT HARD TO GET TO. FRIGGING DO-GOODER. SHE WANTS US ALL TO UNDERSTAND EACH OTHER, TO WORK TOGETHER. SCREW THAT. WE WEREN'T MADE TO WORK TOGETHER. I KEEP TRYING TO TELL THESE MORONS THAT, BUT THEY DON'T LISTEN.

"WHAT DO YOU WANT?" I DEMANDED. "COME TO GLOAT?"

SHE SCOWLED AT ME AND SAID TO "KNOCK IT OFF. YOU'RE SCARING THE KIDS."

"THEY SHOULD BE SCARED," I FIRED BACK. "WE ALL KNOW WHAT HAPPENS IF OUR SECRET GETS OUT."

SHE HELD UP A HAND—LIKE THAT WAS GOING TO STOP ME—AND SAID, "YOU NEED TO CHILL OUT."

I LIMPED TOWARD HER, GETTING RIGHT IN HER STUPID FACE, AND YELLED "YOU NEED TO BACK THE FUCK OFF!" I COULDN'T CONTROL WHAT I SAID AFTER. "YOU'RE A WORTHLESS PIECE OF SHIT. NONE OF YOU HAVE THE BRAINS OR THE BALLS IT TAKES TO PROTECT US. NONE OF YOU!"

That's a lot of anger. I glare at the page. *Hey, asshole,* I write in the margin. Fuck, even our handwriting is different. *Don't talk to Lannie that way.*

Inside me, a little bloom of love blossoms in response.

Oh my God. I *do* have DID. Either that or I have the most overactive imagination.

THEN ONE OF THE KIDS STARTED TO CRY, SO I SLAMMED MY FIST AGAINST THE WALL. "SHUT UP!" I YELLED.

"NO," SAID A QUIET VOICE. "YOU SHUT UP."

IN THAT MOMENT, I FROZE. SLOWLY, I TURNED MY HEAD. STANDING BESIDE LANNIE WAS ALYSS. SHE'S THE ONLY PERSON IN THIS SHITHOLE THAT SCARES ME. I SUPPOSE SHE'LL SEE THIS, BUT IT'S NOT LIKE IT'S A SECRET. SHE'S NOT INTIMIDATING

BECAUSE SHE'S BIG OR EVEN BECAUSE SHE'S TOUGH, BECAUSE SHE'S NEITHER OF THOSE THINGS REALLY. WHAT MAKES HER EFFECTIVE IS THAT SHE DOESN'T REALLY CARE ABOUT HERSELF. WHAT ALYSS CARES ABOUT ARE THOSE DAMN KIDS. THE KIDS AND NOTHING ELSE. THAT INCLUDES YOU, DYLAN.

ALSO, SHE'S FUCKING INSANE. LIKE, HORROR-MOVIE-VILLAIN INSANE.

"RAISE YOUR VOICE AGAIN AND I'LL RIP OUT YOUR VOCAL CORDS," SHE TOLD ME IN THAT CRISP VOICE OF HERS, SMILING THE WHOLE TIME. "POUND ON THE WALLS AND I'LL BREAK YOUR HANDS. SCARE THE CHILDREN AND I'LL EAT YOUR LIVER WHILE YOU'RE STILL ALIVE."

FUCK, I HATE WHEN SHE MAKES HER SMILE GROW LIKE THAT. HER HEAD ISN'T BIG ENOUGH FOR THAT CREEPY SMILE.

AND I JUST STOOD THERE, STARING AT HER, WAITING FOR HER TO JUMP ME.

"UNDERSTOOD, DUCKS? I WILL DEVOUR YOU WHOLE."

You go, Alyss. Threaten her ass into the middle of next week.

MY MOUTH WAS SO DRY I COULDN'T SPEAK, BUT I NODDED. SHE SCARED ME ENOUGH THAT I DON'T EVEN MIND TELLING YOU THIS, DYLAN. YOU OR ANYONE ELSE WHO READS THIS, BECAUSE YOU ALL THINK I'M THE BAD GUY, WHEN THE REAL HARD-LINE BITCH IN THIS PLACE IS ALYSS. SHE'S A PSYCHO. SHE'S THE ONE YOU NEED TO LOCK UP. THE ONE YOU NEED TO WATCH.

CUE THE CONDESCENDING LITTLE SPEECH.

"GOOD GIRL. NOW, BACK TO YOUR TIME-OUT. I WANT YOU TO THINK ABOUT WHAT YOU'VE DONE, AND IN THE MORNING, YOU'RE GOING TO APOLO-GIZE TO EVERYONE IN THIS HOUSE FOR PUTTING THEM IN DANGER. THEN, WE'LL HAVE PANCAKES. HOW DOES THAT SOUND?"

THE DOOR CLOSED IN MY FACE BEFORE I COULD ANSWER. THEY DIDN'T EVEN TURN THE KEY IN THE LOCK. LANNIE KNEW SHE DIDN'T HAVE TO, NOT NOW THAT ALYSS HAS PAID ME A VISIT. WE'RE ALL AFRAID OF ALYSS. YOU'D BE SMART TO BE AFRAID OF HER TOO, DYLAN. YOU'LL FIND OUT WHAT I MEAN THE FIRST TIME ONE OF THE LITTLE ONES RUNS TO HER CLAIMING YOU SCARED OR HURT THEM IN SOME WAY.

AFTER, I SAT DOWN ON MY BED AND DID WHAT I WAS TOLD. I'M NOT STUPID. I THOUGHT ABOUT WHAT I'VE DONE. I'M STILL THINKING ABOUT WHAT HAPPENED WHEN I HAD CONTROL IN THAT BATH-TUB.

AND HOW I CAN DO IT BETTER NEXT TIME.

I slam the journal shut, heart pounding hard in my throat. *Next time?*

———

Dr. Zhao knocks on my door as I'm drawing horns on a de-mon with a strangely familiar face—only I'm not quite sure who he reminds me of.

"That's pretty good," she remarks.

"Thanks."

"You're an art student, yes?"

I nod. "I was. Mom thinks maybe I should bow out for the rest of the year."

"Might be a good idea. You should concentrate on your well-being. I'll see what kind of supplies you can have. Maybe we can arrange supervised art time as a kind of therapy."

I smile at her. "That would make being here a lot easier. Thanks." I show her the journal Izzy brought me. "My friend thought it might be good for me to write stuff in."

Dr. Zhao smiles. "Good friend. Have you written in it yet?"

I hesitate. I should tell her about the note from Scratch. I should let her read it. I should . . .

"No," I say. "Not yet. She gave it to me today."

"Well, maybe before bed tonight you can write about your day. Meanwhile, I have some work for you, if you don't mind." She offers me a clipboard and a felt-tip pen. "Answer the questions as honestly as possible. There are no right or wrong answers. They are only designed to assess the level of dissociation you experience. Inaccurate answers can result in a faulty diagnosis."

"I'm not going to lie," I say, a little indignant.

"It's the same thing I tell everyone," Dr. Zhao replies, smoothly. "I don't think you'll lie, but you might be tempted to skew your answers as we all would be. I'll be right here if you have any questions."

The first form is a series of nearly thirty questions. I have to respond to each with how much of the time I spend feeling a certain way. Like, one of the questions—they're all posed as statements—says "some people find themselves in situations with no memory as to how they got there" and asks me to say what percentage of the time I find myself feeling this way. I'm able to get through most of the questions before Mom walks in. Maybe they should put a revolving door on my room.

Dr. Zhao fills her in on the paperwork as I move on to the second stack. It's larger—roughly twenty pages of questions I'm supposed to answer with yes, no, or unsure. Dr. Zhao has marked the parts that I don't need to fill out, or that are only for her use.

"I left a message for Dr. Mueller," Dr. Zhao informs Mom. "Her assistant told me to expect her to be in touch later this afternoon. As soon as I've had a chance to talk to her, I'll give you a call."

"Dr. Zhao's going to ask them to let me have art time," I add, because it's the best thing that's happened to me in the last couple of days.

Mom's smile is the second-best thing. "Wonderful. D, I'm going to write down the times during the day you're allowed to make and receive phone calls on your whiteboard. Do you need me to get any numbers from your phone? Oh, and you can have visitors so long as they follow hospital rules."

"I doubt anyone but Izzy will visit."

"What about Connor?"

"Would you want to see the girl who started screaming in your ear about . . . all of this?" I challenge, raising my bandaged wrists.

"Depends how much I like the girl," Dr. Zhao answers with that unreadable expression of hers.

"He did ask about visiting," Mom chimes in. "And he's texted me a couple of times to ask after you."

I don't understand. I can't imagine wanting to be with someone as fucked up as me.

"If this is DID, what's the treatment?" I ask. "Are there meds?"

"It's mostly therapy," Dr. Zhao responds. "Medication will depend on whether or not there are other conditions present. I know this must be frustrating for you, Dylan, but first we need to have an official diagnosis."

I study her, looking for an indication of something— anything. "But you think it's DID."

"I think I'll need you to answer all those questions before I can even begin to say."

I catch Mom smiling at her. That vaguely amused and slightly proud smile mothers sometimes wear when someone handles their difficult child in a particularly skillful way. My BPD raises its head for a second. I want to throw the clipboard to the floor. I want to tell them both to fuck off.

Chill out, I tell myself. At least, I *think* it's me who says it. This is so messed up. I take a couple of deep breaths and go back to answering questions. Neither of them seems the least bit aware of how close I'd been to pitching a fit.

Mom and Dr. Zhao talk about the hospital, and Mom starts making a list of things she can bring me.

"Some music would be nice," I tell her. "And books. There's only so much TV I can watch." At least I have one in the room. And I don't have a roommate. I don't even want to know if insurance is covering this or if Mom has to pay for it. Honestly, I don't need the extra guilt, it's guilt I'll wear like some kind of fucking badge.

After I finish Dr. Zhao's papers, she leaves, and Mom

decides to go out and get me some stuff with the promise to pick up dinner before she comes back. When she returns— with a new, glue-bound sketchbook and felt-tip nontoxic markers—I can smell the fried chicken she brought with her. Oh. My. God.

We eat at a table in the visitation area so I can have a change of scenery. It's brighter out there, and we can people-watch. People who are in worse shape than me. I wish I could feel terrible about taking joy in that, but I can't.

"Have you and Mark made up?" I ask, stuffing a piece of juicy, honey-dunked chicken into my mouth.

Mom inclines her head slightly. "I told him I was sorry for how I reacted, because that wasn't okay, but not about my anger."

"And he said?"

She sighs. "That he *wasn't* sorry. So, then I called your grandfather Walker and asked him to have a chat with your brother about how Hollywood feels about misogynists these days."

I laugh. Grampa Walker semiretired years ago, but he's still a lawyer in LA with his name on the letterhead. He's got a real David vs. Goliath complex and loves taking on power- ful Hollywood men and corporations on behalf of those they take advantage of.

"Mark was not happy about that. He looked pretty ashamed by the time your grandfather was done with him. Went straight to his room, which was a good place for him. I didn't raise him to be an asshole and I won't tolerate it."

"He was just mad at me," I say, defending him. "I don't blame him. I must look pretty crazy from where he stands."

Why am I defending him? Am I so screwed up from whatever happened to me as a kid that I'll let the people I care about treat me like crap and then thank them for it?

"That's no excuse to talk to you the way he did."

I know better than to argue when she uses that tone, so I don't. Plus, she's right. My brother has every right to be angry, but not to be an ass about it. And not to act like he's the one most inconvenienced with all of it.

She's brought me some clean clothes—new ones. I guess she decided to go shopping instead of home. It's nothing fancy, only some yoga pants and T-shirts and a hoodie. Oh, and a pair of Chuckie T's with the laces taken out. I guess they're scared of what I might do with them? Doesn't matter. It will be nice to wear things that weren't given to me by the hospital. I'll feel more like me.

She's brought chocolate too and tucked that into the bedside table.

"I sneaked it in," she whispers with a conspiratorial grin. "Don't tell anyone."

Technically, I think any food has to be okayed or doled out through the kitchen or floor staff. Regardless, I'm not about to say a word.

"You don't have to stay with me all day," I tell her once she's put my clothes away. She refused to let me do it.

"I know. I'm going to head out soon. I have an appointment and a drinks meeting tonight."

"Drinks meeting?" Since when does she meet anyone for drinks during the week? "With who?"

She shrugs. "A friend from the city looking to recast the lead in his play."

My mother loves Broadway. Loves theater. Ever since we were little, she's dragged me and Mark to every production she can. A couple of months ago she and I went to see *Wicked* for the third time.

"Mom, that's awesome."

Another shrug. I can tell she's hopeful, though. "We'll see." She straightens the blankets on my bed. "Connor called again while I was out getting dinner. I told him when visiting hours were. He said he'd like to come visit if you're up for company."

"Thanks." If I were him, I'd run as fast as I could in the opposite direction, but whatever. "Yeah, he can come by if he wants."

Mom shakes her head. "Don't downplay the fact that he cares, Dylan."

"Go home, Mom," I reply with a smile.

She kisses me on the head. "I'll see you tomorrow."

"Have a good meeting. Make sure he pays the tab."

She waves her hand. "Oh, honey. That goes without saying. Love you."

"Love you too."

Alone in my room, I lie back and enjoy the relative silence. There's noise—my door is open—but it's a low-key hum of activity. This morning I woke up to the sound of someone screaming, so everything else seems like peace.

I don't get to enjoy it much before the social worker shows up. She doesn't stay long, just goes over a few things in my file and mentions that she knows I'm working with Dr. Zhao. She asks if there's anything I'd like to discuss with her—anything I feel uncomfortable telling someone else.

"Uh, no," I reply.

"Well, if you do, here's my number." She sets a business card on the tray table. "They know how to get in touch with me at the nurses' station as well. If you need anything, give me a call."

"I will. Thanks."

After she's done with me, I open the sketchbook and markers Mom brought me and start doodling. It's a woman. Once I get to the eyes, I realize she's the woman from the house—the one that sits on the porch. There was a serenity to her that I find comforting.

I'm working on a sketch of Kaz done entirely in purple when someone raps on the doorframe. It's Dr. Zhao.

"You're here late," I remark.

She smiles. "I stay a little later a couple times per week. I'm on my way out after this. May I come in?"

"Sure."

She has her hands in her pockets as she walks into the room. She looks like she just stepped out of a magazine.

"I spoke to Dr. Mueller. She's cleared tomorrow morning on her calendar for us."

I raise my eyebrows. "I scored that high, huh?"

She smiles slightly. "There's a lot to support the theory of dissociation, yes. But DID isn't the only disorder on the spectrum. There are still a few things we'll need to look into, and of course, she wants to speak to you directly."

"In case I'm faking, right?"

Dr. Zhao's eyebrows arch even higher. "To make sure you aren't given an inaccurate diagnosis. Why do you think she'd suspect you of faking?"

I shrug. "My brother thinks I'm doing this for attention."

"Are you?"

There's no accusation in her tone and I wonder if she ever loses her shit. I mean, like, throws things and screams. I'd like to see it if it ever happens.

"No." I set down my marker. "I wish I was."

She nods at the book. "May I?"

I hand it to her. She studies the two drawings I've done since Mom left. "Who are they?"

"The one on the left is a woman from the dream I had the other night. The other one is Kaz. I told you about her, I think? She was in the dream, too."

"You're incredibly talented." She passes the book back to me. "You know, one of the things we encourage DID patients to do is open a channel of communication with their alters using journals so they can share thoughts and ideas. Your sketches and the journal your friend gave you may be a great way to encourage that communication."

"Izzy said some of my art looks like it's been drawn by other people."

She thinks about that. "Would you mind if I asked your mother to bring some of that work to the meeting with Dr. Mueller?"

I shake my head. "I'm okay with it. Whatever it takes to figure this out." I swallow. "I'm scared, Dr. Zhao. Something inside me made me hurt myself and I couldn't stop it."

"I can't begin to imagine how that must feel. What's important to remember is that whatever, or whoever, precipitated the attempt failed because you regained control of your body. *You* were stronger."

This woman is really good at making me want to cry. "Okay."

She gives me a sympathetic smile. "You've had a rough twenty-four hours. I'm going to let you rest. Take the evening to sleep or draw—whatever makes you feel safe. Practice a little self-care, and in the morning, we'll begin anew."

I nod. It's not until she's at the door that I speak again. "How high did I score?" I call out after her.

Dr. Zhao shakes her head with a tiny smile. "Get some rest, Dylan," she says, and she's gone.

—

I wake up shivering. All I have over me is a thin sheet. It takes me a second to remember where I am.

The soft light in the room makes it easy for me to see the heavy blanket that should be over me has been taken completely off the bed. Someone—someone inside of me, I guess—has positioned a chair with its back a couple of feet away from the footboard and draped the blanket over the two, making a tent. The kind I used to make as a kid.

Looking at it makes my stomach churn. Scrabbling to my knees, I grab the blanket and pull it down. I don't know what I expected to find beneath it, but there's nothing except an empty candy bar wrapper and a carton of chocolate milk. There's chocolate on the blanket and on my fingers.

Standing, I toss the blanket on the bed and stumble to the bathroom. There's no mirror, because people in the psych ward can't be trusted not to break mirrors and use the pieces to hurt themselves. I wash my hands and use a cloth to wipe my face. More chocolate. What the hell? Did I fall asleep with my face in it? How did I get it all over myself?

When I step back into my room, it becomes clear.

I stand there in my yoga pants and T-shirt and slip-proof socks and stare at the wall where I'd come to. *Someone* has drawn all over it in crayon.

Fuhhhhh-ck.

It's not quality art by any stretch. It's the work of a child—probably one on a sugar high. There are misshapen stick-figures with great swirls of hair standing next to impossibly tall trees and incredibly round . . . horses. I think they're horses.

There's a man standing next to a little girl. I think it's a man, because of the short hair and how he's dressed. The little girl has yellow hair and a pink dress. She's crying. There's something written beside her—circled in white, with a line pointing toward the man, as if he's saying what's written.

"'Its our sekret,'" I read aloud. And beside that, "'Dont tell.'" "Sekret" is repeated over and over in big red letters all around this otherwise innocent drawing.

But it's not innocent. I sink to my knees in front of the drawing and press my fingers to that little girl's face. She was innocent. She was until *he* got ahold of her. She's inside me now, afraid the secret is going to be revealed. Afraid he'll hurt her when it is. I feel her fear in the back of my mind. I want to respect it. I want to take it away from her, but I don't know how.

Rage and pain cramp my stomach. Hot bile rises in my throat. This anger doesn't just belong to me. It's too much for one person. I pick up a piece of the broken red crayon and grind it over the man's face until he's obliterated into nothing but a waxy sheen of crimson.

I want to know who he is. I want to remember. And I want to make him pay for what he did to the sweet little girl I used to be. Because whatever I am now, whatever is wrong with me, or going on inside me—I'm what he made me.

ELEVEN

I have this image in my head of what a doctor is supposed to be. They're professional and polished. They really take care of themselves and work hard to project a professional image.

Then Dr. Mueller walks into my room and I have to rethink my assumptions.

She's maybe five feet tall, with curly red hair that's piled up on her head and held in place with a pencil. She wears a red jumper with a marigold-colored turtleneck underneath and olive-green tights with marigold boots. She carries a battered leather backpack over one shoulder and smiles at me from the threshold of the door. Her nose crinkles.

"Dylan?" she asks.

I nod, too busy studying her from my bed to speak. She's like a character out of a children's book, and because of it, I like her immediately.

She sets her bag on a chair by the wall and offers me her hand. "Dr. Gritta Mueller. Dr. Zhao asked me to visit you this morning. Is this a good time?"

"Uh, yeah," I reply, finding my voice.

She grins. "Awesome. Are you comfortable talking here, or do you want to go somewhere else?"

"Here is good." It's private, and it feels more like my territory.

She turns to grab the chair at the foot of my bed and stops, her attention focused on the wall.

"That's an interesting picture," she comments. "Who drew it?"

"I guess I did." I twist my sheets with my fingers. "It was there when I woke up to go to the bathroom during the night." I didn't want to tell her about the blanket.

She glances at me. "But not before you went to sleep? Did you have any memory of getting out of bed?"

I shake my head.

"So, *you* didn't draw this then. Someone else did, using your body as their conduit."

"I guess so."

She nods, her attention back on the image. "Who is the little girl?"

"Me, I think."

"And the man?"

I open my mouth, but nothing comes out. A voice in my head whispers, *We'll get in trouble if you tell.* It's the voice of a child that's not really a child—if that makes sense.

"Dylan?"

"I don't know who he is," I tell her, blinking. My head still feels fuzzy—a feeling I'm beginning to recognize. I can't quite seem to focus. I try to fight it. It's like being pulled by invisible hands from my body.

Outside my body, I look at myself. My expression is angry—defiant.

"I don't wanna to talk to you," I say, but it doesn't sound like me. It sounds like a kid. "You're not supposed to be here."

I don't know how to get back inside myself. I try to shove my way in, but I'm pushed away.

"It's all right," Dr. Mueller says in a calm voice. "You're safe here. Dylan, if you can hear me, I'd like you to name five animals that start with the first five letters of the alphabet—one for each letter."

"Alligator," I say, but my mouth says nothing. I scream it.

"Alligator," my body repeats.

I push hard again. It's like trying to find my way through thick fog. I don't even know where I'm going, but I am determined to get there.

"Buffalo. Cat."

I push harder. My head hurts and my vision swims. "Dog . . ."

Suddenly, I'm in the bed, looking into Dr. Mueller's bright blue eyes. "Elephant."

She smiles. "Thank you. You slipped away for a bit there. Do you know where you went?"

My head feels fuzzy, but at least I'm in control. "It felt like I was outside myself."

She nods. "And the person who spoke to me, do you know their name?"

I shake my head.

"That's okay," she assures me. "Dr. Zhao told me that you spoke to her about the possibility of having dissociative identity disorder. I've seen the results of the tests she's done. I've spoken to your mother already, and I'd like to chat with you now. Is that all right?"

"Yes."

Over the next twenty or thirty minutes, she asks me a lot of questions I've already answered—some of them many times. A few are new, but none seem to freak out the people in my head.

"Since your MRI came back normal, with the exception of smaller hippocampal and amygdalar volume, I do believe you have dissociative identity disorder," she tells me, finally. I don't know whether to be relieved or panicked. She must see this, because she gives me a kind smile. "I know this must be overwhelming, but with therapy and treatment, there's no reason you can't have a happy, fulfilled life."

"How?" I ask. "There are people in my head who make me do things I don't want to do and don't remember doing."

"The people in your head were created by your mind to help you deal with trauma. They've hidden for years because that was their job—to stay hidden and quiet. That they are no longer hiding tells me that you're ready to hear what they have to say and to get to know them. Once you start, they will get progressively easier to live and communicate with. Some of them might even integrate."

"What does that mean?" Because it all sounds terrifying.

"It's the breaking down of the amnesiac walls between alters, allowing their memories and them to blend together. Some people confuse it with fusion, which is the combining of two alters into a new one. There are therapists who support this as the ultimate goal of treatment—all alters fusing together, leaving only one."

"Is that what you do?"

"I like to start with encouraging communication between you and your alters and letting your system decide the course of treatment. I've had patients who want to integrate or fuse, and others who are perfectly happy to keep their system intact. 'System' is the term we use for the collective personalities living in one person."

I close my eyes for a moment, letting this sink in. The inside of my head feels like it's been through a blender. "I don't remember a trauma."

"It's likely one of your alters holds those memories so you don't have to. You may never recover the memory, or you might. Once you begin talking to the others you may learn what it was and then we can work on how you deal with it."

I look at the drawing on the wall. "I think it's pretty obvious what happened to me." It explains why I don't remember losing my virginity—or at least, what I thought was the loss of it. Someone else took over. It doesn't always happen, but I realize now that sex is something I tend to remove myself from.

"Yes," Dr. Mueller agrees. She pauses a moment, as though she thinks I might speak again. "You are fortunate that you are surrounded by people who support you. Do you feel safe in your home?"

I nod. "It's just me, my mom, and my brother. I have no idea who he is." I gesture toward the drawing.

"Possibly a family member or friend. Perhaps even a stranger."

My stomach lurches as I remember hands reaching for me. "Maybe," I say. The memory is gone—snatched away by someone in my head. It wasn't a stranger, though. I'm certain of that much.

"How do I communicate with them?" I ask. I'm glad for the meds they gave me earlier—one of the pams, I think. Something to keep me calm—all nice and floaty. It's keeping the panic at bay.

From her bag, Dr. Mueller pulls out a stack of papers and a books. "One of the best ways to start is with a journal where you can all write to one another. You may have some alters who can't write, but I know you like to draw, so that will be helpful as well. Dr. Zhao told me a friend gave you a journal, so I'd encourage you to write your feelings in that."

"Okay."

"Many people with DID also have what's called an inner world. For some it's a house or a building. For others it's a town or a park. Basically, it's a place where your alters gather or even live."

"It's a house," I tell her. "A really cool house."

She looks pleased. "You've already been there? That's wonderful. Many hosts—that's the person who has control of the body most often—have a hard time accessing their inner world. Were you welcome there?"

I nod. "I was. Mostly."

"As you learn about your alters, you will probably come to identify many of them as having different roles within your system."

I sigh, considering that. "This is a lot to take in."

"Yes, it's overwhelming, I imagine. I'm sorry if I've added to that. I brought you some articles and a book that I hope will help you."

The book is by a doctor and someone with DID. Its focus is on learning to communicate and live with the people in your head.

My head—which has gone eerily quiet. I can picture them in there, in the windows of the house, peering out from behind curtains, waiting. Holding their collective breath.

It's okay, I tell them. *I'm okay.*

I know you are, comes a reply, loud and clear. Lannie, I think. Hearing her voice validates all of this. It should probably freak me out, but it's comforting.

Dr. Mueller watches me with a small smile. "You can talk to some of them, can't you?"

"Yeah. Lannie. She seems closer than the others, if that makes sense."

She nods. "It does. Very likely there will be some with whom you can easily communicate. Others may take some coaxing or require you passing messages via another alter. Some may resist communication altogether. Start slowly, go at your own pace. Don't push yourself or them."

"Are you going to read the journal?" I ask.

"Only what you want me to read," she promises. "If you'd like, you can have a separate section, or even another journal, for personal, system-only communication. My only goal is to help you and your alters work together so you can live your best life."

"My best life." I can't help the scoffing noise.

"You've done okay so far, haven't you?"

"One of them tried to kill me."

"A persecutor, and they failed. Now that you know, you can be better prepared for drastic attempts to protect your system. They won't feel the need to take such measures. I know it may not be helpful right now, but that alter thought it was the best way to protect you and the others."

I guess I have to take her word for it. I'm not sure I want to know Scratch any better than I do. Pretty sure she doesn't care to know me either.

I need a nap. I want to curl up and go to sleep. Forget all of this and dream the rest of my life away. Just give up.

Don't you fucking dare. It's loud enough to make me wince. Kaz. Her voice is raspy and rough. I have to smile a little. It's nice knowing she and Lannie have my back. Maybe I'll survive this with their help. I didn't even know they existed two weeks ago.

Maybe Dr. Mueller is right. Maybe my "system" wants to be okay as much as I do. Maybe they're ready to heal. Well, maybe not Scratch.

"There are suggestions for how to set up the journal in the book and tips for encouraging conversation. It also suggests you make rules or guidelines for the others to follow, such as dating and signing entries."

God, this is weird. I can't seem to get past that. It's so surreal.

"Our immediate concern is making sure you and your system feel safe and heard. We'll do this together. I'm here for whatever you need. I also want to have a session with you and your mother to address any concerns you might have. I would like to begin that tomorrow if you're ready."

I blink. "So soon?"

She smiles. "You have somewhere else to be? The sooner we begin and get a treatment plan in place, the sooner you can go home. Probably within a few days. I'd like you to remain here a little while longer just in case your persecutor resists treatment."

Fear tickles the underside of my stomach. "You mean she might try to kill me again?"

"She might threaten you or others within the system. A persecutor's job is a strange one. They're often tasked with protecting the system, but they do it using abusive tactics."

"She looks a lot like my mother," I reveal. "Why?"

"I have no idea, but we'll work on figuring it out."

I stifle a yawn. "Okay."

"Looks like we've done enough for one day," Dr. Mueller allows. I glance at the clock. She's been here for over an hour. "I'll be back to see you tomorrow morning. Read as much as you want of the information I'm leaving with you. There's no rush. I will stress again that it's important you do this at your own pace and not try to force your system into facing memories until you and your alters are ready."

I have no idea what to say, so I nod.

Dr. Mueller stands. "This must seem like a lot. I can only imagine how you feel, but you will survive this, Dylan. You've already survived so much."

I guess. But I don't remember it. I'm not sure I want to remember anything bad enough to make my brain split up into new people. I mean, that's gotta be pretty fucked up.

"How does it happen?" I ask. "A lot of people have horrible childhoods. They don't all have this."

"Between the ages of seven and nine is when your personality comes together as singular. Repeated trauma at a young age can inhibit that cohesiveness and cause alters to form. Each of your alters was created by your subconscious to protect your mind from what was happening. It's an incredible defense mechanism. It means you were determined to survive."

"Thank you," I say. My voice is hoarse, but it's still mine. Not Kaz's or Lannie's. I feel them with me, but no one's trying to push their way to the front.

"You're welcome. I'll see you tomorrow."

I watch her leave the room, then slowly start to look at the stuff she left for me. Most of the papers look like things printed off the internet, or photocopies of book pages. They're a lot less intimidating than trying to read a whole book, so they seem like the best place to start.

The first page has the description of DID according to something called the *Diagnostic and Statistical Manual of Mental Disorders, Fifth Edition.* Reading the criteria, I realize it's pretty obvious this is what's wrong with me, but the next article discusses why it's so hard to diagnose DID. Like Dr. Mueller said, the brain is good at protecting the body and hiding the disorder, so people who have it are often misdiagnosed. I've been there and have the paper trail to prove it.

Some of the printouts are from the blog of a woman with DID. As I read it, a sense of ease begins to take hold of me. The tension in my shoulders and stomach lessens. Someone else expressing the same concerns and fears I have makes me feel less alone. She says she was eventually so glad to have the diagnosis because she could work on getting better instead of spinning her wheels feeling crazy.

And then she says suicide is a fear she constantly fights against. Fucking great.

It also says it's a fight she's winning, Lannie whispers.

But I don't feel much like a winner.

—

KAZ

At least I'm going to have some cool scars. And everyone knows how much chicks dig scars, right? That has to make staying in this fucking hospital worth it a little bit.

I trace the puckered line of flesh on my left wrist. It's still red and tender, the stitches tight. I like it. Maybe I can convince Dylan to get a tattoo over the scar to make it look like this. That would get attention. Make everyone think we're such a train wreck. Everyone underestimates a train wreck. Dylan hasn't figured out the power in people thinking you're delicate yet. Maybe I can teach her. Maybe she'll listen to me now.

I lean back against the pillows. I like being out. That has a double meaning for me, but in this case, I mean out in the body. I like the body. It's softer than mine, rounder. Sometimes, I like to touch it because it doesn't feel like mine, but I can feel the sensations. It's like synchronized sex. Whatever I do to the body, it does to me. And it feels nice.

Dylan doesn't get laid nearly as much as I would like. She doesn't take care of her needs like she ought to. I thought we were going to get lucky the other night on the beach with that pretty boy, but no. Doing that after cock-blocking me with Nisha was a real pisser. It's become pretty clear that if I want to get any kind of action, I'm going to have to be more aggressive. It was a lot easier to persuade her when she drank.

"Hello."

It's Dr. Zhao. "Hi," I say. Makes sense she'd show up when I'm looking like hammered shit. She's gorgeous as usual, co-ordinated and polished. My thirsty gaze travels her from head to toe. I'm such a sucker for a femme.

Her heels click on the floor as she approaches the bed. She gives me a smile that reads as sincere. "Is it all right if I visit you for a bit?"

She can stay as long as she wants. I smile at her. "Sure."

"Thank you." She sets her bag on the floor. "Who am I talking to?"

I blink. "Me. Dylan, of course."

Her smile grows a little. "No, I don't believe it's Dylan. If you don't want to tell me your name, that's okay, but I'd appreciate it if you didn't lie."

I can't help but grin at her. "What gave me away?"

"The tilt of your head. Your expression. You seem more interested in what I have to say than trepidatious." She sits down on the chair beside my bed. "Will you tell me your name?"

"Kaz." Someone's yelling at me not to trust her, but I ignore them. I like this woman and that doesn't happen very often. I'm not ashamed of myself or anything I've done, and I'm not ashamed of the fact that I'd pull back the blankets and let her into bed if she asked.

"Nice to meet you, Kaz."

"Nice to meet *you*." I put on my coyest smile. It's probably not good for much when my hair needs to be washed and I smell a little like old fish.

"How are you feeling?"

I hold up my wrists. "Like a rag doll."

"Shouldn't you have bandages on those?"

I shrug. "I like looking at them."

"Why is that?"

"They remind me that I'm real. That I'm alive."

She nods like she understands. Maybe she does. I try not to make judgments about people. "I assume you weren't the one to make the cuts?"

"No. That wasn't me."

"But you know who it was."

I nod. Everyone knows it was "death-solves-everything" Scratch.

"Will you tell me?"

"I'm not a snitch."

She raises a brow. "Your attempted murder doesn't justify snitching?"

When she puts it like that, it suddenly becomes incredibly tempting to tell her everything. *Yeah, Scratch tried to kill us all. Stupid bitch.* I can hear her pounding on the door of her room in the back of the head space. I smile. I get off on knowing she can't stop me from saying whatever I want. I still have bruises from the last time she kept me quiet.

"What's it worth to you?" I ask.

"I don't negotiate where a patient's well-being is involved."

My smile relaxes. "I guess I'm probably not the first to try."

"You are not," she replies with a slightly amused expression. "It was a valiant effort, however."

"Thanks." I jerk my head toward the artwork on the wall. You'd think someone would have tried to remove it by now. "What do you think of my latest masterpiece?"

Dr. Zhao glances over my shoulder. "You drew that?"

I snort. "I hope I have more talent than that. No, it was one of our kids." I probably shouldn't have told her that either, but fuck it. Staying safe is one thing, but underneath the need to protect us is something stronger. Something I haven't felt in a long time—the urge to talk. Because, even if something bad happens to us for telling, we all know something worse is coming. Why else would we get so sloppy and let Dylan find out about us?

"Do you know who that man is?"

I shoot her a sharp look. "Yes."

She looks at me but doesn't push. "I actually came by to talk to Dylan about her session with Dr. Mueller. Is it possible that you might let me do that?"

Is she fucking for real? Who in the hell does she think she is? She's known Dylan/us for what amounts to a few days— hell, a few *hours*—and she thinks she can come in here and make demands of us? Decide who gets to be in the body and who doesn't?

Does she have any idea how hard it is to get control—full control—and hang on to it for any length of time? I'm in the body and no one is trying to fuck me. I can watch TV if I want. Read a book. Not that I read much. Regardless, no one's asked anything of me until this bitch walked in.

I meet her gaze. "No." Dylan stirs inside me, close to the front, but I'm not ready to go. I have a phone call to make. There's someone I want to talk to.

Her gaze narrows as she tilts her head. "I've offended you."

"If I walked into your office and asked to talk to someone else would you be offended?"

"Fair enough. My apologies. I meant you no disrespect. Obviously, I'll need to learn how your system works. Are you able to give Dylan a message for me?"

I nod.

"I would like her to have one of the nurses call me when she's in front again. Will you tell her that?"

Another nod. "I don't keep secrets from her."

"Except for the identity of the man in the drawing?"

Now I feel like maybe I've been played, but I'm not sure. "She knows it, she just hasn't remembered yet. Why are you so horny to bring all that shit back to her anyway?"

"Acknowledging the trauma may help her move forward and heal."

"Or it might make everything worse." Even as I make the argument—pushed by the others in the head space—I know she's right.

"If that were the case, you and the others wouldn't have made it so easy for her to find you. If you don't want her to remember, why let her in?"

"I don't think we had a choice."

Dr. Zhao looks at me like I just said the most interesting thing she's ever heard, and it freaks me out. I don't care how gorgeous she is, I want her to go away.

I shift the blankets off me. "I have to use the bathroom."

"I'll leave you, then," she says. "I hope to talk to you again sometime, Kaz."

I already regret the entirety of this conversation. "Yeah, thanks. See ya." I duck into the bathroom and close the door, waiting until I'm sure she's gone. When I come out, the room is empty. I glance out into the hall before making my way to the nurses' station. That's where the phone we're allowed to use is kept.

"Is it okay if I make a call?" I ask the nurse behind the counter.

She smiles at me. "Of course." She pushes the phone toward me. It's beige and plastic with push buttons, some of which light up. I've never used one like this before.

"Just dial nine first," the nurse advises, seeing my confusion. "Then the number."

"Thanks." I do as she instructs, turning my back to her when someone picks up on the other end.

"Hello?" says a familiar voice.

My heart skips a beat. "Nisha? It's Kaz."

TWELVE

There's a sticky note on the front of my journal when I "wake up." I'm in bed with the TV tuned to some crime show. My right temple throbs with the beginnings of a headache and my stomach growls.

I'm hungry. I turn my head and see a tray on the table, the food on it untouched.

Whoever was out was obviously a fussier eater than me. Or, with my luck, has some kind of eating disorder. It happens to a lot of girls with DID, according to what I've read so far.

Fortunately, the food I'd chosen for dinner is a sandwich and salad, so except for bread that's a little dry and the slightly wilted lettuce, it's not bad. The warm juice is the worst part, so I drink my water instead. I've been "gone" for hours. I'm so tired of this. I hate losing time and not knowing what I've done. It's not like I can get into much trouble here in the hospital, but what if someone came to visit? What if I missed something important?

What if I'm not the host or whatever? What if I think I'm the subject of this piece, but I'm really just background scenery? And why doesn't that thought make me panic?

I pick up the journal Izzy gave me and look at the note. It says, *Let Dr. Zhao know when you (Dylan) are back—K.* I assume "K" is for "Kaz." I guess it was nice of her to leave a message, not that it does me much good at this time of day. It bodes well for the whole journaling thing, which I guess I should start. I open the book to the first page—Scratch's journal entry and I stall out. Should I rip it out or leave it there?

I rip it out but tuck it into the back of the book so it's still there, just not the first thing I—*we*—have to see.

Thinking about what little I got to read about journaling, I try to figure out what to say. I flip through the papers and book Dr. Mueller left for me, felt-tip pen poised over the paper for what feels like forever. Then I begin to write:

This journal is for the people sharing this body. It's meant to be a safe space for each of us. Please observe the following rules when writing (and feel free to suggest other guidelines you think might apply):

1. *Be respectful of one another. No criticism or shaming another alter.*
2. *Please sign and date your entry.*
3. *If you're writing to another alter, please address the entry to them.*
4. *Be supportive of one another.*
5. *Do not offer advice unless it is asked for.*

6. *This journal is for everyone to read. If there is something you don't want read, please mark it as private.*
7. *This journal may be read by our therapist to get a better understanding of us. If you don't want our doctors to read what you have to say, please mark it as private and fold the page.*

I can't think of anything else to add. The information Dr. Mueller gave me on journaling probably has more suggestions for rules, but I'll start with these and go from there. I turn the page.

Dylan, October 13

Hi, everybody. I'm sitting in bed as I write this, feeling a little stupid and kind of lost. I don't know how to do any of this, but I know that none of us can go on the way we have been. I'm tired of losing time and I'm tired of being afraid of what I—or one of you—might do. The way I see it, we're in this together, right? I want to be safe and you want to be safe, too. I also want to be able to live my life without worrying about surprises or getting hijacked.

According to what I've read so far, writing in a journal will help us all communicate better, and maybe even get us to the point that we can have conversations in ~~my~~ our head like we did when I visited the house where you live. I hope that's something the rest of you are into.

I want to get to know you better, but I'm scared. To be honest, you really freak me out, because I know having you in my life means something terrible happened to us and I don't remember what that was. At least, not really. I've started having flash-

backs, I think. They're not fun, whatever they are. I know it's
not going to be easy to remember, and that some of you would
really prefer I didn't remember, but maybe I should.

Also, I would really appreciate it if none of you tried to kill
us again. That's a sentence I never thought I'd ever write! Sui-
cide is something we definitely need to have a vote on, okay?

I feel ridiculous, writing a letter to essentially myself—my
selves. Even though I know the diagnosis of dissociative identity disorder is right, and it's only going to become more ap-
parent as I learn about it, I can't help but feel like I'm lost in
a dream. It's hard to feel grounded in reality when you have
several of them in your head.

I have a feeling most of you know way more about me than I know
about you. I'm hoping you'll introduce yourselves so we can start be-
coming friends and work together to have a productive life. If you have
any questions, feel free to ask. I hope next time I look in this journal
one of you will have replied.

After this I go to another section and start scribbling some
"System Rules." I got the idea from a video I watched earlier
on YouTube. A girl with DID showed her journal and some
of the rules she has with her system and it seemed like a good
idea. I write things like "no unsafe sex" and "no changing hair
color without a vote." Again, it feels insane to do it, but there's
also something weirdly freeing about it.

I can't really explain it, but even though I want to bury
myself under the blankets and sleep for the next year, I feel
hopeful. I know what's wrong. I can stop googling symptoms
of strokes and brain tumors. There may not be a cure, but at
least DID won't kill me.

Well . . . it won't kill me, but one of my alters might. To be safe I write: *No harming the body, physically or mentally. The body is where we all have to live and it's our responsibility to take care of it. This means proper hygiene as well as practicing self-care. We all need to make sure we're getting enough to eat, enough sleep, and enough exercise, as well as brushing our teeth and showering.*

Using "we" feels weird, but it's what everyone seems to agree on. Every article I read or video I watch, the people with DID refer to themselves in the plural. Some of them even seem comforted by it. I hope to get there someday.

My antianxiety meds must be wearing off, because panic is starting to buzz in my chest. Time to stop writing. Time to stop thinking about the crowd in my head and relax for a bit. In the morning I'll get in touch with Dr. Zhao—if I'm me, that is.

Fuck.

There's a knock at my door. I look up to see Izzy standing there. "Can I come in?" she asks.

I open my mouth, but before I can say a word, I burst into tears. She comes at me fast, throwing her things on the chair and wrapping her arms around me in a fierce hug. I grab onto her and hold her as tight as I can. She's the anchor that keeps me from floating away. My rock.

"It's okay," she whispers. "You're going to be okay."

And I believe her, because Izzy's never wrong, and I really, really want her to be right.

——

I've been in the hospital four days when Connor comes to visit. It feels like longer, even though I've been "absent" for a lot of it. The whole losing time thing has gotten worse in here, or maybe I'm just more aware of it. Regardless, I'm glad I was able to shower last night so he doesn't see me with greasy hair.

I'm surprised he actually shows. I thought he'd find an excuse to stay away. I would have. Not because I wouldn't want to see him, but because I'd have no idea what to say.

I'm nervous at the sight of him. He hesitates in the doorway and doesn't bother trying to hide it. I like that about him, his openness. He's not afraid to be vulnerable.

"Hi," I say, my voice raspy.

"Hi." He smiles that cute lopsided smile of his. "Is it okay that I'm here?"

I nod. Everyone who has come to see me seems to share that uncertainty—like I might lunge at them because they dared come visit. Maybe they think I'm like Jekyll and Hyde and if they're here at the wrong time they'll see me transform into something hideous.

Or maybe they're just worried about me and want to make sure they're not intruding. Want to know I consent to their presence, because they actually give a shit. Maybe that.

With all the people I supposedly have living inside me you'd think I'd be okay with being alone, but I'd rather be distracted by people *outside* of me. Almost every waking moment is spent trying to come to terms with my tenants and it's exhausting.

He comes into the room. It's then that I notice the paper shopping bag in his hand. "What's that?" I ask.

Connor opens it and peers inside, as if it's a surprise to him as well. "I brought you some graphic novels, candy, and a voice recorder."

I arch a brow. "Interesting combination. Thank you. You didn't have to bring me anything."

He shrugs. "When Jess was hospitalized, they wouldn't let her have pens or pencils. I figured if you couldn't write stuff down, you could talk about it instead."

Jess was hospitalized? I want to ask what for, but it's not my business. "That's awesome. Thank you. I mean it. It was really considerate of you to bring me anything at all."

He sets the bag on the bedside table. "So . . ." He chews his lower lip. "How are you?"

"Okay, I guess." I hold up my right hand and flex the fingers. "It's getting easier to hold things. Luckily my tendons didn't get messed up."

He winces slightly as he looks away. "That's good." Suddenly, his gaze snaps to mine and doesn't waver. "What the fuck happened?" There's no anger in his tone, at least none that I feel directed at me.

"I'm not sure." I can only imagine how crazy that sounds. "I came to in the bathtub after it had already happened."

He frowns, as if trying to make sense of it. "Your mother says you've been diagnosed with dissociative identity disorder?"

"I don't know if it's official, but that's what they think, yeah."

"So, *you* didn't do it."

"No, another me did." That sounds weird. "Not another me, but another part of me."

Connor's answering nod is slow. I can only imagine how this sounds to him. "So, when you answered my call . . . ?"

"I didn't know what I'd done. I swear. I never would have done that to you. That would be really sick."

"I knew you weren't playing me. You sounded really scared."

"I was. It's kind of a blur, but I was terrified." I meet his gaze and hold it. "I thought I was done."

"Why would a part of you do that?" He moves closer. "Isn't the whole point of DID to protect?"

I shrug. "My doctor says that some system protectors will go to extreme lengths to keep the system safe."

"System?"

"That's what they call the internal society."

He smiles. "I think I like 'internal society' better. It sounds like the Illuminati or something."

I smile back, lighthearted for the first time in days. "Yeah, but 'system' sounds so intriguing, don't you think?"

"True. Maybe you've got like, a Jason Bourne inside you. Superspy."

I raise my brows. "Maybe a Mr. Darcy."

He grins lazily, a curve of his lips that makes my stomach flutter. It's those heavy eyes of his that really get me, though. I think they used to call a gaze like his "bedroom eyes." "It always comes back to that guy."

"Yeah, well, he sets the bar pretty high." Kind of like Connor himself. This guy's too good to be true. I can't figure out why he would waste his time with me, when I'm obviously not even on the scale of high maintenance. They can't measure where I'm at.

"Are you one of those guys who gets off on train-wreck girls?" I ask.

His jaw drops. "I beg your pardon?"

His politeness would be laughable if he didn't look so utterly insulted. I guess that's a good sign.

"I'm just trying to figure out why you're here. Most guys would have cut and run—unless you like telling your friends about the mess you're dating."

"That would make me a real asshole, wouldn't it?"

"Or a mess yourself."

He shakes his head. "I don't know whether I should be mad at you for thinking that of me or feel sorry for you for thinking so little of yourself."

"Split the difference," I suggest.

"I like you, Dylan."

"The girl you like isn't me," I remind him, not meanly. "She's an alter in my head. You really want to hang out with me when you never know who you're going to be hanging with?"

"When I saw you in the coffee shop, I liked the outside you. You told me your name was Lannie and I liked you. I liked you when you told me your name was Dylan and I drove you home." He shrugs. "Maybe I'll like the rest of you, too. I don't know."

"I was on the phone with you in the middle of trying to kill myself."

"And scared the shit out of me, yeah." He chuckles uncomfortably. "But like you said, you didn't know you'd hurt yourself."

"You're crazy for coming here. Crazy for getting involved with this." I gesture wildly in the air around myself.

"Better crazy than an asshole for walking away." Connor tightens his jaw. "I've spent the last few days worried about

you, wanting to talk to you or see you, *to make sure you're okay.*
I think your mom's going to get a restraining order, and I
don't fucking care, okay? If that's crazy, then, whatever."

"What if I'm making it all up?"

A slow blink, followed by a frown. "What?"

"What if the people in my head are . . . imaginary friends?
What if this is all just pretend?" Hasn't he considered that?
I've been sitting here all morning trying to get into that damn
house in my head and I can't help but wonder if maybe I'm
making it all up. I mean, it's in my head, after all.

But if it's make-believe, why did no one answer the door
when I imagined knocking on it? If it were made up, wouldn't
I be able to do whatever I wanted?

"You can't fake the way you freaked out at my place that
morning," he reminds me with a shake of his head. "You didn't
make that up."

"I don't know who I am, Connor." I don't know if I'm
trying to drive him away or desperately begging for help. "I
thought getting an answer would make me feel better, but I
feel like I'm on the verge of freaking out all the time."

He takes my hand. His fingers are warm and strong. "What
can I do?" he asks.

I shake my head. "I don't think anyone can do anything.
I just have to deal."

"Maybe you need something else to think about."

"Like?"

He shrugs. "When I'm anxious I make up stories about
other people. I make up characters. Maybe if you think of
the people inside you as characters and not other yous, it will
help."

A low gasp of appreciation echoes in the back of my skull. My "system" likes the idea, I guess. "You mean draw them?"

"Yeah. They're people, right? Think about what they want. Every character in every book or movie wants something. They have goals and reasons for wanting those goals. And to make a great story you have to set up obstacles to them getting those goals or make them want the wrong thing. So, think about what your people want and why. Then, work on breaking down the obstacles, or changing the goals, but treat them like people outside of yourself—people you want to understand. Maybe the distance will help."

Maybe. I don't think it will make the situation worse. "Thank you," I tell him. "That helped."

Connor smiles. "I was thinking that maybe we could work on something together to take your mind off things. Like a collaboration. A graphic novel or something—like we joked about before."

Before one of my alters tried to take me out. "Okay, but I don't know how much work I'm going to be able to do."

"It's not work. Just something fun."

"Why are you this nice? Most guys would seriously run screaming." He's already validated my ego, but I need him to do it again.

He looks away, obviously embarrassed. "I guess I think you're worth it."

I lift the hand he's holding and press my lips to the back of his. "Thank you."

Still holding my hand, he leans down and kisses me on the

mouth. He tastes like caramel and coffee, his lips sweet and soft. My heart thumps so hard it hurts, and inside me, I feel Lannie's romantic sigh.

And right now, calm and lulled into peace by Connor's kiss, I know that, for the most part, I don't care what's wrong with me. I want to be okay. It's the not knowing if I will be okay that's left me off balance.

"Ahem."

Connor pulls back like someone tased him. Standing in the doorway of my room with a smirk on her face is my mother. "Am I interrupting?" she asks sweetly.

Connor blushes. He looks adorable.

"Yes," I tell her without too much annoyance.

"I brought lunch," she announces, holding up takeout bags. "I brought enough for three." Then she does something that amazes me. She sets the bags on the table, and puts her arms around Connor, hugging him. He hugs her back. I don't think he was exaggerating when he said they'd been talking a lot. I wonder if he realizes how much my mother embracing him means.

Cougar, says Kaz.

Bitchy, much? I ask silently, adding my own smirk.

Love you too, whore.

The response surprises me, but I can tell Kaz is surprised too. We haven't "spoken" since I was a kid. That we can actually have a conversation is amazing. And freaky. Having her so close feels like having my best friend with me. The only thing that would make me feel more stable and loved would be if Izzy walked in. DID isn't all terrifying. Maybe I will be okay.

"Where's my hug?" I demand, when Mom releases Connor. "Hello?"

She wraps her arms around me too, so tight. I breathe her scent deep into my lungs, sighing inside. Kaz echoes the sentiment. Other voices chime in, too. There's only one voice that rises up in defiance, and I barely hear it. Scratch.

She hates my mother—hates her so much. And I can't help but wonder why.

—

October 14

Hi, I'm Lannie. I'm in my early twenties. I have blue hair and wear glasses. I like to be social and hang out. I like to paint with watercolors. Dylan's drawn me a few times, which is pretty cool. I'm not sure what the "professionals" would call me. My job is to protect us and handle social situations that make Dylan, or anyone else, uneasy.

I didn't always know this was my job, but I figured it out. I wasn't always aware that I was part of something bigger either. Like, for a long time I thought I was the owner of the body, for lack of a better term. The first time I looked in a mirror, I freaked out. You see, the face looking back at me wasn't mine. Then, Dali and Kaz explained. That was when I realized that I wasn't my own person. I mean, I'm a person, obviously, but not the person I thought I was. That kinda sucks, you know? That's not a bid for sympathy, though. I've accepted the things I can't change, and I've embraced who and what I am. I was created for a purpose and I'm important.

I've been aware of you (Dylan) for a long time. I've watched you grow up. Watched you fuck up and then try to fix it. I know what's been done to you and what you've done. I've tried to help, but there wasn't much I could do when you weren't even aware we existed. Sometimes I've had to take control away from you, and I'm sorry about that, but it was for the best. I like to think I've kept you safe over the years. Helped you find your creativity and pushed you to do things you were afraid to do. Helped you overcome a lot of fear and maybe have some fun? I tried to keep the bad memories from you. Once in a while, something slid through, but it's my job to protect you, and I take that seriously.

You never would have talked to Connor if not for me. Do you remember? You probably don't. We were in that coffee shop together when he walked in. You thought he was cute—so did I. He looked at us and smiled, and you looked away. You wanted to talk to him, but you were afraid. Afraid he might not be interested. Afraid of him, for reasons you didn't understand. It made me angry, because you—we—deserve to have that feeling in our lives. You deserve to like someone, even if you think you don't.

That's when I took over. If he'd been a jerk, I would have gotten you out of there, but he was <u>nice</u>. A little awkward, but so very, very nice.

We haven't met many nice guys, Dylan. I know you remember some of them. I didn't plan to spend the whole weekend with him, but I had fun. I've never been out that long before. I've never really been able to just be me before.

I always had to pretend to be you. I knew as soon as we started talking that you'd like him. I knew you'd like Jess, too. I really liked her. They're not pretentious like some of the people we've met at school. I wanted to tell them the truth by Saturday night, but it wasn't my truth to tell, and I was scared they'd make me leave. I'm sorry you woke up in a strange place, and I'm sorry I made you miss turning in your work on time, but I'm not sorry for anything else. I didn't even drink much, because of the problems you've had in the past. I vaped a little. It's okay, but it was just so cool to have the choice.

And see? You like Connor and he likes you. He might even like the rest of us! And we don't have to worry about him finding out because he already knows and we can just be ourselves with him. Right? So, that's a good thing, yeah? I really hope it's a good thing and that you're not mad at me. I guess I'd know if you were really mad, but I'm just picking up on your confusion and fear.

I know this must be hard for you. You haven't had time to get used to this like we have. The most important thing for you to remember is that we're here for you. It might not seem like it at times, but we are here to help and protect you, whether we like it or not. I suppose it's whether you like it or not as well. We're in this together, and now that you know about us, we can work together to make the best of the situation.

Because we HAVE to make the best of this, Dylan. There's really no other option, is there? What Scratch did— none of us wanted that. You need to know that. Doing it behind our backs is unforgivable, and I want you to know she's being punished for it.

There's not much else for me to say right now. I hope I didn't say anything that upset you and that maybe we can be friends. I'd like that. I hope you will too. ☺

THIRTEEN

Lannie's journal entry makes me tear up when I read it the next morning. It's hard to think of the people in my head as separate from me, but it's obvious they think of themselves that way. Lannie is much more than a figment of some mental breakdown I had as a kid. Maybe that's not the right way for me to think of it, but it's how I see it right now. She sees herself as her own person. I suppose I need to see my alters that way as well if I'm ever going to have anything remotely like a normal life. I have to stop thinking of them as different versions of me.

Where do I go when one of the others comes out? Why don't I hang out in the house with the rest of them? Maybe I do and I don't remember it? Or maybe I get shut in a box like a doll because I'm not the real me.

Fuck, that's a scary thought. If I'm not me then who is?

This is not something I can think about without a truckload of Xanax.

I've been "switching" a lot these last couple of days. Maybe it's not really a lot. Maybe I'm just hyperaware of missed time now. Or maybe it's the stress of finding out I have DID and wondering what caused it. Stress is a trigger for switching, so it makes sense.

I have to be honest with myself. The whole point of this disorder is to protect me and hide what happened, but I was sexually molested as a child. I just haven't remembered the details. I don't need to remember them. Who the fuck would *want* to remember that? I am very appreciative of the alters who keep those memories so I don't have to dwell on them. I'm able to know it happened, but it feels like it happened to someone else.

Except when I have a flashback. Then it feels like it's happening to me all over again. I've only had a couple, but that was enough. I can feel him. Smell him. And my body floods with nausea and panic.

What kind of asshole hurts a kid like that?

Before the divorce, Mom and Dad had parties at our house all the time. We were always traveling and seeing people. There was always a crowd around. Hollywood and New York entertainment people. Musicians.

There were ones who hung around a lot. Randy and George and Leo. They were good to me. We spent time with Uncle Travis and his friends, too. But none of them stand out.

Who was it?

God, it wasn't Dad, was it?

My stomach lurches at the idea. No. I'd know if it had been Dad, wouldn't I? I love my dad. I talk to him a lot. We get together as much as we can. He's going to be here soon for our birthday. It wasn't him. I refuse to even imagine it. He would never, never hurt me.

Thinking about it starts a sharp throb in the front of my head. Is this a normal headache, or a message from one of my internals? I read that some alters will cause pain when a host gets too close to remembering a detail the alter wants to stay hidden. Scratch is probably digging an imaginary dagger into my brain. She'd like that, I think. She loves making me feel bad. She's a persecutor, I guess. Hard for me to think of her as anything but the worst kind of asshole.

DID's a complicated disorder and I see why some people think it's made up. I meant what I said to Connor—that sometimes I think this is all in my head. There's a reason for that—it honestly is *all in my head*. It's about neural pathways and memory and the splintering of personalities before the self is fully formed. It's all based on my experiences and emotions— a fully customized mental disorder that is completely different from someone else's version of it, despite there being similarities in how symptoms manifest. I've read about four different people so far and each of their stories resonated with me as similar to my own, while the things that go on in their inner worlds have been drastically different. With every new case I encounter I wonder if maybe I don't have DID, and then I realize I do. It's easier to accept and deal with if I don't let myself think about it too much.

But I don't have much else to do in here but think. There's

been talk of sending me home soon, and I can't wait to sleep in my own bed.

Someone taps on the door. I look up, expecting to see Mom or Izzy, maybe even Mark, though I haven't heard from him since he stormed out. But it's Nisha, the girl from the train.

"Hi," I say dumbly. *Kaz, a little warning might have been nice. Sorry. I didn't think she'd come.*

I don't know what's more surprising—that she answered, or that she sounds genuinely apologetic. And then, *Actually, I'm not sorry.*

"Hi." Nisha smiles from the doorway. She's dressed all in black with a red scarf wrapped around and in her hair. Her nose ring glints under the lights. She is an affront to the tranquility this place tries to enforce. Looking at her is like looking at energy incarnate. I can see why Kaz likes her. Personally, I find her slightly intimidating.

She moves into the room like a dancer—all rhythmic grace. I wonder if maybe she knows the effect she has on people and likes it.

"I didn't think you'd come," I say, going on what little Kaz has given me.

She shrugs. "Thought the least I could do is come visit. You asked so nice." Her pale eyes twinkle. Her mother is British, I remember randomly. Her parents met at college in England. That explains that beautiful gaze that looks at me as if I'm something I'm not.

Oh, shit. I don't know what Kaz said to her, and I don't want to know. It already freaks me the hell out that I remember what this girl's skin feels like, and that her smell makes my stomach quiver. It's unsettling, feeling this attraction with someone that *I'm* not attracted to.

I clear my throat. We can't keep leading her on. I can't. "I'm glad you did come. There's something I want to tell you."

Don't, Kaz whispers. *Please don't.*

We can't lie to her. If she's okay, I promise I'll be cool with the two of you hanging out. It's not something I'm totally prepared to honor, but I will if I have to. We were—I was—honest with Connor and he chose to give us a chance. Nisha deserves the same consideration, and so do the rest of us.

"Is it a continuation of what you told me yesterday?" she asks with a sultry smile.

I swallow. "Uh . . . no." *What the fuck did you say to her?*

That's private.

Nisha frowns. "You seem different. You were weird on the train, too. What's going on?"

I push myself a little further up on the bed. The stitches in my wrists pull and twinge. "Did I tell you why I'm in here?"

"You told me you cut yourself." She glances at the bandages. "Looks like more than a simple cut."

"I tried to kill myself."

Her hand catches mine. Her fingers are cool and soft. I can't stop the shiver that runs down my spine. "Are you okay? What happened?"

I can't quite bring myself to meet her concerned gaze. "I got a diagnosis I didn't like." Not quite the truth, but it's a good segue.

"Are you sick?"

Sighing, I force my eyes up to hers. "You know how I seemed like a different person when you saw me on the train?"

She nods, smiling a little. "I thought maybe you were ashamed to be seen with me."

"No!" That's Kaz's voice that comes out, not mine. She's up front and center. I can feel her—almost like she's sitting right next to me, but in my head. She doesn't try to take over, though. She's afraid. Huh. "No, that's not it."

Her thumb strokes the back of my hand. God, it's nice to be touched. "Then, what?"

"I've been diagnosed with dissociative identity disorder. I don't know if you know what that is—"

"Dissociative identity disorder?" Nisha echoes, jerking back. She pulls her hand out of mine. "Are you fucking kidding me?"

I shake my head. "You have no idea how much I wish I was."

"That shit's not real."

I'm a little surprised at the vehemence of her tone. "Yeah, it is."

She scowls. "Are you making this up to get out of seeing me?"

I stare at her. "No offense, but I wouldn't do something like this just to avoid someone. I'm telling the truth. That's why I'm in here. That's why I hurt myself." It's easier to take the blame than try to explain that Scratch was the one with the blade.

Nisha looks at me in disbelief and disgust. "Is your name even Kaz?"

I think of Jess that morning at the apartment, looking at me the same way. She felt duped, betrayed, like I bet Nisha feels. "My name is Dylan, but Kaz is inside me. She's part of me. She likes you. She really does."

"Right." She backs up. "I don't have time for this. You wanna play head games, pick someone else."

"I'm not playing."

"No? 'Cause it sounds like you want to keep me on the line for whenever you feel bi-curious. I'm not interested in being a booty call for someone who would lie to hide who she is."

"I'm not lying!" I hold out my bandaged wrists. "Does this look like some kind of joke to you? Please, will you sit down? Let me explain." I don't know why I care so much that she understands, but I think it's because Kaz is so close I'm no longer sure what's me and what's her. It's like layers in Photoshop.

"I don't want to sit. And I really don't want to listen to any more of this." Her features harden. "I took the train here, you know that? I took time out of my schedule. I had to make an effort to come to you, and for what? To get made a fool of."

"I didn't know you were coming," I argue. "I didn't even know Kaz called you. If I had, I would have called you back myself and explained everything. I'm not telling you this to pull something over on you. I'm telling you because you deserve to know the truth."

"You're messed up," she says, shaking her head. "Really messed up. I'm sorry, but I . . . I can't do this. I won't. Take care of yourself, Kaz—Dylan. Whatever the fuck your name is."

I watch her walk out. Inside me, Kaz's pain is sharp and deep. To be honest, I'm hurt, too. I've never had someone look at me like I was evil.

"I'm sorry," I whisper. She hurts so bad and there's nothing I can do to help her. All the pain she's taken away from me over the years and I can't even spare her this.

Kaz doesn't reply, but I feel her retreat deeper inside. Her withdrawal leaves an emptiness behind that is almost painful.

I don't understand. Nisha seemed like someone who would understand. Someone who would sympathize and support. Maybe she has her own trauma and that's why she can't handle this. Maybe she really did think I was lying. Or maybe she just didn't want to deal. I can understand that. But if she liked Kaz as much as she seemed to, wasn't that worth at least a conversation?

I lie back against the pillows and close my eyes with a sigh. I have a headache and I'm emotionally drained. I need a nap.

The next time I talk to Connor I need to thank him for giving a damn, because I'm starting to realize just how fucking rare that is.

—

DALI

Our house has always been the way it is. The decor has changed, and the floor plans sometimes shift and morph, but it's always been exactly what each of us needs it to be. It's our world. It's always been easier for those of us on the inside to communicate with each other than it has been for us to communicate with Dylan, but there's a consent element. We have to want to communicate with each other.

Kaz, Lannie, Alyss, and myself have always had fairly decent lines of communication. I suppose I should add Scratch to that as well. But Alyss can reach the kids when the rest of us can't, and Scratch has access to the basement where Lannie can't go. There are rules on the inside, even for those of us who have been around since the beginning.

I've always been the den mother. I know where everyone is, and I know all their names. I know of alters buried so deep they might never be found, and I know it's for the best if they're not. I can't talk to all of them, not even I can do that, but I know they're there. And if I pay very close attention, I know what they're feeling. I missed that with Scratch the night she tried to murder us. I won't miss it again.

I stop writing in the journal and retreat into our inner world. I'm more comfortable on the inside these days. When the body was younger, I used to front more to keep us away from dangerous situations, but that changed over the years. Now, most of my time is spent making sure everyone else is okay, not just Dylan. And right now, there's someone I need to check up on.

It's dim in the room when I open the door, only a little daylight coming in through the curtains. She's sitting on the floor in the corner, knees drawn up to her chest. It's not uncommon for her to withdraw, but this feels different than just moodiness.

"Are you okay?" I ask, hesitantly. If she hadn't wanted me to come in, the door would have been locked, but that doesn't mean she isn't in a state.

Kaz raises her head. I can just barely see her tearstained face. "Do I look okay?"

I wince at the harshness of her tone, but don't back down. "No, but I've seen you look worse."

She laughs and I'm relieved. Kaz is the most mercurial of us, and she's never taken rejection well. It hasn't happened often, but the few times it has were . . . *difficult.* If she withdraws, we all feel it. She's a huge part of our community. Our "system" as Dylan is beginning to think of us. If one of us can't do our job, the others have to step in. It causes disruptions, but it can be done. But with Dylan struggling in her position as public face, we can't afford to have Kaz struggle. Lannie and I can't cover for both of them. Not now. And with the damage Scratch has already done, we can't risk Kaz harming the body as well, which she's been known to do when things get dark.

Dylan's birthday is rapidly approaching and a wave of change is coming with it. I feel it. We all do. I'm not sure we are entirely aware of what it means, but we know something is about to happen. Otherwise there wouldn't be this upheaval. I don't know if we let her become aware of us, or if she became aware on her own. I don't know if what's happening is the right thing, but it's happening regardless. I'm just trying to hold everyone together so we can survive what's coming.

The house has undergone some renovations lately. Walls are coming down, and with that, memories are resurfacing. Kaz has been the one to deal with some of the more . . . unpleasant ones.

"Do you want to talk?" I ask.

Kaz shakes her head. "Nothing to talk about. The girl I like can't handle that we're multiple, and Dylan's too much of homophobe to go along with me."

So she's in one of her "it's not me, it's everyone else" moods.

"Don't blame Dylan," I tell her. "She tried to explain. Not everyone's as open as you are when it comes to attraction, sweetie." Honestly, I don't know if Kaz has ever actually cared about any of the people she's had sexual relationships with. Some of them have been pleasing to her, I suppose, and others not so much. Her idea of keeping Dylan from getting assaulted or hurt has been to take on the aggressor role to maintain control.

"You're right," Kaz allows with a sigh. "I'm just pissed 'cause that boy of hers likes her enough to give us all a chance. He won't last, but at least he's willing."

"You don't know that. He seems very nice."

"He hasn't met me yet."

"You are not going to sabotage Dylan's relationship out of pettiness."

She looks offended that I'd even suggest it. "I'm not sabotaging anything. I don't have to. He's not going to have the balls to deal with us. If I don't make him run, Scratch will."

I frown, because there's a lot of possibility in her words. "I'm going to hold out hope."

"You always do."

I lean against the wall. "I'm worried about us, Kaz."

She frowns as she rises to her feet. "Why?"

"Something's coming. I know you feel it. Alyss says the little ones are scared and anxious all the time. I hear noises in the basement. Lannie is afraid Scratch will try something again."

"What are you afraid of, dilly-Dali?"

I smile at the pet name. "I'm afraid Dylan is going to break and one of us will have to take her in." It happened once, a few years ago. Remmie couldn't handle things anymore. Next thing we knew, she was gone and so was Tuesday, and in their place was Alyss—a little bit of them both, but different.

Kaz shudders. "I'm not taking her on."

"We need to help her so it doesn't happen." To be honest, I don't know if any of us have the power to stop it. Each of us is a person in her own right, but we're governed by Dylan's mind. I don't know what would happen to us if she wasn't able to host anymore. She's always been the host.

"Have you talked to the old bitch?"

I grimace. "You shouldn't call her that."

Kaz shrugs. "It fits. Have you talked to her?"

"No." I sigh. "I should, I suppose." I don't like talking to Scratch, though. She's always so angry. Bitter.

"You're the only one of us she respects. Except for Alyss, maybe."

I tap my tongue against the back of my teeth. "She's afraid of Alyss, a fact for which I am very happy."

"You talk like an English teacher sometimes, Dal."

She's teasing me, which is a sign that she's not completely morose over this heartbreak. "Why don't you come sit on the veranda with me? It's too gloomy in here."

I expect her to turn me down, but she nods. "Don't tell anyone else about this, okay?"

"Of course not." I put my arm around her shoulders as we leave the room. I am the keeper of secrets—I never tell anyone what I'm not supposed to. That's what has me so afraid. If all of the walls come down and Dylan remembers, there won't be any secrets anymore.

And no one will need me at all.

—

DYLAN

Dr. Zhao comes by to talk about treatment once I get out of here. My diagnosis of dissociative identity disorder is official.

I'm told I'm lucky that we've gotten a diagnosis because people with DID often go years in the mental health system before getting the proper help.

I don't feel lucky. There's a part of me that wishes it had been a tumor, but I'm smart enough not to say that out loud to anyone who knows and loves me. I did say it to Dr. Zhao, though. She's hopeful I'll change my mind once we begin treatment.

There aren't meds you can take for DID, but there are things you can take to help offset other issues, so I'm going to be sticking with the pills that help my BPD and anxiety. The DID stuff is going to be dealt with through therapy. I'm going to start off seeing Dr. Zhao a couple of times a week, continue with my reading and journaling, and once a month we'll meet with Dr. Mueller. We're going to do this for a few months and then reevaluate.

"How's Kaz?" she asks.

So Kaz *was* "fronting" the last time Dr. Zhao came by. I was right. The realization is comforting.

"I'm not sure. A girl she liked didn't take hearing about the DID all that well."

"Kaz told her?"

"I did. Kaz was . . . co-conscious with me." Look at me, learning the lingo. "I think she knew we had to be honest about it."

"Honesty will save a lot of confusion, but the goal of the disorder is to protect itself and you, so don't be surprised if not everyone in your system agrees with being completely truthful."

"The idea of a lesbian relationship freaked me out." There, I admitted it. "Maybe she picked up on that."

Dr. Zhao smiles slightly, in that sympathetic way of hers. "I can understand that. May I ask what you said to the girl?"

"I told her that I wasn't Kaz, that I . . . *we* have DID and how Kaz really likes her. She accused me of being bi-curious and basically said we were too messed up for her."

The doctor looks impressed with me. "So, even though you are not bisexual, you took Kaz's feelings into consideration, that's good."

"I could feel how much she liked this girl. She still likes her, and I know how hurt she is. I couldn't ignore that."

"Dylan, I want you to know how wonderful it is that communication between the two of you is so open already. That bodes very well for our work going forward. Do you know if Kaz holds or remembers any of the trauma your system suffered?"

I shake my head.

"That's fine. We'll work on that once we're able to resume our scheduled sessions. Now that we have a diagnosis, I'd like to use a combination of cognitive therapy and something called eye movement desensitization and reprocessing."

"Okay." I have no idea what she's talking about.

"Basically, we'll identify areas of trauma and use EMDR to begin working on how your system reacts and processes the experiences. The focus will be dealing with past and present trauma, but also setting you up to deal with any future issues as well."

"So, it will help with flashbacks?"

"That's the goal. I assume since you asked that you've had flashbacks?"

"A couple, yeah. They scare the shit out of me."

"That's because your mind hasn't processed those memories, so it feels like it's happening in the moment. Do you remember what they are?"

"A man reaching for me. His hands. His breath. He hurts me." Talking about it brings them back—flashes in my head that make my heart pound and my throat tight. I can see him, shadowy and vague. His hands reach for me, and the fog around him clears a little. "I think he has a tattoo on his arm."

A sharp pain jabs me in the stomach. I gasp, doubling over in bed.

"It's okay." Dr. Zhao is out of her chair. She offers me her hand and I grab it hard. "You're safe."

Oh my God, it *hurts*. I'm sweating and gasping for air. Then, as sudden as it came, it eases and fades away.

I catch my breath and release her poor hand. Dr. Zhao hands me the glass of water beside the bed and I take a sip. "I'm sorry," I tell her. "I thought my appendix burst or something."

"Most likely an alter," she says calmly. "You got too close to remembering, and they were trying to protect you."

I've only met one so far who confuses pain and suffering with protection. Scratch. "It's a really shitty way of trying to protect me."

"Yes, well, they sometimes go to extremes, as you are aware."

The sweat begins to cool on my forehead as my heart rate slows. It's like nothing ever happened. "Is this going to happen every time I remember something? Because I'll stay ignorant, thanks."

"It may. Perhaps we need to assure your system that you

don't necessarily have to remember the trauma in order to begin healing from it."

"Yeah, let's do that." I sigh. "How are they able to do things like make my stomach hurt?"

"They are limited only by your mind. But the more we are able to increase intersystem communication the less they should, hopefully, feel the need to use physical cues."

"I just want to be normal. Is that possible?"

She smiles again. "Normal is overrated. Let's use the word 'balanced' instead."

"Seriously?" I slap my hand over my mouth. That wasn't me. Scratch, maybe, since she's close? I can't feel her like I do Lannie and Kaz, but I know she's around.

Dr. Zhao chuckles. "How about we look at it as getting you to a good place, then? A place where you feel secure, safe, and content with your system?"

"Okay." Honestly, it's hard to concentrate on what she's saying when I feel like Scratch might be lurking. She fucking scares me. I don't know what she's going to do. *Go away,* I think. *Back off and leave me alone, you fucking bully.*

"Dylan? Are you all right? Are you dissociating?"

I blink and raise my head. "I'm okay. I'm here. Sometimes this stuff makes my head spin. It feels so out of reach and impossible, and I don't understand a lot of what I'm reading and hearing . . ." Yeah, it feels pretty defeating.

"Have you tried watching some YouTubers who have DID?" she asks.

"I've watched a couple."

"I'll give you some suggestions of who to watch—systems who provide verified research in a more accessible way. There are Facebook groups as well, and other social media sites where you can talk to other systems. I would suggest checking some of them out and finding a few you like. It can be very helpful knowing you're not alone."

I laugh at her unintentional joke. "Hard to be alone with a houseful of people in your head."

Her eyes crinkle with laughter. "Yes, I suppose it is." Her smile fades. "I want to help you, Dylan, but how you progress is going to depend on you. I can't tell you it'll be easy, but I can assure you that we'll advance at your pace. I know it's overwhelming, but you can have a fulfilling life."

I nod. She and Dr. Mueller keep telling me the same things in different ways, trying to drive the message home. I can have a meaningful life. Well, yeah. That's awesome.

But which one of me gets to have it?

FOURTEEN

YOU DON'T LIKE ME. I GET IT. SO FUCKING WHAT? NO ONE IN THIS PLACE LIKES ME— EXCEPT MAYBE FOR DALI AND SHE LIKES EVERYONE. LET ME FILL YOU IN ON A LITTLE SECRET—I DON'T FUCKING CARE. I'M NOT HERE TO MAKE FRIENDS, SWEETHEART. I'M HERE BECAUSE YOU CAN'T HANDLE THE THINGS THAT HAVE HAP-PENED TO YOU. SOMEONE NEEDS TO PROTECT THE HOUSEHOLD AND IT'S OBVIOUSLY NOT GOING TO BE YOU, IS IT?

YOU SHOULD HAVE JUST LET ME DO MY JOB. I COULD HAVE ENDED ALL YOUR PAIN, COULD'VE MADE SURE NO ONE IN OUR SYSTEM EVER HAS TO SUFFER AGAIN. NOW, BECAUSE OF YOU, A LOT OF US ARE BEING FORCED TO RELIVE OLD PAIN. FOR THE MOST PART, WE'RE OKAY WITH IT, BECAUSE

IT'S OUR JOB, BUT WHEN YOU START TALKING TO THESE FUCKING DOCTORS ABOUT THINGS, THAT'S NOT OKAY.

WE'RE NOT SUPPOSED TO TELL. HORRIBLE THINGS WILL HAPPEN IF YOU KEEP TALKING. PEOPLE WILL GET HURT. YOU'LL WISH I HAD SUCCEEDED IN KILL-ING US. YOU'LL BEG ME TO FINISH THE JOB. THE BEST THING YOU CAN HOPE FOR IS TO DIE.

—

DYLAN

They let me—us—go home Friday afternoon. I'm scared Scratch might try to hurt me again, especially after reading the journal entry she wrote in the middle of the night (which explains why I'm so freaking tired).

Sleep is going to have to be something we all agree on. I can't be walking around like a zombie.

"Want to have pizza for dinner to celebrate coming home?" Mom asks as we pull into the drive.

"Sounds good," I reply.

"Would you like to invite Connor?"

"Yeah, sure." I look around our yard. "Who put the Hal-loween decorations up?"

"Izzy and Mark. They thought it might be a nice welcome home."

Mom is hopeful, in tone and expression, so I don't reveal my disappointment. It was a nice thought, but I love decorat-ing for Halloween every year. It's always been my job and I enjoy it. I'd been looking forward to it.

"It's great," I say, caught between indignity and shame as I unfasten my seat belt.

Mom's hand gently pats my knee. "I made sure they saved the inside for you, especially with the party coming up. I thought you might like to be in charge."

She gets me. In so many ways this woman knows me better than anyone else. I don't know what I'd do without her, so why does Scratch, the most hateful part of me, look so much like her? I hate it.

And I hate Scratch. So much.

I hug her. "Thank you."

She hugs me back. "I love you, baby girl."

I bite the inside of my mouth to keep from crying. No time for that crap. Halloween—and our birthday—is coming up. My father will be here. Every year I plan the party with Mark's input. Mostly my brother just tells me what he doesn't want, and I fill in the blanks. I have too much to do to wallow in emotions.

I text Connor to see if he wants to come over. He said he'd keep the evening open in case I wanted to do something, which was sweet and also a little scary.

Do I want a boyfriend right now? Is it even a good idea with all that's going on? It feels insane, and yet . . . here I am, texting him, anxious that he will have changed his mind. He's a glimmer of normalcy in my life and I need all the normal I can get. I don't care if Dr. Zhao doesn't like the word.

He responds a few seconds later, as I'm walking into the house. I smile at the reply. "He wants to know what time?"

"Let's say seven. That will give him plenty of time to get here." Mom closes the front door and locks it. "Why don't you go take a shower?"

Not a bath. I guess it's too soon for that. She'll probably never suggest I take a bath again.

"Mom," I begin, and hesitate when she turns her head toward me.

"Sweetie?"

"I'm sorry about all of this."

Her smile melts into an expression of sympathy. "Oh, honey. I know you are. So am I."

I'm not sure what to do when a tear trickles down her cheek, but someone inside me knows exactly how to act, because they shove me forward, giving me no choice but to wrap my arms around her. She clings to me.

"I didn't do my job," she says, her voice thick and low. "I should have protected you better. No one should have gotten close enough to hurt you."

"Mom, there's no way you could have been there every minute of every day."

She pulls back, the lines of her face harsh. "I only needed to be there the right minute on the right day. I should have seen the signs, and there's nothing that can convince me otherwise, Dylan. I didn't do my job and you've paid a horrible price." Her fingers bite into my arms. "I promise you I'm going to do everything I can to make it up to you. I will never let you down again."

Tears run. My nose fills up. I'm a mess. "Mom. You've never let me down. Never."

We hug again, both of us crying. We stand there for a few seconds, just holding each other, before I feel strong enough to let her go. "I love you," I tell her, sniffing.

She swallows, runs her hand over my hair. "I love you,

too." She wipes her eyes. "Now, go get your shower. You don't want to smell like hospital when Connor gets here."

I don't remind her that Connor saw me in the hospital. That's not what this is about. I didn't think that Mom might take any responsibility for my disorder. I'm not surprised she feels the way she does, but the intensity of her guilt hits me hard. She's on emotionally treacherous ground, just like me. We're both one breath from losing it, and the only thing keeping us from doing just that is each other.

"Oh my God, I'll be so glad to shave my legs," I say, and then I hesitate. "Should I use a razor?"

"Epilator," Mom replies. "To be safe. There's a new one on your bed."

"Thanks." I haul myself upstairs to my room and close the door. I'm tempted to crawl into bed and pull the covers over my head, but I don't.

I start to undress as I walk into the bathroom. I stop in the middle of the tiled floor and stare at the tub. It's spotless. Someone cleaned up all my blood. Mom? Jesus, I hope not, but I can't imagine her letting the housekeeper do it.

Fucking Scratch.

Stop whining, she hisses. *You're still breathing. Don't think your mother crying and snotting changes anything.*

"Fuck you," I say out loud, before giving the tap a twist. I start singing to drown out anything she might say back.

I don't take a long time in the shower in case Mom's nervous. It feels good, though. And it's nice to use my own toiletries again. Afterward, wrapped in towels, I sit on the edge of the tub and use the epilator. The first time I used one it hurt, but it's not so bad anymore.

When I get dressed, I choose a shirt with long sleeves. No one wants to look at my arms and I don't want them to. I'm going to have to get tattoos to cover the scars at some point. I'm not sure where the idea comes from, but I kind of like it.

I can't really be bothered to put on a lot of makeup, only a little mascara and lip gloss. I don't even do anything with my hair, just coil it up damp in a high bun. Connor's already seen me at my worst, so anything's got to be an improvement.

I glance at the painting on the easel by the window. It still needs work, but it's past the fugly stage. It's a portrait of Izzy. I started it for Mark. It was going to be my birthday present to him. I suppose it still will be.

As if on cue, there's a knock at my door. It reminds me of being in the hospital. "Come in," I say.

I expect to see Mom, but Mark is standing there like a fucking idiot. "You're home," he says.

"Yes, I am, Mr. Obvious."

He flushes. "How are you feeling?"

I twitch my shoulders. "All right."

Mark shoves his hands into the pockets of his jeans and leans against the doorframe. It's like he's afraid to come inside. Maybe he thinks one of my alters will switch out and attack him like in the movies.

There's a whole genre trope ruined for me—the evil personality. I used to find it intriguing, now it's insulting.

"So, it's true?" he asks. "This dissociative thing?"

"You mean my all-consuming quest for attention?" His flinch isn't as satisfying as I thought it would be. "Yeah. It's true."

"So, you have, like, other people in your head?"

I nod.

"Because something bad happened when we were kids?"

"Yep."

"What?"

My own arms creep around me until I hug myself. "I'm pretty sure I was molested." I expect Scratch to hurt me, but nothing happens.

He looks upset, angry. "By who?"

"I don't know." I'm so close to seeing his face, I know it. "You probably think I'm making it up."

My brother looks me in the eyes and holds my gaze as he steps into the room. He walks straight toward me and doesn't stop until he reaches the bed. Then he crouches before me. He takes my right hand and pushes my sleeve up, revealing the line of puckered flesh beneath a clear bandage. He looks at it and into my eyes again. "These don't look made-up to me. It's some pretty intense method-acting if you did."

"It would be easier if I was making it all up," I offer, remembering what Izzy said in the hospital about him feeling helpless. I would have felt the same way if he'd done it.

He nods. "I was so scared when I came in here and saw the blood. Saw you. It was less scary if I got angry."

"It's less scary for *me* if I get angry."

Mark smiles crookedly. "It's like we're related or something."

I laugh.

He turns his head slightly and sees the painting. I watch as he goes still, eyes widening. "Is that Izzy?"

"Yep." So much for the surprise.

Standing, he walks to the easel. His fingers reach out and

touch the canvas in a gentle, hesitant way that reveals how much he thinks of my friend. He glances at me over his shoulder. "D, it's amazing."

"It's not done."

He stares at it for a few seconds longer before turning around. "What I said to you in the hospital . . ."

I hold up my hand. "It's okay."

"No. It's really not. I've felt like shit ever since."

And he should, Kaz whispers. "I would have felt the same way."

"You wouldn't have been that cruel." He shakes his head ruefully and I don't argue. He's right. "Whatever happened to you, I wish you had felt like you could have told me."

I know that look. He's going to dwell on this—on how he thinks I didn't trust him.

"You and Mom need to stop trying to take responsibility for something someone else did." A twinge of pain in my stomach sets my pulse racing. *Hurt me again and I'll tell everyone I ever meet that we were assaulted.* The pain fades.

Mark shakes his head. "That's probably going to take a while for both of us." And then, "Anyway . . . I told Izzy I'd pick her up. Want to come with?"

And like that, we're good. I don't know if all siblings are like this, or if it's just us, but no one can love or hate one of us the way the other can.

It's not quite five o'clock. We'll be back long before Connor gets here. I could go with him or I could hide in bed like I wanted. Keep going or give up, those are the options.

"Yeah," I say, standing. "I do."

He comes back, catching me in a hug that lifts me off my feet. I squeeze my arms around his neck. "I'm glad you're home," he says. "I love you, D."

I close my eyes, no more tears. "I love you, too. Asshole."

—

KAZ

This is Kaz. I don't know what day it is. Sue me.

This is just a reminder that one of us does not speak for the whole of us.

EVER.

Scratch, babe, you don't get to decide what happens to the body. You don't know what's best for our "system." And you don't get to decide what we talk about or who we say it to. None of us do, okay? That's not just you. We're in this together, and we can all agree that we want to keep ourselves safe and do what's best for _all_ of us. Even though Dylan is the one who will be in the driver's seat for a lot of this, we're all going to be along for the ride, so let's make sure there's gas in the tank and the engine's tuned up—all that car analogy shit. It's the only way we're going to get anywhere worth going.

Okay, I'm done. If you need help, ask for it. Just try not to be an asshole.

And, Dylan? Thanks for trying.

—K

I take a few minutes to gather my thoughts before writing a reply. On the top of the page, I write: *THIS IS A PRIVATE LETTER TO KAZ. PLEASE DO NOT READ IF YOU ARE NOT KAZ!*

Dear Kaz:

I know you've checked out. I hadn't realized how much you're up front with me until you weren't there. I needed to write this letter to you because I'm afraid you blame me for what happened with Nisha. I don't know how else I could have explained the situation to her, but if you want me to try again, I will. I never wanted you to get hurt and I'm sorry it happened. Is there anything I can do to make it better?

—Dylan

Dear Dylan:

Dude, take a pill. It's all good. I just needed to feel sorry for myself for a little bit. It never lasts very long. I guess I have a short attention span when it comes to disappointment. Besides, you think Connor would understand you finger-banging a chick? Probably not. LOL. I need you if I want to experience the world and you need me if you want to experience intimacy, so let's just find a way to work together and make both of us happy, okay? Because I don't care what equipment they're packing. I want the attention, but you . . . you need some love, girl, and you're pretty narrow in your preferences. We'll take it slow, and I promise, it won't hurt a bit. 😉

—Kaz

—

Connor texted me when he was leaving his apartment, but I still jump when the doorbell rings shortly before seven.

"It's your *boyfriend*," Mark singsongs from his seat next to Izzy. "You get it."

I'd forgotten how annoying he can be when he's not acting like a douche. Rolling my eyes, I get up from the sofa and head to the front door.

Connor stands on the steps, the glow of the porch light casting his face as a study in highlights and shadows. He smiles when he sees me, and my heart skips a beat.

"Hey," he says.

"Hi." I move back so he can step inside. Once I close the door, he turns to me as he removes his coat.

"Um . . . so, are you Dylan right now, or someone else?"

He's the first person to ask. Mom, Mark, and Izzy all just assumed. Or maybe they know me better.

He continues, "I read that alters are really good at impersonating hosts, so I want to be sure I call you by the right name."

He's nervous and he's entirely too sweet. I can practically feel Lannie sighing in the back of my mind. "No, it's me. Thanks for asking, though." I take his coat and hang it up. When I turn back, he's still standing there.

"Is it okay if I hug you?"

Is he for real?

Shut up, Kaz. She chuckles in response, so I know she's not really trying to be a jerk. I'm just glad she's back. Weird. A few weeks ago, I didn't even know she existed. A few days ago, I would have been thrilled if she had announced she was leaving. But when she was gone, I missed her.

"Hug away," I say, opening my arms.

He steps in, enveloping me in that sweet, spicy scent of his that smells so very, very good. He's solid and warm and . . .

I am going to break this sweet thing in half.

For fuck's sake. I know I did not just think that. I would never think that. When Connor lifts his head and I come up on my toes to steal a kiss, that's not me either, though I have no objection.

Connor seems surprised by the kiss, but I don't think he minds either. We stand there for a few moments, arms around each other, bodies pressed tight, lips moving together. A noise from the kitchen—someone getting ice from the fridge—makes us step apart.

His gaze is warm as he looks down at me. I tingle all over, little shivers through every nerve ending.

Oh. My. God, Kaz purrs. *I'm so going to enjoy this.*

I ignore her and take Connor's hand to pull him along behind me. Mom lights up as soon as she sees him. Guess she's not going to get a restraining order like he feared. She gives him a tight hug like she's known him forever. He's definitely won her over this past week.

"Thanks for inviting me," he says, handing her a bottle of wine. "That's for you, of course." He laughs self-consciously. He's not trying to suck up, he's just nice. I should be afraid of him, but I'm not. I don't know if it's because Kaz is close, or because Lannie picked him out, but I'm not second-guessing this anymore. Finding out I'm plural rather than single kind of makes everything else less of a drama, I guess.

Which is kind of weird if I think about it, but for tonight I'm not going to. Everyone here knows this part of my story. There's no need to be on guard. I guess the people inside me can finally relax a little, too. Maybe that's why I feel this way. Comfortable and unafraid.

Mom pats his arm. She shoos us into the living room and goes to order the pizza. Mark stands up and shakes Connor's hand like they're a couple of old men or something. "It's good to see you, man," my brother says.

"Yeah," Connor says. "You too." Izzy stands up and gives him a hug like Mom did. I smirk when my brother raises an eyebrow.

I really hope Mark and I stay good for a while. It's exhausting never knowing if he's going to blame me for something. On the drive to get Izzy he told me that he and Mom sat down and had a long talk after she slapped him. He realized he'd crossed a line, and it was during that conversation that he realized he wasn't really angry at me, he was scared. He'd rather I'd be a liar than actually sick.

And then he asked me the same thing Mom had—why hadn't he seen any signs of abuse when we were young? As if I held the answer. Telling him that DID was a protective thing didn't seem to help.

"You didn't see it because you weren't looking," I said. "And I guess I was doing my best to hide it."

His expression went grim. "If I ever find out who it was . . ." I let the threat hang in the air between us. I didn't want to ask him what he'd do. I didn't want to put him in that position. I don't want to know.

He feels guilty because it happened to me and not him, and I had to explain that, for the most part, I don't feel like it even happened to me. That I can't remember is hard for him to get his mind around, and I get it. It's like having a safe but not the combination. Everything in it is yours, but you can't get to it.

Maybe that's not the best analogy. I mean, I'm not really

in a hurry to open this particular safe and see what's inside. Not like it's going to be a million bucks. It's just memories of something so horrible it split my consciousness. Isn't it enough that I know it happened? Can't I work on healing anyway? Why is it so important to know who it was? Am I suddenly in charge of stopping them from doing it again? It's been at least ten years. Chances are they've already done it.

That makes me want to puke, so I shove the thought aside. I'm good at that.

Connor and I sit on one couch while Mark and Izzy sit on the other. It's so obvious they're a couple now. It's strange watching them interact like that when six months ago they didn't even notice one another. I guess I'm happy for them, but I'm also a little mad that neither one belongs just to me anymore.

I don't even belong to just me anymore.

"Did Dylan tell you what we're watching?" Mark asks.

Connor shakes his head. "No. Whatcha got?"

My brother lists off the selections—over a dozen horror movies from the past twenty years. It's our October tradition.

"Every weekend leading up to our birthday we watch our favorite horror films," I explain. "We started it the year we were twelve."

"Enjoying a good bloodbath is the one thing we have in common," Mark says. The color drains from his face. "Oh, shit. Sorry, D. I didn't mean . . ."

I laugh as they all stare at me. I can't help it. It's easier than thinking about the reality of it.

"The look on your face . . ." I laugh harder. Kaz's laughter echoes inside my head. Connor slowly starts to laugh, then Izzy, and finally poor Mark.

"I can't believe I said that," he allows with a chuckle. "Jesus."

Mom comes into the room and finds us in varying stages of amusement. She doesn't ask, just shakes her head and asks if we want anything to drink.

Finally, we settle on a movie—*The Conjuring*. We've all seen it before, but it doesn't matter.

We wait until the pizza arrives to start watching. Mom even joins us.

"Are we going to watch *Spring Break Slaughter*?" Connor asks, grinning at her.

"We have it," Mark informs him. "Mom's got some great stories from the set."

"Really?" Connor's legit interested now.

Mom gives him an indulgent smile. "I thought my career was over at the time, but it was one of the most fun experiences I've ever had."

"Better than the Aerosmith video?" I ask.

She nods, a funny little smile on her face that makes me laugh. I don't want to know.

It's nice hanging out like everything's normal. Other than Mark's hilarious fuckup, no one's said anything about what happened or what's going on with me. They're treating me like they always have, and it feels good. We eat and laugh and comment on the movie. Connor steals the crust I don't eat off my plate and scarfs it down like a starving dog. I have no idea how he manages to eat so much and stay so skinny. When I finish my second slice, I hand him the crust before he can ask.

By the time the movie's over, the four of us have managed to devour two large pizzas, minus what Mom took. I don't even know how many slices I had—it was like I hadn't eaten in ages. Mom goes into the kitchen to get another drink and some dessert before we start *Spring Break Slaughter*.

"Mom took us to the Warren's Occult Museum when we were kids," Mark says. "Remember, D?"

"I do." It's amazing how surprised and grateful I am to realize that. "They had Annabelle locked up in a case. She was a Raggedy Ann doll, not like the one in the movie at all."

"Kinda hard to make a cloth doll creepy, I guess," Izzy ventures.

"I dunno," Connor remarks. "Raggedy Ann creeps me out. It's those dead, button eyes." He grimaces.

Button eyes. Like Scratch.

Mark opens his mouth to say something, but he's cut off by a crash in the kitchen.

"You okay?" Mark calls out.

"I broke a glass," comes Mom's voice. "Don't come out until I get it cleaned up."

My heart feels like it's in my throat, and I have that sensation of being pulled outside of myself. *No, no, no. Not now.* I don't want to switch out. I don't want to lose the rest of my first night home. It was only a broken glass. The memory of Scratch's button eyes.

"Dylan?" Connor's voice sounds like it's being filtered through a dense fog. "Are you okay?"

"I'm dissociating," I tell him, trying to blink him back into focus. "I don't want to go."

"Then don't go."

"I don't . . ." My head swims. ". . . know how to stop it."

"Hey, Mark, can you dim the lights?" I hear him ask. Suddenly, the room is a little darker. "Dylan, can I touch you?"

I nod. My mouth, no longer mine, won't work. Connor's fingers close around mine, warm and strong. I cling to them as the fog recedes a little. He lifts my other hand and puts it on the back of his head. "Feel my hair," he says. "Rub it between your fingers."

It takes all my concentration, but I get my fingers to move. I love his hair, the waves and movements of it. I told him once. Maybe Lannie said it. I don't care, I'm just glad he remembered, because it works. The combination of his touch, his voice, and the tactile sensation of his hair between my fingers brings me back. I don't know who was about to take over, but they don't resist my reassertion of control, and I'm grateful. Maybe they don't like switching in any more than I like switching out. Maybe they realized we're not really in danger.

"How did you know to do that?" Mark asks when I'm almost myself again. I feel vaguely motion sick.

Connor glances up at him. "I've been doing some research on helping people with DID ground themselves."

My brother looks impressed. "Can you send me the site?"

"Yeah," Izzy chimes in. "And me?"

I laugh. "I can probably use that, too." I should be embarrassed that he knows things I don't, but I'm too grateful. I'm touched that he bothered to educate himself. I squeeze his hand. "Thank you."

"It's okay." He looks uncomfortable at all the attention but fuck it. He deserves it. As far as I'm concerned, he's a goddamn hero. He kept me here. I stayed in control, and it makes me want to cry.

I might get through this after all.

FIFTEEN

Right, then. I'm Alyss. I used to be Remmie and Tuesday, but Remmie went full-on mental and couldn't handle it anymore and Tuesday was kinda ambivalent about everything, so the two of them melded together, and the result was me. Don't ask me to explain it, 'cause I can't. All I know is that I came into existence with feelings and memories belonging to both of them, but I wasn't either—I was me. Confusing, it was. Thankfully, Dali and the kiddies helped me adjust.

My 'job' in the inner world is to look after the young ones. I roll my eyes at the thought of being the British nanny, but I reckon stereotypes exist for a reason, right? So, usually I'm a caregiver. I fancy myself pretty good at it too. I'm good-natured and even-tempered.

Except when someone threatens my kids. That pisses me off, and I've been right pissed ever since Scratch tried to snuff us out without so much as a 'do you mind?' I've tried letting go and yoga and all *that shite, but it's still there, simmering. I don't get angry easily. I get aggressive and whatnot, but not angry. Takes a lot to get me fired up, and Scratch is ridiculously good at doing just that.*

I've always thought me and Scratch had us an understanding. She understands that I protect everyone in the house, and I understand that she's absolutely mental. She says she wants to protect us, but I think she really wants to destroy us. All of us. You, Dylan, most of all. The rubbish she says to you is just mean—horrible stuff. She wasn't like that when I first met her, but she changed along the way. She took on all the secrets and shame you couldn't voice and got all twisted up in it. That's no excuse, though. We all have scars from what happened to us, and none of us have ever tried to kill anyone.

How dare Scratch yell at the kids. How dare she try to destroy them. *Poor little mites never stood a chance. Some of them are so scarred and messed up, all they do is cry. They wouldn't—couldn't— hurt anyone.*

But I would, and I will. I meant everything I said to Scratch. I will devour her if she tries that stunt again. I'll chew her up and spit her out—literally. Won't be nothing left.

Since Lannie let her out of lockup, Scratch's been skulking around in the shadows, keeping quiet. Still, I don't trust her, so I keep the kids as far away as possible. It's gotten a little easier to do that now, what with the playground showing up.

It was the weirdest thing. For years, there's been nothing for the little ones to do but play in their rooms or run around outside. Then, you pop by for a visit and stuff starts changing. I dunno if you've done it on purpose, or if things have changed just because you're aware of us, but there's a play area now where there used to be only grass and a few trees. The kids love it. I have to take them out to it all the bloody time. Honestly, I don't mind. I like a good spin on the merry-go-round same as the next person. It's all very bright and shiny and new. Now, if only we had some candy floss, it would be a right good time.

Darla and Rosie play in the sandbox while Christina twirls the ropes of the swing together and spins like a top. She usually keeps to herself because she starts screaming if anyone gets too close. Except for me, that is. Sometimes she'll let Dali come close. I think she's the one that remembers what happened to us with the most clarity, only she's not old enough to understand it. To her it's only fear and pain. She's a good girl, though. They all are.

Anyway, I don't have much else to say. I like sweets and good coffee and I'd be a vegetarian if it weren't for bacon. I figure this journal will make talking to each other easier, and that's a good thing, though I'll probably have to write for any of the kids who want to talk. Christina likes to draw, so don't be surprised if she occasionally abuses paper and pen privileges.

And for what it's worth, I like Connor. Anyone who appreciates the Mighty Boosh is all right by me. He knows about the rest of us and he still wants to hang about, so I figure he might be worth giving a chance.

———

There's this movie Izzy wants me to watch with her, so we make a date to do that on Saturday. It's called *Waking Madison* and it's about a girl with DID. I try not to have any expectations, but Iz says it has fairly decent reviews.

I agree to watch it, not so much because of the subject matter, but because it's only going to be me and her. She didn't ask Mark to join and I didn't ask Connor. In fact, Mark is going out with a couple of friends and I think Connor has family plans.

Because Izzy's going to be with me, Mom decides to have dinner and drinks with an old friend from her slasher-movie days. To be honest, I'm surprised she goes, but her leaving says a lot about how much she wants to trust me—and even more about how much she trusts Izzy. Earlier, she asked if she could write notes to my system for me to share in my journal so my alters would know she's here for them. I almost cried—not like that's difficult for me to do these days—but I don't think she realized how much that meant to me.

Izzy comes over around six. We order Chinese food and spread it out on the coffee table in the living room, eating right from the containers as we watch the movie. It's really good. I don't know how realistic it is, because I can only compare it to my experience, but the director did a good job of trying to convey what it's like to live with other people in your head. Of course, I saw the plot twist coming. Izzy didn't, so that was fun.

The best part? It didn't have to do with sexual trauma, so I wasn't as triggered by it as I could have been. It was still upsetting in spots. Twice I felt myself start to dissociate, but I held Izzy's hand and tried to relax. I managed to stay up front, but the second time Lannie moved into place beside me. It's a weird thing, because I know my body is a singular thing, but in my head, Lannie is right there, her presence so very real and comforting, just like Izzy's presence is comforting in the physical realm. Anyway, it's kind of nice having that support. It was even nicer not switching.

"Did you like it?" Izzy asks afterward. I figured there would be a question-and-answer period following. I don't mean that in a snotty way, just that Izzy wants to know as much as possible so she can help me. I try to remember that when it gets a little overwhelming and my BPD makes me want to lash out in frustration.

"It was good," I say. "Great cast."

"So . . ." She smiles sheepishly. "Was any of it like how it is for you?"

"Yeah. Like, I thought Kaz was my imaginary friend as a kid—probably because that's the title other people gave her? I don't know what it's like in the inner world when I'm not there, but I've seen some of my alters together, so I assume those are the ones who can communicate openly with each other."

Izzy frowns as she processes this. "It's so hard to wrap my head around. I really want to understand, though. Do you mind talking about it?"

Shaking my head, I give her a little smile. "With you? No. I'll tell you what I can, but I'm still figuring this out myself. Ask whatever you want."

"Do you have what they call 'littles'?"

"Kids? Yeah. I have at least three." Something tugs at my mind, a feeling more than anything else. "I think Alyss would prefer I don't talk about them, though. She's very protective."

"Alyss?"

"Yeah. She's like this British goth-chick. I guess she's what they call a protector—at least of the kids."

Izzy leans her elbow on the back of the couch and props her hand against her head. "It's good they have someone looking out for them. From what I've researched, that seems pretty normal."

I laugh. "Normal for all its abnormality."

"Normal within the scope of the disorder," she corrects me

with enough defensiveness that I get serious fast. She's trying to be an ally. I need all of those I can get.

"Sorry," I say. "I don't mean to be an ass. I feel like I'm teetering on the edge of completely losing it almost every minute of the day. Sometimes laughing about it is all I've got."

"I just want to be the best friend I can be to you."

I hug her. "You already are."

She smells good, Kaz whispers.

I stiffen. I can't tell if Izzy notices, but as I slowly pull back, the thought in my head is loud and clear: *NOT HER. NEVER HER.*

Again, it's not words, but a feeling. I know Kaz heard me and understood. Izzy is off-limits. She's the only friend I have. It's dangerous enough that she's dating my brother, I don't need my sexual protector hitting on her. I'm pretty sure Izzy is straight, and I don't need things to be any weirder than they already are.

"What's your inner world like?"

"It's nicer than Madison's," I joke. I tell her about the house, describing it as much as I can.

She smiles. "That totally sounds like a place you'd put together. I wish I could see it." Her smile fades. "I wish I could see them like you do."

My lips press together. "It must be weird when one of the others is up front. My voice, my face, but it's not me."

"That's just it. I've *never* fucking noticed. Like, what the hell?" She holds up a hand. "I know. I know. DID is designed to hide itself. I'm not supposed to know if your alters don't want me to, but you'd know if someone took over my body."

"You've noticed when I've done stuff that was out of

character," I remind her. "But beyond that, my alters have been around a long time. You haven't noticed them because you accepted them as part of me."

She smiles. "And that's how I know I'm talking to Dylan. We're talking about your stuff, and you still want to make me feel better about myself. You've always been like that."

I blink. I've never really thought about it before. "I've always thought of myself as pretty selfish. You know, because of the borderline personality thing."

"You're not selfish. I don't even think your BPD is as bad as you seem to. I mean, not to discredit it."

I laugh. "It's okay. You don't have to be considerate of it. My mental illness has no feelings."

She smiles. "I'm sorry. You're probably sick of people being careful of everything they say to you."

Leaning into the couch cushions, I shrug. "Being treated like you're fragile isn't any fun, especially when you're afraid it might be true. You don't have to watch what you say to me. I mean, Mark made that bloodbath remark."

Izzy throws her head back as she rolls her eyes. "Oh, my God! He brought it up when I talked to him earlier. He feels so bad."

I grin. "Yeah, I might milk it for a while, so be prepared."

"Consider me warned." She smiles. "What can I do to help you through this?"

Reaching out, I take her hand and squeeze her cool fingers before letting go. "Just be you. Say what you're thinking and be there when I need you—like you've always been."

"I can do that," she says. This time she takes my hand in hers. "I love you, Dylan's system."

The lump that suddenly forms in my throat doesn't belong to just me. Tears prickle the backs of my eyes, but I blink them away. "We love you, too," I tell her.

And we do.

—

Monday rolls in quietly. Mark goes to class and I sit at the breakfast table with Mom, working on a sketch for a new painting. I think she kind of likes having me home. Part of the reason neither Mark nor I has moved out yet is because we don't want to leave her alone.

And really, if I'm completely honest, the noise of Manhattan has always given me a headache. Probably because my system is on high alert whenever we go there, everyone on guard. No, I love the city, but I could never live there.

Right now, having a place of my own is one of the farthest things from my mind. The thought of living alone with the people inside me fills me with fear, and it's all Scratch's fault.

According to my journal, I only switched out a few times this weekend—that's if everyone who came out actually remembered to write it down. I take this as a win, though I have no idea if it is one or not. At least the journal is being used. I wasn't confident anyone would write in it.

They upped my dosage of Prozac in the hospital and I feel less twitchy and panicky than I did even a few days ago. It's been over a week—closer to two, I guess—since Scratch tried to murder me, and I feel pretty calm, considering. Obviously, I'm still having trouble with losing time, or keeping track of it, but I'm . . . okay.

I'm still a little in awe of Friday's "grounding." Connor

shared where he got the information and I made a note on my phone of the things they suggest doing to keep from dissociating. Now that I know what it means when I start feeling like that, I'm prepared for when it happens.

"Did you know there are positive triggers?" I ask Dr. Zhao later that afternoon during our appointment.

She nods from her seat across from me. "Yes. Music is a strong one. Scents as well."

"Why would anyone want to switch out?"

"Just because it's positive doesn't always mean it's planned or wanted. Sometimes spotting a toy store will prompt a little to come out, and if they have access to your wallet . . . well, you can see how that might not be welcome."

I hadn't thought of that. "But you can use triggers to encourage a switch?"

"Yes, and that would be useful if you were, for example, expected to go to a function or show up at an event that really doesn't hold any interest for you, but is of interest to an alter. You and that alter could agree to a switch so they could attend the event and you don't have to."

That's kind of awesome. "I wish I'd known about this in high school. I would have gotten someone else to do my homework."

She smiles. "I bet if you could look back on some of your work, you'd find a lot of it was done by one or more of your alters. They come out when they're needed."

"Except for Scratch. I don't need her."

"But you did, at least once upon a time, or she wouldn't exist."

"I don't need her anymore," I declare. And then, "How can I get rid of her?"

"I'm afraid you can't just get rid of her."

I am not living the rest of my life waiting for the psycho inside me to attempt murdering me again. "There must be something I can do. Can't I force her to integrate or fuse, or whatever?"

"Dylan, no. You can't force an integration."

"Well, can I force her to go away or kill her?"

Dr. Zhao looks aghast—like I suggested we go murder some toddlers or something. "No. You can't kill her. In fact, I strongly advise you not to even attempt such a thing. It could have incredibly adverse effects."

"So, she can try to kill me, but I can't kill her?"

"What she did was a defense response. It wasn't a personal attack against you."

This is maddening. "I don't understand. If I created these people, why can't I get rid of them? It's not like they're fucking real, right? I made them up."

She looks at me a long moment, a slight frown wrinkling the skin between her eyes. "Dylan, do you have someone in front with you? These things you're suggesting and the way you're talking don't seem quite like you."

"I don't know," I reply, honestly. "When I first got here, I felt really positive, but now I'm annoyed and angry. I don't know why I'd feel that way, so maybe there's someone else, yeah." I shake my head. "I hate not being able to tell."

"It's okay," Dr. Zhao says in a gentle tone. "Do you need to take a minute?"

I pull a paintbrush out of my bag. It might seem ridiculous to some people, but I've chosen it as something to help ground myself. It's one that I bought during the summer as part of a set.

The synthetic bristles are smooth and sleek between my thumb and index finger. The handle is nicely weighted and shaped just right for my hand. It's not too thick or too skinny. It's one of my favorites for working with acrylics. Closing my eyes, I inhale a deep breath through my nose and concentrate on the feel of those bristles, the weight of the handle. I keep breathing, imagining myself at my easel, painting something colorful.

When I open my eyes, I feel more like myself, but I still don't know if someone else was near the front with me, or if my anger at the whole situation was getting the better of me.

"Better?" Dr. Zhao asks.

I nod. "What do I do about Scratch then? I can't spend my life worrying about what she might do, and I really don't like how she talks to me."

"Have you told her that?"

"I'm pretty sure she knows." I sigh. "I wish she'd go away."

Dr. Zhao shifts position in her chair and leans her chin on her fist. "Perhaps you could show Scratch some gratitude and see what happens."

"Gratitude?" I parrot. "For trying to kill me?" Maybe Dr. Zhao wasn't the right doctor for me after all. I mean, WTF?

"For being prepared to kill herself and everyone else to protect you. That's a pretty heavy burden, don't you think?"

"No, I don't. I think it's crazy."

She stifles a chuckle. "Dylan, Scratch didn't ask for this any more than you did. None of your alters came into creation on a whim. They're all here because you needed them for something. For years, Scratch has believed that silence is what keeps you safe. When you found out about your system, you put that safety in jeopardy."

"Why would she think silence was good? If we'd told someone the truth, wouldn't it have been better?"

Her expression is uncomfortable and sympathetic. "Children are often told something terrible will happen if they tell, or they're threatened with greater harm."

"This is our special time, Lannie. If you tell anyone we'll both be in trouble." The words echo in my head and I frown. That voice. I know that voice.

Why won't you let me remember? I scream inside my head.

I feel his hands on me, smell the stale beer and cigarettes on his breath. My stomach turns. He's there, pushing me down, telling me what a good girl I am. His special girl. And then . . . Oh, God, it hurts. *It hurts.*

Pain in my hand distracts me. This isn't real. I'm in Dr. Zhao's office. She's talking to me. I'm safe. *I'm safe.*

The palm of my hand is bleeding. Splinters of wood stick out of my skin. It doesn't really hurt, though. It's like I'm numb. I broke my paintbrush. I can get a replacement, but that doesn't stop tears from slipping out of my eyes.

"Dylan?"

I look at Dr. Zhao through the tears and swipe at my eyes with the back of my uninjured hand. "Sorry. I remembered him telling me not to say anything. And now Lannie's upset."

The psychiatrist hands me a box of tissues. I wipe my eyes and blow my nose.

"Why is Lannie upset?" she asks when I'm done.

"Because I remembered. I think she's upset for me, not at me." I throw the wad of tissues in the trash can next to my seat. "Can this eye-movement thing you talked about help with this kind of stuff?"

"I believe so. Think of it as a kind of distraction technique. It allows you to deal with traumatic memories by diluting the anxiety response to them. I believe it also limits the amount of information, or memory, that can be retrieved, therefore making it easier to process. Would you like to try it?"

I nod.

"I'm going to take a moment to remind you that this is a safe place. I want you to feel calm and secure here. Do you feel calm enough to continue?"

"I want to try," I tell her.

It's hard to describe what happens next. I talk about the flashback I had while Dr. Zhao taps me on one shoulder and then the other, all while reassuring me that I'm safe and asking me questions like how disturbed I feel on a scale of one to ten. She asks me if any new thoughts emerge.

And here's where it gets weird. I do have new thoughts. All she's doing is talking to me while I think of being assaulted as a child, and while it's disturbing, I'm able to look at it as if it happened to someone else. I guess that's where the whole DID thing comes in handy. Regardless, I'm able to talk about it and realize that it's not happening to me right now. I still can't see his face, but that's not the point. The point is that it's gone from terrifying to very upsetting. Not a great leap, but enough that I'm encouraged.

It takes a while. It's not like she pokes me a few times and suddenly everything's okay. But by the end of the session, I can think about that experience without being actively in it.

"Eventually I'd like to teach you some techniques so you can guide yourself through any traumatic memories that arise when we're not together."

A headache's knotting up above my right eye and I feel completely drained of emotion. It's kind of a nice feeling. This kind of numbness is why I used to drink. My head is quiet. I like to imagine the people of my system are in their living room, gathered around the television, watching with their mouths hanging open. I want them to be astonished by me.

I want them to realize I don't need them and then maybe they'll fade away. Not very realistic of me, but it's something to work toward, maybe? Something to hope for.

"Please consider what I said earlier about Scratch," Dr. Zhao says as we stand. "Write her a letter in your journal or engage her in the head space if possible. Really try to get a dialogue going. It may prove very healing for you both."

My first response is to tell her I doubt it, maybe roll my eyes at the idea, but I don't do either of those things. I can't, because that memory I had? The one that freaked me out and took the rest of the session to get even passably okay with? That's one memory of what happened to me. Us. Lannie has some of them, and I know how upset she got because I started to remember only one. Scratch has all of those horrible memories. Or, at least I assume she does. She has more than me, that's for certain. My brain created her to hold those memories so I could go on. She's a product of my abuser telling me not to tell. Fuck, she's the embodiment of it. That's enough to make anyone a psycho.

"I will," I tell her, and I mean it. I am going to try to reach out to Scratch. Hopefully I'll survive it.

SIXTEEN

On Tuesday, I amend the "System Rules" section of my journal:

The body needs at least six hours of sleep a night. No fronting after 1 a.m. unless discussed!! Littles need to have a bedtime and be monitored so they do not take over the body at night. It's dangerous for them to be out unsupervised. If the littles can't read this, one of you older ones please tell them. If a little wants playtime, we can work something out during daytime hours when there is someone home in case something happens.

I really don't want a mural in my bedroom like the one in the hospital, and I've already found doodles in the journal and stick figures painted on my good watercolor paper. One of my tubes of acrylic paint was left out without a cap sometime late Sunday night. It didn't dry out completely and acrylic is relatively cheap, but that's not the point. The point is, someone was playing with my stuff.

On Monday after therapy with Dr. Zhao, I got Mom to stop at Walmart and I picked up kid-friendly art supplies, which are kept in a plastic bin next to my easel. I made sure everything is as bright as possible to attract the attention of my little alters, and my good supplies are in the cabinet, now with a combination lock on it.

I have no idea if any of this works. No one's used the new art supplies yet, but no one's used my professional-grade stuff either. I don't feel as tired this week, but I'm also still napping, though not as much. Short of setting up cameras in my room, I don't know what else to do.

Maybe I should set up a camera. It would be interesting to see what the people inside me get up to when I'm not around. I mention it to Mom. She's already set some stuff up, so she knows if I try to leave the house at night. I don't take it personally. After "waking up" in the ocean that one time, I'm all for being monitored.

I've written a note to Scratch—nothing big. I just asked her if we could talk. I want to see if she'll come to me in a dream, or maybe I can find my way into the head space. I haven't done that at will yet. Maybe she'll be a voice in my head, I don't know. She has to agree to it first. I suppose I could have just written her a letter thanking her, but I want to see if I can make meeting face-to-face work.

I have to give it a shot. I can't live my life knowing there's something—someone—inside me that thinks we'd be better off dead. If I don't do something, she's going to try it again, and next time she might succeed. She hasn't responded to me yet, but at least Dr. Zhao will see the note the next time she reads my journal.

The next thing on my list of Managing My Dissociative Identity is joining some groups and meeting other people with the disorder. I find what looks like a great group on Facebook that says they want to focus on reducing the stigma around DID and raise awareness. They also say they want to create a safe place for those of us with DID to come together and talk frankly about things. I click on the button to join the group and fill out the short questionnaire that pops up. An administrator has to approve my membership. A few weeks ago, I'd be annoyed that I have to wait to join a group, but now I appreciate the process. At least they don't let just anyone sign up. I really don't want to deal with hecklers while working on my mental health.

Mom comes into my room Wednesday morning. "Come on," she says. "Get dressed and let's go."

"Where?" I ask, looking up as I make my bed. I never used to care if it was made or not, but I've decided my life needs as much routine and order as I can get.

"Girls' day. I've booked mani-pedis and hair appointments for us and tea at the Ritz."

"Are you sure? What if something happens?"

"Like what?" she asks.

"Like I switch out or something?"

"I assume you've done it before around me and I was too dense to notice, so I'll have to pay attention. Other than that, what's stopping us? It's only going to be a problem if whoever comes out doesn't like tea." She smiles when she talks, but I know she's nervous. "Two weeks ago, we wouldn't have thought twice about it. We can't stop living our lives because we're afraid of what might happen."

She's right. "Give me five minutes."

"You can have ten."

I get dressed as quickly as I can, run a brush through my hair, put on some mascara and lip gloss, and meet her downstairs.

We drive to the train station, stopping at a Starbucks along the way for coffee and hot chocolate. Mom likes to take the train because she hates driving in the city. She's always talking about how the cost of parking in Manhattan is highway robbery, and how every car there has dents and scratches on it from getting hit by someone else. We get our tickets and wait on the platform. It's a sunny day—chilly, but bright. It's hard to believe it's going to be Halloween soon.

It's past peak travel time, but the train's still pretty full as it pulls into the station. I watch the cars as they slow to a stop. A girl meets my gaze through the window.

Nisha.

She stares at me. I stare at her. She looks away first.

"Not this car," I say to Mom and walk off toward the next one.

"Dylan?" Mom follows after me. "Who was that?"

I don't say anything until we're on the train. A man in a suit gives up his seat and the empty one next to him for us. Mom flashes the smile she usually reserves for fans who recognize her. The poor guy looks like he's been hit by a truck. He stammers something and moves two rows back to sit with another man.

"I think you made his week," I tell her as the train rolls away from the platform.

"Oh hush. Now, who was that girl? Don't tell me no one."

I sigh. How much more does my mother really want to know about my foray into bisexuality? How much do I even know about it? "She's someone I thought could be a friend. Turns out I was wrong."

She touches my leg. "I'm sorry, sweetie. That's something that hurts no matter how old you are."

"I guess you've had a lot of experience with false friends, huh?"

"Oh, just a bit," she says with a laugh. "I've made some real ones too, though." She rattles off the names of a celeb couple she's been meaning to catch up with.

It's surreal that my mother has famous people she socializes with every once in a while. It's surreal that my mother is a somewhat famous person herself. I remember a few years ago, she was in a Blumhouse movie. We went to Comic Con in New York and she had a line of people waiting to get her autograph and tell her how much they'd wished for a friend like Addison in high school. Almost every one of them told Mark and me how lucky we were to have her for our mother.

They were right.

But there were also people there who only wanted a piece of her. You could see it. She was exhausted by the time the signing was over, and even though it was the staff who said she had to go, there were people who still blamed her for leaving.

"Do you want to see if Connor wants to meet us later?" Mom asks as the train jostles along the track.

I do, but I don't. "Nah. I want to hang out with you," I tell her with a smile. The look on her face is worth it. She's still smiling when the conductor shows up for our tickets.

We're in the middle of discussing possible nail colors and if I'm going to refresh my pink or try a new hair color when a shadow falls over us.

Nisha.

And suddenly, Kaz is right there in the passenger seat of my mind. My head swims with her sudden intrusion. *Oh, shit,* she says.

Nisha braces a hand on the seat back in front of me as the train moves. "Hi."

"Hi," I repeat, Kaz's voice echoing in my head. "What's up?" I'm aware of Mom watching us while trying not to seem like she's watching us. She looks at her phone instead.

"I . . . um . . ." Her heavily lined eyes narrow as her dark lips purse. "I saw you at the station and I wanted to tell you that I'm sorry for how things went down at the hospital."

"Yeah," Kaz and I agree. "Me too." And I'm sorry that I'm going to have to explain to my mother that this is the girl I don't remember sleeping with.

"How are you feeling?"

I nod. "Pretty good. Glad to be out."

She nods too. "Yeah, I bet." This is so awkward. She glances down the aisle, as if looking for someone, or something. Maybe an escape route.

"Where are you headed?" I ask. Dragging this out is painful, but Kaz isn't quite ready to let go.

Her attention comes back to me. "Class. You?"

"Mom and I are headed into the city."

At this, Mom looks up with a smile. "Hi."

Nisha looks at her with an expression I've seen a million times before. It's the face of someone who thinks Mom looks familiar but can't quite remember where from. "Nice to meet you."

"Do you want to sit?" Mom asks, nodding at the seat across from us.

"No. Thanks. I should get back. My friend's watching my stuff." Then, to me, "I just didn't want to leave things the way they were. If you still have my number, maybe text me sometime?"

I expect Kaz to freak out with happiness, but she doesn't. I'm not sure how she feels. I want to tell this girl to forget it. She's not going to get a chance to hurt Kaz again. I don't care how fucking sorry she is.

But that's not what Kaz wants either. At least, I don't think so. She appreciates my wanting to protect her, though. She's surprised by it.

"Sure," I say with a nod. "Maybe I will."

Nisha smiles in a way that makes me feel almost guilty for thinking badly of her. "Okay, well, see ya."

"Bye."

I watch her walk away. In my head, Kaz sighs. I rub my paintbrush—the broken one—between my fingers, trying to keep myself up front and grounded. If I let go, Kaz would go after her—or tell Mom even more things I don't want her to know.

Mom, still focused on her phone, says, "*That* was not the kind of exchange you have with someone who is only a friend, my love."

My sigh echoes Kaz's. "It's complicated," I explain.

She looks up and gives me a sympathetic smile. "It always is, sweetie. It always is."

—

Mom and I don't get home until early evening. After tea at the Ritz, we wandered around and did a little shopping.

Our last stop was Barnes & Noble, where I picked up a couple of books about DID and dealing with trauma that were on a reading list suggested in the Facebook group I've joined. I also snagged a couple of art books and two novels I've been wanting to read. Not having classes anymore has given me a lot of free time. I'm pretty sure I'm eventually going to miss school, but I can't imagine trying to drag myself to class on top of figuring out how to deal with what life's tossed at me.

In all honesty, I don't have any business dating Connor, either. He deserves someone who can be there for him. I don't even know *who* I'm going to be, let alone if I'm going to be present for him. I should concentrate on my health, but I'm selfish and he makes me feel almost normal.

Mark is home when we get there, so the three of us cook dinner together, something we haven't done in forever. It's nice, like old times.

"Have you decided on a costume yet?" he asks me later, when we're sitting around the table, eating.

"I've narrowed it down," I reply. "You?" Having Halloween for our birthday has always been fun, but it means finding *the* perfect costume every year. You can't go half-assed when it's your birthday.

"I'm thinking Thor." He grins. "I'm trying to convince Izzy to be Valkyrie."

They'd look amazing, but Izzy isn't one for calling attention to herself. "You could split the difference and go as agents H and M."

His expression makes me chuckle. "That's brilliant," he says, pulling out his phone. "I'm going to ask her."

"Oh, lord," Mom moans. "Can we have dinner without cell phones, please? You can text her after we've finished eating."

My brother sets the phone on the table beside his plate. "Sorry."

It's perfect, this moment. I know it won't last—it can't. Eventually Mark will get mad at me for something, or I'll think he's an ass and Mom will be caught in the middle. Or, she'll get a gig and it will just be me and him here, fighting. It's what we do. Then we'll make up and we'll have a moment like this that I'll want to hold on to.

Or, maybe we won't. Maybe this is what it's going to be now. Or maybe he and I will try harder because we're not kids anymore.

After dinner Mark loads the dishwasher while I put away leftovers. Then he disappears into his room and Mom curls up on the couch in the living room with a cup of tea and a script her agent sent. I take my shopping bags upstairs to my room and set them on the floor. What I want to do is soak in the tub and start reading one of the books I bought, but I'm still leery of taking a bath. It sucks, because I love my tub.

So, instead, I put my hair up and take a quick shower. Then, in my pajamas, I climb under the blankets and text Connor. He has a class tonight and is going out with friends after, so I don't expect to hear from him, at least not right away, but I want to say hi.

I open one of my new books to the first page. It's a fantasy, something fast-paced and easy to lose myself in. When I read, sometimes I hear the words out loud in my head. I'm not sure if everyone's like that, or if somewhere along the line I decided to read "aloud" to my alters. Regardless, I feel some of them coming closer as my eyes travel the page. It's story time with Dylan.

Fun fact—DID means that you're never completely alone. Even if my alters are quiet, they're still there. It's not quite like being with friends, though. I'm starting to think of it as living in a one-room house with a bunch of extended family. Or, in an apartment with a lot of nosy neighbors.

An hour into the book, I get a text from Connor. He's at the coffee shop where he and I—well, Lannie—first met. He sends me a selfie of him sitting at a table with a huge cup of coffee.

I smile at the sight of him. He's so adorable and hot at the same time. How is that possible?

Connor: No sleep tonight.

Me: Have fun. Early night for me. <3

Connor: *kissy face emoji* I'll call you tomorrow.

I fall asleep reading, I guess, because the next thing I'm "aware" of is standing outside the house in my inner world. For whatever reason, it's easier for me to come here in my dreams than it is for me to access it when I'm awake. But is it really a dream?

Dali is on the porch where she always is—the gatekeeper. She's the sentry that guards the house and looks over everyone else. I'm starting to figure out the roles everyone plays.

"Hey, stranger," she says as I walk up the steps. "What brings you by?"

"I'm not sure," I tell her, except . . . "Is Scratch around?"

She looks surprised but doesn't ask questions. "Last time I saw her, she was going to the basement. Shall I get her for you?"

"No, I'll find her."

Dali arches a brow. "You probably shouldn't venture into the cellar."

"Why not?"

"Because it's dark down there. That's where the unwanted are."

Oh, yay. More of us. "I should probably know who they are, don't you think?"

She shrugs. "We're all here so you don't have to know things. I'm not a good one to ask, but if you want my opinion, you already have it."

Right. Stay out of the basement. "I appreciate it, thanks. Can I get to the basement from inside?"

"Probably. If there's a door, you'll find it."

It is my house, after all. I guess if I want there to be a door to the basement inside, there will be one. I don't know if I'll ever get used to this combination of conscious and subconscious thought.

I open the door and step over the threshold. Inside, the house is dim and quiet. Peaceful, almost. Somewhere above me I hear the sound of children playing, but that's the only thing I hear. There's no one around and my footsteps echo as I walk down a long corridor, lined with paintings. Most of them I recognize as my own. Others are by my favorite artists.

At the end of the corridor is a giant, carved door with a large dead bolt on it. The entrance to the basement, I'm sure of it. I slide the bolt out of its hold—it's heavy but moves smoothly. I turn the knob and pull.

Sconces line one side of the descending wall, torches flickering and illuminating the dark stone staircase that leads down into the cellar. I hold on to the banister as I cautiously place my foot on one step and another, drifting down into the darkness.

At the bottom of the stairs, the area opens up. The basement has rough stone walls that hold more torches. Against the back wall is a stack of boxes and crates, but ahead of me is a wide hall with rooms on either side. No, not rooms. Cells.

It's a dungeon.

This is why Dali told me not to come down here. If Scratch is allowed to walk free among the others and she tried to kill me, WTF is locked up down here?

I hear them—their cries and moans. Somewhere beyond me, someone sobs, deep and anguished. I take a step toward the sound and freeze. I am unable to move. It's like someone bolted my feet to the ground.

"Not a good idea," comes a voice. Scratch steps out of the darkness between the cells. She's dressed entirely in black, her hair pulled back in a tight bun. She looks at me like I'm something she scraped off her shoe. It's amazing how much malice buttons can contain.

"Because they'll scare me?" I ask.

Her dark red lips curve into a sneer. "Because you'll scare them. It's your fault they're down here."

"I didn't even know this place existed. How is it my fault?"

She tilts her head. "Everything that's happened to us has been your fault." All that's missing is the "duh" at the end.

"You're tripping," I tell her. "I didn't ask for any of this. And I sure as fuck didn't ask for what caused it."

Confusion flickers across her features. My contradiction has thrown her. According to both Dr. Zhao and my research, Scratch is what's known as an introject—an alter that's based on a real person. She's also a persecutor/protector. She protects me and the others by preying on all the negative things I've been told and believe. Since I've always listened to her in the past, she doesn't know what to do when I don't behave appropriately, so she does something like try to kill me, or freeze up completely, which is what she's doing now.

"I didn't ask you to meet me so we could fight," I tell her.

"Then why are you here? To tell me to go away?" There's a hint of a tremor in her voice, along with a heavy dose of derision. She hates me so much, but in a weird way, I think she equates hate with love, or at least caring.

Maybe Dr. Zhao is right. Kindness is the only way to approach Scratch. It's worth a shot, because telling her to leave or trying to do violence against her isn't an option. Not just because it could be harmful, but because at this moment, I don't think I could do it.

I take a step toward her, my feet able to move again. "I wanted to talk with you about all you've done for us, how you protect us."

She snorts. It's bizarre, because she looks so much like Mom, but she's nothing like her. It's like Mom got cast as the villain rather than a victim in a horror movie. "Did Alyss put you up to this?" she asks. "That bitch is always yanking my chain."

"No, I came here on my own."

Scratch frowns. "I don't believe you. You've always been a fucking liar."

She sounds like a hurt child—a defensive kid trying to act tough.

I take another step forward. "Can I hug you?"

She looks suspicious but gives a small nod.

"Thank you for being prepared to take your own life to protect the rest of us." I put my arms around her. She's stiff as a board, and I'm not much better, waiting for her to bury a knife in my back. She can't hurt me in a dream, can she?

Then I feel it—tentative arms around my waist. She lets go of a shuddering breath and hugs me, before pushing me away.

"What do you want?" she asks, stepping back. She wraps her arms around herself. I don't know if it's because she misses mine, or if she's traumatized.

"I want to get to know you better," I offer. "I want to understand why you are the way you are."

"I'm this way because you're a broken little . . . girl." She frowns, and I know she couldn't bring herself to say what she truly wanted.

"Why do you look like my mother?"

"Isn't it obvious? Because she should have seen what was happening. She's supposed to protect us, and she didn't."

So she hates Mom almost as much as, or more than, she hates me. "Protect us from who?"

Scratch shakes her head. "I can't tell. I can't ever tell." She looks away.

I touch her shoulder, but she jerks back. "Don't fucking touch me!"

I hold up my hands. "Okay, okay. I'm sorry, I should have asked."

Sucking in great bursts of air through her nose, Scratch nods. She takes another step back—well out of my reach. "It's fine. But don't grab me like that again."

He used to touch us like that. I don't remember it, but I know it. He would put his hand on our shoulder, and we'd know what it meant—that he had control over us.

"I'm sorry," I repeat. "I didn't mean to scare you."

She scowls at me. "You didn't scare me, bitch. You fucking pissed me off."

Smiling gently, I shake my head. "I don't believe that, but if you'd rather be angry than afraid, I get it. That's something we have in common."

Silence stretches between us and I let it. I don't want to antagonize her any more than I have. I don't know how she'll react, and I'm still tender from the last time she got upset.

Turning so that she's in profile, Scratch shakes her head. "I wasn't always like this, you know." Her voice is tired and raw. "I started out as a guardian. I protected everyone and Dali played house mother. Then, the more anger you formed toward your mother, the more I changed. I suppose I changed so you didn't have to. I took the anger, so you didn't have to feel it. Life wouldn't work right if you resented the only protector you had left in your world. Honestly, I've always thought it's your brother you should resent."

"Why?"

"He was there. He should have realized the danger we were in, but I guess we were already good at hiding it by then. And we didn't want anything to happen to him. Didn't want him to hate us, and we knew he would, if he found out the truth." She looks me in the eye. "And he will, you know. He'll hate you so bad."

I ignore the warning and the hard thump my heart gives in response. "What truth?"

"I can't tell you." She shrugs. "You could torture me, and I wouldn't be able to say it, even if I wanted to. I'm a secret keeper."

If only some of my friends had been more like this. "I wish I could remember."

"No, you don't," she says, looking at me in disgust. "You wouldn't have us if it hadn't been more than you could tolerate. I hold a lot of those memories, and trust me, little girl, you don't want them. I remember *everything* he did."

Tears burn my eyes. "I'm sorry."

Scratch stares at me. I watch as her expression softens. Not only her expression, but everything about her. She literally changes before my eyes. Her hairstyle becomes a little looser, her features less sharp. Even the lines in her face fill in, making her look more like Mom—the Mom I love. I stare back. I can't believe it.

She presses a hand to her heart as though to quiet the pounding there and frowns. "You need to go," she says softly.

"But—"

She cuts me off. "Please go."

Before I can argue, she pivots on her heel and disappears back into the darkness between the cells. Once again, I'm aware of the noises made by the alters in this prison, and I realize that Scratch is far more comfortable with their pain than she is with my attempts at kindness. I still don't like her, but I understand her better. I feel for her and she knows it.

I think maybe she likes it.

SEVENTEEN

*D*eer Dillin I am soury for drowing on yor wall. Pleese forgive
me.

—

KAZ

There's a note in the journal asking which of us would like
to talk with Connor, the boyfriend. He wants to meet some
more of us, if we're up for it. I was like, "Bitch, don't have to
ask me twice." If there's a chance of getting some, I'm sure as
hell going to take it.

Dylan is nervous as shit before we switch out. She doesn't
know what to do to lube up for the switch, so to speak, and
she's worried I'm going to do something to embarrass her. I
try not to be hurt, but it's not like she's never done anything

to upset me, and I can't stop her from being in control ninety percent of the time.

In the journal I suggested she play some music to help and listed a few of my favorite bands and songs. This is what I found written in response:

We need some rules about how things are going to go when you're with Connor. Like, I don't want you coming on to him. I also don't want you scaring him away. It's not that I don't trust you, but I've been uncomfortable with situations that have come up when you front and I'm anxious. I'm sorry.

Of course I have to respond.

Look, sweetie—it's going to be okay. You and I don't have to completely trust each other yet. What we have to agree on is that we don't want to hurt each other, the body, or anyone else. I may be way more sexual than you, but that's not all I am, okay? Connor wants to meet more of us, and I want to get to know him better, so that's all this is. Although, if he wants to fuck . . .

Oh my shit, I'm joking. LOL. I'm not going to sleep with him. Promise. Pinky swear, whatever. He will be completely safe in my presence, the precious little boy.

And then:

I'm not sure that makes me feel any better.

To which I say:

Suck it up, buttercup. We have to start trusting somewhere. You did me a solid with Nisha, now you either trust me to do this, or you don't.

I'm not sure how long I have to wait for a reply. Time moves differently in the inner world. But the next time I'm hovering even close to the surface I convince the body to check the journal and I see:

I do.

It makes me stupid happy—more than I'll ever admit on paper. So, with that *finally* decided, we make plans to have Connor come over.

Connor shows up at seven. Dylan's mother is out with a "friend" and Mark is at a movie with that deliciously sweet Izzy. That girl has been such a good friend to us and doesn't even know it. I used to have a thing for her, but now I love her too much to ever try anything. And Dylan would never forgive me if I fucked that relationship up. I've already messed up with so many others. That doesn't mean I don't tease her about it sometimes, though.

"Hey," he says when Dylan opens the door. I'm as co-conscious as we can get. Like, if Dylan was driving the bus that is us, I'd be sitting on her damn lap.

"Hi," she replies. Her heart rate amps up when he looks at her—it's cute. He looks at her like she's the prettiest thing he's ever seen. Like she's something amazing. Has anyone else ever looked at us like this? Other than the mother and father, I don't think so.

I'm kinda jealous, because even though he's looking into the same eyes I'm looking out of, he's not saying it to me. I don't look anything like Dylan, not in my world, anyway.

"It's me," she says. "Kaz is still up here." She taps her head with her finger. "She's really close, though."

He smiles. "I thought so." He opens his arms. "Hug?"

I want to roll my eyes that he asks, but he's such sweetie. Is he still a virgin? He's a little old, but I can't help but wonder.

Most guys I meet are horndogs and this one, while definitely interested in us, is just so stinking respectful.

We step into the hug and wrap our arms around him. He doesn't *feel* like a virgin, but I'm not sure I've ever felt one. His hands are warm on our back and his grip is just firm enough that I want him to hold us tighter, maybe get a little rougher. He doesn't, though.

"I thought we could hang out for a bit before Kaz comes out," she says. This is news to me. How long am I supposed to just hang here until she decides it's okay? I could force my way out, but that doesn't always work and usually ends up with whoever's up front having a shitty headache.

Instead I hover while they sit on the couch and talk. He holds her hand, kisses her knuckles. I want to scream at her to grab him and give us both what we want. I don't, though. I just watch, bouncing from jealousy to disbelief to awe. He's not playing. He's sincere.

Eventually, she says something about switching. She plays some of the music I suggested—it's the easiest way to bring me out. I'm a sucker for something with a good beat. I love to dance, and if the music makes me feel sexy it's even better. Right now, I'm into Lizzo and Cardi B, but I also like old-school stuff like NIN and the Offspring. It's all about the energy.

It's the difference between going from the passenger seat to the driver's seat. Like looking through glass and finally opening the window. One second I'm a bystander and the next I'm in control. *Oh, yeah.*

As I dance around to Lizzo, a wide smile spreads across my lips. "Oh, I love this song," I say.

Connor's eyes widen a fraction as he looks at me. "Kaz?"

I stop dancing. "What gave me away?"

"Your voice is a little different, and the way you move. It's just . . . different."

"Well, aren't you a smarty-pants." There's no reason to pretend now that he knows. "You want to dance with me?"

He hesitates.

"One dance," I say. "Then we can talk about whatever you want."

Connor smiles. "Okay."

He's a good dancer, not self-conscious or stiff. I'd love to go out clubbing with him. He twirls me around and steers me through some steps I've never done before. I laugh out loud at how much fun it is to be out and enjoying myself. He grins at me, those green eyes sparkling.

I grab him and kiss him—hard. He pulls back. "What was that for?" he asks.

"Fuck conversation," I say. "Let's get naked." So much for all that trust BS I tossed at Dylan.

The smile melts off his face. "What? No." He steps back, and the spell is broken. "That's not what this is about."

Exasperation sighs from between my lips as I turn the music off. "What is it about then? Twenty questions?"

"Maybe. I don't know. I just want to get to know the rest of you."

I laugh. "You're a trip, you know that." I flop onto the sofa. I'm a little out of breath. "Okay, fine. What do you want to know?" If I'm not going to get laid, I might as well enjoy the attention. Maybe if we spend enough time doing what he wants, he'll give me what I want. And what I want is a reason not to be nervous around him. I want to find that weakness in him that makes him like all the others. I *need* to find it, otherwise . . .

Otherwise, he's too good for me.

He sits down beside me, closer to the edge of the cushion, hands on his knees. Angles toward me. "What are your hobbies?"

I frown. "Hobbies?"

"Yeah, what do you like to do in your spare time?"

I prop a foot on the coffee table, spread my knees a bit. "Fuck." Yeah, okay, I say it mostly for shock value.

Connor doesn't seem impressed. "Look, you agreed to this. If you only did that so you could have control of Dylan for a while, then I can go and leave you to it."

I sit up. I don't want him to go, I realize. I want to talk to him. I want him to know me. No one outside of this body knows me except maybe Nisha, and we didn't talk that much.

I clear my throat. "I like music, and I like to dance. I also like to draw."

"Yeah?" He relaxes a little. This common ground between me and Dylan is obviously a good place to start. "What do you draw?"

I shrug. "I like stuff like Tank Girl."

His eyebrows go up. "You like graphic novels?"

"Well, yeah. Doesn't everybody?"

We talk a bit about Gaiman and Ennis, Moore and Miller. He seems really surprised that I'm into it. That's when I find out he's as into the writing as I am the art form.

From there we cover music and movies. He's a huge movie geek. When he starts talking about books, though, I have to cut him off. "If it doesn't have pictures, it won't hold my attention. Though Dylan read something the other night that was pretty good."

"Could you read it, too?" he asks.

"More like I could hear her reading it. She says the words aloud in her head. She does different voices for the characters, so it's fun."

"Can I ask you what it's like in the inner world?"

Suspicion creeps in. Trust isn't something I have in large supply. The primary objective is to protect the system. Always. "Have you talked to Dylan about this?"

He nods. "Some. She's told me that you live in a big house. I've been reading about DID in an effort to understand you all."

I smirk. "You sweet thing. Maybe you should tell me about myself then. What's my role?"

He stills—like a deer in the sights of a rifle. Takes a second to gather his thoughts. I can almost smell the smoke. "You're a sexual protector, I think."

"How does that make you feel?" I ask. "Sitting here, alone with the sex fiend that inhabits your girlfriend's body?" I lean closer so he can see down my top. He doesn't look.

"It makes me feel like you're testing me. Is that what you're doing?"

"Kinda, but it's a legit offer. It's going to be me you have sex with anyway. Dylan's not going to do it. Sex is one of those things that freaks her out. I always have to help her out. Although . . ." I smile, feeling nasty. "She did rub one off not long ago while thinking about you. That was a surprise."

He turns the most adorable shade of red, but he holds my gaze. "Then maybe it won't be you after all."

I laugh. He got me there. "You willing to wait until she's ready? From what I've heard blue balls isn't a comfortable state."

"I'm more uncomfortable with the idea of Dylan doing something she's not ready to do. I'd rather deal with sexual frustration than hurt her."

I admit, I'm not used to being shot down. It kind of pisses me off. "So, what's the plan, man? You going to do this song and dance with us all?"

"If I can, yeah. I want to meet as many of you as possible."

I shake my head. "There's some of us you don't want to meet, trust me on that."

"Okay, I will. If you'll trust me."

"That's a hard one for me to agree to. Just the fact that you're a guy makes me trust you about as far as I can throw you."

"I have to trust you with Dylan. I trust you to protect her. You can do the same."

"You want to ask me what happened to her, don't you?"

He looks at me with an expression that makes me reevaluate my opinion of him. He's not that naive after all.

"I have an idea of what happened, and if Dylan wants me to know, she'll tell me. I'm not using any of you to get around her."

"Right answer." I smile. "I liked this girl, but she couldn't handle that we're multiple. And here's you, being all chill about it."

He shrugs. "I'm not sure I'm chill, but I'm keeping an open mind."

"I want to hate you for it. And I kind of want to give you a blow job, too."

His eyes widen in a way that makes me laugh. "Um, thanks, but I'm okay."

My gaze narrows. "You got a side piece or something?"

"What?"

I straighten. "Is there someone you're doing on the side? Is that why you're so easy about all this?"

"No." He shakes his head. "Wow. You haven't met too many nice guys, have you? We do exist, you know. So, I don't think with my dick, I'm not a fucking unicorn."

I laugh—a real one, not the kind meant to ingratiate me or win someone over. "You're okay, Connor. I might like you. Don't disappoint me."

"I'll try my best. Anytime you want to talk Sandman again, just let me know."

Arching a brow, I don't bother trying to hide my surprise. "Are you saying you'd like to hang out with me again?"

"Yeah. Is that okay?"

"Yeah," I say, my throat suddenly tight. "Yeah, it is. Okay, I'm starting to feel like we're done here, and Dylan is getting anxious. Why don't you get the ginger ice cream out of the freezer and a spoon? Dylan loves that stuff, and I don't. It should be easy to coax her back out, especially if I'm ready to give up the driver's seat."

"Are you sure?" he asks. "I can go if you want to stay out, or we can watch a movie or something."

"Fuck me," I whisper. "You really are a nice guy, aren't you?" His confused expression is more of an answer than any words could be. "Get the ice cream, sweetie." He's too clean for me. I'm starting to feel dirty just looking at him.

I watch him get up off the couch and leave the room. Dylan deserves a guy like him. And the rest of us, well, we deserve a friend like him. Maybe Dylan will let me date him, too. Sharing might be fun. Regardless, I won't be calling Nisha again, not when we have a chance with someone like this.

—

DYLAN

My father is here.

Mark and I go to JFK to meet him, his wife, Angie, and our little half-sister, Bella. We find parking and manage to get to arrivals just as they've collected their bags. Their flight was ahead of schedule.

"Hey!" Dad exclaims happily, coming toward us with his arms out. He's gotten a little grayer since the last time I saw him, and he looks leaner. He and Angie decided to start going to a nutritionist or something a few months ago. I don't ask, because I don't want to know what kind of freaky LA stuff they're getting into. Dad's a director, but Angie is an actress, so she's always right there with the latest health craze trying to look her best. She's already gorgeous, but I guess having a kid kind of messed with her self-image and now she's obsessed with healthy eating—but not in that "everyone has to do it" way that some people get. She just does her thing without trying to make me, which I appreciate. My brother, on the other hand, always wants to know what she's doing and how it works.

Our father grabs us into a three-way hug. A second into it, I feel something press against my legs. I look down and see sweet little Bella, plastered against me, her arms stretching from my legs to Mark's.

"You're getting so big," I tell her. "How tall are you, eight feet?"

She laughs. "No. I'm seven feet."

At five, she is probably the most adorable kid I've ever seen, but I'm biased. I pick her up so I can give her a better hug. She looks even more like Dad than I do, but has light hair like me, so our coloring is the same. Her eyes are huge, and she has this thing for crossing one while the other goes all over the place because she knows it weirds me out and makes me laugh. She also likes to "do voices" whenever we FaceTime. I'm pretty sure she's going to be in entertainment. I adore her, and the kids inside me like her, too. I feel one of them excitedly hovering near the front, enjoying Bella's energy.

She hugs me tight, then crawls from me to Mark. Angie has joined us, so I hug her. too. Mom and Dad splitting up was a good thing, we all agree on that. Dad finding Angie—and having Bella—was definitely the best thing that came out of it. Angie might be obsessed with her looks, but she's good to him and has the same way of thinking. Plus, she's awesome with Bella. I can even forgive her for naming her after the *Twilight* character.

Oh, yeah, Angie's sixteen years younger than my dad. So, even though he's pretty great, he does have that stereotype against him. Whatever. Secretly, I'm hoping Mom finds someone younger, too. I'm certainly not going to mind if she brings Liam Hemsworth home, or maybe Diego Luna.

"How are you doing, babe?" she asks me before letting me go. Angie's real big on making eye contact.

"I'm good," I tell her. "Mom filled you guys in, yeah?"

"She did, but your dad and I want to have a sit-down with you so we can better understand—if that's okay with you?"

"I'll explain as well as I can," I tell her. "I'm still figuring it out myself."

She squeezes my arm. "You'll figure it out. I know you will."

I swallow past the lump in my throat. "Thanks."

Bella wants Mark to give her a piggyback ride, so that leaves me to help with luggage. Thankfully, Dad has a cart that he loaded up with their bags. The only thing I have to carry is Bella's Disney Villains backpack, because it's too "portant" to go on the cart with the others. Why don't they make stuff like this for big kids? I'd love to have a backpack with Maleficent on it.

We get them to the car-rental section, where Mark and I play with a wound-up Bella while Dad and Angie get their keys. Our little sister has a meltdown when she realizes that Mark and I have our own vehicle, so I end up traveling to the hotel with them while Mark meets us there.

Bella falls asleep five minutes into the drive.

"She's exhausted," Angie explains, as if that wasn't obvious. "Everything's been very exciting and overwhelming."

I can relate. "We can postpone dinner," I suggest, casting a glance at my sister. Is it okay that her neck's bent at that angle?

Angie waves her hand. "She'll be fine when she wakes up. Plus, I don't want her to sleep too much. We're still on LA time, remember."

Right, it's three hours earlier there. I don't tell her I doubt Bella will wake up that soon. Seriously, the kid's *out*.

"So, how's therapy going, Lannie?" Dad asks, glancing at me in the rearview.

Now that I know about a different Lannie inside me, it seems weird to be called by that name. I glance at Bella, wondering if maybe I could wake her up so I don't have to have this conversation. "It's okay. Lots to get through, obviously."

"Yeah, I can only imagine. Do you need anything?"

"I'm good, thanks."

"You know, whatever you want or need, your mom and I, and Angie, we've got you, right?"

I nod, holding his gaze in the mirror. "I know, and I appreciate it."

"I don't know much about DID," he goes on. "Only what I've seen in movies."

"Well, if you're expecting James McAvoy to show up, you're going to be disappointed. It's not really anything like that. No superpowered villains inside of me."

"God, I hope not!" Angie laughs. She peers back at me from between the front seats. "But I wouldn't mind if McAvoy stopped by for a visit."

I smile. When she and Dad first got together, I hated her. I planned to keep hating her for my entire life, but it's hard to hate someone who is so genuinely nice, and she won me over. I held out longer than Mark, though, which is a weird position of pride for me. Like, my loyalty to Mom was stronger or something, even though Mom encouraged us to get along with Angie from the beginning.

"I watched a movie called *Waking Madison,*" Angie tells me. "Have you seen it?"

"Yeah, I watched it last week. It was pretty good."

"Did you find it accurate?"

"I'm not an expert," I reply with a nervous laugh, "but, yeah. Mostly."

"I'm sorry." She reaches back and pats me on the leg. "Are we being too much too soon?"

"No, it's cool. It's just . . ." I glance out the window at the darkening sky. "Everyone's been so supportive and it's a little overwhelming, y'know? Like I can't catch my breath."

"I do. When I had postpartum depression after Bella, I felt like such a failure as a woman and a mother, but my friends banded around me, and your dad was fabulous." She gives him a loving look. "I felt like I didn't deserve the help or love they gave me. I felt smothered by it even though I was desperate for it."

"Yeah," I say, a little hoarse. "That's pretty much it."

Angie smiles back at me. "Just take the love. Whether you realize it or not, you need it."

I force my trembling lips into a smile. "I can do that."

"And then, if you need space, just let us know." She turns to face the front. "Okay, so we've got the party this weekend and a couple of Broadway shows during the week. I also can't wait to go shopping. Oh! Is that Indian restaurant we liked so much still open?"

Oh, thank God she changed the subject.

"If it's not, I'm sure we'll find another one just as good," Dad assures her with a smile.

"It's still there," I say. "I was there a few weeks ago." It feels like a million years ago now.

Angie claps her hands. "Yay! And are we going to meet this new guy of yours?"

Poor Connor. He might be ready for all of me, but I'm not sure he's ready for all of my family. "He'll be at the party. He actually lives in the city, so maybe he can join us for dinner?"

"I don't see why not." Dad's gaze peeks into the rearview. "What's going on with Mark and Izzy?"

Oh, finally! Some people like to talk about themselves, but

I'm not one of them. Which is too bad, I guess, since I have so many selves to talk about. I love it when the conversation turns to someone else.

"Didn't see that one coming, huh?" I ask, grinning.

He chuckles. "Hell, no. I thought Izzy was too smart for that. I didn't even know he'd broken up with Kristy."

"Kirsty," I correct him. "Yeah, he ended that insanity months ago. She was a real piece of work."

"That's why I'm so surprised to see him with sensible, grounded Izzy. The boy does seem to like difficult women."

I laugh. It's horrible, but true. Mark has an impressive track record of dating girls who are completely high-maintenance and demanding. Like, I can name four easily, and that's just ones he's dated in the last two years. They never last long.

"He better not break Izzy's heart," I say. "He won't be able to ghost her like he did the others."

Angie groans. "He didn't."

"Of course he did." I'm spilling *all* the tea now. "Mark never met a text he couldn't ignore or a phone call he couldn't send to voicemail. One of them showed up at the house one night." He's going to kill me, but I don't care. I proceed to give them the tawdry details of how Mom and I had to tell this girl to forget about Mark and find someone who appreciated her.

It's not that Mark's a jerk, more like he's a coward who doesn't like to hurt people. Unfortunately, he can be really good at it—which I know firsthand—so he'd rather avoid it if he can.

Still, it's no excuse to just fuck off on someone, so I don't mind outing him to our father. And if Dad tortures him a little, then great. Maybe he'll think of that before pulling the same moves with my bestie.

As we pull into the hotel parking lot, Bella wakes up, bright-eyed and ready to go. It's like someone pressed her "on" switch. I don't know much about kids, but I think she's going to crash hard later.

Mark's already there when we get out of the car.

"Speed much?" I ask him as he approaches.

He smirks. Dad looks at Mark with a raised brow. "No, he wouldn't speed. That's reckless and dangerous. That's the kind of thing that causes accidents and Mark would never do that."

"Yeah," Bella chimes in loudly. "Mawk would nevuh do that."

My brother gives me a mean look as the rest of us laugh. I hand him a suitcase to carry. "Oh, yeah, I told them all about Kirsty, too," I inform him in a bright tone. "I hope you don't mind."

The look on his face is priceless. If I had my hands free, I'd take a picture.

"I'm going to milk the sympathy card of dragging you out of that bathtub," he says, for my ears alone.

"Milk away," I say. "You deserve all the praise and sympathy you get, but if you treat Izzy like your past girlfriends, every last person inside me is going to make your life miserable."

"You're threatening me *now*?" His tone is incredulous. "You were fine before."

I smile as I swing a carry-on over my shoulder. "That was before I knew I'd have backup."

EIGHTEEN

*R*oses are Red
Violets are Blue
Go fuck them all
Before they fuck you.
Happy Birthday, Bitch. Don't do anything—or anyone—
I wouldn't do. Save me a piece of cake.—Kaz

—

I had elaborate plans for our party and the costume I would wear. It was going to be epic, the best costume *ever*.

Funny how a mental health crisis can suddenly make all those plans seem kinda . . . well, less important. Still, I manage to pull it together.

Since Mark and Izzy decided to go with Thor and Valkyrie as their costumes—much to my surprise—they wanted me and Connor to do the matchy-matchy thing with them. Connor was game, so I figured, why not? To continue the Avengers theme, Connor's coming as Loki and I'm going to be Black Widow. What points I lose in originality I make up for in effort, because I *really* worked on the makeup and wig.

Both Connor and Izzy arrive before everyone else to help with last-minute details. Not that there's much for them to do. Mom's hired caterers for the evening. Jennifer Tate never half-asses a party.

I help Connor with his costume. He needs some extensions put in his hair, since it's not as long as Tom Hiddleston's was in the movies. It only takes a few minutes to snap in the waves and blend them with his natural hair. Then I rub some product between my palms and smooth it all back from his face. The horned helm goes on next. It looks like it weighs a ton, but it's actually really light. The horns shine under the lights in my bedroom.

I'm not one of those Loki girls. Never have been. But, when I see Connor all done up, hair brushed back from the exquisite architecture of his face . . . Well, let's just say I'm a Loki girl now.

"You're gorgeous," I tell him.

He blushes. "Thanks. Do you need help?"

"Yeah, you can help me with the hair." I pull my hair back and tug on a wig cap before pulling on a bright red wig. It was one Mom had in her closet—real hair. We'd cut a couple of inches off it and styled it to look like what Scarlett Johansson had in the first Avengers movie. Once it's on and I've set it in place with a bit of wig glue, Connor helps me perfect the style before spraying it. After that I pop in some blue contacts and quickly do my makeup. I don't really look like ScarJo, but covering my real eyebrows and drawing them on a little lower, plus overlining my upper lip, helps.

Finally, I go into my bathroom to zip up into the suit. It's pretty basic—a black, formfitting one-piece—but I add some pops of red and strap some fake pistols to my thighs. It looks pretty good. Thank you, YouTube makeup gurus/makers and your Halloween tutorials. You're freaking awesome. I'm ready to show Connor.

"What do you think?" I ask, doing a little twirl in the middle of my room. "I'd do a high kick, but I'm afraid I'd rip the seam."

He stares at me.

"It's me," I say when he stares at me a little too long. "Dylan."

"I know," he tells me with a wide grin. "I'm just taking it all in. It's . . . a lot. You look amazing."

"Makeup," I say, preening under the praise. "Is the outfit okay? Seriously? I don't usually wear anything this tight."

He raises his eyebrows. "It's incredible. And hot. I want to wrap you in a blanket or something."

I lean closer, feeling brave and liking the way he looks at me. "Will you get in the blanket with me?"

The brightness in his eyes shifts in a way that makes my heart skip a beat. I'm not sure if Kaz is close, or if this is me feeling comfortable, but I like it regardless.

"I will do whatever you tell me to do," he promises, his voice so low it raises the hairs on the back of my neck.

Sweet Jesus, Kaz whispers.

I can't even laugh at her. I'm too caught up in the promise

in Connor's gaze. All those years I wasted dating jerks who didn't care if I got off or not when I should have been dating nice boys who actually give a shit.

"Promise?" I ask.

He kisses me on the lips, lightly, but with intent. "Promise."

I exhale a breath. "Okay, I need a drink."

Laughing, Connor hugs me and then we walk to the bar set up in the living room and get a couple of sodas.

People start showing up shortly after and keep arriving in a fairly steady stream. As usual, Mom has invited a lot of people. Most are friends and family, and each of them makes their way over to say hi and wish me a happy birthday at some point. Connor grabs my arm as a famous model walks in and gives Mark a kiss on the cheek. "Is that who I think it is?"

"Yup," I confirm. "They dated in high school—back when she had braces and he had acne."

"And that guy with your mom . . ." he says a few minutes later, jaw hanging open.

"Definitely the guy from that movie you saw. He and Mom used to date back in the day." I smile. "Want to meet him?"

"Maybe later." He looks at me. "Any of your famous exes going to show up?"

I arch a brow. "I don't have any. You may have noticed I'm sort of the black sheep of the family."

"I'm cool with that. Izzy doesn't look the least bit bothered by Mark's fan club."

It's true, my brother does have a few girls gathered around him, including the model ex, and my friend looks totally at ease with the whole thing. "Izzy's a rock star," I explain. "She knows her worth, and even if she didn't, she'd never let on."

When she glances in my direction, I blow her a kiss. She grins and rolls her eyes. That's when my brother reaches down and takes her hand in his. Maybe he's not as dense as I thought.

I turn my attention back to Connor. "Hey, my dad's here. You ready to meet him?"

He straightens. "Sure. Where is he?"

I point across the room to the man dressed as Wolverine—the leather-jacket-and-jeans version. "There. That's his wife, Angie, with him." Jean Grey, of course. We have a thing for superheroes in this family. I think Dad just likes the Wolverine thing because all he needs to do is get the hair right. And it's an excuse to grow out his sideburns.

For what it's worth, I've never seen anyone react to my father the way Connor does. I swear, all the muscles in his face go totally slack as his jaw drops.

"Your father is Eric Walker?"

"Well, yeah." I thought he knew. I must have told him at some point, hadn't I? Maybe I didn't. To me, Dad's not that big a deal, but then again, neither is Mom. They're just my parents.

When he looks at me, disbelief shines in his gaze. "He wrote season one of *Dark Falls*."

"He created it," I reply—and yeah, with a certain amount of pride. *Dark Falls* premiered on HBO last year and was one of their highest-viewed shows. Dad was showrunner. Season two is due to start airing in December.

"I have his book on screenwriting. I've read it more times than I can count. It's brilliant."

"So . . . I guess you *do* want to meet him, then?"

He shakes his head. "Fuck, no."

Laughing, I take him by the hand, and pull him across the

room. "Dad," I say above the music—it's not so loud that people can't talk. "I want to introduce you to Connor."

Grinning around the stub of a cigar, Dad offers Connor his hand. "Nice to meet you, Connor. Dylan says you want to be a writer."

"Yes, sir," Connor replies. He's so nervous; it's adorable. "It's so awesome to meet you. I'm a fan."

"My ego thanks you. You're joining us for dinner on Wednesday, right? We can talk shop."

Connor looks like a small animal trapped in the headlights of an oncoming eighteen-wheeler. "That would be great."

Angie gives me a little smile. She's seen this before. Dad's not being overly nice for my benefit, though. I don't think he's ever realized that he's famous, because he just thinks of himself as a guy who spends way too much time in front of a computer. He really does love talking about writing to any-one who will listen. He's going to enjoy it just as much as Connor. Maybe more.

We talk to Dad and Angie for a few more minutes—long enough for Connor to relax a little—and then an old friend of Dad's comes along to say hi, so we drift away.

An hour later, Mark and I blow out the candles on our cakes to applause and cheers. Mom has it arranged so that there are precut pieces for everyone already set out, along with a selec-tion of ice creams—kept in chilled containers so they don't melt.

"You realize this is like something off of an eighties sit-com?" Connor remarks as we scoop ice cream onto our re-spective slabs of cake.

I'm not offended. My mom grew up on an eighties sitcom.

I enjoyed a really comfortable life thanks to that sitcom and the kinda cheesy movies that followed. "Where do you think she got the idea?"

He looks around with a grin. "It's incredible. Thanks for inviting me to be part of it."

"Thanks for wanting to be part of it," I reply.

He cuts into the cake on his plate. "Where are all your friends? I've met Mark's but so far the only friend of yours I've met is Izzy."

I shrug, poke the icing with my fork. "I don't really have friends."

He stares at me. "What?"

This is awkward. "My . . . issues have made it hard to make and keep friends. A few people have tried, but I succeeded in driving all but Izzy away."

He leans in and nudges me with his elbow. "Well, you know, me and Izzy are worth like, twenty regular friends, so you're actually doing pretty good."

"Yeah," I agree, honestly. "I think so." I hold his gaze long enough for him to get the hint and lean in and kiss me. Kaz sighs. For someone who claims to be all about sex, she's really kind of a romantic.

After cake we do presents. As usual, we get a stupid amount of stuff. I get a lot of art supplies, which is nice, especially since most of them are pretty high-end. Mark and I are fully aware of how spoiled we are. Full disclosure, what we can't use will get donated to a local shelter, the same one we volunteer at every Thanksgiving. Aren't we precious? It started as a pub-licity thing set up by Mom's agent, but she discovered she liked doing it, and it became a family tradition when Mark and I became old enough to join her.

My favorite gift is from Connor, though. It's a scarf designed by one of my favorite artists that features her artwork. It's simple and beautiful, and most of all, thoughtful. It shows he's paid attention. Kaz and Lannie really like it, too, and it's just dark enough that I think even Alyss would approve.

Around nine o'clock I start to get a little tired of the talking and the people. My focus isn't what it ought to be either. I'm dissociating off and on and feeling loopy as the party over-stimulates my system. I can't tell if someone else wants to come out or they want me to come in.

Then the doorbell rings, signaling a late arrival.

"There's the surprise," Dad says, with a smile. Frowning, I turn my gaze toward the doorway. Surprise? Isn't everyone here? Who are we missing?

And then I see him.

Uncle Travis. A bigger, younger version of my father. He looks like a more rugged Ben Affleck with longish hair. He was a stuntman for a while, then got into directing. I adored him as a kid. He used to always be around, taking me and Mark places, hanging out. He always had a different girlfriend but got married not long ago. Or, I thought he had, but there isn't anyone with him.

There's a moment of joy when I look at him. And then he looks at me and my stomach rolls. The room swims around me, and for a second—it couldn't possibly be any longer than that—I'm somewhere else. Somewhere with Uncle Travis and I feel his hand on my shoulder . . .

Oh, God. The weight of that hand . . . all the memories it holds. Inside me, I feel the tightness of half a dozen held breaths.

I've got you, Lannie whispers.

And there's Scratch, hovering. Angry, terrified. I blink as they tug on my consciousness, all of them pushing toward the front. I guess they're showing support, but it just makes me dizzy and my head starts to ache.

"Who's that?" Connor asks.

"My uncle Travis," I reply. "Dad's brother. I haven't seen him in years."

"Cool that he came for your birthday, then."

It should be, right? I watch, throat clenched between two invisible hands as Travis greets Mark with a hug and a grin. They talk for a few seconds before clapping each other on the back. Then he looks at me.

I can't move. He's coming toward me with that charming smile of his and I can't fucking move. My heart is going to break my ribs and I'm going to die right here. Scratch won't have to do a damn thing.

He stops in front of me. "Dylan, happy birthday."

I swallow, choking on the knot in my throat. "Thanks," I whisper.

He comes closer and puts his arms around me. The mother-fucker *hugs* me. As soon as he touches my body, I retract into my mind. I literally feel myself withdraw. He destroyed my life, and he has the balls to put his hands on me in front of all these people? I want to ask him why he did it, but my mouth won't open.

Someone inside me starts screaming.

US

No one inside will
ever disappear.
We're all real.
We all matter.

—JOAN FRANCES CASEY

NINETEEN

'm not sure what's happened. I'm not at my party anymore. I'm somewhere else. The party has to be close, because I can hear it, like I'm in an apartment building and it's happening the floor above me.

"Hi," says a voice.

I whirl around. "Who the fuck are you?" I demand. The girl before me is young and tall, with long red hair and a beautiful, flawless face.

She arches a perfectly shaped eyebrow. "I'm Monet. What are you doing here?"

Monet. I'm in my head. Seeing Uncle Travis must have triggered a switch and I'm in the head space. This is the first time I've come here that it wasn't a dream, or maybe those other times weren't dreams at all.

I glance around me. We're in a small theater—six recliners in front of a large movie screen. "You tell me. What is this?"

She watches me closely. I feel like I should know the answer, but maybe it's a trick question. "This is where we keep the memories of what he did to us. If you're here, it means you want to see them."

"No, I don't." The feelings are bad enough. I don't want to fucking see anything.

She shrugs. "Need to see, then. You're here, I'm here. This is what is supposed to happen."

"We'll be here with you," Lannie says from behind me.

I turn. She has Kaz and Dali and Alyss and Scratch with her, though Scratch looks like she's about to freak out.

"Who's fronting?" I ask, panic gripping my heart. "Not one of the littles?"

Alyss looks offended that I even suggested it. "Of course not. Vincent's got control of the body."

"Who the hell is Vincent?" Just how many people do I have inside me?

"Vincent is who always stepped in to play sports when you were a kid, or fought with your brother," Kaz replies. "Don't worry about it. He's cool."

"He's a protector," Lannie adds, giving Kaz an exasperated look. "He's not afraid of Travis. You're safe with him up front. We're *all* safe."

I look at each of them, and they all meet my gaze, even Scratch, though Alyss has to nudge her. "Fine," I say, and sit down in one of the recliners.

"This isn't a good idea," Scratch says. "I don't like it."

"Sit down," Alyss hisses. "None of us like it, you old fool."

The two of them take seats at opposite ends of the row. Dali sits next to Scratch, and Kaz and Lannie sit on either side of me. Lannie offers me her hand, and I take it gratefully. Then Kaz offers me hers. I grab on tight.

When everyone is seated, the lights dim and the screen flickers as the film begins to play.

They're images—memories. Most of them don't even feel like they're mine, but I know they are. Just like I know the eyes through which I'm seeing them are technically mine, but when Lannie makes a small noise, it's obvious who is really being held down.

Family vacations. Get-togethers. Holidays. Travis touching me when no one was looking. Coming into my room late at night. Taking me places, or going on rides with me, all the while his hands go places they had no business going.

My heart pounding in the dark, my mind splitting— becoming someone else when it goes further. Kaz, taking the shame away. Lannie, taking the pain. Alyss telling me everything is going to be all right. Dali reading me a story. Vincent reminding me it wouldn't have happened if I was a boy, so I let him take over. Monet promising to make it all go away. And Scratch . . . Scratch telling me no one is coming to save me, so the best thing to do is stay quiet and hope it stops, because everyone will say it was my fault. Just stay quiet and still.

I remember. Even if it doesn't feel entirely mine, I remember. It happened to all of us, and we sit here holding hands in the dark as our abuse looms larger than life before our eyes.

He told us he loved us. Told us we were his special girl, and then he betrayed our love and trust in the worst way. How could anyone do that to any child, let alone one they claim to love?

When the credits roll and the lights come up, we exchange glances. Tears run down our faces, except for Scratch. She's dry-eyed, but her fury is as obvious as our tears. Our fingers are still entwined as one by one, they draw closer to me. Kaz and Lannie rest their heads against mine as Monet and Alyss crouch before them. Dali kneels at my feet while Scratch stands back, arms folded over her chest. The six of us bow together like buds of a flower waiting to bloom as Scratch bears witness. We cry. We remember.

I'm never going to forget again.

—

VINCENT

At least the kids are quiet. *Too* fucking quiet, but I can't worry about that right now. I have to keep the body functioning like nothing's wrong when everything is so very, very wrong.

What the fuck are we wearing? Of course it would be a costume party and we'd wear something that shows off our curves. I see how some of the guys here are looking at us. It makes me want to punch them in the nads, and go upstairs to change.

Instead, I stick close to Connor. He seems like an okay guy, and he likes Dylan. He'll provide a buffer between me and everyone else, especially that slimy asshole who had the balls to hug us earlier.

I wish this body looked like I do. I'd kick the snot out of him for what he did. I'd fix him so he'd never hurt anyone ever again.

"Hi."

I look up to find Connor watching me. "Hi," I say. Shit, had he been talking to me?

"What's your name?" he asks.

Kaz said he's good at noticing when Dylan's switched out. Too good, maybe. There's no point in trying to lie to him when he obviously sees me, and I'm too stressed to be bothered. "Vincent. Vin."

"Nice to meet you, Vin. You don't look like you're enjoying the party."

"I'm not much of a party person."

"Then why are you here?"

I shrug. "I guess Dylan needed a break or something."

He watches me with a narrow gaze. He knows something's up. Dylan might like this pretty boy, but he ain't nothing to me, so he better just step the fuck down.

Suddenly, Mark appears beside us, grinning like an idiot. "Come on," he says.

Connor and I exchange glances, but we follow him to the back door where Izzy's waiting with a couple of heavy blankets. She smiles when she sees us. "Mark started a bonfire on the beach." She shows us the six-pack of beer hidden under the blankets. It's not nearly enough to get us feeling good, let alone drunk, but that's not really the point.

I follow the three of them out the door and down the low bank to the beach. It's cold but there's very little wind, which is good because this outfit isn't made for warmth.

The fire snaps and flickers in the darkness like a living thing. I feel the heat of it before we get close.

Mark and Izzy share a blanket as they huddle on one of the logs near the fire. They both take a beer and hand the others our way.

There's only one other blanket. Connor gives me a questioning look as he opens it. There's no way either of us can sit in this cold without an extra layer, even with the fire. Dylan wouldn't think twice about sharing with him. She'd like it.

I sigh and sit down next to him on the log. I peel a beer out of a tab for him as he drapes the heavy blanket over my shoulders. This would have been the perfect time to out me as "not Dylan" but he doesn't. Instead, he chooses to protect us.

"Thanks," he says before popping the can.

I hope he doesn't expect to get any love while I'm in control of the body. I'm not interested in him. Now, if we were sharing this blanket with Nisha, that would be a different story. Too bad that went the way it did.

To his credit, Connor doesn't try anything. He doesn't even touch me—not that anyone would really be able to tell beneath the blanket. He'd have to be kinda gross to paw the body with other people around anyway.

Travis would definitely take advantage of the situation, but we're too old for him now, I bet.

"You should let Dad read some of your work," I say, holding up my end of the charade.

Mark grins. "Yeah, you should. He's got a lot of friends in Hollywood, man. He can help you get a foot in."

"Unless he thinks I'm a talentless hack," Connor replies. There's enough sincerity in his voice that I frown. He doesn't strike me as someone who has confidence issues.

"He's not going to think you're talentless, because you're

incredibly talented," I say. I don't know this, but that's how Dylan feels, and she's read his work.

"Yeah," Izzy chimes in. "D's told me how good you are."

There was a time when I had the biggest crush on Izzy, but thankfully that went away, along with the resentment I used to feel every time she believed I was Dylan. I realized that it wasn't that she didn't notice the changes in our behavior, because she did. She just thought it was a "mood" or something else, because she saw us only as Dylan, her friend. She didn't think we'd lie to her about who we were, and so we continued to lie. It was easier.

And she was still the first to figure out what was going on. You don't figure out our kind of situation by not paying attention. We underestimated her.

"If he asks to see my work, I'll show him," Connor allows, "but I'm not going to throw myself at him. That's just desperate and rude."

Mark lifts his beer in acknowledgment. "Welcome to the entertainment industry."

We all chuckle. I like Mark when he's relaxed and happy like this. We've always gotten along fairly well, even when he used to pick on Dylan when they were kids. Sometimes I had to come out to give him a slap upside the head, but for the most part, we've always had fun when he's not being moody. We don't spend as much time together as we used to. I miss that.

"Hey, how awesome was it to see Uncle Trav?" Mark asks, his gaze on me.

I swallow a mouthful of beer. It's bitter and hides the real reason for my grimace. "Yeah. Awesome."

"Apparently he's doing some work in New York while he's here."

"So he didn't come home for our birthday." Of course he didn't make the trip for his "special girl." There had to be something else to lure him back. After all, they have little girls in Europe, too. It makes my stomach roll thinking what he might have done on his travels outside of the U.S.

Mark gives a tiny smirk. "I guess this way he can write the trip off as a tax deduction. Anyway, he'll be at dinner Wednesday night. I want to hear all about his trip to Iceland."

I take another drink. "Mm." I could not fucking care less. I'd be happier if the asshole stayed in Iceland. I wish he'd fallen off a fucking iceberg.

"He's your dad's brother?" Connor asks.

Mark nods. "Younger by a few years. He was around a lot before Mom and Dad split. He used to do a lot of stuff with me and D. The fun uncle, you know."

Connor's gaze is heavy as it settles on me. "Were you his favorite?"

I turn my head to look into his eyes. "No."

Mark laughs. "Yes, you were. He called you his princess."

Beer and birthday cake are not a good combination. If this conversation doesn't stop soon, I'm going to be spewing both all over this blanket and stupid costume.

Connor must notice, or maybe he's sick of talking about Travis, because he holds his beer aloft, can glinting in the firelight.

"A toast: To Dylan and Mark, happy nineteenth birthday. I hope it's followed by many, many more."

"Yasss," Izzy enthuses, raising her beer. Then she turns to

Mark and kisses him on the mouth. Oh, hell. I look at Connor. He looks at me and shrugs. Sighing, I give him a peck on the cheek.

"Thank you," I say in my best Dylan-voice.

He stares at me intently. I feel bad for him. I really do. "Is she okay?" he asks.

I pat his knee. "She's going to be fine." I raise my beer. "Happy fucking birthday to me!" I shout.

Izzy hoots and Mark shouts it back at me. Only Connor is silent. To be honest, I'm thankful for Izzy and Mark's noise, because all I can hear inside our head are my girls sobbing.

And it breaks my heart.

—

LANNIE

The next morning, I wake up in the body. Dylan apparently needs some more time to process what she learned last night. It wasn't my idea for her to find out like that. I wanted to tell her, prepare her. But I . . . *we* couldn't. It was against the rules. I can't imagine what it must have been like for her to have to face those memories. It was bad enough for us to see *him*, especially the littles. Christina screamed for hours afterward. Poor thing. When he hugged us . . . I shudder . . . it was like we were back there again, under his power, being held down. Being hurt.

The shock of the memories forced Dylan to switch out and threw us into chaos. I don't know what we would have done if Vincent hadn't stepped up. No one else was fit to front. Who knows what Scratch might have done. There was a moment when Travis looked into Dylan's eyes, and I swear he could see inside us. He's the one thing we're all afraid of.

Everyone but Vincent. But Vincent doesn't like to front much since the body matured. It gives him dysphoria if he's out too long. So, here I am, up front and in control.

I stretch under the blankets. I enjoy the feeling—the heaviness of the body's limbs. However, I don't enjoy the feeling of a full bladder, so I slip out from the warmth of the bed and hurry to the bathroom. The tiles are cool beneath our feet.

"Our." I'm doing that more, referring to the body or parts of it as "our" instead of "mine." We've become more of a unit since Dylan discovered us, since we came out of the shadows and let her know we're here. I don't care how angry Scratch is at me for it, I'm glad I did.

Once I'm done in the bathroom, I find a pair of fuzzy socks and pull them on our cold feet before slipping on the robe draped over the foot of the bed. Then I go downstairs, following the smell of freshly brewed coffee.

Dylan's mother is in the kitchen making pancakes.

"Smells good," I say.

She glances over her shoulder at me and smiles. "I thought you'd sleep in a little while longer. You were up pretty late last night."

Were we? I yawn as if on cue. "Had to pee. And I smelled coffee."

She laughs. "I thought maybe it was the enticing aroma of these pancakes I've made from scratch."

Our stomach growls and I grin. "That too. You made bacon?"

"Of course. After fifteen years of having it the morning after your birthday you shouldn't be so surprised."

Yeah, but this is the first time I've ever gotten to be the one who gets to eat it. I'm excited. Dali would run screaming— she's a vegetarian.

"Can I help?" I ask.

"Nope. Just about ready. I'll make Mark's when he comes down."

Jennifer fixes both of us plates at the counter while I pour coffee. This puts her right in front of the cupboard where the sugar is kept.

"Jennifer," I begin, "would you mind—"

"Jennifer? Since when do you call me . . ." Her face loses some of its color. She stares at me. I hate the realization that tightens her features. "You're not Dylan."

"No," I reply with a slight smile, gripping the coffee cup in front of me like a shield. "I'm Lannie."

"Lannie." She slowly nods and sets the spatula on the counter. "That's what your . . . Dylan's father used to call her."

"I know."

She clears her throat. It's obvious she's thrown—bothered— but she's trying to roll with it. "So, what's your role within Dylan's . . . system?"

"I'm a protector."

A frown creases her forehead, deepening the lines there. I want to hug her, but I don't think touching her is a good idea right now. "Does Dylan need protection right now?"

We haven't agreed on what we were going to do, and I have no idea how much I'm allowed to tell. It would probably be so much easier for me to say what happened, but I refuse to be the one who tells this woman what her daughter suffered at the hands of a man she trusted. "She needs a break. The party was overwhelming." I nod. "All those people."

She doesn't look like she believes me. I wouldn't either. Plus, this isn't like lying to a stranger, this is Dylan's mother.

Jennifer doesn't look at me. "You know, I used to ask her if something had happened. When she was little, there was a change in her. I can't quite describe it, but she wasn't as happy as she used to be. I thought maybe it was the trouble her father and I were having." She makes a scoffing noise. "Funny how we make things about our own issues, isn't it?"

"I remember you asking questions."

"Yes, you probably know me much better than I know you."

I smile. "I doubt that. You just don't know how well you know me."

"No." She smiles as well. "I guess not. I'm sorry, you were asking me for something."

"Oh, the sugar. Would you hand it to me?"

"Of course." She reaches into the cupboard and hands me a covered dish.

"Thanks." I add two spoonfuls to my coffee. "I'm not much for candy and sweets, but I just can't drink coffee without sugar in it."

"I'm sorry." Jennifer gives her head a shake. "This is so . . . *weird* for me."

"Yeah, I bet it is." I tilt my head in the direction of the table. "Want to sit?"

"Mm." She hands me a plate and I take it to the table, sitting down in our usual spot. "If it makes you feel any better, this is strange for me as well. I've never been able to be myself in front of you before."

"That must be hard for you. I can't imagine."

I think for a moment. "Maybe you can. Imagine if you had to be Addison whenever there were people around. And you could only be you when you were alone."

I guess it wasn't the right thing to say, because she looks horrified. "Oh, my God," she whispers. "That's horrible."

Our hand falls over hers. "No, it's not that bad. Not really. You've made it nice."

Jennifer wipes her eyes with the back of her free hand. "That's sweet of you to say."

"It's true. We're all very comfortable in front of you." Except for Scratch.

"How many of you are there?"

This is tricky territory. "I'm not sure. Hasn't Dylan told you about us?"

"She has. I thought maybe you would be able to elaborate, since you're more familiar with things."

I let go of her hand to take the top off the maple syrup bottle and pour a small lake of it onto my plate. I guess I can't eat pancakes without sweetening them up either. Surely answering her questions wouldn't hurt? But I can't tell her things that Dylan hasn't discovered yet.

"There's nine of us." That Dylan knows of, not including the littles, and I'm not telling this woman about the littles.

Her mouth drops open for a split second before snapping closed. "Nine?"

Yeah, good thing I didn't tell her the truth. "Yes. These pancakes are *really* good."

"They're your—Dylan's—favorite."

"I think they might be mine too." I smile but she doesn't return it. "Would you feel better if I pretended to be Dylan? I can do that."

"No." Her tone is adamant. "I want you to be you. The collection of you has been a secret long enough. I want you all to feel safe and comfortable here, with me. It's the only way for any of you to heal and move forward."

I'm pretty sure she wants us to go away. That's what she's hoping, at any rate. I can't say I blame her. "That's nice of you," I say instead. "You know, you've handled all of this really well. A lot of people would have freaked the fuck out. Sorry."

She laughs. "Sweetie, at this point, you dropping the f-bomb is the least of it."

I laugh too. "I guess so. I tell you what—I'll answer your questions if you eat your breakfast. Pretend we're two friends who haven't seen each other for a while that are hanging out."

For a moment, I expect her to bolt, but her shoulders relax. "Okay." She takes a deep breath. "How old are you?"

"Twenty-one. I have blue hair, not pink. And my eyes are also blue." I take another bite and shiver when the rich sweetness hits our taste buds.

"What do you like to do?"

"I like art, like Dylan, but I prefer pencils to paint."

She turns her head toward the hall. "You drew my blackbird."

Joy bursts inside me. Jennifer might not think she knows me, but she *knows* me. She knows all of us. "I did."

She stares at me. "I love that drawing."

"We gave it to you for your birthday two years ago."

Tears bead on her lashes, but she blinks them away. "How long have you been with Dylan?"

"Since she was six, I think."

"So Kaz came before you."

I nod, again, impressed. "Kaz was here first—after Dylan herself, of course."

"And the one who tried to hurt her? All of you?"

"That was Scratch." Normally Scratch would yell at me for saying her name, but she's silent. They're all deep in the head space trying to figure out what to do.

"I'm going to have to write your names down." She smiles wryly.

I shrug. "Dylan's keeping a journal. I don't see why you can't, too. Have you read hers?"

"I wouldn't do that without her permission."

"You should ask. Most of us have written in it as well. It might help you."

Setting down her fork, Jennifer shakes her head. "It might also make things worse. I'm having a very hard time . . . Lannie. You're very nice, and I appreciate you talking to me, but I can't help but think I could have prevented you from ever coming into existence."

I tilt our head. "What could you have done, though, Jennifer? Read Dylan's mind? Watched her every second of every day?"

"I'm her mother. I should have protected her from the monster that hurt her." I watch as her expression changes from anguish to a raw, dawning realization. "Did something happen

last night? That's why you're here and not Dylan. You're protecting her because something happened that upset her."

I force a tiny smile. "Yes."

Silverware clatters as she grabs my hand in a tight grip.
"What?"

Pressure bears down on our throat, making it hard to
breathe. "I can't tell you that."

Her fingers tighten around our wrist. "Yes, you can. Just
tell me what it was so I can help."

The familiar buzz of dissociation starts vibrating around
the edges of my brain, trying to drag me inside. Vincent, our
knight in shining armor, wants to come out and protect us.
He's such a boy. I give him a little push. I can handle this.

I place my hand over hers. "I don't mean I won't tell you.
I mean I literally can't. Dylan won't let me." I frown, trying
to think of the right words. I'm not going to tell her that her
daughter is trying to choke me into silence. It might not even
be Dylan doing it. But she's close and doesn't want me talking
to Jennifer before she's ready.

"I know this is hard for you to understand, but we can't
fill in the blanks and make Dylan whole again. This secret—
this horrible, horrible secret—is hers. My job is to protect her
and the trauma she's hidden all these years. Even if I could
tell you, I wouldn't without her permission. It would be a betrayal." I look deep into her eyes, willing her to understand.

She nods, gaze drifting away. "Is there anything I could
have done to protect her as a child?"

I feel so bad for her. I really do. And I don't know how
to answer her questions. I don't know if there even is a right
answer.

"I don't think so," I reply. "And even if there was, it's not like you can go back now and do it, you know?"

The look on her face makes me wish I'd stayed quiet. Makes me wish I'd never called her by her fucking name. I should have pretended to be Dylan. Why had I thought it was safe to be myself?

"No," she says in a hoarse voice. "I suppose not. Enjoy your breakfast, Lannie. Excuse me."

The legs screech against the floor as she shoves away from the table. I watch her leave the kitchen with a heaviness in my stomach that's almost painful. For the first time in my existence, I resent Dylan for making me front.

But mostly I resent everything that happened to that little girl that made her need to hide behind me.

TWENTY

November 1

Dear Dylan—I'm kind of freaking out here. It's not un-
usual for one of us to front for a day or two, but this is the first
time in a long, long time that we've switched out because you
didn't want to be present. That worries me, so I hope we can
talk about it.

So, you and I have been together for as long as I can
remember. I don't have any recollection of time without you,
and I don't think you have many memories that predate me.
You are the OG, and you've always been up front the most.
You're the host, for lack of better term, but still one of us.
Your job has always been to be in control the majority of the
time, to be our constant. You've never backed down from that,
until now. I'm worried about you.

I want you to know that even though it's scary—the idea

of doing this without you—it's okay if you need a break. It's okay if you need to step away from being host. Someone will step up and take over if that's what's needed, but in case you were wondering, we need you just as much as you've needed us, and we'd really like it if you'd at least talk to us and let us help. Hiding in your room doesn't benefit any of us, and I hate knowing you're struggling. Please, come out.—Lannie

—

LANNIE

Day two up front. Dylan's still in hiding, but I can feel her moving around in the inner world. She can't hide in there forever, that's not how this works. Right? Somehow she's managed to avoid us, but there's no way she can keep that up.

Near the front, Kaz shrugs. She doesn't know what's going on either. I'm glad she's sticking close in case I need her. Usually being up front is fun for me, but this isn't fun. This makes me anxious.

What if we see *him* again? Christina is traumatized. She's still screaming. Alyss and Dali don't seem to be able to get her to stop. And I'm *livid*. Not at Christina, but at *him*. For years we haven't had to face our feelings about him, and then he just walks in like he fucking owns the place, like he's *wanted*, and puts his hands on us.

I get to the toilet just in time to vomit up what little food was in our stomach. I shudder. God, that's horrible.

I sit on the bathroom floor, resting our head against the

vanity. It's nice, being still. Quiet. I can't stay here forever, though. I have to get dressed. I don't move right away. Instead, I pick up our cell phone from where it dropped on the tile floor and open my texts.

Me: It's Lannie. Still here. She's okay. Will update you after appointment.

I hit send and use the toilet to help get to our knees. *Ugh.* I'd better flush that puke.

The phone dings while I'm brushing our teeth.

Connor: Thanks. Here if you need anything.

I sigh, shoulders relaxing. I doubt he has any idea how much that means to me. I like Connor—not like Dylan does, obviously. I'm not sure I'm capable of all that romance stuff. I've never really been attracted to anyone. But Connor has become a friend, whether he knows it or not.

Connor's the only one other than Jennifer who knows I'm not Dylan, but he doesn't know why. He suspects. Vincent said as much. Connor hasn't put the questions to me, though. I told him Dylan isn't ready for any of us to talk. She might be quiet in there, but Dylan made it very clear that she didn't want anyone to know anything was even up before our appointment with Dr. Zhao today.

Connor was pretty understanding. Worried, though. Poor guy. I feel a little guilty for even dragging him into this, but also very impressed with myself for choosing him. Obviously, he's a good match for Dylan—for us. Even Kaz thinks he's

worth having a conversation with. And Vincent allowed that
he was a "good guy." The others don't really care either way,
I don't think.

I reply to his text telling him I'll call after therapy. I have
no idea if it will be me calling or not, so I set an alarm on our
phone. I hope it's Dylan who makes the call. She can tell him
as much or as little as she likes.

I finish getting ready and go downstairs. I grab a bottle of
water from the fridge and a granola bar from the pantry, so I
have something if I get hungry.

"You look tired," Mark says from where he's sitting at the
counter. He's got a script in front of him. I don't know if it's
something he's got an audition for or if he's reading for plea-
sure, and I don't want to ask. Dylan would probably know.

"I didn't sleep well last night," I tell him.

"You're not getting sick, are you? We've got the family dinner on Wednesday."

Our stomach lurches. Right. Travis will be there. What
are we going to do?

"No," I say, voice hoarse. "I'm not getting sick." Though
if I'm still up front come Wednesday, I might fake it.

"I figure I'll drive the three of us in," Mark continues, un-
aware there's anything amiss. It's not his fault. We've been
fooling him for almost fourteen years. He's gotten so used to
us that we'd have to do something shocking to get his attention. "Parking will be cheaper than the train and then we can
stay as long as we want."

I nod. "Sure. Connor's going to meet us there." I can't leave
Connor to go on his own, I realize. And talking to Dylan's
father is a big deal for him. I have to go.

Dylan better get her ass out here by Wednesday. That's all I can say.

Jennifer drives us to Dr. Zhao's office for our three o'clock appointment and comes up the elevator with me.

"After you talk to Dr. Zhao, you're going to tell me what's going on, right?" she asks as we enter the waiting room.

"Right." Or Dylan will, or someone. This appointment is about figuring out the right way to handle things and how to get Dylan to front again.

We sit down to wait. Jennifer flips through a magazine while I scroll through our Instagram feed. Vincent posted some nice photos from the party, including a really nice one of us with Connor. No one would know it wasn't Dylan in the shot. In fact, it might be Dylan in that one.

"Dylan?"

I look up. Dr. Zhao is in the doorway that leads to the therapy rooms. I put the phone in my coat pocket and stand.

"I'll be right here if any of you need me," Jennifer says.

"Thank you." I give her a small smile and follow Dr. Zhao. As soon as she closes the door, I stick out my hand. "I'm Lannie. I don't think we've met."

She doesn't miss a beat and accepts the handshake with a firm grip. "Hello, Lannie. Would you like to sit?"

I sit in Dylan's usual place, kick off our shoes, and tuck our knees up to our chest. "You need to help us."

She frowns, creasing the normally smooth skin between her eyes. "What's happened?"

"We saw him. He was there at the party, and now Dylan won't come out."

"Him?"

I roll my hand in a circle in the air at her. "Travis, the guy who abused us. Dylan's uncle."

The frown gives way to slight alarm. "He was at Dylan's birthday party?"

"Fucking right he was. Sorry." I'm shaking. I clench our hands into fists. "He hugged her. Us."

"That forced you out?"

"No. Vincent switched out when Dylan decided to bail."

"Vincent's a protector?"

"Yeah. He comes out sometimes when we feel physically threatened or need to feel safe. Then, Dylan found Monet and accessed our memories."

"What did she remember?"

I have to hand it to her for keeping up. "What he did to us. Specific occasions." I hug our arms around our knees. "We all remembered."

Her expression doesn't budge from serene sympathy. I appreciate it. "That must have been very traumatic for you all."

"It was. But Dylan locked herself in her room and refuses to come out. I need you to help me get her back out."

"Why is it important to you that Dylan assumes control of the body?"

"Because I don't want to be in control. And this is Dylan's chance."

"Chance for what?"

Do I have to spell it out? "To tell what happened. To out the asshole."

A dark eyebrow lifts. "You want her to reveal the abuse?"

I close my eyes. "Yes. Fuck, yes." It feels good to say it out loud, but there's going to be hell to pay for the confession later.

"Lannie, has this been your intent all along? To convince Dylan to talk about what happened?"

I look at her. "I've always wanted to tell, and now that he's here, we can make sure he doesn't hurt anyone else."

You bitch, Scratch whispers. *You promised we'd never tell.*

I clench our jaw. *I lied. Shut up.*

"Is someone talking to you?" Dr. Zhao asks.

"Scratch is giving me grief for wanting to tell."

"So, you haven't discussed this with the rest of the system?"

"No, I did. I just didn't discuss it with Scratch." In the head space, a string of foul expletives are shouted at me. I ignore them. "Dylan is our primary concern. I want her to have some justice." Scratch can be as angry as she wants, but the rest of us are in agreement. Telling sets us on a course of healing, and we want to be better. We want Dylan to be better.

"How long have you had control of the body?"

"I've been fronting since late Saturday."

"You've had control for several days before."

"Not because she was afraid to come out." I slump in my chair. "What do I do?"

"I'm not sure there's anything you can do except be patient. Dylan blocked memories of what happened because they were too painful for her. Now, she's remembered what happened. You were already aware of these memories, but they're new to her. She needs time to accept and adjust. She needs your support, not pressure to return to the front."

I rub my fingers over our forehead. "I was afraid you'd say

that. Okay, how do I keep from freaking out and pressuring her?"

"Let's talk about your anxiety a bit. What's the worst thing that might happen if Dylan stays inside for a while?"

"She'll miss the chance to tell everyone what Travis is."

"She can do that when she comes out. There isn't a deadline for that, is there?"

"I guess not. I just want her to do it while he's here."

"Do you want to see him arrested?"

"I don't know. I want him to pay, so yeah, I suppose."

"What does Dylan want?"

"I don't know."

Her expression softens. "Maybe that's where you should start."

I really hate it when someone else knows what's best for us. Usually that falls on me or Dali. "I can't talk to her while I'm out—she won't respond to me—and I have to be out because of Scratch."

"Are you afraid Scratch might try something drastic again?"

"Yeah." That's pretty obvious, I think. "She can't take control from me, though."

"Why not?"

"I have no fucking idea. I just know she can't." I sigh. "Jennifer expects me to tell her everything when this session is over, but I don't feel like that's my place."

"Okay, tell her that. Perhaps you can explain that you would rather let Dylan explain, or let Dylan decide how much she wants to reveal."

"Could we do that together?" I ask, not the least bit ashamed.

Dr. Zhao leaves the room and comes back a few moments

later with Dylan's mother. Jennifer takes a seat next to me and gives me a comforting smile.

"Jennifer, Lannie respects your concern for Dylan and knows you only want to protect your daughter, but she feels revealing Dylan's secrets would be wrong of her. She thinks Dylan should be the one to tell you what she wants you to know about the past."

Dylan's mother gives me a sympathetic, slightly guilty look. "I admit, I'd been hoping maybe therapy would bring Dylan back out, or if not, that Lannie would share," Jennifer remarks. "What do you think, Doctor?"

"I agree with Lannie. It's very important to allow Dylan to do this at her own pace and as she sees fit. She had no control over what happened to her and so she ought to have complete control over how she deals with and shares it."

I'm so relieved that I could kiss Dr. Zhao. Kaz wouldn't mind.

Jennifer turns to me and offers me her hand. I take it. "Lannie, I don't want you to feel any pressure from me. That's not how I want our relationship to be. I want you to think of me as a friend and someone you can trust. Someone who will do all she can to keep *you* safe. You can talk to me about anything without any worry of repercussion."

"Thank you," I squeak as tears flood our eyes. "You have no idea how much that means to me." I swipe at the tears with my free hand.

She squeezes my fingers before letting go. "Dylan is my priority, but I realize that both of you understand this situation better than I do, and I'm willing to take your advice, even if it chafes my maternal instincts."

"Dylan just needs to deal," I explain. "Then she'll be back." I really hope I'm not lying to this woman, who has never been anything but kind to me my entire existence.

"Can I hug you?" Jennifer asks.

I practically throw the body into her arms. I need a hug. *We* need a hug. Her arms close tight around me, and I imagine strength and love pouring into me. Into the body. Into the head space.

I hope Dylan can feel it, too.

—

DYLAN

Hiding out in here is nice. I don't have to deal with anyone, don't have to face anything . . . It's actually a little boring. The time—when I'm aware of it—passes slowly, and it's really easy for me to avoid everyone. I know they want me to come out, though. It's like I've grown more aware of what they feel.

Christina hasn't stopped screaming. Alyss finally had to segregate her from the others because she was getting them wound up. So, while Alyss and Christina are gone, Dali is looking after the rest of the kids, which leaves Vincent in charge of the porch and overall security of the head space. Lannie is fronting, Monet is in the back with all the secrets, and Kaz . . . well, Kaz just wants to go out and bang the first person she finds—preferably someone who will treat the body like shit. If someone didn't need to watch Scratch, I think she'd do just that.

They feel like it would be better if I'd go back out front.

Well, I don't want to go. I'm tired of being the one in charge. I want to hide. That's what I tell myself, anyway.

I suppose I'd feel guilty for bailing on my friends and family if I thought they'd even notice I'm gone. Connor might, he hasn't spent as long thinking my alters are just moods. But honestly, I don't care if people notice or want me back. I need a fucking minute to process everything.

My uncle—*my hero*—abused me. My father's brother, who should have been my friend, my protector, hurt me in ways that can never be healed. He betrayed me, my father, and everyone else in the family who believed he was good. That he could be trusted. He destroyed my innocence, fractured my mind, and abused my body when I was most vulnerable.

I'm so angry I can't stop shaking. The others think I'm afraid, but that's not it. I *am* afraid, and I'm horrified by what Travis did to us, but most of all? I'm fucking pissed. I'm not afraid of what he'll do to me, I'm afraid of what I want to do to him.

I know what I should do—report his ass and tell everyone. But then what? *Maybe* he gets arrested? Let's say the police *actually* believe me and take him in. Let's pretend that no one thinks my DID makes me unreliable and they're all on my side. Finding out what Travis did would hurt Dad. It would hurt Mark.

And what if they don't believe me? What if Dad thinks I made it up, or that I'm confused? What if they hate me? What if they think it's my fault and blame me? What if Travis is set free because I'm just *some crazy girl*?

If my family turns against me, I won't know what to do.

But, if they believe me, I'll have to file charges. My mother is semi-famous. My father is current in Hollywood. Travis is well known in his field. It will get reported on at least a couple of news sites. Nothing ever goes away on the internet. Do I want that kind of exposure?

Yeah, that's all a pain in the ass, sure. But what I really want to do is kill him. I'm serious. I want to torture him to death, I'm that angry. And I don't really know if all that anger is mine, or if it belongs to the others, too.

So, I'm hiding, because I can't trust myself to do the right thing, and I don't know how much of my thoughts are mine. I want to hide until it goes away. Until he goes away, and it won't matter anymore.

The door to my room opens. Shit. I thought I'd locked it. Kaz stomps into the room wearing a pair of black shit-kicking boots.

"Get out of here," she commands. "You don't belong here."

"I belong here as much as you do." More, even. I built the stupid place.

"No. You don't. You belong out there. That's *your* job."

I can't argue with that, not really. I'm the host. It *is* my job to deal with daily life. "I needed a break."

"You're hiding. You may as well be dead."

I fold my arms over my chest. "No, Crazy, I may not."

"I'm not crazy. You're the one who split into different people because you couldn't handle it."

"I was a kid."

"You're not now, so stop hiding behind us."

Wow. That was a good hit. "You know, you could have made that point in a much less mean way."

"No, I don't think I could have."

Is that supposed to be a joke? "I don't want to deal with it," I tell her. "I don't want to see him. I don't want to have to pretend. I don't want to lie to my parents to protect them, or him. I'm happy letting one of you handle it."

"Lannie's covered your ass enough in the past. It's time for you to step up."

"Why?"

"Because we've protected you for fourteen years and you fucking owe us."

"*Seriously?*" All the anger in me is close to bubbling over. "I never asked for any of this. I never asked for any of you."

Kaz doesn't back down. "Actually, you did. Vincent wouldn't exist if you hadn't figured out that your uncle wouldn't hurt you if you were a boy. I wouldn't exist if you hadn't needed someone to deal with your guilt over sexuality. You may not have said the words out loud, but you asked for us, Dylan. Don't you ever forget that."

"Fine." Her words sting more than I want to admit. I guess we're both right. I didn't ask to split, but I asked for help. I just didn't ask the people I should have asked; I looked for it inside myself instead. A little kid doesn't know the right way to deal with that kind of crap. "What do you want me to do?"

She grabs me in a tight hug. For a second I'm stiff, surprised—then I hug her back. Strange how she feels solid and real. It's easy to forget she's not a physical person in the outside world.

"Walk out that door," she says, close to my ear. "And show him that you're not a scared little girl anymore. Don't let him have that power over us. Show him what we've become." She lets go of me.

When Kaz opens the door, I have a choice to make. I can

stay here and hide and fight with her, make myself a liar, or I can "step up," as she always says, and face the world. Face my fear and my rage.

Is it horrible that I'd really rather be a liar?

I sigh and walk out the door.

The moment I'm in the hall, I hear sounds from the outside world, muffled and distant. I walk toward them, down the stairs to the front door. Vincent is there, all chiseled and buff. He nods at me as he opens the door. I guess Kaz wanted to make sure I made it outside.

Or maybe she wanted me to know that my alters were with me every step of the way.

Lannie is on the other side. Her voice is louder than the other sounds. Once I cross the threshold, I'll be able to see what she's seeing, hear what she's hearing. I'll be able to take over, and she'll let me.

I hesitate in the doorway. Lannie knows I'm close. She's dissociating. I step out onto the porch. The wood crumbles away beneath my feet and the scene around me fragments as my consciousness slides against hers. For a second my two worlds—inner and outer—meld together and bleed through one another.

I blink and focus. I'm back in my body. I look up.

Dr. Zhao and my mother stare at me. Mom has that look on her face that means she's trying really hard not to cry. She squeezes one of my hands in hers. "Welcome back," she says.

I force a smile. "What did I miss?"

TWENTY-ONE

Wednesday night rolls around, like we knew and dreaded it would. We go to an Indian restaurant that we've gone to for years because they have the best vegetarian and vegan options for those who want them. And because the food is that good. It's one of my favorites and I'm not going to let anyone ruin it for me.

Mark drives us in. Izzy sits up front with him and I'm in the back. It's hard for me to pretend I'm not nervous, like there's nothing wrong.

"You're quiet, D," Izzy remarks when traffic slows us down. "You okay?"

"Just tired," I tell her.

"You've been tired a lot," Mark joins in. "Maybe you should see about something to help you sleep."

"I think I just need more exercise," I reply. I mean, it might help, who knows?

"We could go for a hike this weekend," Izzy suggests. And then, "Hey, how come your mom didn't come with us?"

"Dunno," Mark tells her. "She said she'd bring her own car."

Mom's been coming to the annual dinner since Mark and I turned ten, I think. It took a couple of years for her and Dad to be able to socialize without getting catty, but it was nice once it happened.

Traffic in the city isn't too bad. And it's right after rush hour, so we're able to find parking in a garage only a couple of blocks from the restaurant. I have to hand it to my brother for driving in Manhattan. I wouldn't do it. I would be triggered all over the place.

It's a chilly night, but nice. Warmer than it probably ought to be in early November. I love this time of year.

The restaurant is busy when we get there—mostly the members of our family who have already arrived. Our arrival is immediately met with a loud cheer that I can't help but smile at, especially when Bella runs up to say hello.

A few minutes later, Connor walks through the door, his cheeks flushed and hair tousled. The sight of him is grounding for us. I should probably be concerned at how attached we're getting to him, but I'm not. A lot of things scare me, but Connor's not one of them.

He walks straight toward me, that wide grin on his face. When he hugs me, there's a second when everything is fine. Great, even. He holds my hand while he says hello to those he knows and gets introduced to those he doesn't—like my cousin Vanessa and her boyfriend, Rob.

Maybe it's just me, but I feel like Vanessa wants to avoid

Uncle Travis, too. She stands with her back to him and keeps inching toward Rob. I don't look at Travis at all. To be honest, he doesn't seem to have that much interest in me either.

Is it weird that there's a part of me that's almost disappointed at his lack of attention? That after all he did to me, I would like to think it made me special, or something? Like I really was as incredible as he used to say? That I meant something to him? Instead, I realize I was just a way to scratch a shameful itch. I also realize that it really wasn't my fault. I wasn't some child seductress luring him into darkness, making him do unspeakable things. It was he who had the problem. He who should carry the guilt he tried to place on my small shoulders.

Connor knows, I can feel it. Maybe it's because he is special, or maybe it's because he's the outsider. He's new and everyone else has some sort of relationship with Travis or awareness of him as a good man. Connor doesn't have any preconceived misconceptions. He's able to see us all through a clear lens rather than a smudged filter.

"If you get overwhelmed or need to leave, let me know immediately," he tells me in a low voice.

I squeeze his hand. "It's okay, I'm good." For now. There are a few people close to the front. I'm not sure if they're here to watch, or if they're worried I'm going to bail, and someone will need to take over in a hurry. Or maybe, they're here for support. I'm not sure with all the noise. Regardless, Kaz won't mind if she has to take over—she loves Indian food.

The big surprise of the evening is that Mom brings a date! It's obvious from her posture and how she's glowing that she likes him. His name is Jake and he's a playwright, and it's obvious from the way he looks at my mom that he likes her back.

He's around her age, tall with reddish-brown hair and green eyes. He's really good-looking. It's funny, because Dad looks almost relieved to see Mom with someone, while Mark wears his indignant face. I have to laugh as I explain to Connor.

"It's not like we got to meet Angie before Dad started dating her. Mark didn't seem to mind that at all."

"Your brother sees himself as the man of the house, I guess," Connor offers. "He's protective of your mom."

"Mom is the last person who needs anyone to protect her."

"I don't know." He smiles a little. "I think we all like knowing someone's looking out for us. It means they care."

I glance at him. I have a lot of people looking out for me—including the ones in my head. I admit that I still have trouble thinking of them as individuals rather than imaginary friends. I may have created them, but they evolved on their own, and they do care about me, even if some of the ways they show it seem contradictory.

"Why do you keep staring at my uncle?" I ask.

Connor's smile fades. "Because I want to punch him in the face and I'm waiting for the right moment."

We stand there, staring into each other's eyes, the space around us our own little world. "No," I say, finally. "It's not wrong, but it's not something I'd want to explain to everyone here, either."

I can see the muscle clench underneath the skin of his jaw. "I understand. I'll wait until he's alone."

I'm not sure how he manages to make jokes but also be so aware of the seriousness of the situation. He seems to know how to keep me from getting stressed out, but also let me know that he's got my back.

It's nice having someone figure it out on their own and not force me to break my system's vow of silence. It's so goddamn nice to not have to carry this around inside and hide it. I don't want to talk about it, but I can, *if* I want. Really, it's just awesome having someone *see*.

"He outweighs you by a good sixty pounds," I remark. "Make sure you have a crowbar or something."

Connor shrugs. "He's also at least twenty years older than I am. Pretty sure I'm faster. But sure, a crowbar works. They must have a chair I could use out back."

I actually laugh, but I don't get a chance to reply because that's when Dad lets us know that our table's ready and we're taken into the private room he's booked for the evening.

It's one long table for all of us. Bella wants to sit across from me and Mark, so it's Connor, me, Mark, and Izzy on one side, and Uncle Travis, Bella, Dad, and Angie on the other. Great. Why couldn't he have sat somewhere else? Haven't we established that I'm not special anymore?

My heart seizes as if stabbed by a shard of ice. I may not be special, but Bella is.

Nonononononono.

Across the table I watch as Uncle Travis pretends to pull a quarter out of Bella's ear. She laughs in delight, a sound that makes my stomach spasm. The way he smiles at her slithers over my skin.

Just relax, I tell myself. *He's not doing anything wrong.*

"Dede, look!" my little sister cries, holding up the coin. "Uncle Trav hid this in my ear!"

I smile at her. "That's awesome, B!" Then, looking at him: "Uncle Trav is great at hiding things."

Did he just turn a little pale? Hard to tell beneath all that tan. I force my smile a little brighter. *Asshole.*

My cousin James sits next to Travis and he asks him a question about some work he did on a show in Prague. I don't mind that my uncle doesn't have to face me anymore, because it also means he can't focus on Bella either.

With my uncle distracted, Bella engages Connor in conversation. "Have you seen *Coco*?" she asks him. "It's got bone people in it."

"I haven't," he replies. "I heard it's good, though. Should I watch it?"

"Oh, yeah. You and Dede should watch it with me. I can sing all the songs, but I don't cry when the gramma dies."

I glance at Connor with a smile. "Spoiler alert." I am hyperaware of how much this kid means to me at this moment. At how far I'd go to keep her safe.

Menus get passed around for drinks, but dinner is a buffet based on items Dad requested. Bella holds my hand as we get in line to get plates.

"I'm going to see the Wicked Witch tomorrow," Bella announces.

"Right, you're going to see her onstage." Of course Dad scored orchestra seats for *Wicked*. "You're going with Dad and your mom?"

"And Uncle Travis." She beams up at me. "He's my date."

My stomach lurches. "That's great, B. You're going to love the show. It's one of my favorites."

I don't take much food, even though Indian is one of my top fives. Mentally and emotionally, being around my uncle isn't as bad as I thought it would be, but he definitely has a physical effect on me. My stomach feels like I'm on a carnival ride. He can't hurt her in a crowded theater, right?

Christ, what if he already has hurt her? I almost choke on the food in my mouth.

Sometime during dinner, I happen to glance across the table and see Uncle Travis lean down to say something to Bella. He puts his hand on her shoulder.

I feel the weight and heat of his fingers, feel the bite of his grip. He used to touch me like that. Sometimes he'd do it before leading me off somewhere for "special time," or he'd do it if he thought I might say something, although those times he'd use more force.

I blink as the memory tears through my brain, put there by Monet's home movies. Suddenly, I feel a shift inside.

No, says Scratch. *No fucking way.* Her rage floods my mind like fire from a flamethrower.

I get up and walk around the table. Stopping by my uncle, I bend down. "Hey, Trav," I say in a low voice.

He looks up at me. Bella's talking to Connor, who keeps looking at me out of the corner of his eye.

"Take your fucking hand off her."

His eyes widen, but he does what I—with the help of Scratch—say.

No one else heard me. No one else will.

"You're not going to do to her what you did to me, asshole. I'm going to make sure of that." I give his shoulder a good squeeze before heading off to the bathroom, where my trembling knees finally give out.

I think I love you, I whisper to Scratch as I hold on to the sink and get my legs underneath me again.

It's about fucking time, she replies. And then she's almost laughing. *Did you see the look on his face?*

I smile before splashing a little cold water on my cheeks. Then I use the facilities and take a few seconds to compose myself before returning to our table.

Connor looks up at me questioningly as I sit down. I squeeze his hand. "I'm good," I tell him. Then I notice that Uncle Travis's seat is empty. Thankfully, Bella is still in hers.

"Hey, what are you doing tomorrow?" Angie asks me as she taps a spoonful of rice onto her plate.

"No plans, why?"

"We have tickets for *Wicked* and Travis had to bail. Want to come with us? Bella says it's your favorite."

Suddenly, my appetite returns, and I smile. "I'd love to."

———

There's a piece of me that doesn't want to ruin Uncle Travis's life. I don't know why I feel like he deserves that consideration, but I do. Regardless, I can't let him hurt Bella the same way. I can't let him hurt any other kids. Who knows how many other little girls he's abused? It would be naive of me to think I was the only one. I probably wasn't even the first.

I have to tell.

I know it's the right thing to do because Scratch hasn't even kicked up a fuss. She wants to protect my sister—and other possible little girls—as much as I do. Not even the threat of what will happen if we tell is enough to cow her into submission. But she might change her mind, so I have to act fast.

On Friday, the day Bella goes to visit with her cousins, I

ask everyone to meet me at the house so I can tell them what's been going on. Do I want to do it? Nope. In fact, I'm really hoping either Lannie or Dali will come out and take over for me so I don't have to deal.

But that doesn't happen. So, with my family and Izzy gathered in the living room, I sit on the edge of one of the big armchairs.

"I know you have all wondered what happened to me to cause me to develop DID," I begin, my voice trembling. I dig my nails into my palms to help steady my nerves. "And I— I'm finally ready to tell you. I was sexually abused as a child. By Uncle Travis."

All the color drains from my father's face. Mark looks like I hit him with a brick. "What?" His voice is small, shocked.

Mom comes and sits beside me, reaching between our chairs for my hand. Her fingers are warm around mine and I cling to them.

Dad protests, but Angie stops him with a hand on his leg. He puts his hand over hers and looks at me. He's wrecked. Confused. Pissed. I don't feel like any of it is directed at me, and even if it was, that's his problem, not mine.

Taking a deep breath, I tell them that Uncle Travis began abusing me when I was five, and it continued for a brief time after the divorce. I don't give much in the way of specifics— they don't need those details in their minds.

"This is what caused me to develop alters," I explain. "It's why I don't have many memories of being little."

"Oh my God," Mom whispers, pressing her hand to her mouth. She turns toward me. "My sweet girl. I'm so sorry."

There are tears in her eyes, and pain and regret in every

line of her face. If she hugs me I'll lose it, and I can't do that, so I hold her at arm's length. "I know, Mom. Thank you."

"Why didn't you tell us?" Dad asks, his voice raw. His face drawn and pale.

Angie leans into him, but her focus is on me. There's love and support in her gaze.

I swallow. "He told me you'd all hate me and that I'd get in trouble. That he'd get in trouble." I frown. "I didn't tell because he told me not to, and I trusted him."

"My brother." Dad shakes his head. "He's my brother. I can't believe he'd do something so . . . monstrous. Sweetie, is it possible—"

"Don't you dare, Eric," Mom interrupts, voice shaking with anger. "Don't you question her. She was doing okay before he showed up. The morning after the party, she was someone else. She didn't come back for days because of him. I bet this is why Marsha left him."

Marsha? I remember the name. She was my uncle's girl-friend years ago, but they broke up.

She had a daughter.

"I'm sorry, Dad," I say. "But it's true. I remember most of it now, and when I saw him with Bella at the restaurant the other night, I knew I couldn't let him do the same thing to her."

"Bella," Angie whispers, horrified. "He's been alone with her."

Dad jumps to his feet and bolts from the room. A few seconds later we hear the muffled sounds of retching from the bathroom down the hall.

"I don't think he's done anything," I tell her. "But I recognized his behavior."

Poor Angie hugs herself. She's so pale I think she might be sick as well. But not my mother; Mom looks mad as hell.

I look at Mark. He seems as astounded and angry as everyone else.

"Did you know?" I ask him, throat tight.

Mark's eyes widen, and his mouth falls opens. For a second, he just stares at me, horrified. "No. Fuck no. How can you even ask me that?"

"Because you always hated me for getting his attention."

"I was a jealous kid. If I'd known what he did to you . . ." Tears fill his eyes. "I would have told, D. I wouldn't have let him do it!"

Izzy puts her arm around him, but his gaze stays on me. "I didn't know," he whispers.

I nod. I believe him. My brother has his faults, but he wouldn't have let it happen. He would have told. God, I wish things had gone that way.

"What do you want to do?" Mom asks me.

"I don't want to cause trouble," I whisper. Fuck, that's not me, it's one of the kids. Gritting my teeth, I fumble for my paintbrush, my thumb stroking the bristles while my other hand clings to Mom. I'm not going to switch out. I can't.

"You're not, sweet girl. You're not. Whatever you do will be the right thing."

If I let him walk away, he'll do it to another kid, and another and another. He'll be a monster until the day he dies. When I was little, I didn't know that, but I know it now. If I don't do something, the next little girl he hurts is on me.

I glance at Izzy. She gives me a half smile and blows me a

kiss. She's got my back. She'd tell me to make sure my uncle never gets to hurt anyone ever again.

"I want to call the police," I tell Mom. "I want to make sure he doesn't do this to anyone else."

I've already looked it up. Even though the abuse happened when we were living in Connecticut, he can still be arrested in New York.

Mom takes her cell phone out of her sweater pocket and stands up. She walks a few feet away to make the call. Izzy comes to me in her absence. I stand up and we hug. She holds me so tight I think my spine might crack.

"I'm proud of you," she whispers. "Whatever you need, I've got you. You know that, right?"

"Does Mark hate me?" I hate the whiny sound of my voice. It's one of the littles again. I'm dangerously close to switching out, and I do not want to be a child when the police get here. It's going to be bad enough having to explain my situation to them.

"No, of course not!" She shakes her head as she pulls back so I can see the disbelief on her face. "If anything, he thinks you hate him for not seeing what was going on."

"He was only a kid."

"You both were." Taking me by the hand, she pulls me over to where Mark sits. He looks at me for a second. I don't know which one of us moves first, but the next thing I know we're hugging each other like our lives depend on it. A few moments later, my father—smelling of toothpaste—joins, putting his arms around us. Then Angie, and finally my mother, once she's done with her call. Mark and I pull Izzy into the group as well.

Inside my head space, I feel something similar happening. One by one, the alters I know embrace each other outside my reach, but close enough to let me know they're there. I no longer feel like switching, though, grounded by my family and best friend.

For the first time in my life, I feel safe and protected. Supported. Like everything's going to be okay.

TWENTY-TWO

By the time the police leave, I'm exhausted and dissociating all over the place. Even my poor broken paintbrush is having a hard time keeping me grounded.

I expected the police interview to be a clusterfuck, to be honest. I figured once my DID diagnosis came out they'd call me a nutjob, pack up, and leave. That's not what happened.

The detective who came by deals with cases of child sexual abuse. She told me that straightaway, as we sat alone in Mom's office. I'm not the first case of DID that she's seen, and she's accustomed to people who remember childhood abuse having spotty memories.

"You don't have to prove yourself to me," she assured me. "Just tell me everything you can remember."

So, I did, repeating to her what I told to my family, and then some. I told her details of what he did. She had no reaction to the horrific things I shared but an expression of sympathy. Sometimes, it's better telling these things to a stranger.

We probably talked for at least an hour as she took my statement and asked me questions. Then she talked to Mom and Dad and Angie.

"If you can talk to your daughter and make sure he hasn't made overtures toward her, that would be appreciated," Detective Fulton tells them. She has her notebook in her hands. "And can you give me the name of that former girlfriend again? Marsha? Do you have contact information for her?"

Once she leaves, Dad and Angie aren't long leaving as well. Angie wants to be with Bella, and I don't blame her.

"I don't want to leave you," Dad says when he hugs me goodbye. "Are you going to be okay?"

"I'm good," I tell him, and I mean it. A part of me— probably Alyss—figures that what's been done is done. They can't fix it, but if Travis has done anything to Bella, they can help her. They can make sure she doesn't turn out like me.

Not that I'm all that bad. I mean, how many people get their own built-in support group? We just have to work on the memory loss and set up some boundaries and we're going to be something else. I have to believe that, and for the most part I do.

Mark and Izzy hover over me like a couple of hens after Dad and Angie leave. It's sweet, but I'm over it.

"I'm going to take a bath," I tell Mom. "I'll take the baby monitor in with me." Although I really doubt Scratch is going to try anything. The secret's out and she seems okay with it.

I fill the tub with hot water and a mix of soothing oils and submerge myself up to my chin, leaning my head back. I've missed this.

The wounds on my arms have closed up, the skin pink and healthy. I've already started working on tattoo designs to cover them.

I fall asleep in the bath. I don't dream. I jerk awake almost an hour later with the water lukewarm and my skin shriveled.

Once I get out of the tub, I towel off and dress in a soft, fuzzy sweater, leggings, and fuzzy socks. I feel like a cozy Muppet. I could take a nap, but the one I just had has jacked me up enough to know I won't fall asleep anytime soon. I go downstairs and find Mom sitting at the kitchen counter, sipping a cup of tea.

"Water's hot," she tells me.

I make a mug of chai and sit down across from her. She gives me a tired smile, her eyes crinkling at the corners. "With your hair up like that it reminds me of when you went through your Eliza Bennett phase. Do you remember that?"

"Mr. Darcy rocked my world." I take a sip of tea. It's hot and spicy as it goes down, and I shiver.

"I always liked him." She reaches over and takes one of my hands in hers. "How are you doing?"

"I'm good." Getting a little tired of being treated like I'm fragile, but I don't tell her that. "You?"

"I've been better," she replies, surprising me with her honesty. "I'll be good once Travis has been arrested."

"Can we not talk about it? I'm so tired of it."

"Sure. What would you like to talk about? Connor?"

"Why don't you tell me about Jake?" That's the guy she had with her at the dinner. "Is he Mr. Darcy material?"

She blushes a little. How sweet is that? "I'm not sure. I think so. I like spending time with him."

"Is he funny?"

"Very funny. And smart. And nice." She smiles and raises her cup to her lips. "And a good kisser."

I laugh. "But does he have his own estate?"

"He has an apartment in the Village that's paid for."

"Close enough." Manhattan real estate is ridiculous. "I'm happy for you, Mom. You deserve someone nice."

"Thank you, sweetie. So do you." She takes a drink. "Is Connor as nice as he seems?"

I nod. "I think so. Either that or he's into crazy girls."

"*Dylan.*"

"Okay, okay. I take it back." I laugh. "Yeah, he's really great. You know, he can tell when I'm not me?"

She frowns. "He can?"

"Yeah. I guess it's because my alters don't really feel like they need to protect me anymore? I don't know. But he always knows."

"I suppose that makes sense. I just assume you're always you, because even when you're different, I recognize it as what I believe to be you. Does that make sense?"

"Barely," I say with a laugh. "They're getting more and more comfortable with switching out and being themselves. They'll probably start telling you."

"Well, Lannie seems perfectly lovely."

"Yeah, she's cool. Where are Mark and Izzy?"

"They're in his room. Your brother was pretty upset."

I run my finger around the rim of my cup. "He blames himself."

"We all do, sweetie. I'm surprised you *don't* blame us."

And for that reason, I will never, ever tell her how Scratch came to be. Never reveal what Scratch looks like. "I just don't. Okay, change of subject. I'm sick of talking about this stuff. I'm sorry, but I can't do it anymore."

"You know what? You should go out."

I raise my brows. "Excuse me? Where the hell am I supposed to go?"

"Why don't you see if Connor wants you to go to his place? Or, I'll get you a hotel room—go be somewhere else. Take a mini vacation from this."

I stare at her. Has she lost her mind?

"You want me to go spend the night with my boyfriend."

"I want you to be somewhere you're not reminded about this every waking moment. I want you to have five minutes of wonder and special."

I can't believe she's even suggesting it—she who got a baby monitor so she could hear me if I needed help. But . . . it's a good idea. I glance at the clock. It's only four. Maybe Connor doesn't have plans for the evening, or maybe he wouldn't mind if I invite myself along.

I pick up my phone and start typing.

"But don't tell your brother," Mom says, sipping her tea. "I'll handle him."

Mom has never had a lot of hang-ups when it comes to sex. She sat both Mark and me down at fifteen and gave us "the talk," which included telling us—in graphic detail—about a friend of hers who got venereal warts from a famous actor, and why we should always use condoms. She took us for testing, got me birth control. Kaz must have loved it.

My phone dings. I glance down at the screen.

Connor: What time do you want me to pick you up?

—

Connor picks me up around six. I told him I could take the train in, but he and Mom seem more comfortable with him coming to get me.

Mom was right. I need a little distance between me and my family right now. I'm so overwhelmed by all of the emotions. I don't want to talk about it, and they need to, so if I'm not there, they don't have to worry about me overhearing. I don't want to be part of that. I've told them what they need to know. I'll keep the rest to myself or save it for therapy. They're the ones who need to process.

Right now, what I want is to be with someone who doesn't have any guilt over it, and won't inadvertently make my trauma about them. They don't mean to do it, but I know Dad has to be wondering how his baby brother could do this to *him*? To *his* child? According to the very sage voice of Dali, it's human nature.

Mom, Mark, and Izzy can share their feelings with each other, and I can maybe have a few hours of normalcy. And Mark and Izzy can have a night together without worrying if I'm a third wheel.

I'm nervous when I get into Connor's car. This will be the first time I've stayed at his place as me and not Lannie. It's the first time I've stayed anywhere other than home since getting out of the hospital. It feels like we're taking our relationship to another level, and I guess we are. We haven't talked about Travis since I told Connor what happened, and I appreciate that he isn't suddenly treating me differently. I mean, he'd already figured out what I'd gone through, so me verifying it didn't change anything.

He won't let me pay for gas, so I offer to buy him dinner instead. We park at his apartment and take my stuff upstairs before walking a couple of blocks to a little Vietnamese—a shared favorite—restaurant. It smells delicious when we walk in, and the waitress smiles and calls Connor by name. She tells us to sit at a table near the back and brings us a pot of tea.

It's a cold night, so we both order spring rolls and pho.

"Thanks for letting me stay with you tonight."

He folds his arms on top of the table and gives me a little smile. "You can stay with me whenever you want. That goes for any of your inner posse, too."

I smile. "My inner posse?"

He shrugs. "'System' seems so clinical. 'Posse' sounds fun."

"If you say so. Are you disappointed you're getting me and not Vincent?"

"No offense to Vincent—he's great to share a blanket with—but I'd rather spend the night with you."

I know how he means it, but there's an unmistakable sexual implication in the phrase. I swallow. "Good to know."

Connor is oblivious to how my stomach has tied itself in knots at the idea of getting physical with him. All we've done up to this point is make out. It's just now occurring to me that maybe he has expectations as to what's going to happen between us tonight.

It's okay, Lannie whispers. *He's not that kind of guy, remember? He's safe.*

Of course he is. I know that. But . . . what if I'm that kind of girl? What if I want to have sex with him? What if I want something good and sweet and someone of my choosing to cleanse what's happened to me in the past?

Our food comes out quickly and I dump hot sauce and hoisin in my soup before snapping up bean sprouts and tearing up leaves to sprinkle on top.

"Oh my God, this is good," I praise after slurping down the first mouthful.

He winds noodles around his chopsticks. "Right? Told you you'd like it."

"I think this is the best pho I've ever had."

"I come here at least once a week. Jess makes fun of me for it."

"Will she be at your place tonight?" The idea of seeing her again makes me a little nervous.

"She's at her boyfriend's. She says hi, though." He smiles a little. "And she hopes to be home before you have to leave tomorrow."

Okay, so we're going to be totally alone. That's good. No added stress means less chance of me switching out. Co-consciousness is okay, but I'd rather not alter-jump if I can help it. Not just because of the amnesia that comes with it, but also the headache.

I feel like I'm actually sloshing when we get up to leave, so I'm grateful for the walk back to the apartment. Once we're inside, Connor pops a game in the PS4 and hands me a controller.

We play a racing game that I absolutely suck at but is stupidly fun. I spend most of my turn laughing and trying to get my on-screen car out of the bushes I've driven it into. It's mindless fun and exactly what I need.

After the racing game we spend an hour hunting zombies in a game that, while incredibly gory, is insanely well rendered.

"Look at that anatomy," I say, pointing at a shambling brain-eater. "That's amazing."

"She's going to eat your face if you don't shoot her," Connor advises. So, I shoot her, much to my dismay.

After games we look for a movie on Netflix and talk about graphic novels and art.

"You know, it might be fun for us to work on something together," he says. It's not the first time he's brought it up.

"Or, it might drive us to kill each other." Seriously, I've seen joint projects ruin relationships.

"But think of how fun it would be up until that point."

We find a movie and cuddle on the couch. His shoulder is warm and solid beneath my head. He's hands-down my favorite person to cuddle with.

And he smells good. Everything about him is good. Being this close to him makes every nerve ending I have tingle and burn—in a good way.

I didn't need to be anxious about him wanting to have sex—turns out *I* am the one itching to make a move. What if I do and he turns me down? Like, what if he thinks I'm too fragile or something?

Just kiss him, you idiot. He's not going to say no. Anyone with half a brain can see how much he's into you.

I smile. I should have known Kaz wouldn't be far. *I want this,* I tell her. *I want it and I'm terrified. Will you help me?*

I got you, Boo, she replies. *I'll be there with you. Promise I won't watch.* She chuckles as she settles in beside me. She's not quite co-fronting, but she's there. It's like she's mentally holding my hand, but not sharing the experience.

So, I make my move. I start by kissing his neck and moving my way up to his jaw. He turns his head and covers my mouth with his. He has the softest lips.

I could probably list half a dozen reasons why I want/need him the way I do, but I don't. Instead, I pull him down with me as I lie back on the sofa. The lean length of his body settles on top of mine, and I slip my hands beneath his shirt, touching the warm, smooth skin of his back.

We're both breathing a little faster. Connor kisses my neck and I shiver. I press my hips up into his and he gasps softly against my jaw. He kisses me again and our bodies move together in a way that's delicious and frustrating. Finally, I grab his hand and guide it down between us.

"Tell me if you need me to stop," he whispers against my lips.

"I will," I say. It's not like I haven't done this before. Of course, I don't remember most of those times.

He pushes up onto his elbow as he unfastens my jeans and slides his hand inside. His gaze is locked on mine and I can't look away. We don't have sex. He just touches me and kisses me and holds me and tells me how beautiful I am. He doesn't pressure me to reciprocate, though I do. I can't help myself. A couple of times he wraps his fingers around my wrist and guides my hand away, placing it on his back or at my side before turning his attention back to me.

I've made myself orgasm before, so it's not like it's something I've never experienced, but oh, *fuck*—it's something else entirely when someone else does it. I shudder and shake as Connor kisses my face and shivers at the noises I make.

I open my eyes when he kisses me, and as he comes into focus, I realize Kaz isn't here. Somewhere during that incredible buildup, she slipped away and let me experience it on my own. I'm so grateful for that, and for Connor's sweetness, that tears fill my eyes.

He wipes away the ones that spill over.

"I want to do something for you," I murmur.

"I'm okay," he tells me. "I liked being here for you."

But he doesn't stop me when I unfasten his jeans. "I don't expect anything," he tells me. "You don't have to—"

I cut him off with a kiss. "I *want* to." And I do. When I touch him, he stops protesting, and I watch the changes in expression flicker over his beautiful face.

Afterward, we lie together, arms around each other, just kissing and idly touching whatever bare skin we can find. We might not have had actual sex, but it feels pretty damn significant all the same. I wonder how many people take for granted being present for every moment of their lives? I've lost so many of mine—a lot of which I'm thankful to have lost.

"You okay?" he asks.

He's so good. Sweet and nice. I'm thankful the world has people like him in it. I wish there was one of him for every person like me, but I know there's not, and it makes me feel very, very lucky.

"I'm good," I say, and I kiss him again.

—

The next morning, I wake up in Connor's bed for the second time, but I remember every detail from the night before.

After our "almost sex" we messed around some more

before getting up and going in search of food. We sat in the living room and watched TV while eating cold pizza. We stayed up until 2:00 A.M., and when I started dozing off, Connor helped me off the sofa and waltzed me to his bedroom.

I had the best sleep I've had in weeks snuggled up against him. No dreams, no nightmares. No waking up wondering where I am or feeling lost. I wake up feeling happy and relaxed. Almost giddy.

Connor's awake and watching me with a smug smile.

"You look way too pleased with yourself," I tell him.

"I am way too pleased with myself," he replies before kissing me, slow and deep. I don't even care if I have morning breath—that's how far gone I am where he's concerned.

We make waffles for breakfast and a pot of coffee.

"I eat a lot when I'm with you," I remark.

"Eat as much as you want. I don't care. I like it."

I'm pretty sure that makes Kaz scream inside, but I smile regardless. I have enough issues without adding food to the mix. Let's leave that alone.

After breakfast, we sit together on opposite ends of the sofa, our legs entwined in the middle. He writes on his laptop while I draw in my sketchbook. Occasionally, I poke him with my toes, forcing him to pay attention to me.

You're so needy, Kaz teases.

She's right, so I don't argue. I just smile and poke him again. Grinning, he closes his computer and sets it on the floor. I put aside my drawing supplies and meet him in the middle of the couch. We kiss like we haven't seen each other in months. I don't remember having this kind of connection with anyone before.

We end up in his bed, and this time, I'm ready to take things further than we did last night. Honestly, I don't know if it's me or if it's Kaz who wants more, and I'm not sure it really matters. What matters is that I'm present for it—all of it. I feel Connor against me and inside me and I can touch him and kiss him and be there for every moment of it. There's no disconnect.

Afterward, I bury my face in his chest to hide the tears that fill my eyes. I don't want to be one of those girls who get emotional, but this is really special for me. I also don't want him to know that, because I'm afraid it will scare him away.

"I have to meet my granddad for coffee," he tells me a little while later, when we're getting dressed. "Do you want to come? I can drive you home if not."

It's the first time he's mentioned me meeting anyone in his family. "Sure," I say. I don't want this to end yet. I'm not ready to return to reality. "If you don't mind."

"Wouldn't have asked if I did. I have to warn you, though, Gramps thinks he's a charmer. He'll flirt with you, but don't take it seriously. He thinks it's fun. If it makes you uncomfortable, let me know."

"I'm not that fragile," I tell him with a wry smile. "An old man being flirty isn't going to send me over the edge."

"I don't think you're fragile. I think *he's* starved for attention."

When I meet Patrick O'Brien, I see what Connor means. His grandfather has been incredibly lonely since losing his wife two years ago. He tells me about her between bouts of old-fashioned flirtation and teasing. I like him immediately. Both of my grandfathers are loving and kind, but Mom's dad is really quiet, and Dad's father is a football nut. Neither of them has ever been eager to engage me in conversation, though I'm well aware they love me.

Mr. O'Brien wants to talk and be talked to, and he doesn't give a sweet damn what we talk about. And he's not terribly concerned about being politically correct, but it's not because he's an asshole. He's just out there—if that makes sense.

"Do you cook, Dylan?" he asks me. "Because I'm hoping you can fatten the boy up a bit."

I arch a brow. "Sir, have you seen how he eats? If he's not fattened up yet, it's not going to happen."

"So, you don't cook, then?"

"Nothing you'd want to eat."

He laughs as if it's the funniest thing he's ever heard. He and Connor have the same eyes and the same unselfconscious laughter. "My wife could burn water," he confides. "It was one of the things that drove me crazy about her. And one of the things I miss most."

"How long were you married?" I ask.

He gives me a sad, sweet little smile. "Not long enough."

God, he breaks my heart. It's pretty obvious to me now where Connor gets his goodness. Turns out Mr. and Mrs. O'Brien lived in the apartment Connor now has when they first got married. That sentimentality is what made him buy the building when it came up for sale years later.

When we leave, Patrick hugs me. This is after he makes us let him pay for our coffee. "It was nice to meet you, Dylan. My grandson doesn't usually trust me to meet his lady friends. Thinks I'm going to run off with them."

I smile. Nice of him to tell me that he hasn't met many

of Connor's girlfriends. "I don't blame him, Mr. O'Brien. I wouldn't trust you either."

More laughter. "Call me Paddy. I hope to see you again soon, dear."

"Me too." And I mean it.

"Was he too much?" Connor asks when we're in the car.

"He's adorable," I reply. "You're right, he's lonely."

"Gram was his world."

"How did she die?" When he hesitates, I continue, "I'm sorry. Never mind."

"No, it's okay." He checks traffic before making a right turn. "She got dementia about a year before she died. It progressed pretty quickly, and we knew she would have to go into a home, but before we even found a place she took a fall and broke her hip." He shook his head. "She didn't last long after that. I think . . . I think she knew what was coming and wanted to still be her when she died. He was with her at the end. So was I."

I press my hand against my chest to ease the sudden tightness there. "Oh, my God. Connor, that's . . . I'm so sorry."

He gives me a sad smile. "Yeah, it sucked, but it was what she wanted, y'know?"

I don't know what to say, so I don't say anything. Instead I rest my hand on his thigh. I keep it there until we pull into my driveway.

He comes in long enough to say hi to Mom and Mark, and then leaves. He's got work for class tomorrow. I walk him to the door and kiss him goodbye.

"I'll talk to you tomorrow?" he asks.

I nod. "You can talk to me whenever you want."

He smiles and kisses me again. Then he's gone, and with him all his magic. Sighing, I close the door and join Mom and Mark in the living room, where they're waiting for me.

"So?" I ask. "What did I miss?"

"The police arrested Travis," Mom informs me. "He told them he didn't know what they were talking about."

Mark's jaw clenches. "He said that you were a 'troubled little girl' who needs help."

Mom looks at him like she wishes he hadn't told me that. It doesn't bother me. "I am," I reply. "And it's all his fault."

"Then," my mother continues, "they told him that they talked to Marsha, who revealed how her daughter, Cassie, told her Travis had touched her when she was younger. That's when he asked for his lawyer."

Mark jumps in. It's like they rehearsed this or something, the way they're sharing dialogue. "After that, the asshole admitted to everything. He changed his story and suddenly he became the sick one who needed help." Rage and disgust thicken his voice.

"Whatever," I say with a shrug. "I don't care." Don't care what he says, or how he tries to cover his tracks. He has no power over me anymore.

I have so much to tell Dr. Zhao in our next session.

I do a little searching on Google later. Turns out pedophilia is considered a mental disorder. Uncle Travis really *is* sick. That's so unfair. He shouldn't get to play that card, and I really, really don't want to have anything in common with him. I don't want to feel sympathy for him, but I do, a little, because of that disconnect where the abuse I suffered is concerned. It doesn't feel like it happened to me, and that allows me to feel for him, until I remember and get mad all over again.

It's going to take me a while to work through that, I think.

Mom sticks her head in my doorway that night when I'm in bed, reading to my headmates.

"Did you have a nice time at Connor's?" she asks.

My face turns hot. Can she tell? "Yeah," I say, voice hoarse. "I did. I met his grandfather this afternoon."

"Oh, how lovely. I'm glad you had fun, sweetie. You should invite Connor for dinner Saturday night. He can stay over if he wants."

"Who are you and what have you done with my mother?"

"I can't let Izzy stay with Mark and not let Connor stay with you. What kind of mother would I be?"

"Maybe you should invite Jake for dinner. He can stay over, too. We can all get some."

I'm not sure, but I think she blushes. "This is where I say good night. Love you."

I smile. "Love you, too." She blows me a kiss and closes my door. I turn back to my book and pick up where I left off. Inside me, there's a lightness I haven't felt for a while—a hopefulness.

I hope it lasts.

TWENTY-THREE

Dear Dylan,

 Alyss, here. I'm going to try to give you as many details about what happened as I can. I know only what Darla told me and what little I saw myself, being up front enough to keep an eye on her.

So, last night we went to visit your father and Angie at their hotel, as you probably remember. Bella wanted to show us her dolls, which caught Darla's attention and triggered a switch. Your sister was absolutely delighted to have someone to play with and she and Darla had a lovely hour of Barbie hijinks before your father's phone rang. I don't know who it was that called, or what they said, but your father was _very_ upset by the conversation. He came into Bella's room where the girls were playing and told them to stop.

"You need to go home," he told Darla. "You need to go _now_."

This scared Darla, who was afraid she'd done something wrong, and she began to cry. Your father didn't know what to do with us then, so he called your mother, told her what happened, and demanded she come get you. He still hadn't realised that "you" weren't you. And can I say that, while his grief and shock can excuse that to an extent, I still think he's a fucking git for not seeing that it was obviously a small child in control of the body. I see where Mark gets his bouts of insensitivity and boorish behaviour.

But I digress. Darla's distress brought me closer to the front and into co-consciousness so I was able to soothe her and take partial control. With Bella and the dolls still present, I wasn't able to wrest her away completely, plus she's a nosy little thing. Regardless, here's what transpired next:

We continued to play dollies with Bella until your mother arrived. It seemed to take forever for her to appear, but I suppose that was compounded by my sharing the front with a six-year-old and really wanting to get the hell out of there.

As soon as Darla saw Jennifer, she quieted and receded into the inner space, allowing me to take full control. I'm not that comfortable out front, as you know, but I assumed you'd take control soon. I packed up our things, gave Bella a hug, and got the bloody hell out of there, because frankly, your father gives me the shits.

Once in the car and on our way out of Manhattan, your mother asked if I was okay. I introduced myself and expressed my confusion as to what had even happened. She took it in stride, brilliant creature that she is. That's when she advised me of the night's events.

"Dylan's uncle attempted suicide," she explained.

"Travis?" I asked for clarification. (I have no idea how many siblings either of your parents have.)

"Yes," she replied. "They found him in his cell. He's in the hospital now."

When I enquired as to his methods, she told me she didn't have all the details. I expressed my disappointment, which may have disconcerted her somewhat. Please extend my apologies if so. I did advise her that my lack of any sort of familial feeling for the bastard prevented me from mourning his condition in any way, shape, or form. She seemed to understand this and told me she didn't plan to cry over him either. I do quite like your mother.

So, there you go, that's the extent of what I know. When we arrived at the house, I came immediately to your room to write this down. Now that I have done that, I am going to attend to the list of nightly ablutions you have detailed elsewhere and prepare the body for rest. I hope that if you have not returned to the front by the time I put us to bed that you will be here by morning. Let me know if the bastard makes it.

—

I'm digging through a drawer looking for the s'more tongs when Izzy arrives on Saturday. She came over early so we could hang out without the guys. It's important to us to still have our friend time, and I appreciate it more than she could ever know.

She gives me a hug and helps me put everything together so we can make s'mores later.

"It's going to be cold on the beach," she comments.

"I'm going to build a fire in the pit on the patio," I tell her, because she's right—the beach will be too cold, and it's also a pain to lug everything down there.

"Is your mom's boyfriend joining?"

I grin. "For dinner. Not sure what their plans are for the evening. I think I freaked her out when I suggested they stay here, too."

She laughs. "Perv." Her smile fades. "So, what's the word?"

I shrug. "He's alive, but now his lawyers are concerned about his mental state. Doesn't matter. It's not up to me anymore—I was a minor and the state doesn't fuck around with that stuff."

"Good. I hope he ends up in gen pop."

I can't help but smile at her slang. "Look at you knowing all the lingo."

Izzy shakes her head. "I don't know how you can be so relaxed about it."

I think about it, choosing my words. "Because even though I know it happened to me, to my body, I still don't have a lot of those memories. I guess it allows me to stand back a bit. My main concern is keeping him away from Bella. And other girls. Any punishment he gets is icing."

From the way she looks at me I can tell she doesn't quite get it. "Okay. I got the update. New topic." Her eyes sparkle. "I haven't seen you since you spent the night at Connor's . . ."

I flush. "No fair. I don't ask about your sex life."

"Because I'm sleeping with your brother."

"Ugh!" I cry, covering my ears with my hands. "Lalalala!"

She pulls my hands away and holds them, her dark eyes twinkling. "Seriously, D. Are you okay?"

"I'm better than okay," I tell her. "Connor and I are good. Like, better than I ever expected."

Her face lights up with interest. "Really? That good?"

My face is already hot, so who cares. "Better." We giggle a little. Seriously, I never thought of myself as a giggler. Of course, a few months ago I wouldn't have thought of myself as multiple either. I thought my brain was defective; now I know it's just . . . compartmented.

"I'm so happy for you," Izzy says, giving my hands a squeeze before letting go.

"What are we happy about?" Mark asks as he saunters into the room. He's wearing sweatpants and a Henley and somehow he still looks like he crawled out of a catalog, the ass. Meanwhile, my hair's puffed up like a mound of cotton candy on top of my head.

My brother grins at me as he tugs on a strand of it. "You look like one of those troll dolls."

I snap at him with a pair of tongs. "You smell like a troll."

Connor arrives a few minutes later, followed shortly after by Jake. The six of us decide what takeout we want, and Mom places the order; then we play a board game while we wait. Turns out Jake is very competitive.

Turns out so is Lannie, and she and I take turns switching in and out throughout the evening depending on what's going on. It gives me a low-grade headache, but it's worth it. The last time I switch, I find myself in the bathroom brushing my teeth, dressed for bed, the smell of woodsmoke clinging to my hair. Connor is in my room, making a bed on the floor.

"What are you doing?" I ask.

He looks up. He's wearing track pants and a T-shirt.

"Lannie was out," he explains, blinking. "I was going to give her the bed."

"Well, she's gone now, and it's not like you haven't shared a bed with her before."

"I know, but it felt . . . weird." He shrugs. "I don't mind taking the floor if you want."

"You're not sleeping on the floor."

I finish in the bathroom, then let him do what he needs to do as I crawl into bed. He joins me a few minutes later also smelling of toothpaste and smoke.

"Does this feel weird?" I ask him.

He shakes his head. "Maybe if your mom was still here, but I relaxed a lot after they left. Lannie teased me about it."

"You know, you're the only guy who has ever been in this bed," I tell him in a mock-sultry tone.

Putting his arm around me, he pulls me close. "Yeah?"

I nod. "I even changed the sheets for you."

He laughs. "I'm honored." He smooths my hair back from my face. "I don't have any expectations, just so you know."

He tells me that a lot. "I know. You're a really nice guy, do you know that?"

Twirling a strand of my hair around his finger, he smiles. "Yeah, I know. It's how I was raised."

"Remind me to thank your parents when I meet them. If I meet them," I correct myself.

"You can meet them whenever you want," he tells me. "They've been asking when it's going to happen. Apparently, my grandfather sang your praises the last time they saw him."

I grin. "Really? That's so sweet. I'd like to meet your parents."

"Next weekend, maybe?"

"Yeah." I stifle a yawn. "I'm sorry. I don't know why I'm so tired."

"You were switching out a lot tonight. That has to be exhausting. By the way, Lannie should not be trusted near fire. Just saying. You should see how she likes her marshmallows."

"Burnt?" I guess.

He nods. "It's a crime."

I wrinkle my nose. "I like them burnt, too."

"No." He makes like he's going to get out of bed. "I don't think this is going to work."

Laughing, I grab his arm and pull him back. It doesn't take much. I wrap myself around him as he pulls the covers up, and we snuggle together in the middle of the bed. We kiss.

"If Lannie or Kaz came out right now and said they wanted to have sex with you, would you do it?" I ask.

"No," he replies. "That's something we'll need to talk about, I guess. Right now, it would feel weird—like I was cheating. Maybe when I get to know them better? If that was something you wanted. I mean, if you were okay with it."

"I don't know," I reply honestly. "You're right, it's something I guess we'll figure out. You, me, and the Posse."

He grins. "I love that you're calling them that."

"It was your idea."

He kisses me again, his expression turning serious. "So, since you're you and *not* Lannie or Kaz . . . you want to take advantage of me?"

I do. I really do. I'm not naive enough to think it's always going to be this way, but I'm smart enough to know to take advantage of it while it is. I crawl on top of him as he reaches for the light.

"No," I say with a smile. "Leave it on."

—

DALI

I look for Scratch in the cellar, but she's not there. Vincent's working out in the gym and says he hasn't seen her; neither has Monet, who has been busy recataloging memories with the help of Kaz. I'm not completely sure, but there might be something romantic developing between them now that Monet has stopped avoiding the rest of us. It would be nice for them to have someone to spend time with. Monet has been so cloistered, and Kaz has spent so much time looking for a connection with someone—anyone—that I've often worried she might bring herself, and the rest of us, to harm.

Before Dylan discovered us, it had never occurred to us that we might find happiness inside our own world. Things have changed a lot over this last month and a half. Most of it has been good, and some of it we're still trying to figure out. It's early days, though.

Finally, I look outside. To my surprise, I find Scratch sitting on the merry-go-round, gently moving it from side to side with her feet.

"It's more fun if you get it spinning and hop on," I tell her as I approach.

She looks up, squinting into the sunshine that turns her hair bright as gold. I can't remember the last time it was such a nice day here. For years it's been perpetually overcast. Not unpleasant, but certainly not like this. The children love it. "I don't like to get dizzy. It feels too much like when one of you kicks me out of the front space."

I smile. "I guess it does sort of feel like that, yeah." I sit down on the segment beside her and lean against the metal bar. "It's a beautiful day."

"It's been like this ever since we told the truth." She gives me a look. "Coincidence? I think not."

Her voice has changed. I don't mention it, however. I'm sure she's aware of the changes that have taken place in her over the last few weeks. Of all of us, Scratch has gone through the most metamorphoses over the years. "It was a good thing you did, letting her tell."

She makes a scoffing sound. "I couldn't stop her. No, that's bullshit. I didn't want to stop her. For the first time in my existence, I was angrier at him than I was at her. I'm not sure what that means."

"We've all felt a change. I suppose it means we're healing."

She lifts her face to the sun, eyes closed. "I'm not sure I like it, but I could get used to this weather."

I chuckle and shut my eyes, tilting my chin up. Never mind the brightness that permeates my eyelids, the warmth of the sun does feel good. I'm going to miss it. I wait a few moments before speaking. I want to enjoy this moment. "She doesn't need us anymore, Scratch."

"Don't be stupid. She needs someone to watch out for her."

Opening my eyes, I use my hand to shield them from the sun as I roll my gaze toward her. "Yes, but not you. Not me. Not like we did, anyway."

She stares at me. "What the fuck are you saying?"

I hold out my hand. "We need to talk."

Scratch doesn't hesitate, she puts her hand in mine. She knows she can trust me. I've never betrayed her, never lied to her or let her down. "You want me to leave, don't you?"

"No. Yes." I sigh. "You and me, we know where she's weak and where she's strong, but she's figured that out for herself. We knew how to keep her safe, but now she's doing that on her own."

"She's pretty shit at it."

I laugh. "Maybe, but she wants to take care of herself, and of the others. She can't do that with you putting her down and me fussing over her. A system is only as good as the sum of its parts and you and I have become obsolete. She needs something new. Someone to have her back and support her while she makes her own way."

She doesn't look surprised that I've included myself in this equation. "You want to integrate?"

Integration, or fusion. One of the two—whichever one is less painful. "What do you think?"

She looks away but doesn't let go of my hand. "I don't know if I'm ready for that."

Get in line. "I don't think it matters if we're ready, sweetie. Dylan is."

"You bitch." Her jaw tightens, but there's no violence in her tone. "I don't want to go."

"I know. Neither do I, but we won't really be gone, will we? We'll still be us, just together. I can think of worse things."

"You sure you want my memories?"

"No," I reply honestly, smiling. "But you'll have mine, too. Think of what we might become."

Leaning back against the swing set, she turns her head to meet my gaze. "It might be nice, not being so pissed off all the time."

"And I think it might be nice actually feeling a little anger now and again."

She smiles. "You losing your temper is something I'd like to see. How do we do it?"

"I don't know. We don't have to rush. Let's just sit here for a minute." So, we do, leaning against opposite sides of the same bar, eyes closed, and hands clasped, enjoying the beautiful weather until I float away into what feels like a dream.

The light is warm and bright and I let myself dance toward it, as invisible fingers pull invisible strings, tugging me closer and closer until I whirl into the light itself and become one with it, the edges of me evaporating into the nucleus of its brilliance.

I don't know how much time has passed, but I open my eyes to find Alyss hovering over me, a frown on her face. "What's wrong?" I ask, blinking.

Her frown deepens. "Who the bloody hell are you?"

—

Deer Dillin, Thanke yu for the swing set. I kan go relly high now. Im nut afrayed anny more.

DYLAN

A few days before Thanksgiving, I found out that Christina has stopped screaming. She still won't allow anyone to come near her other than Alyss, but at least it's something. I'm going to take whatever wins I can get.

I have so much to learn. So much to figure out. There are more people inside me that I don't know, like Vincent, who recently started talking to me. And there are the people in the basement. I have to do something about them. I have to help Christina. I have to do right by Lannie and Kaz and even Scratch.

It's weird, Scratch being gone but not gone, here but not here. I didn't really get the chance to know Dali very well, so her loss hasn't hit me the same way.

The new alter hasn't told me her name yet. She hasn't said much of anything. I've written to her in our journal, but no response as of this morning. I wouldn't even know about her if Alyss hadn't told me. It freaked her out, finding someone new where Scratch and Dali had been sitting a few minutes before.

I'm still trying to understand how my brain works. How does it do this stuff? I've got so many books on dissociative identity disorder and dealing with trauma that I don't know how I'll get through them all. I have a new notebook—a binder—so I can take notes on what I read and put them all together in one place for my reference. I keep it in the living room so Mark and Mom, or anyone else, can read it when they want to get a better understanding of our system.

Because of all that reading, I know the new alter will reach out when she's ready. I have to be patient—not one of my strong suits. Lannie spoke to her briefly and told me she seems nice. Apparently, she spends most of her time outside tending to the flower garden she's planted. It makes sense to me that a caretaker like Dali would transfer that sense of nurturing to something else. And a garden is something Scratch could have complete control over. Anyway, I hope she feels comfortable enough to introduce herself soon. It's important to welcome her to the system, even if she's technically always been here.

Someone—I think it was Mark—suggested I start a You-Tube channel, but there are a lot of DID-awareness channels out there that are much better than anything I could put together. I don't feel like I could offer much more to the topic, and unlike my brother, I'm not that comfortable in front of a camera.

Probably why Mark got another commercial recently. This one's for a designer cologne. It's pretty cool, because it's going to plaster his face all over network TV and maybe even lead to some magazine work. I don't think he ever gave much thought to doing modeling before this, but living this close to Manhattan, it can't hurt to at least give it a go. Who knows? It might lead to some acting gigs.

So, while Mark gets his chance at the spotlight, Connor and I are working on a graphic novel about a character with DID, and Mom suggested I look into having a showing of our art. Pretty much all of us like to draw or paint, and we each have our own style and preferred medium. She's going to check with a friend who owns a gallery. I'm excited. Even if it doesn't work out, it's still something to work toward.

I'm also going to start taking some art classes in the new year. Nothing too strenuous, mostly some online stuff that I can do at my own pace. They have a forum where students can talk and share their work, and that's mostly what I want it for, so I can talk to other creators. I miss that. One of my favorite things was being in a class where we all drew the same thing and yet every drawing was completely different. It's kind of what it's like inside my head.

Bella video-chats me once a week. Sometimes I talk to Angie or Dad for a few minutes. I'm so happy my half-sister is okay. Travis never got a chance to hurt her, and I give myself full credit for that. He's been released on bail. Obviously, somebody put up a lot of money to get him out, but he's not allowed to go near any places where there might be kids. He's going to trial in the spring, and when they find him guilty, he's going to be a registered sex offender in addition to doing prison time. I'm okay with all of that.

Oh, yeah. Two more girls have come forward and said he molested them as well. Fucking bastard.

I'm not sure if Dad has forgiven me yet. It's not like he blames me for anything that has happened to me, but I know there's a small part of him that blames me for not telling him when I was a kid. It's tied up in his own guilt, though. I didn't need Dr. Zhao to tell me that, so I don't claim any responsibility. That's on him, not on me. And I'm not mad at Dad for feeling the way he does. It has to be hard finding out your brother is a monster. You can't just wipe out years of love no matter what the person you love has done, not even if you've already begun to hate them.

Dad said that Travis "couldn't live with the guilt" and that was why he tried to end his life. But he was living with the knowledge of what he'd done for years. I wasn't the only kid he abused, and he lived with that knowledge just fine. It was the idea of having to *pay* for what he'd done that drove him to it. I don't have any sympathy for that.

"You saved Bella," Angie said to me before they left for

LA, and she hugged me so tight I couldn't breathe. "Your dad knows that, too."

I nodded. Dad and I will be okay, eventually. I know that. Some night he'll call and we'll talk and probably have a cry. I can't imagine finding out that Mark hurt my kid like Travis hurt me and would have hurt Bella. I wouldn't want to believe it, even if the truth was undeniable.

I'd be lying if I said it wasn't a relief when Dad, Angie, and Bella left for LA. It was like checking off another box in taking as much stress as possible out of my life.

There's been some press. Not too bad, because Mom hasn't made her big comeback yet, and no one else in the family is a major celebrity. Still, it's out there, along with the fact that I have DID. FORMER CHILD STAR JENNIFER TATE'S PERSONAL TRAGEDY was one headline. Mom's gotten some phone calls and emails from various gossip rags looking for quotes. I told her that if anyone from Oprah's network calls, we're taking it. I don't care if it means talking about my disorder in front of millions of people. I'm not ashamed, and I want to meet Oprah, damn it.

But until that happens, I've been keeping busy with art and therapy. I've also started trying to stay on top of eating well and exercising, because it's all supposed to be good for mental health. I've even taken up yoga. Mom and I go to a class a couple of times a week. She's going to be starting rehearsals for her play in the new year, but until then, I have a workout buddy. She and I have always been close, but lately we've gotten closer. She's been getting to know the others as well. I can't imagine what that's like for her, but I appreciate the effort.

Mark and Izzy are still together. They're getting pretty serious. I don't mind that she spends so much time with my brother, because we still make time for each other. She and Lannie have become pretty tight as well. Mark has started making himself available more, especially for Vincent. The only one he won't hang out with is Kaz. He says she's too weird. I have no idea what that means, and I'm afraid to ask. Kaz just laughs whenever I try to ask her, so . . . yeah.

Connor and I have started having dinner every couple of weeks with his grandfather. We'll pick up takeout or grab some groceries and cook at Paddy's house. It's fun. He likes to dig out photographs or old movies and show them to us. Connor says he's gotten to know his grandmother better in death than he did in life. I think that's kind of sad, but also sweet.

I don't know how long Connor and I will last. I want to believe in things like forever, but Mom and Dad wanted to believe in forever when they fell in love, too. I know I can't compare us to them, but I don't want to have unrealistic expectations.

Can't you just enjoy what you've got? Lannie wants to know. *He likes you and you like him. Stop overthinking it.* She's right, but I don't tell her that.

If someone had told me a couple of months ago that I'd learn to like the people in my head, I would have told them to fuck off. I do like them, though. They're my friends. Yeah, sometimes they're a pain in the ass, like when they switch out when I don't want them to, or they stick their faces into my business, or buy things without permission, but sometimes they're a comfort, a source of love and security. That's pretty cool.

Actually, I guess family is the better comparison. You don't get to pick your family, but you can choose how you decide to deal with and interact with them. That's what "the Posse" and I are working on. We're slowly making it work, and the more we get to know each other, the easier it's becoming. Is it perfect? Not by a long shot. I still spend most of my time exhausted and confused because someone's been out when they shouldn't have. It's better than what I had before, though. And now there's no one in my head telling me I'm terrible.

Maybe we'll have more integrations in the future, I don't know. There are people who seem to think that's the way to go and others who think all you need is good system communication. I'm not sure what side of the fence I'm on, but I do know that we'll figure it out.

Together.